Praise for Caroline Corcoran

'A rival to *Gone Girl* for its addictive, twisted plot'
STYLIST

'[A] successful foray into *Girl on the Train* territory, replete
with jealousy, stalking, gaslighting and control-freakery'
THE GUARDIAN

'A deliciously twisted thriller'
RED

'This atmospheric read really ramps up the
pace as it nears its chilling end'
GOOD HOUSEKEEPING

'Corcoran maintains suspense throughout and is
brave enough not to opt for a fairytale ending'
DAILY MAIL

'A well-paced, insightful but ultimately
twisted look at modern life'
SUN

'The narrative flows effortlessly as the tension ramps up'
MY WEEKLY

'I could not put it down . . . a fantastically written, deeply
dark story that raises important issues'
THE COURIER

THE BABY GROUP

Caroline Corcoran is a freelance lifestyle and popular culture writer and editor. She has worked for most of the top magazines, newspapers and websites in the country, and also as a copywriter for brands and websites. After 14 years in London, Caroline recently returned up north to the Wirral because she had a baby and there was more free grandparent babysitting available there. You'll often find her feeling travelsick but still trying to write on a Virgin Pendolino into Euston.

You can follow her on Twitter here: @cgcorcoran

By the same author:

Through The Wall

THE
BABY
GROUP

CAROLINE CORCORAN

Published by AVON
A division of HarperCollins*Publishers* Ltd
1 London Bridge Street
London SE1 9GF

www.harpercollins.co.uk

A Paperback Original 2020

First published in Great Britain by HarperCollins*Publishers* 2020
2

A catalogue copy of this book is available from the British Library.

ISBN: 978-0-00-833512-0

This novel is entirely a work of fiction. The names, characters and
incidents portrayed in it are the work of the author's imagination.
Any resemblance to actual persons, living or dead, events or localities
is entirely coincidental.

Typeset in Bembo by Palimpsest Book Production Limited, Falkirk, Stirlingshire
Printed and bound in UK by CPI Group (UK) Ltd, Croydon CR0 4YY

MIX
Paper from
responsible sources
FSC™ C007454

This book is produced from independently certified FSC™ paper
to ensure responsible forest management.

For more information visit: www.harpercollins.co.uk/green

The Originals: Mum, Dad and Gem

'Let her cover the mark as she will, the pang of it will be always in her heart.'

Nathaniel Hawthorne, *The Scarlet Letter*

Prologue

Scarlett

It's a strange thing, thinking about who released the sex tape of you while you eat a blueberry muffin next to your baby.

My mind ticks away, somewhere else entirely while Cora, Emma and Asha – the friends I made at NCT antenatal classes – rock their own babies to sleep, pick up slobbery teacake from the floor, grumble about daily grinds, everyday problems.

Not like mine, I think. Not life-destroying.

A shriek from Cora brings me back to the present with a jump because I am nervous at the moment, edgy.

I look at my friend, and see her mouth full of large veneers, white as toothpaste.

It's surreal that I'm still functioning here, in normality.

'I told you!' Cora yells at Asha, loving being right. 'Told you it was her.'

Asha is standing up, trying to rock her baby back to sleep but disturbing the smooth rhythm with shoulders shaking in amusement.

Emma points to Asha's mint tea. Raises her eyebrow at her in silent question.

'Yes please,' Asha says, through her laughter.

Her own hands are too full of baby to hold a drink so she sips from the tea Emma holds out to her as though she's an elderly relative in the care home: mouth a little dry, darling.

My own hands – barring the muffin – are free, a rarity. My

daughter Poppy is sleeping next to me in her pram under a bright green blanket gifted to me through my parenting blog, Cheshire Mama. Poppy snores lightly through Cora's shrieking, the whirring of the coffee machine and a contentious elderly book club on the next table.

Lucky girl. Her mother can't nod off despite blackout blinds and severe sleep deprivation at the moment.

I think of the sex tape again. Feel my stomach plunge.

Then I'm back, Cora brandishing her phone in my face.

'See!' she yells, victorious. 'We do get exciting things happen here. Sally from *Home and Away*'s best friend circa 1995, just over there burping her baby. Like we do! She's not even rubbed in her dry shampoo so her roots look grey! And her, a celebrity.'

I raise my own eyebrow.

'I'm not strictly sure we'd call her a celebrity . . .' I say.

Cora rolls her eyes.

'Here we go,' she says. 'Cue name-drops from Scarlett's glamorous former life in the fancy millennial office in Manchester.'

Former life. That bruises.

'Says the WAG,' I mutter.

My regular mocking of Cora for her pre-marriage days dating a subs' bench regular from one of the lower league Cheshire clubs washes over her like a spray tan. She waves a dismissive hand, nails concluding at violent points in bright red. Squeaks as she crosses her legs, one over the other, in leather leggings.

Suddenly a baby – not mine – lands in my lap.

'Need the loo and he's just woken up,' mutters Emma, tiny hint of a Welsh accent. 'Thanks, babe.'

I sit Emma's son Seth up on my lap. Push my turmeric latte further away across the table so he can't reach the hot drink.

Seth smiles up at me, knowing my face and clearly reassured.

There are people who know Emma better than we do. We only met her – and each other – fourteen months ago. But time scales alter when you've crossed to a new life plane.

2

I watch Asha place a sleeping Ananya like a glass vase into her pram and ruffle Seth's hair as she sits down. As Poppy wakes up, I hand Seth over to Asha and pick up my girl and it's Cora's turn – her daughter Penelope still asleep – to feed me a giant chunk of that blueberry muffin. On the one hand, it exacerbates the nausea that's constant for me at the moment. On the other, I need the sugar to ease my trembling. Also constant.

Out of nowhere, Poppy brings up a bit of milk and I don't have a cloth. Three muslins appear in my line of vision, along with wet wipes and antibacterial gel from Emma, now back from the toilet.

We've just sat back down when Cora starts looking twitchy.

'Can I tell you a secret?' she says suddenly, like it's bursting out of her.

She leans in, conspiratorially. Emma follows. Asha next. We meet in the middle like the hokey cokey.

'Is it that you don't really make your cupcakes?' I whisper, hammy, about her bakery business. I have never seen Cora and those nails stray near a mixing bowl. I'm fairly sure there are zero-hours workers in her outbuilding currently shoving choc-olate buttons in icing.

'Don't worry,' I carry on, deadpan. 'I won't expose you to the Cheshire Mama crowd. It'll be just between us.'

I often promote Cora's Cupcakes on my Instagram. She does the same for Cheshire Mama on hers.

Cora gives me a death stare. Then smirks.

'Actually,' she says. 'I'm sleeping with someone else.'

If the look that would normally accompany this revelation would be guilty, Cora's face with its extra long eyelashes and its possible fillers and definite Botox bucks the trend. She is kind of . . . proud.

I glance at Emma. Did she know? She and Cora have been friends for a long time, way before NCT, so she must know Cora's husband. But Emma may look the most shocked.

'Seriously?' says Asha.

'Who?' I ask.

Cora's smile fades; she looks taken aback at the question. She rallies quickly.

'He's the teacher at hot yoga,' she says, speaking the way she pours champagne, quickly, spilling over. 'Hunter. Utterly dreamy. Exceptionally bendy.'

'Bloody hell,' says Asha. 'I was not expecting *that*. How long for?'

'Since Penelope was four months old.' Cora laughs. 'I know, it sounds crazy.'

'How could you be *bothered*?' I ask. 'When Pen was that young and you were so knackered.'

Cora shrugs. 'Gave me something to make an effort for. I was sick of the leggings. Sick of the giant pants.'

We all nod in recognition. New mum life is the opposite of an illicit affair.

There are gags, then, about Cora's downward dog and we annoy the book club with shrieks of dirty laughter.

'Come on then,' Cora says. 'That's my biggest secret out. We've known each other long enough now. Anyone else got any? The babies are nearly one. Time to liven up this mum chat.'

My heart begins to smash into my chest.

Poppy's tights are damp where my palms touch her.

And it's on the tip of my tongue, then, burning like hot coffee.

Could I tell them? Now?

It would be a relief, to have it out there. It would be awful, knowing that they know.

Asha. Emma. Cora.

I look at them.

Is it possible to keep it from them anyway, now it's out? Is it better for it to come from me?

4

It rewrote everything, becoming a parent, and friendships were one of the areas that had the strongest edit.

I thought I had to accumulate mum friends when I had a child so my real friendships could still be sexy on the other side, with their Pinot Noirs and their gossip, and without everyone thinking, *Yeah but remember that voice she sings 'Wind The Bobbin Up' in*, as I danced at a grown-up party in my mini dress.

But that wasn't what happened.

Instead, those 'real friendships' faded away, their place usurped by my mum friends, and there are no women I am closer to than Asha, Emma and Cora, even though we're chips-and-salad different.

And yet, I haven't told them about this thing that consumes me.

About the sex tape that almost everyone in my life was sent just over a few weeks ago.

I saw it, first, in the boardroom at work on my first day back from maternity leave.

The film played, bad quality from a second in time just before the world was viewed through flattering filters and cute effects.

I stared at the screen.

A woman; two men.

My ex, Ollie.

A friend of a friend of ours, Mitch.

The woman: unmistakably me, albeit a different me.

In that room in central Manchester, I looked down at myself: cobalt blue midi, large diamond on my ring finger, nails painted carefully in two layers of black. In the mirror opposite, long legs crossed, bright white trainers. The resting bitch face I'm told intimidates people. Big brown eyes, hard eyes.

I looked back at the screen.

The me on there wasn't the one that commuted in from the countryside with bags under her eyes. Not the one that buys gender-neutral, organic brands for her baby girl. Not the one

5

who puts the broadsheets in the recycling bin and runs 10k for fun at the weekends.

But the old one.

Party Scarlett, who if she by some miracle had money in her bank account, spent it all on drugs. Harder drugs, more drugs. Party Scarlett didn't feel fear; there was nothing to be scared for.

Party Scarlett flitted between jobs in pubs and got sacked for not turning up. She spent summers working in clubs in Ibiza. She slept all day and eye-rolled about fidelity and marriage and people who had sensible jobs because none of that was *fun*. She stayed out later than you, partied harder than you, was more, more, more than you, but felt less than you really, so much less.

The Scarlett I had tried so hard over the years to bury.

I glance again now at my friends, alternating between analysis of Cora's affair and the placating of their babies.

That Scarlett, they have never known.

And they never would have.

Except that now, that Scarlett has been exhumed.

I don't know why or by who but I know something: bringing old Scarlett back from the dead like this is about to smash my carefully curated world apart.

1
Scarlett

Before

4 May

Fourth of May, Pay Day, my husband Ed and I have nicknamed it. Today is my first day back at work after almost a year of maternity leave and the day our finances, even if they're still less stretched than most people's, stop taking the battering of being one salary down.

Leaving my eleven-month-old daughter will be torture; not having to ask my husband for pocket money won't be.

This morning I have been awake since 5 a.m., fuelled by worry and newness and the running through of which items are going in which of Poppy's bags like I am on an excruciatingly dull quiz show.

At five thirty Poppy joins me, sitting in her highchair and grinning with her new top teeth on show as I spoon-feed her Weetabix. I feel my stomach lurch. She slaps her lips together for a kiss and I lean in, coating my face in slobbery cereal mush.

'Love you, Pops,' I tell her. I wipe my mouth though. It's still gross, even with the love.

As I carry on feeding her breakfast, we listen to Noughties dance mixes like we always do when we're alone and Poppy shrieks with delight at the familiarity of 'Lola's Theme'. I am too tired to dance, but I smile at her as she tries to and I'm glad that she loves it like I love it. The beat has always soothed me. It's even helping a little this morning.

'Right,' I mutter, to Poppy or maybe just to myself. 'What next?'

This process of breakfast takes fifty-five long minutes, during which one person poos (not me, as if I have time for such luxuries) and I pay an overdue payment for Poppy's sensory class and order new baby sleeping bags.

As Poppy gums on a banana, I take out the pile of washing that's in the machine, hang it up and put on a load of baby vests. I try to have a conversation with my daughter as I walk around the kitchen because I read that that was crucial for speech development, even if she responds with babble. I pronounce my g's when I do it, in a way that isn't natural for me and my Manchester accent but in a way I am determined to do because I want better for Poppy, more.

I dash back to my phone on the table to chase up the date for Poppy's one-year check then I walk around the room trying to identify a weird smell I eventually place as tuna in the food bin.

'Shit,' I mutter, as I drip bin juice on the floor taking out the bag, then keep my fingers crossed that swearing doesn't count towards speech development.

I open the front door, do a quick scan then Usain Bolt it to the outside bin in my dressing gown. As I mop the bin juice up back in the kitchen, I hear the shower turn on upstairs.

'Take your time, Ed,' I mutter, about my husband who is just getting up when I am on task number 345 of the day.

I think about how I'm about to leave my funny, bright Poppy all day with the childminder and feel like I can't breathe. I think about remembering how to do my job, and feel similar.

Turning the radio volume down and flicking over to Radio 4, I switch the day to Ed mode. Ed can't bear dance music and I gave up trying to persuade him otherwise long ago.

8

The radio presenter informs me that it is 6.45. I look up from the mop as though she has personally offended me.

Now I am in a panic that I will be late, which is ridiculous, since I have been up since 5 a.m.

I calculate.

To get to the childminder then the station and be at my desk in central Manchester on time from my home in Sowerton, our small village in Cheshire, even if the normally fuckupable train line fucks up, I need to leave the house at 7.05 a.m.

Right.

Okay.

Twenty minutes. That's doable.

'Morning, darling,' says Ed, walking into the kitchen. He kisses my head then pours out coffee from the pot I've made for him. He holds it up. 'Thanks for this.'

He takes a gulp.

'Fourth of May, Pay Day.' He smiles.

'Don't talk to me about it,' I snap. 'I'm too nervous.'

I look over at my own coffee – made far earlier – that sits uncupped by human hand and chilly on the kitchen table.

I have been waiting for the holy grail of a window when it is hot enough to comfort but cool enough not to burn my child, causing social services to take her away and my life to be lived under a cloud of horror and guilt. It's a difficult balance to nail. There's no time to drink it now.

I glance at the clock.

6.50.

Oh God.

I still need to shower, whack some eyeliner on – the rest I can do on the train, but my eyeliner requires a proper mirror especially when I am out of practice at looking like a human existing in the real world – and get dressed.

I shove Poppy at Ed, pause, then come back for an extra kiss and crazy mum smell of her head.

'Don't drink that coffee while she's near you,' I shout, flying upstairs into the bathroom. 'And have you seen my coat?'

Ten minutes later I am back downstairs and shouting. 'You must have moved it!'

'Calm down a second,' says Ed, putting a hand on my arm from where he sits at the kitchen table drinking his second coffee as I pass.

I stand still.

'Right,' he says. 'Speak to me. Are you still on about the coat?'

'I laid it out last night,' I reply, trying to stay calm so I don't get sweaty. 7.01. This carefully curated 'back at work and still dressing like a non-mum, don't write me off' midi dress and new trainers outfit doesn't need sweaty. 'Right there.'

I gesture to the kitchen chair.

'Your denim jacket is on the coat rack,' he says like he's come up with an ideal solution, standing up and putting some bread in the toaster. My heart is hammering in panic. 'You can wear that!'

I stare at him.

'I cannot wear *my denim jacket* on my first day back in the office, Ed,' I hiss. Poppy is on the floor with her chunky little arms in the air, asking to be picked up. I pick her up. I have my dressing gown back on over my dress: this child knows when to projectile vomit. Dry-clean only silk Whistles is just her thing.

7.03.

'Why not?' said Ed. 'Just ditch it as soon as you get there. No one will notice.'

He smiles.

'And you always look lovely in a denim jacket.'

I stop for a second and smile back.

Yes, *in beer gardens*, Ed. When the sun stops warming us at 10 p.m. over a G&T.

I don't have time to explain to him that if I turn up to work in anything less than new, slick attire, my obscenely young team will tuck me away in that mum file.

Since we had Poppy, he still wears the same suit on his same-sized middle. When she was born, he took no more time off than a colleague who went on a summer trip to Majorca. There has been no seismic shift. It's one of the ten thousand or so double standards in our life now.

She's been on maternity leave, they would think. She's not a serious player any more. Expect her to leave at 4.59 p.m. for pick-ups; one eye on the clock. She's a mum now and that explains the denim jacket. Next week: meeting in her Ugg boots; work wines in her baggy leggings.

The sweating starts again.

'I'll just have to go without a coat,' I bark, before asking the digital speaker what the temperature is outside.

'Quicker to stick your head out of the door,' mutters Ed.

'Luddite,' I mutter back, as I shove a dishwasher tablet in and whack the machine on while brushing my teeth.

Why is the dishwasher still my job, I think, when I am going to work now too?

Ed bends down to kiss Poppy in my arms and I notice his hair is greyer than before.

'Good luck, darling,' he says, as he kisses me too, hard on the mouth, one hand on my bum cheek. Even in the chaos, I think, I still fancy you.

Ed leaves for work. Like he is used to doing; like is normal to him.

'Thanks,' I yell as the door slams and I collect a handful of bags while holding a wriggly Poppy.

The speaker says it's fifteen degrees but I leave the house without a coat anyway.

Piling a babbling Poppy into her car seat, I mumble to myself. 'A denim bloody jacket.'

11

As Poppy and I drive in silence to the childminder's house, I think about Ed, now on his own in the car to work. It's only a thirty-minute drive away but he needs to be in early today. He looked distracted this morning, like he often looks distracted these days, and I wonder if it's work or something else. I frown.

He needs order, Ed. Not chaos and lost jackets and Weetabix on the floor and lateness.

I have a pang of regret that I can't provide that for him but another pang of regret that he doesn't play a role in making that happen in our house himself.

Because in my enthusiasm for meeting a respectable, handsome man with a proper job and a close family – a man who also looked at me like I was the hottest woman he had ever seen, and the feeling has always been mutual – I overlooked the fact that he is Radio 4 traditional and I am . . . not.

The differences weren't so noticeable when we rented in a city and ate Deliveroo for tea but now we own a house in the countryside and have a child? They're sticking their head above the parapet, about chores, about parenting, about work, and sometimes it's like I'm a Trotskyist in a coalition with the far right. But still, I think, we love each other. We don't have to agree on everything.

A few minutes later I pull up outside the childminder's up the road. Ed hadn't offered to do it but I wouldn't have let him anyway. This was my multitasking horror show; no one else's. *I* wanted to settle her in. *I* wanted to mourn the end of maternity leave. I wanted to write lists and pack seventeen bags last night like a ritual and huff about it. Parental gatekeeping, I think the books call it.

Apt for a gatekeeper, I make Poppy hold on to the gate of Ronnie's house with her tiny Peppa Pig backpack on and snap her from behind so I can use the picture for a back-to-work post on my parenting blog later.

'Is it okay?' Ed asked, concerned at first when I launched Cheshire Mama. 'Privacy wise, to show off our home and our daughter?'

But I swept away his concerns.

'Oh, everyone does it, Ed,' I said dismissively. 'It's the twenty-first century. Life's online. I'll keep an eye on it, make sure there's nothing weird posted on there.'

Ed didn't raise it again. He trusted me. I worked in digital marketing, did a lot of social media. This was my world. Plus we saw kids' films for free in the best seats when they first came out and a fancy coffee machine arrived by courier. I told him that potentially, this blog and my Instagram could start to make us money. That was enough to stem any objection.

It gathered pace, the numbers rolling in.

'We'd get more followers if we showed the whole family off,' I told him, with a grin. 'You, topless at the coffee machine should do it.'

I raised an eyebrow, questioning.

Based on the number of women who stared at him on the street though, I knew a *lot* of women would enjoy staring at him in the privacy of their own homes. And funnily enough, when I did start to include him, it boomed fast.

'You do that all the time,' my half-sister Josephine tells me whenever I give that verdict about the brand's success. 'Give Ed all the credit; don't give yourself any. Cheshire Mama is successful because it's a *good blog*. You have the eye, you're funny, you know your stuff on social. The whole leaving the city and being new to the countryside is relatable.'

I drop my phone into my bag. 'Okay, Pop, got it!' I say. She's used to posing for my iPhone by now.

I take her hand and we walk in.

Ronnie was recommended to me by Emma, whose son Seth goes to her too. I've met Ronnie twice. She seems lovely. She also obviously has, you know, paperwork and things.

But I am leaving my child with her all day. Is this insanity? Is it legal?

'Good morning, Poppy!' singsongs Ronnie in her gentle Brummie accent as we walk in, heaving four bags and a suitcase-load of anxiety. 'And good morning, Scarlett.'

She looks at me with pragmatic empathy. It's a very specific expression.

'Big day today, I know,' she says. 'But we're going to have fun, aren't we Poppy?'

I fend off tears by speaking fast, with no let-up.

'She doesn't have a dummy except for her nap, which will be at eleven, eleven thirty but definitely not after three because otherwise sleep is a *nightmare* later,' I ramble.

I realise why I am shattered all the time despite Poppy, finally, sleeping well. It is the level of detail in my head. The tiny things I know about my daughter's needs and her day and that I am tick, tick, ticking and checking and balancing all day long.

The parenting stuff is often left to me. It's my head that's crammed full of its mundanities.

Ronnie smiles.

'Got it,' she says. 'We do naps straight after lunch anyway. All tickety-boo.'

Serene. Experienced, both at childminding and looking calm in front of irritant mums, I suspect. Meanwhile it is me versus the sweat again.

'Milk, water, snacks in the Peppa rucksack,' I say as Poppy crawls to the doll she can see in the living room.

'Change of clothes, nappies, Doggy Dog – that's what she calls it, it doesn't have a name – all in this one.'

I gesture wildly at one of the eighty-five zip compartments in my changing bag.

I look up at Ronnie. Still serene.

I point at bag three.

'This one is toys.'

Then I look at Poppy, yanking the doll round the room by its hair in one hand as she crawls, and my face goes red.

Ronnie smiles.

'I know you have toys. But in case she wants *her* toys.'

Bag four.

'Stickers, books, crafts . . . I guess this bag is the calmer stuff. For when she needs to relax. Perhaps around three thirty?'

'Perfect,' says Ronnie kindly, gently, like she is trying to deflect a toddler from a tantrum. 'We'll do some of that later.'

I've overdone it. Even I know it. But if you pack enough bags, the feelings of guilt can perhaps be squashed under their weight. If you buy enough stuff, perhaps what you can't purchase – time with your daughter, sanity, a mind that isn't running away with thoughts about the right time to get out Doggy Dog – isn't as obvious.

Serene, serene, serene. I can't hear any other children; we must be the first. This is early. Poppy will spend so many hours here. *Oh God*.

I stare at Ronnie. On the surface: maternal, cosy. Her hair is short in a way that says practical and efficient. Her clothes would be able to go in the boil wash that her job probably requires. She's about to turn fifty, has children of her own who are in their teens now and has been a childminder, I know from the chats we had at Poppy's settling-in days, for upwards of sixty kids. Seth has survived; *thrived*, Emma says.

Everything seems right.

But I panic.

Does Ronnie's mask slip when the others arrive and then she loses her shit, desperate for everyone to shut up? Would she ever lose it with Poppy?

Me versus sweat, me versus sweat.

But then I remember my pièce de résistance.

My document.

15

This document that will make everything okay and keep everyone happy.

Mostly me.

But also everyone else.

Okay really, just me.

'This is a schedule of Poppy's whole day,' I say slowly, unrolling the document like I am presenting a degree, so that Ronnie gives this masterpiece the gravitas it deserves.

In my head, I am already having a conversation with Asha in which she is congratulating me on multitasking to such a level that I have documentation on my daughter's oatie bar consumption.

'You. Are. A. Machine,' she will say. 'How you have time to do your job, keep on top of house stuff AND write a schedule of Poppy's day is beyond me. It's beyond all of us. It's beyond womankind as a whole.'

But, bursting my bubble, Ronnie is kind of . . . *ushering* me out of the door.

'Don't worry about a thing,' she says. 'It's going to be smooth sailing here.'

I glance down. My document is bunched up in her hand. I have a deep-seated suspicion that Ronnie will never read it.

And meanwhile the one who matters doesn't care about the document either.

Instead, Poppy is sitting next to Ronnie's foot, poking her moccasin slipper and pulling at the bottom of her leggings. I bend down to say goodbye and Poppy's rosebud lip wobbles.

My insides feel as though they have a hand roaming around in them, jiggling things about, perhaps performing some sort of surgery that involves the removal of an organ. I feel emotions that I can't name, tormented at the idea of walking away from her.

I have heard so many people talk about this feeling when you leave your child but I'm sure mine is worse. The worst.

I push past Ronnie and gather Poppy up, stroking that short fuzzy brown hair and smothering her in I love yous. She's come dressed for fun: leggings and a T-shirt, ready to play, make mess, do all the things that Poppy likes doing. It's going to be okay. It's going to be okay.

I take a deep breath.

'Right, chicken, you have the best day,' I say but she doesn't look convinced. She knows something's unusual. And she's suspicious of Ronnie.

Gulping back a sob, I plaster on a pretend smile.

'Mummy's going to work for a while now but I'll be back later to get you,' I say.

She doesn't *quite* cry.

'She'll be fine,' says Ronnie, softly. 'And so will you. Hey, by the way are you the one who does the Cheshire Mama blog?'

I nod, distracted by Poppy. Not now, Ronnie. Do I look like I can hold a conversation?

'I love that blog!' She smiles. 'About time we got something local to us. Well done.'

I say thank you, then kiss Poppy ten, twenty, possibly thirty more times before I drag myself out of the door. If I don't leave now I will be late and then I will be officially bad at parenting and work, which is really everything, so I will be officially bad at everything.

I cry so hard on the drive to the station though that the windscreen has the visibility of mid-thunderstorm. On the train, I had planned to do the back-to-work post on my blog and reply to a backlog of messages and comments on my Instagram.

The numbers have been growing so fast that I'm starting to make a tiny bit of money from it with affiliate links but that means there's more pressure to keep up. And days like today, I don't have it in me to be visible. If I post, I have to be ready to do the follow-ups, replying and responding. Being *on*.

Instead, I turn off and go insular, blasting house music into my ears as loud as it will go and carrying on with my sobbing.

I wait for it to ease but the further away I get from Poppy, the worse I feel. I calculate how long it will take me to get back to her if she needs me, all the routes and ways I could get there. I google taxi companies at each town we get to, to see if that will get me there faster than the train back to my car.

Further away, further.

The ache is deep in my insides, around the same place Poppy used to live in utero before I brought her into the world then abandoned her to a stranger.

Further away, further.

How am I going to do this?

Every day.

And further.

I look out of the window at suburban Cheshire stations with commuters clutching coffee in flasks brought from home. It is May, with its telltale juxtaposition of boots and sandals, parkas and bare arms. T-shirts hang out with roll-necks, newly waxed legs and thick socks stand side by side on the platform. It is too early to know what the day will bring so everybody is guessing, balancing weather apps with the chill they still feel and the comfort they need when they're craving two more hours' sleep.

I stare at them. That one, who thinks everyone wants to listen to his TV show out loud. That one, falling asleep standing up. I wonder, whether they have bare legs or jumpers or boots or visible toenails, if anyone is feeling close to how I feel this morning.

Slowly, the tiny stations make way for the edge of the city. The flasks are replaced with branded coffee cups and the platforms are crammed full, the people younger, cooler, edgier. Like my colleagues at New Social, one of the city's biggest digital marketing agencies. I glance at my trainers, doubtful now about the brand.

Everyone moves more urgently here. My heart starts racing watching it all and I have the edge of a headache. I used to be comfortable at the heart of this picture; pushing past, boots stomping at pace, latte aloft, tut tut tutting if you strayed into my path. Now I feel distant from it all. Maternity leave days have required me to get to one place at 10.30 a.m. and make small talk while singing nursery rhymes. We spoke slowly, the other mums and I, trying to drag out our coffees because otherwise what would we *do* for the rest of the day? We had tried to kill — stake out and murder — time so that it could be the evening, when husbands would be home and wine would be poured and we would feel, for that tiny window, like the old us.

'That was my shoulder,' hisses the woman next to me at a man who had passed by in the aisle. She could have been me, I think. Not so long ago. 'City wankers.'

She looks at me in solidarity but I feel nervous of her wrath and also like a fraud. This doesn't feel like my world any longer. Doesn't she know that I am normally still in my pyjamas around now, singing 'Row Row Row Your Boat' or hanging up row after row of tiny socks while a child sleeps? I'm not a real commuter, I think. If only you knew.

A surge of anxiety pulses as I think about how in an hour or so, I will be expected to do my job as Digital Marketing Manager. To be current in a sea of twenty-somethings. To run meetings. To dash out of the office to eat pancakes for brunch with a client.

I will be expected to be the straight-to-the-point 'this creative isn't working for me, we need another option for first thing tomorrow' version of me that I am not sure hasn't been written over with toddler songs and baby babble. With photographing my turmeric latte for Cheshire Mama's Instagram and calling that 'work'.

I feel a sensation in my stomach akin to a bad hangover.

Oh, Poppy. My best mate for the last year. I've never spent as much time with anyone as I do with her, with those long walks in her pram, us dancing round the room to our songs.

Just then my phone beeps and I leap on it because, almost definitely, it's a message telling me that Poppy had escaped out of Ronnie's back garden or is in an ambulance with a life-threatening condition, probably brought on by the trauma of being left behind by her mum.

But it's just Emma.

She checked in last night too, even as she dashed from putting her son to bed to her weekly Slimming World meeting. I was what she had done with her spare thirty seconds and I felt touched. And guilty, because sometimes I think I don't make enough effort with Emma. But I want to speed her up, and tell her to speak up. She gets lost, even in our small crowd.

Gd luck today S, her message says. *You're going to smash it!!!*

I smile, picturing Emma bursting in to baby music class – where I'm normally headed on Monday mornings too – muttering apologies for her tardiness. Emma is ten minutes late for whatever she does.

I smile at the thought of them all, my mum friends.

Emma is thirty-five, only a few months older than me, and sometimes I forget that she has a husband. He doesn't come up often but when he does he sounds uninvolved and removed from her and her baby's life.

Our virtually teenage (fine, twenty-nine-year-old) friend Asha messaged this morning at 5 a.m., up early to call her sister in Melbourne. Asha is tiny, less than five foot. She likes to question things and research them and come back to you when she has firmed up her arguments. She would never fight a cause unless she was an encyclopaedia on the subject. Even after wine.

And finally there was Cora, communicating as always via a list of her favourite emojis, sent while I was at Ronnie's. Cora, unlike Emma, likes to do everything fast, but especially talking, which she does tripping over her own thoughts, flitting to a different point, pulling a compact out of her bag to check her eyelashes but still speaking, then asking you quickly if her hair looks okay while also sending a text. Cora is a whirlwind; the kind of WAG I thought I might run a mile from when I first saw her stomp in in giant heels and faux fur to our antenatal class.

The four of us met last year, when our babies protruded from our middles. When we sat in a room feeling increasingly panicked about things we hadn't bought, learned or read, and to plan for a birth that could never be planned for.

Emma and Cora sat together on the parents' evening-style chairs, hands on bumps, already friends. While Ed and I came together, they massaged each other's backs with tennis balls instead. 'My other half's at work,' Cora said. Then she tipped her head in Emma's direction. 'Hers just isn't into this whole thing.' Then she'd rolled her eyes, while Emma's cheeks reddened.

'You know each other already?' I asked, in week one.

Everybody round Sowerton – where I had lived for less than a year – seemed to know each other.

My heart sank. I had been hopeful for a fellow ex-city dweller to find some things in common with.

But Cora nodded.

'Em was in South Wales when she was a kid but after that, we both grew up round here, hon,' Cora told me, leaning into Emma. 'Same school, the lot. We've been mates for years.'

Even at first impressions they were a wonky juxtaposition. I looked at Emma, the pretty blonde with chubby cheeks who blushed when I spoke to her and couldn't meet eye contact. And then at Cora, who'd told me that her wedding cost £60,000 and she has a nanny 'just to help out' about ten minutes after meeting me.

I suspect it worked for Cora like those types of uneven friendships always do. She dominated and talked; Emma listened.

Emma's stories would never compete with her tales of Hunter, her WAG past. Like having a therapist, for free. And for Emma perhaps Cora made her life easier, found the baby groups they should go to, made the friends on her behalf, formed her life then sent her out an invite for it.

'You've not been in Sowerton long, I take it?' asked Cora.

I nodded. 'I'm from Manchester really. Chorlton. I work in town.'

It seemed important that they knew. That they didn't think I was just . . . you know, *Sowerton*.

But Cora was nonplussed, checking her lipstick in a mirror, nodding vaguely.

'Is it just us three?' I asked our teacher, Cath, and she looked at her notes.

'One more starting next week but that's it,' she confirmed. 'We don't get big classes round here. Not like in your cities.'

She nodded at me.

And I sat back and hoped that mystery mum number four brought some balance. Or wasn't already mates with everyone else, at least.

Then in week two, as I swigged Gaviscon from a bottle and Emma got out an emergency KitKat, Asha arrived, little and serious and dressed for the gym with a notebook. Her husband Aidan held her hand.

'Sorry we missed last week,' she said. 'We were visiting family.'

I heard her London accent.

It wasn't Manchester nostalgia, but it would do. I'd cling to a city transplant like a life raft.

'Aidan grew up round here,' Asha said when she introduced herself to the group, nodding towards her husband and I was glad to see another man too, for Ed. I smiled at Aidan. 'Got me with the house prices, obviously. It's been about a year now.'

Cora wasn't listening.

'Let's add your number to the group chat,' she said, brusque; there was no option. But Asha nodded happily, squeezing her husband's hand. This is what we'd all come for, after all. We could learn to change a nappy from Google; it was the mates we were paying for.

So we swapped numbers and arranged, after our babies were born like painful dominoes, one after the other in the space of one week, to meet up.

And we did. We had the same desire to pour the caffeine we hadn't been allowed for months and now needed ferociously into our veins and so it became a regular thing, easy, us all heading for lattes, meet-ups, soft play as the babies got older. New baby lives curated by Cora, who shoved cards for her cupcake business into our hands, friended us on Facebook, asked questions, made sure our friendship gathered pace. And checking in too, after jabs, if our babies were sick, when we went back to work.

I lean back against the train seat and sigh.

My NCT friends haven't been around long but they get it. They understand how my insides feel today. This isn't theoretical to them, it's close. Some have been there, some will be there, some just know how it would feel to be there because they feel a version of it when they lose sight of their child for a second at soft play, or drive away as they wave at the window at grandparents'.

A full set of messages from my mum crew but absolutely nothing, I realise, from Ed. To ask how Poppy settled in, or how I'm coping.

He's so busy at work today, I reason. Give him a break.

Instead I reply to my mum group chat.

I can't stop sobbing, I type. *I feel awful. I hate this.*

It's much more exposed than I usually am. Usually, I prefer to put on a together front. I'm told with that resting bitch face

23

it can seem a bit cold, a bit superior. But at least people don't think I'm weak. At least people don't pity me. I am struggling to react normally to anything today though.

Typing quickly as I'm at BMT, writes Emma. Baby music time. Everything has an acronym when you're a parent. There's no time for full words.

Don't do that! I reply. I feel terrible, distracting her from one of her days off with Seth.

It's fine, whole class is car crash, she replies. *Everyone's on phone. But P will be having the time of her life! Ronnie is great. In a week this will feel normal. It's just today that's weird. Firsts are always weird.*

Thank you, I reply. Emma's emotional intelligence on messages is special. I must make more effort to chat to her as much in person.

The train pulls into the station and I shove my phone in my bag, take a deep breath and join the throng to step off.

Thanks to Emma, I am feeling ten per cent less likely to sprint back to the countryside to sling Poppy over my shoulder and leave work forever.

And somewhere under the rubbish tip of anxiety, I realise, there is a tiny bag of something approaching excitement. I will drink a mint tea today at my desk, slowly instead of chucking coffee down my throat like a pill. I will go into a meeting where people will respect me and somebody junior will be a tiny bit intimidated by me and ask me questions to which I will – hopefully – know the answers. I will reapply lipstick in the bathroom because I will always have thirty seconds to spare and hands that have no other responsibilities to tend to.

I will eat real food, not a child's cold leftover sticky pasta shoved in as I stack an overfilled dishwasher. I will go to shops on my lunch break and make small talk that isn't about weaning but about a date somebody went on and the film they saw, or the risotto one of the social media managers ate on a much-Instagrammed break in Puglia.

There were pluses, weren't there. I needed to hold on to them tightly today.

I make a mental note to message the NCT girls too and tell them what a difference their support made this morning. But the message never gets sent; the sentiment never gets shared. Because it's less than an hour later that something blasts into my world that ruins my relationships, my life and my mind and which I am not sure I can ever find a way back from.

2

Scarlett

4 May

My feet ache as I walk into my building; they have had a chilled-out time on their year-long commuting break and they are mad as hell about getting back to the grindstone.

'Scarlett!' says our giant Aussie Charlie on reception as I walk through the revolving door. 'First day back?'

I nod, bouncing from one foot to the other and unable to keep still with nerves.

'How's the baby?' he says, standing up to high-five me. 'Congrats. I've got three. You've got fun ahead.'

'Thanks, Charlie,' I reply.

I'm twitchy. Now I'm back at work, I want to be back at work.

'Get on, yep, get on.' He nods. 'Get there on time so you can get out for the nursery pick-up, right? All different now. Go!'

He shoos me towards the lift and I dig out my pass, call it and wait. In a few minutes I will see Felicity and the thought calms me. Felicity is my boss but also my mate. Felicity came to my baby shower; I went on her hen do. She'll talk me through what's happened in the last year, give me the low-down on the new people and we'll drink coffee and eat the fancy donuts and everything will be easier because of our

26

relationship. And because of the donuts. Calm, Scarlett. This will be okay.

The lift opens and I catch sight of one of the finance guys, Jared, walking past. I know everyone in this building – it's the best and worst thing about a business that values team-building away days and boozy Friday lunches highly – but Jared a little better than most; Ed was in his department when he used to work here.

That's how we met, Ed and I, at work, or through both spending lunchtimes in the gym next door.

On rare Manchester sunny days, we'd meet outside and go for a run together instead, sprinting the last one hundred metres, competitive with each other. Then Ed got offered a job at another company and took it, both of us thinking that was probably sensible anyway, now we were spending most nights at each other's flats. Jared got promoted. He and Ed kept in touch, meet for a pint regularly. But as I wave at him from the lift, Jared keeps his head down. Mustn't have seen me.

Eventually we get to my floor and I step out, straight into a waiting Felicity.

I fling my arms around her even while I know it is unprofessional.

'Flick!' I exclaim, relieved, and she hugs me back hard.

'Good to see you,' she says and I pull out and look at her.

'You look amazing,' I say because this, for unknown reasons, is how you reacquaint with female friends. I love your earrings. Your shoes are *hot*. Where's that lipstick from? Et cetera, et cetera. Start with the pawing of the new coat and the stroking of the cashmere, then you're ready to move on to real subjects.

'Nice shirt,' I add. 'And thanks for the welcome committee.'

She smiles but it's close-mouthed.

'Come with me,' she says. 'There's something I need to talk to you about. We'll grab a boardroom.'

The goose bumps are worse than the ones I had without a

coat in Sowerton this morning. A boardroom means we need privacy; our office is open-plan. So what is it? Redundancy? Can they do that when I'm on maternity leave? Or is that the point – I'm not any more, so they can?

But I can't ask because Flick is marching off now, past the beanbags, towards the room I presume she has booked, a hand on my lower back to guide me there too. I quickstep to keep up, new trainers threatening blisters.

On the way we pass my colleagues, ten or twenty of them.

'Sara!' I say, excited to see a long-term desk buddy. But Sara just smiles awkwardly and ducks her head.

Freddie doesn't look up at all.

Sanjeeta rummages in a drawer.

I think about Jared.

Something odd is happening.

'Is the company folding?' I whisper to Flick, half-laughing. 'Why is everyone being strange?'

She doesn't answer but ushers me into the room and shuts the door, flicking on the lock.

The trainer situation dictates that I sit down immediately. Flick stays standing.

'Firstly,' she says. 'Welcome back.'

She gives me the only genuine smile I've seen since I walked in here. 'It's lovely to see you. I'm sorry I've not made it over in a few months.'

I look away awkwardly. She visited when Poppy was small. It was about nine months ago. She was one of my closest friends.

'Well, firstly too it's nice to be back,' I say. 'But I think we had better get to secondly. There's a disconcerting vibe in here?'

Flick nods, seriously.

And then she does sit down, and jiggles her mouse to make her computer come alive.

She clicks onto something, then looks at me.

'I need you to steel yourself here, Scarlett,' she says.

28

My stomach lurches. Redundancy, then. I think about the size of our mortgage and regret following Ed's lead despite my nerves and maxing ourselves out on our four-bed pretty listed building on the winding country road in our idyllic Cheshire village. How long will it take me to find something else? How big will my pay-off be?

'Go on,' I say, needing the conclusion as I try to do sums with no facts.

She sighs. Clicks again.

'I was sent a link to this in the early hours of this morning by somebody I don't know,' says my friend, my boss. 'And so was everybody else on the team.'

I nod.

'Right,' I say, searching her face for clues about where this is going. But Felicity cannot meet my eyes.

'It's a sex tape,' she says.

My eyebrows shoot up. Jesus. *That* explains why everyone is in a strange mood; my return isn't the headline this morning. A sex tape!

'Whoa,' I say. 'Do you know why you were sent that?'

Flick doesn't say anything else. Instead she wipes her dark-rimmed glasses on her expensive blue silk shirt to – I'm sure – try and steady hands I notice are shaking.

But then she composes herself.

'I didn't open it at first because it was an unknown link. But I came in early and asked IT to take a look at it, because of the title.'

I nod. Yep. We are always being told to be careful what we open. Makes sense.

Flick bows her head, as if in prayer.

'I did send a memo to everybody, to tell them not to open it,' she says, looking tortured. 'I tried to act, as fast as I could. But it wasn't fast enough, evidently. They'd either already looked or they were too curious and ignored me.'

I reach a hand to her then.

'It's okay,' I say. 'It's not your fault. They shouldn't have done that if you told them not to look at it.'

Would I have looked, though, I wonder? A sex tape isn't normal Monday morning fodder.

Flick's prayer ends and she looks at me.

'Scarlett,' she says. 'The video clip was titled with your name. You're in it. It's your sex tape. You and . . . two men.'

I laugh at first, in disbelief.

'That's impossible,' I say.

But then I look at her screen, from a chair where I usually sit with a cup of coffee in my hand looking at the Google Analytics and I freeze with a memory of something that happened in a different time, to a different me.

Fuck.

Sitting in the chair next to my boss, I am still and I am ice. Flick's hand is hovering over a video clip.

'I can show you, if you want me to, but I understand if not,' she says quietly.

Perhaps if she weren't my friend, or if she were a man, it would be different. But something compels me to watch. I lean forward and click play myself.

Flick stands up to pull the blind down.

I stare at the movements on the screen and at the three naked bodies – one of which is my own – having sex with each other, in various shapes and combinations.

Fuck.

I wrap my arms around myself and try and hold the parts of me together.

My head throbs, my vision blurs.

Felicity, moving back towards me, looks alarmed.

She tries to touch me but I shake her off.

'Let me contact medical,' she says, concerned.

We work in a large building, with lots of other creative

companies. There is a nurse in a small room on the second floor. It's a forward-thinking place to work. Good mental health is a key focus so he would get me a cup of tea and ask if I need the in-house counselling service phone number for a referral and I would sit there and reply with what? That it's not too many working hours that's the problem here, but the fact I just sat in a boardroom with my boss and watched myself have sex.

I shake my head.

'No medical,' I manage. 'I just need a minute.'

She nods.

I know it happened. I do remember it, somewhere in the recesses of my mind.

Felicity has turned the sound off on the video, or it doesn't have sound, but for whichever one of those is true, I am grateful.

One long minute later I look back at my boss's bowed head. She is still wiping.

I continue to sit, my heart feeling like it could injure me with its drumming; migraine kicking in. My back is sweating like I have just completed one of the ten marathons I have run in my lifetime. My face is hot like I've opened the oven on a bubbling lasagne – ready-made, knowing me – and peered right inside.

'It was posted to a website but they sent the video link too,' Felicity says, under her breath.

So it's not just an email to be deleted but this video is accessible to whoever, whenever. For those people to laugh at me or be turned on by me or to use me for whatever they need.

My eyes, which sting with the urge to weep like a toddler who doesn't want to share, can't take themselves off the video.

My hands and my legs shake harder, deeper.

It was pointless, I think, to try and reinvent myself as I look at the woman on the screen. Same arms, same legs, same me.

You attempt so hard to be something, to leave something

behind but image is fragile and now my shiny new one is on the floor.

Can someone pop in to sweep it up? You've left a shard in the corner. That's it, all gone now.

The video finally stops.

'Stay,' says Felicity weakly, as I stand up to leave. 'Let's talk this through.'

But I laugh and she dips her head. Because we both know that what she is saying is preposterous. How can I put either of us through that? What would 'that' even involve?

The only option here is surely to run, run, run as fast as I can.

I fight the urge to throw up.

Even if some people didn't open it without the private IT favours Flick asked for, they would try the link later, at home; less wary, too curious.

To walk to the lift I have to walk past all of them, the colleagues that now know what you would get if you peeled back every single item of clothing that I am wearing.

It feels like that's exactly what has happened.

3

Scarlett

4 May

Breathe.

Remember to breathe.

I feel discussed and disgust and I am outside the office, calling Ed and sobbing hard as I walk towards the train station.

Ed answers on the first ring and I know the second he says hello.

'I was about to call you,' he says. He sounds altered, in the way you do when the seismic stuff happens.

'They sent it to you,' I say, stopping still on the street amongst angry shoppers and people running late for work who have to swerve around me.

'Yes,' he says. 'You know then. Shit, Scarlett.'

We are silent, in shock.

When he speaks next, it's quieter.

'Who else was it sent to?' he asks.

'I don't know,' I say. 'You're the first person I've called, obviously. But my work colleagues, for starters. I've just come out of a room with Flick. Can you leave work and meet me at home?'

'Yeah of course,' he says. 'I'll leave now.'

He'll get home sooner than me from his office in Warrington, only half an hour from Sowerton.

'I'm sorry,' I say, guilty at bringing this into our life. 'I know you're busy in work today.'

He doesn't reply.

'See you soon,' he says, then hangs up.

Is that it? I think. No *I love you*. No *We'll get through this*.

Wait until you get home, Scarlett, I think. He probably just wants to see me face to face. It's not easy to get into this without being in the same room.

On my phone, I am googling lawyers as I walk to the station, bumping into angry people who curse at me.

'Look where you're bloody going, love,' says a city type in a too-small suit.

I stare at him blankly; no capacity to reply.

Finally I arrive at the station and on the platform fire off five emails to different law firms.

I am desperate to pick up the phone to them to speed this along but how can I have this conversation next to a mum with her toddler or the retirees excited about their day trip for a walk and a fish and chip lunch?

A minute after I board the train, one of the lawyers pings back. I have an appointment next week.

Okay. Okay. I'm doing something at least. I'm taking action.

I look out of the window and try now to calm down slightly, to exhale.

Then my phone rings.

It's one of my closest friends, Martha, and so I pick up, hoping for the comfort of her voice.

'Hey,' I say. 'I'm on a train so I might cut out. Did you speak to Flick?'

I met Martha when she worked at our company. She and Felicity are still close too.

'Yeah,' she says. 'I did. Fuck I'm so sorry, Scarlett.'

I sigh. 'Thanks. Just trying to sort out a lawyer now.'

There's a beat of silence that feels odd when there should be a flurry of reassurance and solidarity and 'Oh, Scarlett, this is awful, what can I do to help?' and the like.

'Martha?'

'Scarlett, I'm sorry. It was sent to me too.'

My phone beeps then and I glance at it while Martha is on the line. Because I have a horrible, desperate feeling. It's a text from a friend asking me to call her when I'm free. Then another. Followed by a message telling me I have a voicemail.

From my dad.

It's gone everywhere. To everyone. Or everyone, at least, who matters to me.

My *dad*.

I gag.

'Scarlett? You still there?'

'Martha, I'm going to have to call you back,' I say. 'Talk later.'

And I sink into the chair and sob, avoiding listening to my dad's voicemail and hoping, desperately, that he is phoning about something else.

Oh, to be this exposed.

My phone is no longer the mind-numbing comfort it was on the way in. Instead it's a grenade.

I search my ex Ollie's name on Facebook. I blush when I think about why I'm starting with him, not the other man in the video, Mitch. Because the reason is that I don't know Mitch's full name.

How much will everybody judge me? I'm even judging myself.

Was Mitch a nickname? It's not a very good one, especially not for a DJ. A surname, then? Part of a surname?

I know this is out of the blue, I type to Ollie but think – is it? Is it? Not if you uploaded and sent that video, it isn't.

But I need to speak to you, urgently. Please get back to me ASAP.

No pleasantries; no context.

Another friend tries to phone me. I let it ring out. The bald man in the tie across the aisle glances at me, his face red with irritation.

I would turn my phone off and throw it out of the window, I think, if it weren't for my daughter crawling around a stranger's house and needing me.

The man looks at me again, disapproving. I stare back at him. Why is he going home early? Feeling sick? Forgotten his laptop? Whatever it is, I think, you are having a better day than me. You are reading your newspaper and grimacing at others. This is not, for you, one of those days that alter lives.

I push my fingers into my temples, terrible headache overwhelming me.

And then I think *Poppy*.

I contemplate gruesome images of her as a teenager, being shown or told about the video by crude classmates.

The feeling inside becomes an ache. The gag threatens to go further. The bald man turns away.

Knowing I can't avoid it forever, I listen to the voicemail from my dad.

'Love,' it says, and he sounds like he is delivering news of death. 'I've been sent something awful. Phone me when you have a minute.'

The sobs come harder and the man across the aisle softens, offers me a tissue. I shake my head no and bury it in my hands.

My phone beeps. Ollie.

Bloody hell. Bloody hell. Scarlett! Okay. Yes, let's meet up. When?
It takes three attempts to type my reply with trembling hands.
Tomorrow? I say.
Away for work, comes the reply. *Day after?*
We agree to meet at a pub in Shropshire, in between me in Cheshire and him in – apparently now – Birmingham.
Can you tell me what this is about? he says once the meet-up is sorted. *I'm married.*

Yes, of course – if he didn't do it, that is how it sounds.

I'm not trying to come on to you, I type, cringing for all of the nearly middle-aged married people who are coming on to past loves, right now. *I'm married too. Happily, thanks*.

I think about telling him that I don't have a twelve-year-old that I haven't mentioned either, but decide it can't hurt for him to wonder. Disarming him could make sure he doesn't lie. And make sure too that he comes, shows up, and sits in front of me to answer my questions. My question.

Explain when I see you, I reply quickly.

I stare at the screen and at his name, popping up over and over. The oddness that a collection of letters can make me react so strongly by association; I'll never see a message ping in from Ollie and not be twenty-one and besotted and obsessed with every word he ever said to me. Hairs on my arms stand up straight and tingle.

For God's sake, Scarlett, this man might have ruined your life. Time for the rose-tinted youth glasses to come off.

An hour later, I walk into our large, open-plan kitchen and see Ed standing in the corner by the window like he is trying to disappear into the exposed bricks.

'Oh, Scarlett.'

He looks at me.

I stop where I enter the room.

I can't go to him; I am too ashamed.

He doesn't come to me.

He doesn't speak.

I cry and he doesn't comfort me. He is pacing.

'Have you contacted these men?'

He looks like he might throw up.

'I'm meeting my ex in two days,' I say. 'Hopefully he can put me in touch with . . .' I trail off. Somehow, this seems less real without names.

'Have you contacted a lawyer?' he asks, moving again, hand to his forehead. 'You need to get this taken down. Fast.'

I nod my head, chastised. 'Appointment next week,' I say, pleased to please.

'I'll find you something sooner,' he says, taking his phone out of his pocket. He starts scrolling, searching. 'That video has got to come down. *Now*. For fuck's sake. Why would they do this to you?'

He looks at me. Sighs.

'Scarlett, why didn't you tell me this had happened?'

I flush. 'I did!' I protest. 'When we first got together and we were drunk at that wedding in Spain. I told you that Ollie and I had a threesome.'

Something flashes across his face. 'You told me you . . . I thought . . . fuck, Scarlett, I assumed it was with another girl, not a guy.'

I look at him.

'Is that different?' I ask, frowning.

'Of course it's *different*, Scarlett,' he mutters.

It was okay when he thought it was something a seventeen-year-old boy might fantasise about. But when the picture's less socially acceptable, I'm slut-shamed by my husband.

My sobs come harder.

'How am I going to go back to work?' I cry. 'My colleagues have seen it.'

His phone beeps and he reads the message.

He slams his hand on the kitchen table.

'What now?'

'My parents,' he says, bleak. 'My parents have been sent the video too.'

His phone starts to ring.

He punches the wall this time, just to the left of our large framed wedding picture.

'And by the looks of that call, Liam too.'

His older brother. I cry harder then, because the breadth of this is unbearable. How can this be happening to me? I'm not a celebrity – not unless you count a very low level of attention that I get from Cheshire Mama and I don't – and not a controversial figure.

My skin is smarting in desperation of how much I long for my husband to hug me but I know he won't. He's not in a hugging kind of mood. Ed gets like this sometimes, when he's focused on something practical. He can't step outside it to the emotional.

I look at him, and suspect that however I get over this, I will have to get over it by myself.

'I'll go and get Poppy,' he says.

And it's only then that I think about Ronnie, my daughter's childminder, and if she has been included in this circle around my life that has seen the video. How can I ever ask, as babies roam around and Peppa Pig toys go flying and the picture is such innocence?

I nod.

Even though it is too early for pick-up and Ronnie will ask questions, I let Ed walk away because I know he needs to move, away from me. And because I do not want to have to beg him to come back.

Anon

She's alpha.

That's the first thing I think when I meet Scarlett.

I don't think I've ever thought before about the definition of an alpha person but when she stands in front of me, rubbing that baby bump, it is the only word in my mind and it shouts itself, loud.

Alpha.

Alpha.

Alpha.

Scarlett is not necessarily the loudest in the room, but she is the most comfortable in her own skin. Sitting back. Appraising the situation. Cringing, ever so slightly, when you say something she deems stupid before swooping in to put you right.

Tall but not the sort of tall that means older relatives suggest she wears flats to make men feel more at ease.

'Good tall,' people say, nodding approvingly.

The victim bit? Give me a break. It's hard to swallow when you've seen the way Scarlett walks into a room, presuming all eyes are on her and very happy with that.

When Scarlett's daughter was born and she went on maternity leave, she wanted to keep herself busy so instead of eating fifteen biscuits at a time in front of bad daytime TV, she started Cheshire Mama, a painfully smug parenting blog. She uses any window she can to shoehorn a mention of Cheshire Mama because her blog makes her feel special; a local celebrity. Scarlett likes that.

Even though there are thousands of parenting blogs already, *millions*, Cheshire Mama is successful. It would be; Scarlett's kid's cute and her mum will happily flog those pudgy legs and hair that looks like it was cut in a pixie for a free designer changing bag. Often her husband features too. Beautiful, over six foot and positioned with the kid next to a pumpkin, a Christmas tree, a baby lamb, a swimming pool; insert as appropriate for the season.

It's unbearable.

Scarlett's child has the coolest buggy, and her shoulder has the coolest bag, and her kitchen has the coolest coffee machine. It sits right there, see, on top of the coolest kitchen island. They plant vegetables together in their wellies, the Salloways, but only so they can pose for the picture, a snap for a thousand hashtags.

I see her smugness when I stand with Scarlett in her kitchen. As I watch her, she is barefoot, pink toenails, picking up the coffee cup and flicking on the radio.

I smile at her, tell her I love this song.

Scarlett is pretty. Slim. God, she even has this thick, glossy hair when everyone else's is falling out like it does after you have a baby. If she's casual – often, actually – it's in a way that doesn't apologise for itself. When it rains on her dark brown bob she shoves it in an up-do that looks good without a slide or even a mirror.

It's not that she is the fanciest – that's sort of the point. She's just . . . well, alpha.

Scarlett moved round here a few years ago, relocating from central Manchester. When you need a restaurant recommendation in the city, Scarlett knows the only three places you should go this year. Watch out if you suggest somewhere else; that face she pulls will make you want to drown yourself in her turmeric bloody latte.

We all know that Scarlett thinks she's better than people without even having to try, and that irks. It irritates. It enrages.

4

Scarlett

5 May

The next day Poppy is with Ronnie, and Ed and I are in the waiting room of a lawyer's office in central Manchester. My phone beeps.

How's work going? asks Asha on our group chat. *Sending loads of positive vibes*.

They don't know.

The only people close to me that haven't been sent the video, as far as I can tell, are my mum friends.

Maybe they are new enough in my life that whoever did this doesn't know about our closeness; doesn't know they are part of my inner circle. Maybe there's one area of my life in which I can take a break from this. If there is, I want to keep it protected; keep it safe.

So I don't say a word. Or reply at all. I put my phone on Do Not Disturb and turn to Ed.

'I wish the lawyer was a woman,' I whisper, as we sit alone in the waiting room.

He looks up from his phone.

'Why would that matter, Scarlett?' he bristles. 'The important thing is getting this done, as soon as is humanly possible. Jesus. Priorities.'

He goes back to his email.

I sigh and look down.

I have worn a high neckline today and a long, formless skirt to negate as much as possible of the image that I am convinced this lawyer has already formed of me based on what he knows from our phone call. When I gave the woman on reception my name, I try to mute my broad Manchester accent and sound like I grew up in Kent. Or at least the edge of Cheshire.

I open my mouth to explain the difference between talking to a woman about my sexual past versus a man and of knowing that they have seen my body but close it again when I realise there is no point. We're here now and Ed's right. We need to just get this done.

'Scarlett Salloway?' asks a short man in his fifties. He pumps Ed's hand and then mine and leads us through to an office.

'Can I offer you something to drink?' he says. 'Tea? Coffee?'

We both shake our heads, eager to get on. Our hands are clasped to each other's.

'Okay, thanks for explaining to me on the phone what's happened,' says Mr White. He looks at his screen.

'We just appreciate you seeing us so quickly,' says Ed.

'Handy cancellation,' he says. 'So here's the situation.'

I'm glad he's brusque, at this hourly rate brusque is ideal. And I really don't want to go over the whole story again.

'You can report this to the police, but that would make whoever has done this alert to being investigated, which means evidence could be deleted or destroyed.

'So first, I would suggest that you try to obtain strong evidence on who did this – and I'm presuming in this situation you have a good guess – yourself.'

I nod.

'I'm meeting Ollie – the man, one of the men – tomorrow,' I say.

Ed's whole body cringes next to me. His fingers loosen in mine.

'And the other?' asks Mr White.

I try again to remember Mitch's proper name.

'Working on it,' I mutter, head low, mood lower.

'And what about in terms of getting it down?' asks Ed, letting go of my hand altogether and leaning forwards. I sit beside him, meek, playing with my wedding ring.

'Yes.' Mr White nods. 'Obviously important. Must be traumatic for you and your wife and everyone close to you.'

I think about my dad. I still haven't called him back, despite his multiple attempts to get through to me. Ed has his head bowed. I think of his parents, and how eventually I'll have to see them too.

'What you want to do is contact the operators of the website that it's on directly,' he says. 'Some will remove it, some won't on the basis of freedom of speech.'

I see my legs begin to shake beneath my skirt.

'What if this one won't?' I ask. 'What then?'

'Well, it's a more complicated process but you can make an application on the basis of privacy law. You can also make an application to Google to delist all videos from search results. It'll be easier if it's a UK website operator.'

Ed is nodding seriously.

'There's only one,' I say. 'That I know of.'

Mr White nods, matter-of-fact.

'Yep and hopefully it'll stay that way but don't be surprised if it pops up elsewhere,' he says. 'If that happens you'll just have to go to them individually.'

Ed looks at me, checks I'm getting it all. I nod but I'm shaking harder now. More websites. The video spreading wider. Further. It hadn't even crossed my mind.

'So you will sort this?' Ed says, turning back to Mr White. 'One way or another?'

'Yes,' says Mr White. 'It may take time but there is only one video. In many cases there are hundreds, posted to different websites. This should be simple. The most important thing though is finding out who did it.'

I nod at Ed and at Mr White and think that the situations aren't too different, right now and in the video.

Me, with two men, longing to be anywhere but here.

We leave then, but not before Mr White hands me a glass of water, concerned that I look faint.

5

Scarlett

6 May

Early Noughties house music plays loudly in the car and the window is down. My head doesn't nod rhythmically, automatic, like it would normally do. This has taken even that away from me. Shocked my urge to dance into stasis.

I push my sunglasses up a touch on my nose. Notice that the guy in the car next to me is staring.

You think I'm somebody else, I think. You think I am Scarlett 1.0, the girl in the video. Ollie's 'bird', party hard, probably high, definitely drunk, life and soul. I won't sleep with your boyfriend but I'll probably flirt with him. If you have a proper job, I'll roll my eyes and call you a sell-out.

I am doing it.

I am on my way to meet Ollie.

I shove my hand in a giant bag of Haribo that I bought at a petrol station earlier in the journey and shovel them into my mouth.

We met, Ollie and I, when we were both twenty. I worked in a pub; he drank in the pub. I had spent the years since my pre-teens careering through life, unloved, unloving. My dad, at capacity with his young child, believed me when I said I was fine and didn't push me when I turned down invites to come for minty lamb or a cup of tea or to build a sandcastle with my sister as we shivered on the beach in Blackpool.

I had friends. But they were really drug dealers or party buddies.

I got into university but I partied too hard and I fucked up my degree and so I worked at the pub full time instead of part time and shrugged my shoulders and partied harder. Got kicked out of my flat for not paying my rent. Moved into what I suppose was called a squat. Partied even harder. Took the drugs you aren't supposed to take. Did the stuff you aren't supposed to do.

At the pub there were lock-ins. There was a lot of haziness. But in the middle of the haziness, I met Ollie and wanted to be lucid to impress him and to remember being with him and he brought me back from the brink. From the cracks on the edge of society that in retrospect, I had already started to disappear down.

'Scarlett, Scarlett, there is no one like Scarlett,' he would sing to me as we danced on the streets, at bus stops, bars, wherever we were. We were together for three years of dancing when he stroked my face, held me close and where sometimes I would cry out of nowhere because I was happy, for the first time in years, years, years.

Ollie and I moved for the same music and it was a uniting factor, but it was music that even though I had taken it down a notch, still went with being drunk, high, out of it.

We were young enough to handle that though. Just. We weren't old enough to have to analyse why we got so out of it, or consider our behaviour as destructive. We didn't see therapists or make up for it at the weekend with a fast day. Chaos was just what you did until something happened that stopped you being chaotic.

And when, twenty-three and in shock, I told Ollie one day that that vomiting episode hadn't been a hangover but a baby, we grinned at each other. Because we had our reason to stop being chaotic.

It wasn't on the script but we loved that scene. We would do this.

He kissed my hair and whispered to me: 'Thank you.'

'They'll be funny,' he said, grinning like I'd never seen him grin. 'Like you. They'll be funny and beautiful and confident and a big adventurer, just like you, Scarlett Scarlett Scarlett.'

Ollie started looking for a proper job, and he thrived with the purpose. I stopped drinking and getting high. Until our baby was born too early and didn't make it and then I drank more, took more, pushed the boundaries and tried desperately to rewrite myself back into the party girl I was before, not the mum I had been planning to be.

I wanted to be out every night.

I wanted to try this club, and that club.

I wanted to submerge myself back in that world so that I could pretend I had never left it, even in my head, and maybe that would work; something had to, God it had to.

Because I wanted to die, really.

I wanted to have the threesome because a threesome seemed like the opposite of planning to be parents. Debauched. Irresponsible. Maybe it would be the thing that worked.

'Really?' said Ollie, concerned as I whispered it to him late one night on a dance floor.

'Yes! Yes! Why not?' I said, kissing his face, whirling him around the club.

'It will be fun! An adventure! You always say I like adventures!' I slurred. Except normally they involved impromptu flights to foreign music festivals or a big night out on a Monday. This was left-field.

But we could reclaim our messy young lives. Fully see off these sensible nearly-parents we had turned into. Live, so that the alternative stopped sidling into my head.

'I don't think it's a good idea, Scarlett,' he said, soft in my ear.

'We've been together for three years,' I told him. 'We don't want to get *old* and *boring*.'

That was exactly what we had wanted to get.

But in the absence of that, this.

Ollie looked concerned.

'But *now*?' he said, glancing down my so recently pregnant body. 'Now?'

Now. Exactly now. That was the point.

And I snapped at him that just because I wasn't at my skinniest, didn't mean that our friend's mate Mitch didn't want to sleep with me.

'Mitch made that clear actually,' I said, sullen.

'That's not what I meant, Scarlett,' said Ollie, sadly. 'I meant physically, mentally. When you're still healing.'

Well, was Ollie in, or was Ollie out? The implication was that I was doing it, either way.

He finished his vodka.

I was insistent and Ollie agreed, reluctantly, like he agreed to most things I said around that time in a desperate bid to make me smile again.

The next morning though, what had happened and what we had done when we were still grieving for our baby born only six months before had felt shocking. And for us, it marked the beginning of the end.

I shove in more Haribo. More. More.

After an hour and a half, the sat nav tells me I have one left turn to go. My stomach registers all of the sweets in that second and I fight the urge to vomit.

Ollie. I'm about to see Ollie.

You have arrived at your destination.

I take a deep breath and turn off the engine.

Out of the window, I see a man walking into the pub who looks like Ollie, except he doesn't because he is in his early twenties and giddy and Ollie is in his thirties and by the look of his Facebook picture going grey and by the sounds of his messages, wary.

I unclip my seatbelt and get out of the car.

Deep breath.

Head in.

And it has to be one of the oddest things in life to walk into a pub and see your first love, all grown-up.

For me, Ollie is frozen in time, his arms in the air on a dance floor moving to Basement Jaxx with a lazy smile on his face. He has a bottle of Stella in his hand as he leans forward to touch the birthmark on my ear in a bar. He is naked, getting out of bed to walk to the kitchen to get us some water the morning after. He's bringing in greasy packages of chip shop chips that we will devour to ease hangovers.

But now, he's defrosted. It's twelve years later and there is a tired-looking man drinking a coffee next to a pub window. He may well have had soya milk — he's that kind, looks after himself even if he's exhausted. The BMW in the car park might be his, but then perhaps it's the Skoda with the Baby On Board badge in the back window.

He wanted children. I know that.

But with your first love you don't know, you see, if he has a baby on board, because you do not know him, this man who took such a role in forming your whole life. Who is the reason you drink your coffee the way you do because you started drinking coffee when you were together. Who is the reason you get goose bumps from certain songs and cry at certain films.

You have thought of this moment, though, so many times, as you went to sleep, as you daydreamed on the bus, as you saw a date on the milk that made your stomach flip and realised it was his birthday. You have thought of telling him how well you're doing, and looking good when you did it. You have thought how odd it is that you're thinking all of this because *why*, when it's so past and you don't want him back.

You have thought *Not now*, when you have gone out with no make-up on and seen someone who looks like him from the back.

You have thought about not needing him any more, and how freeing that is.

And then you have wondered if that is real, if it would be, were you to see him again because what if first loves are like tornados; what if they obliterate everything in their path when they come along, even if on a calm day, when the sun shines, you can't imagine their power? Perhaps you will always need him.

What am I doing?

You have thought of the romance of it all, of the depth of that immature love, and of all of that dancing. You have heard songs, and felt tears that contain seven different types of emotions.

You have thought of his skinny legs and his polo shirts and you have thought of his Midlands accent. He's gone back home, Ollie, now he lives in Birmingham. To get some help with childcare for his children, perhaps? For extended family to be close to his own new one?

You have thought of that first love telling you that he wanted to be with you forever, and how that can have derailed. You have thought that well, it's good that it did because look at you now with your real life, but also that it's bad because look at you then, so in love and how can that not be sad, that it didn't last.

You have thought how old the daughter you had together would be now, and now, and now, and now, and nothing has ever hurt like that does, every time.

You have thought everything, because twelve years is enough time to do that, and then suddenly there is no more thinking because he is there.

Before he spots you he is on his phone, because of course, what else.

We didn't do that the last time I saw him. Phones were functional, still, for contact not time-wasting.

And so you stop for a second to try to make your heart stop

racing and breathe so that your voice sounds normal, and so that you don't seem rehearsed, like you haven't played this out a hundred times, which of course you have because yes, twelve years. Twelve years of thoughts.

While you do that, you stare at him, at his head bowed, because he hasn't yet realised you are there.

Could you have done that to me, I wonder? Are you capable? The man I know is not capable but look at him: his face has shifted. It's not a leap to think his character may have shifted with it.

The anticlimax, though, when a moment that was so nostalgic, so loaded in all of those scenes you played out, is dominated by the mundane.

'Hey,' is the first word I say to this man, this man who adored me, my first baby's father. 'Do you want another coffee?'

He looks up and says nothing, but his face contracts.

'I'm going to order one,' I say eventually, swallowing hard.

I walk away but when I get to the bar I am shaking and so I order a glass of wine. Red, large.

It is very, very like having an affair, except that the sex part is out of the way and I regret it already. The one time, with Mitch I mean.

Then I sit back down next to him and we are silent, taking each other in and recalibrating. I want to fling my arms around him tightly and tell him how much it all meant, but it's odd and not allowed and we're grown-ups now and there are boundaries.

So we observe them. We talk about our journeys today, distances, parking. We move on to houses, locations, jobs.

'You're quite big news in the mum blogger world, I see.' He smiles, almost proud and I think that's okay. He can be proud – he helped to form me.

I laugh.

'Apparently so,' I say. 'Who'd have seen that coming?'

I am gentler with you, I think. Soft.

I am enjoying his company like I always did and I have to remind myself to be suspicious of him, wary.

'Just going to the loo,' I say and when I'm there I check my lipstick and add a little concealer.

'So you're married?' I say, back at the table, and Ollie nods.

'Rose,' he says. 'We've got two girls, Holly and Jade.'

I am oddly unmoved. This new life of his feels unreal; something unmoored from me, floating around far away. I can't quite believe it.

'And you have Ed and Poppy, I see.' He smiles. 'Easy to find out all about your life from Instagram. Not that I was stalking but once you got in touch, I did have a look.'

I nod. Of course I know it's out there but it suddenly hits me how exposed I am.

We sit for a second. Now For The Main Event, says the pause.

Ollie breaks the silence with something he has obviously practised. It masquerades as a joke, but his eyes say terror.

'So you didn't have a kid that's mine then?'

There's a beat as he realises what he's said.

'I mean . . .'

I shake my head to tell him it's okay but my smile falters.

'No,' I say eventually as I compose myself. 'I would probably have mentioned that earlier.'

He's a good actor, if he did send the video.

'Do you really not know?' I say suddenly, downing the last of my wine and fighting the urge to order another one, despite the fact I have to drive home, 'why I contacted you?'

He shakes his head. Smiles at me. He keeps doing that, a really big, genuine smile like it is nice to see me, and it is contagious and I do it back before I remember, each time, why I am here.

'The kid was my best guess,' he says.

'Serious?' I ask.

'God knows,' he mutters. 'I could see they weren't on your

53

Facebook but maybe that was deliberate. I don't know. It was pretty out of the blue.'

He reaches for my hand.

'And we had managed it once before.'

His eyes fill with tears as mine do and we think of our baby girl, just for that second, together. I wonder if that means as much to him as it does to me. It's such a relief.

We sit then again in the company of that shared experience and shared loss. There is calm from being able to think about my first baby with the only other person who understands and I tighten my other hand around his. He squeezes back, and it feels like clinging.

'I know,' he says. 'I think about her.'

It takes a few minutes to regroup.

I let go of his hand and go to the bathroom again. When I come back he stares at me.

'So. Come on then. Tell me what it is, new strait-laced Scarlett. Scarlett, Scarlett, Scarlett.'

There it is. That singsong. We smile.

And I realise I would look strait-laced to him in fresh make-up, drinking a glass of red without the wide eyes and the bare legs.

My heart pounds. He DJ'ed sometimes, too. Staring out at me from the decks as I danced for him. What an odd thing, to go off and live life and procreate and move on, but to leave a bit of you back there, twenty-two and besotted.

He repeats my name. 'Scarlett, Scarlett, Scarlett.'

I'm still back there, which means I can't speak here, now.

'What is life like now then?' he asks. He leans forward, onto the table, looking in my eyes. 'Is it all book clubs and organic kale? Are you . . .'

He does a hammy gasp.

'Are you . . . respectable?'

I blush, like I've been caught out. Like the police have come to the door to arrest me for something I did twenty years ago. I'm a fraud, I think. Whatever facade I've put on, it's not convincing.

But his teasing is warm. And it's nice to break the sadness of earlier.

'I am actually, yes,' I say after a while. 'And I like it. Like you say, respectable. People respect me.'

My eyes fill with tears.

'Or they did.'

He raises an eyebrow.

'Tell me if you did it, Ollie. Tell me if you shared the video.'

But when I look up, sobbing, I know he didn't.

Because while his hair has greyed, his eyes haven't changed.

'Fuck, Scarlett, what happened to you?' he says. He goes to touch my face and I see him stop himself, think, about his wife probably, and how this would look, might have looked, as he sits in a pub with his ex. But then he does it anyway.

I tell him what happened.

He slumps back in his chair and I realise for the first time that this affects him too. Sure, I'm female, and so I bear the biggest load of it, but it's his body, his sexuality that's up there too.

'Rose,' he says, looking queasy. 'My parents. The *kids*, even, when they're older. The thought of people seeing that . . .'

He looks at me.

'Why would I do that?' he says. 'To myself as well as you.'

I flounder now, defensive almost.

'Oh come on, Ollie, everyone knows it's not as embarrassing for a bloke. There's no shame for you. Maybe you wanted to get revenge. For me leaving you.'

He looks at me.

'After all of this time?' he says. 'You think I'm that bitter?'

Then, quietly and sad. 'You didn't really think it was me?'

He says it hoping.

I say nothing.

'You did,' he says, devastated, and I duck my head.

If Ollie didn't do this, then it isn't over. And it means I have to contact Mitch.

'Do you have a number?' I ask, wincing.

Ollie looks up from the dregs of his coffee.

'For Mitch. Do you have a number?'

He shakes his head.

'Sorry, Scarlett,' he says. He thinks. Scrolls through his phone contacts. 'I don't keep in touch with anyone who knows him either.'

I can't make eye contact with him because now, more than at any other point in the conversation, we have to picture it. The night that I tried to break our grief, not understanding myself well enough to know that I was really trying to break our relationship, by bringing someone else into our private sphere. Self-destruct didn't cover it; it was relationship destruct, life destruct.

I was sad and I had been through something no one should have to go through, not least when they are twenty-three and living in a shared flat and working in a pub and also have done their share of pain already, *surely*, losing their mum from breast cancer when they were barely able to remember her.

I'd pressed a button I needed to press to get out, away from Ollie and clubs and grief and drugs and vodka and music and sadness. It was a grim method of making those things happen because I didn't know how otherwise. That was my whole world.

Mitch, that friend of a friend, was up for it. God knows how drunk you have to be to have that conversation, but however drunk that is, I was it.

And Mitch was gorgeous. Grass-green eyes, auburn hair, a cheeky smile. A party boy, another sometime DJ – weren't they all – an overgrown child, like all of our friends.

My C-section scar was still pink when I took my clothes off. Mitch didn't notice. It stung when he touched me. He still didn't notice.

Ollie flushes red and I know he is remembering too.

How it broke us, sharing us and our bodies and our world, especially at that point when all of it was so fragile.

How that had been the point.

Because perhaps if it hadn't been for that night and the awkwardness afterwards, we might have made it. But I didn't want to make it. I wanted to run away from every memory of our girl and her existence. Including the man who made her.

I picture it.

Mitch's closely cropped hair. His legs, skinny like Ollie's. But he was different to Ollie with his gym-honed upper body, young enough that it could still work out in the mornings after brutal drug and alcohol binges.

I remember when we went home together – the same night we discussed it – to mine and Ollie's flat. I remember chunks, but nothing clearly. Mitch watching as Ollie and I had sex. Sobering up just enough to see Ollie's face as Mitch touched me. Feeling oddly removed, like I had from all of life for that previous six months too, as I had sex with Mitch. Seeing a look of alarm cross Ollie's face like he couldn't believe we were doing this. Could we love each other at that moment?

I force myself to come back to the present.

I ask Ollie, despite my shame.

'Can you remember much about that night?' I mutter quietly.

'Yes,' he says with emotion. 'I remember Mitch filming.'

I think of the quantities of vodka I had drunk. The quantities of vodka I drank a lot of nights. Of how much we used to drink and of how little we used to consider consequences or the future, or the impact of anything on anything.

I nod. I had vague memories of Mitch filming too.

I hadn't cared. This was twelve years ago. The world had barely coined the phrase 'revenge porn'. It was a bit of fun. We thought the worst a camera phone had to offer was some dodgy pixilation.

The truth is that when someone was filming the video that

would ruin my life, I might as well have turned to the camera phone, grinned and winked.

'Did he send you a copy?' I ask Ollie, cringing.

He looks appalled. 'No! God. Of course not.'

I tried to remember more. Did Mitch send it to me? Did I have a copy in the days before I took computer security seriously? Ever show it to anybody? I don't think so but I couldn't swear to it. I was drunk, it's been years, life was blurry then. Life has become blurry again now.

We sit in silence for a few minutes.

'You know you said you were having trouble tracking Mitch down?' says Ollie eventually. 'I know Mitch was short for his surname. Mitcham. If that's of use.'

And it is. There was no formality with Mitch. He wasn't someone you put in your address book and wrote Christmas cards to. You couldn't imagine him having an oven. Everyone just knew him as the DJ, thingy's mate, y'know, *Mitch*. This is more than that. This helps.

I walk out of the pub loaded with a wedge of guilt, for accusing Ollie, and for inflicting this on him now too.

We hug for slightly too long and I feel tipsy from what I know, really, was too much wine for a stomach only lined with sweets and too much emotion for a woman and her ex and all the nerves of meeting him in the first place and an increasing feeling of unsettledness for where the hell this mess will end.

And in the car I email Mr White.

Met Ollie, I tell him. *He denied it and I believe him. Just working on a contact for the other man. Think it's much more likely to be him.*

And then I shove my hand back in the Haribo, turn the music back up and start my long drive home, hands trembling on the steering wheel.

6

Scarlett

7 May

DJ Manchester Mitcham.

And it's easy, then. Those two extra letters do it.

I find him on Twitter, still pedalling his DJ skills at the odd fortieth birthday party. I send him a short DM, asking to meet up.

All right love, he replies. *That's a blast from the past. But yeah, sure. Everything okay? D'you know the Anchor pub in town? Could meet you there after work tonight?*

I'm meeting up with the other guy, I message Ed, who's at work. I feel victorious. This has to be it, despite the friendliness of Mitch's messages. If it's not Ollie, who else? And I never knew Mitch well. Who knows what sort of person he is, what motivation could have led him to this? The story will unravel soon, I'm sure of it. *So hopefully some answers soon.*

Keep me posted, he replies. *And send me the details of where you're meeting. I can come, if you want?*

Jesus, I think. Imagine.

Best if I go alone but I'll keep in touch, I say. I tell him the name of the pub.

I pick up the phone to Mr White, who I speak to often enough now that he has become Jonathan.

'Made contact with Mitch,' I say.

'Great news,' he says, jovial. 'Keep all the notes. I'll ask Lynne to book you in for later this week. We can go through everything then. Let's get him, Scarlett.'

I get to the pub early.

Poppy is still going to the childminder until I figure out what the hell is going on with work; until I'm out of this limbo. Then Ed took her straight from Ronnie's to Liam's house so she can play with her cousins.

I check the clock above the bar. Most likely Ed is watching Poppy create a crime scene from a bowl of pasta about now. I smile thinking of her with tomato sauce smeared around her soft mouth, then take out my phone to scroll through pictures and distract myself. This time, I stay away from wine and order strong coffee.

I rip the top off a sachet of sugar and see that my fingers are shaking. I'm not sure they have stopped since I met Ollie. This has to be it, surely.

I try to decant half of the sugar sachet and then think of all the ways my life is now out of control and so I pour the lot in, adding a second.

Things used to be measured, I think, so recently.

Oily fish on allocated days and takeaways reserved for weekends. Now they are so out of control, so unordered, it is impossible to imagine getting back on course.

When Mitch walks in, I see him instantly. He is still large, though now it's a largeness that speaks of pints and chips for dinner, and having not seen a vegetable for a long time. Before it was a largeness that spoke of whole afternoons in the gym and protein for breakfast at a time when the rest of us thought health food was a sugary cereal bar.

'Mitch.'

He looks weathered, Mitch. Old. Like the DJ's packed up and the bar has closed but he's still at the party, telling twenty-two-year-olds that they are lame for going home; that it wasn't like this in his day. To stay! Stay! Have one more! Let's do pills!

'All right,' he says awkwardly and I'm surprised by how clearly I remember his Manchester accent, strong even for someone who had lived in the city their whole life like me. 'Drink?'

I shake my head and Mitch heads straight to the bar, while I sit and wait.

He comes back and plonks himself in the chair with a bottle of beer like a thirteen-year-old who's just been picked up from a party earlier than they wanted to be. I stare at him. Confronted by the man who I am sure ruined my life, I am struggling to keep calm.

He looks up at me, raises an eyebrow.

'So then?' He smiles. 'What's this about?'

I would never have struggled with this confrontation before; would have been powered through it with rage. Now though, I am dealing with the maternity leave confidence crisis. Too much time in my comfort zone; too much time in pyjamas.

I hide my hands under the table, so that Mitch does not see them vibrate.

'I'm not sure how well you remember me,' I begin.

'Yeah sure.' He grins, amiable. 'We hung out a lot, back in the day.'

We did, from a distance. In a wider circle, often at the same parties or the same nights out. It was only that one night though that we moved in closer.

My nails are out from under the table and in my mouth. I long for something stronger in my coffee. I am remembering, and I am angry with younger me for having sex with this man for performance not pleasure. For doing it when what she actually craved was a hot water bottle.

I hate that I was playing a part. Party girl, boundary pusher, fun girlfriend and, mostly, non-mum. It hurts that I did that to myself.

'Yeah, so,' I say, trying to get it together. Wishing for a friend to squeeze my hand. Wishing for kind eyes to meet mine and tell me I am safe. Wishing for Ed, on some level. 'A video has been posted of me, you and Ollie and sent to my friends.'

Please don't make me explain, I think but when I look up, I know I don't need to.

'Of me, you and Ollie . . .?'

'Yeah. My boyfriend. I mean my boyfriend *then*. Yeah.'

I only get one second to do this so I need to do it right. I stare at him, analysing his face and trying to work out if it was him. I look at his clothes, try to decipher if he's short of cash; if that could be the reason he's done this.

I have been thinking about this more and more – if at some point something worse will be threatened and I will be black-mailed, and that's where this is going.

My stomach dives. I know what it is I'm thinking about; the thing I fear being revealed. The story Ed can never, ever know.

Mitch may know it. It's possible.

I look again. His clothes are nice, new. I look at his face. Try to work out in that second if he's an attention-seeker, or stalker. If he's cruel, or odd, or both.

But all he seems is normal.

'Jesus,' he says. 'I'm sorry. Did Ollie post it?'

'No,' I say, oddly defensive of Ollie now. Ollie at least cared about me. 'Ollie wouldn't do that.'

But I had thought it. I had thought Ollie could. And now he wasn't in front of me, I wondered it again. It doesn't take long for human beings to become theoretical when you can't see their eyes.

'Sure?' he asks.

'Sure,' I say, unsure.

'So who?'

There's a beat when he gets it but I spell it out anyway.

'You, maybe,' I say, with a tremble in my voice. 'I thought maybe you.'

His eyebrows shoot up. 'You serious, Scarlett?' he says.

I nod.

'No,' he says. 'I didn't do that. I wouldn't do that.'

He sighs.

'Look, I don't mean this to sound rude, honestly I don't but . . .' he says. 'Well, I must have slept with fifty people since you. What happened between us, it wasn't that big a deal to me to be thinking about it or . . . *posting* it, all these years later.'

I flush red. I'm in ballet pumps and cropped jeans. My dark brown hair, hacked bluntly at the nape of my neck, has lost its gloss and is in a tiny ponytail. My bag is tan and large and designer and contains nappies. I clutch it close to me like a child and colour again.

Most of these women he sleeps with are younger than me, probably. Hotter. I no longer sparkle. So why would he target me? Because I'm rich now? Because Cheshire Mama has made me visible? Because visible and exposed and rich is a tempting combination?

'But it has to be you,' I say. 'You were filming.'

He sighs, infuriated.

'Was I? Well, I still didn't do it,' says Mitch, and swigs the last of his beer.

'Ok then, did you share it with anybody else? Send it round to your mates?'

He shakes his head.

'Not my style. You might want to go back to Ollie about this. Maybe he was filming too. Or got hold of my phone or some-thing. I saw him around a bit for a while. He was *broken* when you left him. You sure he wasn't angry enough to take some revenge? It happens, you know. Being dumped can do bad things to a person. Maybe his life didn't go that well. Maybe he blames you. Maybe he never got over you.'

I can't confront him further, can't press him, because suddenly all I can think is how I need to be home with my child.

Everything has an added layer of shame when I think of my daughter, who has a mother who did this. I'm not clean enough for her. I'm not good enough.

I run out of the pub and jump into my car as Mitch – who

sounds genuinely concerned as he shouts after me to ask if I am okay, if I am safe to drive – tries to catch up with me.

In the car park, I put my head on the steering wheel and turn up the Noughties house music that's been the soundtrack to my life, in secret the last few years, replaced in public with more middle-of-the-road music, news headlines or even – Ed's preference – a little afternoon play on Radio 4, like we are sixty-five and slowing into our retirement.

But now, what's the point in turning it down? Turn the real me up; blast her out.

If Ollie didn't do it, and Mitch didn't do it, I think, then who the hell did?

Suddenly there is a knock next to me on the window and I leap. Mitch indicates to me to wind my window down. He leans on it. I turn the music down.

'Just one thing,' he says, palms up in a gesture that tells me he means no harm. 'When you got in touch, I googled you. You're very *out there* online now with that blog and the kind of numbers you have and it doesn't take much of a glance at the pictures of your house and clothes and whatever to see that you're pretty loaded. Maybe someone worth blackmailing? That could be where this is headed.'

He shrugs. 'Just a thought anyway,' he says, and then he walks away, out of my life again.

And I think again of the secret I'm still keeping close and feel my whole body start to tremble, an earthquake at my core.

It's another twenty minutes until I am capable of driving home and I spend the journey wondering if it all has to go now: Cheshire Mama, my side-hustle and the thing I have been clinging to since I walked out of work three days ago. I need to deal with that too. Answer Flick's calls. Make some decisions. I'm drowning.

The noise hidden beneath the beat of the music, I cry so hard as I drive that it feels like my face is bruised and like my life is bruised, way beneath its skin.

Anon

She drives past me, that evening, no Poppy in the car.

Where are you going, Scarlett? She hasn't mentioned anything in her messages and it's a pretty big deal if one of us makes it out in the evening at the moment, with our young babies making 8 p.m. feel like midnight.

Out of her window blasts a song that is too familiar to me. My stomach lurches.

I only get a quick glance through the open window but Scarlett has bare shoulders; lipstick on. She doesn't make that effort for many people. As I said, Scarlett prefers to be (very deliberately) 'effortlessly' casual.

I watch as her car moves further away, heading towards the station. Into town, most likely.

After-work drinks with old friends?

Or the other thing?

I stare after her, until her car disappears from sight.

7

Scarlett

8 May

I open my eyes at five thirty when Poppy stirs and I sense a tiny flicker of energy; a trace of fight.

I am a grown-up, I think. Grown-ups can't quit their jobs because they feel embarrassed. This isn't serving double vodkas on offer in a bar in my twenties. We have a child. And a horrifyingly large mortgage.

I haven't told Ronnie anything yet, so I still have childcare.

I could just go to the office. Stand tall. Reclaim my life.

I dress plainly, in jeans and a thin grey knit. The white trainers that make my heels pinch.

Ed walks into the kitchen later and sees me wearing eyeliner; Poppy dressed.

'You're not going to work?' he says, eyes wide.

'Where else would I go?' I say, taking a coffee pot off the hob. 'We have bills to pay.'

I nod towards the pot.

'Your coffee's there when you want it,' I say, then start sweeping up toys from the floor.

Ed stares at me but doesn't say a word.

I drop Poppy at Ronnie's and it's been easier the rest of the week, in a ludicrous way, because I am too distracted by obsessing over whether the childminder, in between cutting up my daughter's carrots for snack, has seen my sex tape, to focus on being away from Poppy. I avoid Ronnie's eye contact. Dart out of the door quickly.

I distract myself on the train journey by doing that back-to-work-and-traumatised Cheshire Mama post I meant to do the other day. Most people will never know — I hope — exactly how traumatising that trip back to work really was. I do some housekeeping on my Instagram — so close now to the magic 10,000 that would make me a real player in the social media world that it would be a shame to neglect it — and post the picture of Poppy I took at Ronnie's gate. There, like it all happened today. If only I could pick and choose what time slot I exist in in real life so easily. Zoom back to a week ago.

On the train, I message Flick to warn her that I'm coming in and then I email the website operator again, as I did as soon as I got home from the lawyer's yesterday.

'Just chasing!'

I delete my exclamation mark when I realise I have never written an email I want to exclaim in less.

When I get off the train, the reality of what I'm facing by returning to this office hits. I feel my body start to shake. I walk the five minutes from the station and by the time I am there, it's worse.

'Hey,' I say to Sanjeeta as I sit down. And she is so eager as she leaps up from her desk to hug me that I feel like she has been told to make me feel included. She is my junior; she pities me.

Freddie does the opposite, staring straight ahead, apparently intrigued by a social media graphic.

I turn my computer on and wait for it to power up.

I think about the time I spent painting layers of thick respectability over my messy years and what a fucking waste of time that was. I'm swearing a lot more in my head the last few days. Drinking more. Old me has risen from the dead online, I think, and now she's making a play for my real life.

'Morning, Scarlett,' says Felicity, matter-of-fact as she powers over in skintight jeans and high ankle boots that still don't make her anywhere near as tall as me. She ushers me straight into a boardroom. As I walk through the door, I see glances exchanged, eyebrows raised.

'Morning,' I say.

I sit down and put my hands on my lap. They tremble. It's not subtle. Felicity sees it too, and looks away. She nudges her glasses back on her nose. Twirls her ruby wedding ring. It's embarrassing for us both, and I hate that I have piled this on her. My role as Digital Marketing Manager is a senior one, one rung down from the top, AKA Flick, our MD. I am a professional person, an adult. I'm not the woman who hauls her relationship problems to the office or the guy who gets too drunk on tequila at every single leaving do and insults people.

I can be relied upon. 'One of the grown-ups,' Felicity used to say with a wink because there are *a lot* of twenty-two-year-olds in high-tops in digital marketing. I am a grown-up. I put the bins out. I sweep up the toys. I have a grown-up house and husband and life. I have a grown-up job.

And now I am this.

'Scarlett, I'm so glad you came back,' says Flick, smoothing down her T-shirt. 'I would have hated for you to leave like that, over something so . . .'

She struggles for a word.

'Sordid?' I offer. 'Grubby? Disgusting?'

I am angry with her, for reasons unknown to me. Maybe I'm just angry with everybody.

She stares at me, hard, and thinks.

'Something so past,' she says, after a while, crossing her legs to the other side. 'Something so unrelated to your work. Which is brilliant by the way, as you know.'

I don't know why this makes me cry, but it does. It feels like a loss. Felicity hands me a tissue then lowers the blind so the rest of the team can't see in. I wipe my eyes but then I get up.

'I need to get on,' I say, decisive. I throw the tissue in the bin. 'It's time to work.'

I take out a compact and wipe away AWOL mascara.

'Not too rough?'

She smiles and hugs me, then gets the door.

'How is Ed doing, by the way?' she says, casual. 'Can't be easy for him either.'

Flick and Ed aren't close but they've known each other for a long time, as long as I've known Ed. After-work drinks when he worked here, the odd double date with whoever Flick was seeing at the time.

'It's nice of you to ask.' I smile. It connects the dots of my life. Sometimes it's like Ed exists in a vacuum. My mum friends barely know him. 'Typical Ed. Shutting down on the emotional stuff.'

'That must be hard,' she says. 'For you, I mean.'

I shrug. 'You know. That's what I have mates for.'

She winks at me and squeezes my hand and I head out to work. But it's outside in the huge open-plan office with faces and voices and eyes everywhere that it gets me.

I sit at my desk and know that most people in this room are looking at me and speaking about me. A colleague asks if I want a cup of tea and I see him smirk. I log into my email and feel my skin crawl, thinking about them all, logging into their accounts that day, clicking the link, eyes widening, heads tilting, realising who it was and that this was the gossip of the *decade*.

Because whatever anyone says, I know. I would have felt the same if it had happened to someone else. Of course it's gossip. We're human.

Do they still have it? I wonder. Can they picture it? Bring it up for a laugh at 11 p.m. when everyone's had one too many wines and then they watch it in the pub like a Man United match? Are they messaging about it right now? I glance around. My phone beeps. A group chat message from Asha, asking if anyone is signing up for bloody Tumble Tots. But I reply to it because I want to speak to them, want to be in their reassuring company. Want to be in conversation with people who don't know. People who care about me.

I go to the kitchen. I need to breathe. Make a cup of mint tea. Calm down. But as I round a corner, I hear Flick's voice. She's in a boardroom but the door is ajar.

'I get it,' says Flick into the phone and I see the back of her head lean up against the glass wall. 'But it's not Scarlett's fault your guys feel awkward. It's not her fault the video is out there in the first place, Dom. Jesus!'

I am like a child playing musical statues. Stopped where I first heard her. Unable to move.

Dom is a client on a soft drink brand. I won his business and we've worked together for four years now, a good working relationship that's crossed over to a semi-friendship over time. We use meetings as an excuse for brunch and a Bloody Mary; I know the names of his kids and ask about his wife's start-up. When I was on maternity leave, he kept in touch a bit, a few likes on Instagram, the odd message to see how it was going. He'd been one of the people I was looking forward to catching up with most.

'Okay okay, yes, I do get that,' says Flick, gentler, head still back against the wall. A sigh. 'I know it's not coming from you. Yes, I know you do. We all care about her. She's one of my closest friends, Dom, but trust me I still get it – this is awkward all round. There's not exactly a precedent here.'

Dom and his team have been sent the video. Or heard about it at least.

Flick bows her head forward now.

'Okay,' she says with a sigh. 'Maybe we can do that. Temporarily. I'll speak to Sanjeeta. See if she can work on the account. Subtlety is going to be key here though, Dom, to not make Scarlett feel any worse than she does. I can spin it as needing Scarlett elsewhere now she's back but *please* let's exercise some discretion from your end too.'

And as if things aren't bad enough, now I'm a work pariah, making things awkward for my boss, my clients. Junior members of staff covering for me. Things being spun so I don't realise the truth. It's difficult to remember a time I have felt so pathetic.

I turn back and return to my desk.

There, my breath gets shallower, rasping, audible. Something tightens in my throat, and moves down to my chest. It sits in my stomach too, in a way that makes me feel like I need sugar. Or perhaps vodka and a couple of lines of coke.

It's how I've been known to deal with this feeling, when it's happened in the past.

It happened in the past, often. But I thought my panic attacks didn't get me any more.

It turns out instead that they were there all the time, dormant under the surface like fleas.

Now I look around and the perspective of the room is wrong.

I go to the toilet and run straight into Joshua, a senior guy from a sportswear client that I had secured last year. Must be here for a meeting.

'Scarlett!' he says, taking hold of my arms as I slam into him. I shudder, remembering how he does this every time anyway, touches without warning, creepy, handsy. I leave meetings with him feeling uneasy. He tries to flirt, with no encouragement. Now, I have handed him an easy win by charging into his body.

I look up.

And I know, in that second.

Him too.

Word has spread, and all of my clients – or enough of them at least – know about the video.

Joshua smiles.

'I'm so sorry, darling,' he says. 'About the video.'

He still holds on to my elbows.

I am frozen to the spot.

'I shouldn't have said anything,' he says. 'I didn't expect to see you. You caught me on the hop. But I'm . . .'

And I run then and I don't care who sees me fleeing my workplace like a crime scene as long as I don't have to finish this conversation, or any of them.

I stop only to grab my bag and when I get outside I gasp the air like I'm being resuscitated.

An hour later I walk through the door of my house and see Ed, who is working from home, at the table in the kitchen. He turns in surprise. He's barefoot and bare-legged in shorts. His eyes are heavy.

'The whole industry knows, Ed,' I say. 'Not just New Social. But my clients. They sent it to my *clients*.'

He throws his head back, desperate.

We sit in silence for a minute.

Hug me, I think. Hug me, hug me, hug me.

Ed has seen me in the aftermath of panic attacks the odd time. He knows that's what this is. He knows that I don't want to talk. He knows that what slows my brain down is touch, a hug. But lately, I rarely get one.

'Ed, I don't think I can go back to work,' I say eventually.

My job is central to my self-worth. Walking into that office, sitting in those brainstorms is *101* of being me. Plus, I think, there is always the chance this *is* heading towards blackmail. To the threat I'm most scared of. And if it does, I'll need money of my own; money that's not Ed's so that I can try desperately to keep a lid on it.

But work is one of the areas of forest that this fire has burnt through most determinedly. Can I put a mask on and charge back into that burning building?

I sigh, deeper.

No.

I can't get past that level of humiliation.

My clients.

That dickhead Joshua and his team, watching me on their away days.

I am not going back to work next week, next month, ever. My skin isn't thick enough. Those fires have charred it to dust.

Whatever my worries about money, I'll have to find another way. Delve into the savings we have left from my mum. Forget shutting it down, I need to monetise Cheshire Mama, grow it into a genuine business.

I feel a sharpness in my chest.

There is no coming back now.

Whatever this job meant to me, it can't mean that any longer.

Ed nods; grimaces.

'I'll go and work in the other room,' he says eventually, and scoops up his things.

I sit on the kitchen floor for an hour, too tired to move, or even to cry, willing him to come back. But he doesn't, and I message the girls – Cora, Emma, Asha – instead, and tell them I had a hard day at work, so that the comfort comes in, the warmth, even if it's the virtual kind when I am longing for hands and breath on my ear and a voice, gentle, to calm me.

I email a formal resignation to Flick and I weep as I do it, saying goodbye to a slice of my life.

Anon

Subjects in our group chat today: fussy eaters, childminders v nursery, is this too early to think about having another baby, anyone know a good waxer, am I too old for leather trousers, how can my child still not sleep, where's the best place to order pizza from? I've accidentally double-dosed on Calpol HELP.

Subjects Scarlett wants to talk about: her bad day at work.

And there you have it. Scarlett, in a nutshell. Me, me, me.

8

Scarlett

9 May

It's been a day since I ran out of the office for the second, more final, time. Felicity has messaged and called repeatedly since I sent my resignation. I don't reply.

At home I function at the lowest level I can for Poppy, no Ronnie to help as it's the weekend. Ed has gone to the gym, says he needs to burn off some rage. Me too, Ed. I guess I'll load the dishwasher a bit more aggressively than normal, then?

I phone Ronnie. Tell her that my company have given me a little longer off; that we won't need her childminding services after all.

'Not a problem at all, Scarlett,' she says, but sounds surprised. She's the Beyoncé of childminders; no one cancels. 'But you know I need notice normally so I will have to take a couple of weeks' pay?'

'Of course,' I say, glad cheeks aren't visible on phone calls, or for that matter pyjama bottoms with stains on them. 'Sorry to mess you around.'

But also, this is the upside. No more leaving my girl. No more traumatised train journeys. No more pondering the effect on a child of not seeing their parents all day before the age of one.

I end the call and pick up Poppy, who squirms away from me as I try to cuddle her.

I should take her outside, I know. But I am fearful of leaving the house, wondering if every face I see has watched the video. So we are stuck here and the walls are shifting inwards.

I look down at Poppy, who is optimistically holding out a small ball that I barely have the energy to take from her.

'In a few minutes, Pops,' I say, and she crawls away as I lie back on the sofa.

A message pings in. Flick.

'Please reconsider,' it says.

Delete. I've never told her about overhearing her chat; never will.

At 3 p.m. Ed walks in, looking like I look: smaller, broken down, tortured.

'Jared has seen the video,' he says without a hello, as he walks into the kitchen. He slams his hand down next to the hob. '*Jared has seen the video of you.*'

Ed's friend, the guy from the lift, who still works in my company. I didn't even think.

This keeps finding new ways to torment.

I groan, vicious.

'It was a horrible conversation, Scarlett,' says Ed, ignoring the sound.

I nod. Yes. Horrible.

'I'm sorry,' I say, and he says nothing back.

'Are you ashamed of me?' I ask quietly, as I've wanted to ask all week.

The tears are wide and chunky, saturating my face.

He winces. 'Of course not,' he says with a sigh.

Stock answer. What else would he say?

'It's not your fault, is it?' he says but it's like he's reading from a script, approved for use in a #metoo generation. 'You're allowed to have a sexual past.'

He stumbles over the words. Ed's family don't discuss things so uncouth as sex. Ed is repressed, but he tries.

'You're allowed,' he says, head lowered. 'To have made mistakes.'

My own face snaps upwards.

Because was it a mistake? Or just a part of a full, messy life?

'It happened because of what Ollie and I went through, Ed,' I say.

He knows that Ollie and I lost a baby when I was seven months pregnant.

'Do I need to transfer money for the lawyer?' he replies.

I stare at him. 'Did you hear what I said?'

He nods and reddens. Takes his laptop out of his bag and opens it.

I probably wouldn't have told him, to be honest, but while a man you sleep with once after untold amounts of vodka might not notice your C-section scar, your husband does. I told him weeks after we met, tears rolling down my young un-made-up face, as we lay hungover in bed and he asked about my scar, finger near its edge. And of course, when you come to have a baby together, you tell midwives and doctors about it in front of him too. *Yes, I have been pregnant before. No, it wasn't a successful pregnancy.*

Ed looks up.

'I know it sounds crazy,' I say, trying to explain. 'But I didn't want to be this victim who had lost her baby, who everyone pitied. I wanted to be back to the me from before. The party girl who liked adventures. But *more* extreme, *more* wild, *more* crazy. That's how we ended up doing it. It was my idea.'

I blush. Because Ed knows I used to like three-day festivals I couldn't remember much of and coming home at 7 a.m. But I gloss over the drugs I took; how dark things got sometimes, how grimy. Ed wouldn't want to think that about me, prefer-ring the version that beats her PB on her lunch break and sets the table in a fancy way for a dinner party and paints her nails neatly, so I spare him, keep his mind clear of the images.

'I went too far,' I say. 'Obviously. But in retrospect I was pushing the self-destruct button on that whole life. Taking it to an extreme so that I could get out of it and move on and start again.'

Again, he wouldn't want to know that yes, that's all true, but also it *was* the kind of crazy thing we did anyway; the kind of debauched time we had.

Best to focus on this part.

I give him a hint of a smile.

'Start again with you, and our life.'

But this doesn't please him. In fact, Ed's face is contracted in discomfort. Of not having it in him to be compassionate, despite the fact that this is one of only a handful of times I have spoken to him about the baby I lost.

'I knew Ollie and I wouldn't come through that, not with the grief too,' I say, voice catching now too.

I stare at Ed.

He looks like he would do anything to walk away from this conversation and exist anywhere but here.

Well, Ed, I think, I have to deal with this so you have to deal with this too. That was part of the vows.

'So was it a mistake then?' I push. 'Because it brought me to where I am now. Sparked a change. Like things do in life.'

But Ed looks at me, incredulous.

'You're saying that doing . . . *that* on film wasn't a mistake?' he asks.

I stare at him.

To him it's one plus one equals two, as life always is. It was a mistake. I shouldn't have done it. If I wanted to leave the relationship and the life I was living, I should have left. I shouldn't have got drunk and high and had sex.

I look at Ed again.

Did you ever go wild? I think. Did you ever go crazy?

He is staring at the floor.

It's been less than a week since the video but the chasm that's opening up between us is vast and that shocks me. It should be a moment we are pulling together, tight. Surely.

Hug me, I think again. But Ed walks out of the room. He pauses by the door as though to turn, but it's like he physically can't. I hear him go up the stairs as I stand with my arms wrapped around my own body. But you can't hug yourself, no matter where you position your limbs.

9

Scarlett

10 May

Scarl, says a message from the only person in the world who calls me Scarl because there is no word he doesn't shorten, first thing that Sunday morning. *Can I come over? We really do need to talk about this.*

I turn back to the bathroom mirror and tie a bobble in my hair. I glance at my puffy eyes in the mirror. Poke at a spot-cum-boil on my chin.

I look back at my phone and sigh. Everyone's messages are difficult at the moment but this one is the worst.

Since I replied to my dad's voicemail with a text, I've been avoiding speaking to him directly about the video. I told him I was consulting a lawyer, I was sorry he received it. He told me not to say sorry, never to say sorry, please would I answer his calls. I made excuses.

But I think I've run out.

He's seen the video. My dad, who calls me Scarl and tried to plait my hair and be interested in my ballet classes after mum died, has seen the video. I struggle against the urge to be sick again.

Since I left work that day, a steady drip feed of friends has messaged to tell me they were sent the video too.

Some are concerned, some are disbelieving, some are angry,

some send me links to revenge porn articles as though reading about revenge porn is now my hobby. Some, incredibly, act as though it's something we should be laughing at. Come on, it's *hilarious*, Scarlett. They're generally the richer ones, to whom sex has always been funny. Sex hasn't always been funny to me. It's been grimy and embarrassing and a currency and a stain.

But yes, the pattern is set. If you're a major part of my life, you've been sent the video. My family. Ed's family. My old friends. My colleagues. Not the NCT girls, though. As far as I know – and Cora, for one, would be telling me if she had seen that – they've still not had it.

I think of the lawyer telling me that if I'm even going to think about taking this to the police, I need evidence first. Of Ollie denying it; Mitch too. Of the dead end I stand in front of.

Yes, Dad, I reply, weary. *Come round. But there's not much to update you on.*

I turn to Ed.

'My dad is coming over,' I say.

He inhales sharply at the thought of being involved in that conversation.

'I'll take Poppy out,' he says.

What's the only thing more awkward than speaking to your dad about your sex tape? Your husband being in the room while you do it.

'You go out,' I agree. 'But leave her here for protection.'

I give him a wry smile.

'Will you be okay?' he asks, gentle. In between his pragmatism and his pacing, there are moments of softness, of old Ed, and that is all that's getting me through.

I nod, unconvincing. What counts as okay?

But surely there's only a certain level of brutality that this conversation can reach if a nearly one-year-old is cruising along the sofa. She's an unlikely defender, as she blows raspberries over and over and tries to eat her own foot, but she's my best hope. 'It's probably best you're not here. Get another gym session in or something.'

Once upon a time Ed and I were fit. Ed lifted weights and drank protein shakes. I ran the grimness of my past away in twenty-six-mile increments, all over the world. The Chicago Marathon, the Paris Marathon, the Berlin Marathon and in between as many half-marathons and 10ks or stints on the treadmill at the gym as I could. If I could have run a marathon every day, I would have. I'm a person of extremes; always have been.

Now, of course, we're made of Americanos and blueberry muffins and sausages stolen from a toddler's plastic plate. We've abandoned tending to our own bodies for a while, as we help to grow somebody else's.

Ed is already packing his rucksack, grabbing the opportunity to work out and the even better opportunity to get away from this.

And I'm relieved.

As I wait for Dad to arrive, I try to steel myself but I'm made of materials that are the opposite in form to steel. Plasticine maybe. A big lump of Play-Doh.

And when my dad arrives, I lose my shape fast.

It's thirty seconds since he walked through the door and we are standing in the hall with my head bowed on his shoulder as I weep.

He is holding me tightly, and the sobs are coming violently now. It's a release.

'I'm sorry,' I say when I come up for air. 'I'm sorry.'

'Nothing to be sorry for,' he reiterates, rage all over his face.

'It's that piece of shit who posted this who's to blame. You were young. We all do daft things when we're young. We'll have a pint one day and I'll tell you some of the stuff I did in the Sixties.'

I try to smile. Manchester born and bred, utterly working class, my dad. I can believe him. There would be a plethora of stories.

We move into the living room and sit on the sofa. Normality goes out of the window. I don't offer drinks; I haven't tidied up. I wear leggings that once were black. Sport hair that once was washed. Mascara that once was on my eyelashes. I'm a bleak homage to what once was.

This is an emergency summit. The gloss of life – manners, politeness, routine, ceremony – is gone.

'The problem is,' I say to my dad, 'that piece of shit is currently unidentified.'

'But it's him obviously?' he says, brow furrowed. 'That ex of yours?'

I sigh. 'He says it isn't,' I mutter, knowing how naive I sound but believing it, fully.

But also, I can't accept that somebody who used to whisper all the things he liked best about me into my ear until I slept when I had insomnia, could go for me like this.

Ollie and I were together from when I was twenty to twenty-three. We discovered Eighties teen films together and shared a deep love for dance music. We drank one-euro red wine from plastic bottles on European campsites at festivals. I loved the dollop of freckles on his thigh. He loved that birthmark on my ear. But we loved each other beneath our skin too. We were young and obsessed.

My dad would know this, surely?

But then, I think back to the time Ollie and I were together and it was when my dad and I were furthest apart. I had dived into the world to drink and get high and be hedonistic and dance until I was ready to come up for air in whatever part of the grown-up universe I had figured out was for me.

Meanwhile he was at home in the world that he'd rebuilt.

A few years after my mum died, Dad went to French classes

to keep himself busy and met his new wife, Faye, over irregular verbs and extra-curricular Cremant. Tentatively I was introduced to Faye and the three of us spent summer holidays in Brittany and Bordeaux. In between, I peered down the stairs when I was supposed to be in bed, watching them get to know each other, only seven years old and my tummy nervous about what their closeness meant for the future.

Faye started leaving her toothbrush and her blender and eventually her nightie and we were polite but not close and eventually she moved in and they got married and people got weepy at my flower girl dress and it seemed impossible after all of that that we *still* weren't that close but we weren't, even though she tried, and sometimes I wasn't even polite.

It affected my dad and me too and until I had a family of my own, we weren't as close either.

And so when I was with Ollie in my twenties, my dad wasn't in my day-to-day life enough for me to go to him with scan pictures when I got pregnant or, later, howling grief.

Dad was excited for me, and then sad for me, but from a distance and I did most of my crying away from him, then I went travelling and arrived back to him in a different form. Ta-da. Good as new. Mended. I've always been more comfortable presenting a polished version of me. I hate exposing my pain.

But here we are. Consider it exposed, Dad, I'm out of polish. I look at him then, sitting on my sofa, face red like the socks that he is wearing beneath the jeans that have sneaked up his crossed leg. Red like an emergency.

'I believe him, Dad,' I say, sighing back into a cushion and pulling Ed's hoodie sleeves over my bitten nails. The hoodie smells of Ed and I am nostalgic for us before Poppy. For us before the kind of shame that sends you to opposite corners of the house. 'And he did love me.'

My dad raises an eyebrow.

'He did,' I say firmly. 'I don't know many things as fact, but that I do.'

He nods, grimly.

Then he goes to put the kettle on. God, I think, there's no sign that you are in the middle of a catastrophe as clear as someone else putting on your kettle.

'I take it there's none of those fancy cakes you normally get in,' he says. Wry smile. 'I'm going to waste away. Tell me there's a biscuit at least.'

'Nothing,' I say, weak smile. 'You're sorry you came now aren't you?'

There used to be brownies that I would buy from our local deli. A spotless hob.

I glance out of the window to see weeds that would come up to my knees. If we stopped living the day that Felicity showed me the video six days ago, other things have grown up like those weeds in our place. Grime, mess, distance.

I flush pink because my relationship with my dad goes like this: we meet up, I spend the entire time proving that I am not the car crash I once was. I tell him stories of presentations I have given at work, I dress my child in overpriced clothes because I am middle-class and successful. I tick as many boxes as I can, without even realising what I am doing. I am like product placement, attempting to sell you something without you realising it. I am as good as the one I think of, truthfully, as your 'proper' daughter, the subliminal message goes, love me, love me, love me.

I spray some Dettol on the coffee table and wipe it down and wish they sold a human version. If only it was so easy. I touch the grease at the top of my hair, self-consciously, where the greys peek through. The kettle boils and Dad goes out to get it.

He comes back into the room and hands me a mug that I usually reserve for builders, containing tea when I rarely drink it.

'Okay then so what about the . . .'

He looks away from me before he continues his question.

'. . . other fella?'

I cradle my hot mug away from her direction as Poppy pulls herself along the sofa.

'Well done, chicken.' I smile as she takes her hands off for a second and stays upright. I reach down to stroke her hair and kiss her. 'Well done, clever girl.'

The other fella you were having sex with at the same time as this boyfriend who loved you. No wonder this is difficult for my dad to compute. Not for the first time I think of my half-sister Josephine and how much cleaner she is than me. How much more glossy. How much less ruined. She must have been sent the video, Josephine, but she hasn't said a word to me. I can't face asking her. I can't face adding another layer to this conversation and asking my dad. I think about Josephine's upcoming wedding, and how she is at the start of things, unblemished. I scratch at my skin. I've covered it in expensive moisturiser and fancy bath oil for a few years now but it's still me under there.

'Well,' I say, with a cough. 'He says no too.'

'But it has to be one of them, doesn't it?' he says, looking astounded that the daughter who takes the phone off him when he calls his utilities companies to take them down and make them quiver and offer refunds would be so *meek*; so accepting.

I sigh.

'Dad, you're not ashamed of me, are you?' I ask.

I look down at my odd socks, a tiny hole forming at the ankle. I think of the chaos in my kitchen. I picture my ethereal sister, kindly keeping her sex life hidden from view so no one has to think about it.

Then I feel myself enveloped, so tight it is hard to breathe but I don't want it to stop.

'Now you listen here,' my dad says, firmly. 'You never say

that again. I have never been ashamed of you for one day in your whole life and I never will be. Don't let anyone make you feel ashamed, my lovely girl, ever. You're smart, you're funny, you're bloody gorgeous. You're a huge success at work, you're making money somehow from posting pics on the internet even when you're on maternity leave, which I don't fully understand but sounds bloody savvy to me. And you made that perfect girl.'

He nods towards Poppy then pulls away from me.

'You make me proud as punch. Every single day. As much as Josephine, but we will always have our special bond – me and you, my love – we will always have that. And I will look after you, because your mum can't, and that's not bloody fair.'

I cry hard then because I want her, for the first time in years, and it's horrific that I can't have her, but it's also the biggest relief that she has left my dad behind to put his arm around me.

'Now listen,' he says, as he pulls on his trainers to leave. 'I know that Jos is a bit off radar, with all her wedding admin. "Wedmin", she tells me it's called, you heard that?'

I smile, at this strange word coming out of my dad's mouth.

'But do you have friends to spend time with, to keep busy now you're off work?' he carries on.

I nod. 'You know the mum friends I made at antenatal classes?' I say. 'They've become very close. They do stuff for me – babysitting, helping out, we spend a lot of time together.'

My dad nods, fierce. 'Well I like the sound of these girls,' he says. 'Keep them around. Get all the love you can get at the moment, poppet.'

10

Scarlett

11 May

It is 12 p.m. on a Monday and I am in a pair of flannel pyjamas that I sniff occasionally, suspicious. My insides feel achy. Poppy is napping in her usual star shape on her stomach in her cot.

My phone rings. Jonathan White.

'Sorry you had to cancel the meeting, Scarlett,' he says about the catch-up we had been due to have after I saw Mitch.

I couldn't face it. The trip into town, the eyes on me.

'Just easier to do it on the phone, you know, with childcare,' I reply in my lawyer voice; swift, aware I'm being charged. 'So I'm just giving you the update as requested. Mitch says it wasn't him, same as Ollie.'

'You believe him?' I hear him consult his notes.

'He was pretty convincing,' I say. 'But who knows. I've lost all perspective.'

'Keep going,' he says. 'Figuring out who did it is the key. You'll find them. No one can hide in this day and age.'

I hang up on Jonathan with a sigh at how little this has moved on in the week since I first saw the video. Poppy's still sleeping. Now what?

I click onto my Cheshire Mama Instagram.

With more suspiciously scented pyjamas than dreamy family outings, I am doing a lot of motivational quotes and throwbacks.

I fling myself into replying and commenting on other influencers' posts and liking, liking, liking. How okay I sound, I think. How *fine*.

Lots to like online, not a lot to like off it.

I sit back against the cushions on the bed. Sigh.

I need structure in this new life of mine.

This morning – a lot of mornings lately – feels too close to the old life without order. Pasta was served with potatoes after Mum died because Dad was too sad to consider a balanced plate. Washing wasn't divided into colours because grief trumped white washes. Sometimes you were allowed TV before dinner; sometimes you weren't. Depended how the day had gone. Rules ebbed and flowed.

And we all know that a lot of my twenties didn't follow much of a routine either.

But my thirties? So far they've thrived on systems.

I run a bath and lie in the last of a jar of expensive bubbles, still scrolling social media, when I see a post by Josephine.

I had been blocking out how weird it was that I hadn't spoken to her since the video, but seeing my dad has brought it to the forefront of my mind. I can't put it off forever. Even if a little sister and a sex tape is another level of shame.

How's wedmin going? I message.

I reach over the side of the bath for a glass of water but even that turns my stomach.

I have to do it.

You've seen it, haven't you? I write while she is still typing her response to my other message.

There's a pause.

Yes, it was sent to me, I'm sorry, she says. *You poor thing. I didn't know whether to get in touch. Dad said you and Ed were dealing with it privately. That you didn't seem to want to talk about it. I didn't want to be an extra person for you to deal with, someone else phoning. I also didn't want to freak you out that I'd seen it too but I can't lie to you xxx*

It's horrific, even if it's not surprising.

I think of her watching me having sex with those men and my skin flames.

Josephine as a little girl would come into my teenage bedroom to ask me to play with her dollies or tell her why elephants were called elephants.

Little sisters aren't far behind dads and husbands in the list of worst people to see your sex tape. I shudder, despite being in a bath so hot it had made me gasp on entry. That had felt oddly like what I needed.

Dad and Faye had Josephine when I was nine, Faye pregnant soon after they got married.

He told me I was getting a half-brother or sister in a pub over burgers, with a tiny bit of ketchup on his chin. It made me laugh because getting tomato sauce on your face didn't seem like something that would happen to a grown-up.

'Scarl, I've got something to tell you,' he said, hand playing with my ponytail as the two of us, on a rare excursion alone, sat side by side.

'Faye is going to have a baby,' he said gently and I knew suddenly why he had made the effort to make this one happen, where so many other dad-daughter days had fallen by the wayside.

I stopped laughing.

It was like the future was about to rewrite our history with my mum, and I felt unanchored.

Josephine arrived and I did anything to avoid this new family that had sprung up and usurped mine. It felt like a small price to pay.

'Why don't you play ball with the baby?' Faye would ask and I would roll my eyes and stomp out of the door, no idea where I was going other than away, away, to somewhere where the hurt I didn't understand eased enough to bear.

As she grew up, it got worse. I hated my dad going to

Josephine's sports days. I hated her calling him 'dad'. And oh God, I hated her having a mum.

Technically, what I had looked like a family. People were relieved. A sister, too! But somehow, Dad and my weird double carb unit of grief and tenacity had felt more like home.

Now I saw my one-man family share himself with a new crew. If other teenagers were pining for boys in their maths class, it was my dad I was heartbroken over. My dad who had, it felt like, abandoned me.

No one noticed that I wasn't doing my homework; no one cared enough that my grades were dropping.

I became a teenager and looked older than I was and I got into clubs with even older boys who didn't ask much in return for the help with the fake ID but in retrospect they asked a lot with those kisses that hurt a bit and hands that strayed unwanted up skirts.

I could get on, and I did, and then I got on some more, and more, until I fell out of the door of our house and into my next life.

But by the time Josephine was an adult too, we had grown a friendship, even socialised together sometimes.

My sister changes the subject.

You're looking gorge on Cheshire Mama by the way, she types. *All my friends tell me they want to be you when they have kids, true story.*

I pick my phone back up.

Ha! I type. *Is that the equivalent of 'I want to be you when I grow up?' AKA 'You're really old'. It's fine, I'll take it as a compliment . . .*

No WAY! she says. *That one of you and Pop on the farm makes you look about twenty-two. Anyway, got to go, am at a dress fitting. But this will blow over. I promise. So sorry I can't help more. Love you.*

I nip over to Cheshire Mama to look at the post she is talking about. Hmm. Twenty-two is generous. But I do look all right. Confident. Together. Taken before this all happened, obviously. Now I would need more than a filter to get rid of eye bags, matted hair, knitted brow, sad mouth. All the evidence disaster has happened.

I lean back in the water.

Sigh.

Something is gnawing at me. Something else.

Since this happened, a week ago, nothing else has come up. No email follow up asking for money. No second video.

And I can't believe that is it; that this is just sent out into the world and stays there, stagnating.

What would be the point of it remaining stagnant?

Where, then, I think, is this going?

If somebody hates me enough to send that video to my friends, my family, my workplace, *knowing* the impact that would have, they aren't going to leave it at that, are they?

Like Mitch said too, I am out there.

Should I be deleting Cheshire Mama, I think, instead of attempting to grow it, be out there more?

I think of how it looks, our life.

We are quite wealthy now. My own salary might be modest but Ed, high up at an accountancy firm, earns a lot and there was the money I inherited from my mum. We bought a big white listed house on a private road; it looks like something from Escape To The Country. The cars in our drive are fancy. Will this descend to blackmail? It would be worth bothering to ask me for money; from the outside it would seem like I might well have it.

I run my hands through wet hair; think.

And come back to the thing that's been chewing on my insides since this happened.

I glance at the door of the bathroom.

If Ed thinks a sex tape is my only secret, he is wrong.

I have other secrets, from the past.

Worse secrets.

My worst secret.

My heart starts to pound.

If this person has access to the video, do they know that one too?

Is that where this is headed?

The bath starts to feel chilly.

I submerge myself and wonder if I could do it and stay under. But I picture Poppy's face, and I just about come back up to the surface.

Anon

She's starting to break apart, Scarlett, just small pieces of shrapnel coming away, and that's satisfying. I look at her hair sometimes, and see oily roots, white residue from a rushed application of dry shampoo. Ugh.

I see her eyes starved of sleep, heavy. A brief expression of self-doubt that says her confidence had been delivered a blow. Less alpha, more beta. They are fleeting, but I cling to them. Smile as she walks away. This is what I wanted.

But it isn't enough. Because Scarlett still functions; the building blocks of her life still in place.

Would money help? Stripping her of that?

The Salloways' house is a four-bedroomed listed building on a private road and Scarlett calls it 'the cottage' like we'd all have to stoop to get in there before we sit, shivering, in the three-foot-squared kitchen eating jacket potatoes with own-brand margarine. Ha.

'I'm working class!' she protests when she is boozy, her accent deliberately at its strongest.

But there is no evidence of it, this working-class core she claims.

It is another thing that is hard not to roll your eyes at because Scarlett orders the most expensive wine on the list without thinking about it. Clicks order on designer bags while she watches TV. And we all know there is cash, inherited from her mum.

Money isn't what this is about though.

It's about so many things, the unfairness of the world, those rolled eyes, a man I love, but money isn't one of them.

Or it wasn't meant to be, at least.

11

Scarlett

14 May

Poppy is looking at me, eager. Earlier she brought me her shoes like a puppy desperate for a run around the park.

'Okay,' I say, seized by familiar guilt. 'Come on.'

'Yeah,' she says, whether she understands me or not. 'Yeah yeah yeah.'

By 2.30 p.m. we are at bounce and rhyme at the library, and Poppy is on the floor making duck noises.

'How old is she?' asks the mum to my left, smiling down at our children, not me, as parents at baby groups do.

'Turned one a couple of days ago,' I reply. I am not looking at her though but at my phone, which has just beeped. My fingers quiver slightly, as they always do now.

'Aw,' says the woman I haven't looked at yet. 'Did you do anything nice?'

'What?' I say.

My phone beeps.

I leap on it, somehow always hoping for an answer, from somewhere.

Just Ed, saying he's out for drinks tonight. It's happening a lot lately. Gym, drinks. Anything but home.

I realise I sound rude.

'Cake, few presents,' I mutter. I look at her for the first time.

Smile. 'There are plenty of years for the crazy parties aren't there?'

Or we didn't do anything major for Poppy's birthday because there was a deep air of misery heaving its way around our house. It's not like we were the Waltons before, but we marked occasions, did the celebrations. We blew out the candles, cracked open the Cava.

This time, Ed and I had stood next to each other as we sang 'Happy Birthday' to Poppy and helped her open her presents, all of which I had bought and all of which Ed was as in the dark about as Poppy as we hadn't spoken about it, hadn't spoken about much at all lately except lawyers' fees and sex tapes.

'You couldn't *buy* a cake, could you?' Asha had said to me, casually, a few days earlier.

Her big brown eyes were earnest, her trace of a London accent fading with every month that passed.

Everyone nodded in expected agreement.

'You *have* to make one, right?' she said. 'It's just a mum thing.'

Is it? Waitrose does great cake though.

But I added crafting Peppa Pig from icing to the mental list of things I needed to be good at.

Not a problem.

After all, I'd crafted a wife and mum from a woman who used to be eighty per cent vodka and a handful of pills. How hard could a cartoon pig be?

Four hours in the kitchen later as Ed watched the golf highlights on TV, Poppy had her cake. Ropey but done. I presented it to an unenthused Ed and then went to bed, exhausted. Those precious evening hours spent on something that would have been better from a supermarket. But no matter. I had done it. It was *a mum thing*.

I think of Poppy's face though, when she saw that Peppa Pig cake.

Back at the playgroup, Other Mum sniffs at my low-key approach.

'Oh we're going big for Jacob,' she says. 'It's Fireman Sam themed.'

She leans in conspiratorially.

'Fireman Sam *is coming!*' she whispers and I want to explain to her that her ten-month-old son can't be on the receiving end of spoilers on the basis that he can't yet speak and also that *you do know Fireman Sam is a fictional character?*

Instead I look down at Poppy and see her trying to take off, she is waving her hands so excitedly. I love this, being with her, and it's painful, the twitching of my brain and how much I wish I could be *fully* here, immersed. I feel another wave of guilt about her birthday. For not throwing that party that I couldn't face, with the eyes of family and friends on me, all at once, and the loudness, and my paranoia.

I feel a twist of rage again. Fuck you, whoever did this, stealing my daughter's party from her. And for what?

'Come on, Pops,' I say, scooping her up as the final song finishes. 'We're off.'

We leave quickly without goodbyes and I am pushing Poppy's buggy home when I see him, across the road and just cutting through the lane behind the doctor's surgery.

Mitch.

Mitch, who I hadn't seen for all these years, then saw so recently.

Mitch, my co-star in the sex tape.

I stand and stare.

Because as a woman he is speaking to shifts around, bringing her profile into view, this picture gets weirder.

Mitch is speaking to my friend Asha.

Asha, without the daughter who is almost always with her in a sling or feeding, as she's passionate about attachment parenting. Asha, for once, is alone. And she looks intent, focused.

No. Rephrase that. Asha looks angry.

I run down to the crossing and push the button over and over then glance back at them but they have parted ways, and I can see them both getting into separate cars. *Come on, lights.* But they are driving away. When the lights finally change, I run fast with the pram, to try to see into the car Mitch got into. Poppy thinking it's a game and whooping.

But if I was right and it was him, he's gone. More likely it wasn't and I'm losing it, I think. This is too much. I stand catching my breath in the middle of the street.

Mitch isn't in Sowerton, chatting to my mum friends in the street. Come on, Scarlett.

Unless he's stalking me, and he lied, and none of this is a coincidence?

'More more!' shrieks Poppy but I stand still, out of breath and taking in what just happened and how fast my brain invented a scenario that couldn't have been real, couldn't have been a genuine picture. Could it?

My heart pounds as we walk down the silent streets towards home. I glance over my shoulder before I go inside. Double lock the door.

Inside, I pull off my tights and replace them with my pyjamas. Human contact for Poppy: done. Now I can retreat again. I put Poppy in her highchair for raspberries that she smears over her face and I log into Instagram to post her bright red face on Cheshire Mama. Work: also kind of done, in its new guise at least.

My numbers are creeping up; the only success story in my life right now.

I message Asha.

I think I just saw you in the village, I say. *By the doctor's?*

She replies yes, says she parked there while she nipped to the shop. That she's sorry she didn't see me.

And what next, I think? I can't ask her about the guy she was speaking to, without sounding odd. Without flagging what is happening to my life, which I am still desperate to keep from my mum friends just so I have respite, somewhere.

I put Poppy down for a nap, drink a strong coffee and then – far earlier than there should be – there is a key in the door.

'Hey,' I say, confused. 'What's wrong?'

Ed sighs. 'We need to talk,' he says, business-like in the entrance to the kitchen.

My first thought is *You're leaving me.* Another woman? Those long gym visits, the after-work drinks, I know the tropes. I thought the video was the reason we were distant; perhaps the truth is more clichéd.

'That sounds serious,' I say, smiling nervously, trying to defuse. He doesn't smile back.

Instead he sits down next to Poppy, kisses her then wipes raspberry from his lips. I let our kitchen island bear my weight. A few seconds pass, where things feel oddly calm. All I can do is wait. Even if he is leaving me, I am too tired to fight. I could deal with the marriage break-up later, if I could just sleep.

'Any updates?' he asks, perfunctory.

I shake my head.

'No point in the police, not until I figure out who did it. And beyond the two guys, I have no clue where to start. It's maddening.'

'Okay,' he says. 'Well, in the meantime, we need to make sure we're doing everything else we can.'

He looks up at me expectantly.

'Latest on the website operator?'

And the way he speaks to me, like I'm in an update meeting at work, makes my edges shake with rage.

It's horrible to feel such disdain towards someone that you loved. It's horrible to think about how you raced each other to beat your 10k times and bored your friends with monologues about their face and about how now, you can feel such loathing towards them.

100

I look at Ed.

Does he grasp how many emails I have sent to the website provider about taking the video down, how many hoops I have to jump through, how humiliating every single one of them feels?

I wonder if he pictures the video pinging into people's inboxes, spreading like the snotty noses at Poppy's playgroups, in his nightmares like I do.

I stare at my husband with these new bags under his dark eyes. I know he is suffering too. But as much as me?

'I'm chasing them constantly,' I say.

'So no update then,' says Ed, frowning, and I am not his wife but an employee who hasn't done as well as had been hoped. Called in to the office for a warning.

He looks up. 'Also, you need to be making money now you've left your job, from Cheshire Mama at least.'

'Fine,' I say, wanting this to end. 'I will try and monetise the blog. Done?'

Now 7,200 followers; 10,000 is the magic number. Ten's what I need to start properly making cash, to ease my guilt at what I've done to our family finances.

I pine again for work, for that job I love so much. Work fished me out of the sea when I was floating aimlessly in my twenties. Since then, it's been fundamental. My first job, at a small start-up. Then New Social, where I've worked my way up to this role, working with companies on their digital marketing, educating them on social media. Building relationships with clients so that they trust me. And now what? I have to shrink away from people. Hide. Retreat. I think of Dom on the phone to Flick and wince.

'You can go back to work when this has died down,' says Ed, kinder now. 'We'll get the childminder back too.'

But it's half-hearted and Ronnie is in demand, plus I know Ed's mum stayed at home, and her mum stayed at home, and his brother Liam's wife stays at home and I feel irrationally like I have been tricked.

I look at him then. I think of how distant he is. How much more appealing those women at the gym will be, or have been already, than me, at home again in his old hoodie. I know how much Ed fancies me, but it's the me in on-trend jumpsuits heading to work or skintight lycra after a run.

The last few weeks, I have only put my head above the parapet – or the literal version, the Marks and Spencer duvet – for Poppy.

Playdate this week? I type to my mum friends. I've already told them I'm taking more time off than planned; couldn't cope with being away from Poppy.

That bit is true at least.

And when she sits on the floor playing with bricks and catches my eye occasionally and I know that she loves me being there and I think *Would Ronnie have got that same look?* I am happy, deep in my insides.

It's just that I am also struggling, since letting Ronnie go, to have the physical capacity to look after her. To pick up the bricks. To stack the rings. To cut up the toast.

I wonder again why the video didn't go to my NCT friends. Because they are seen as unimportant to me, an add-on to my real life, when this person wanted to attack the centre?

If so, that's wrong.

Lately, it feels like my 'real friends' have retreated into the background. Meanwhile my mum friends have stepped right into the middle.

Anon

'Love you,' I say as I hug her goodbye. Because that's what we do, now. We hug, we kiss, we throw around the L word like honeymooners.

I can see too that after a sceptical start at NCT, Scarlett is starting to warm to us. Even rely on us.

I can see that what we faked at first – a crew of friends, just because we happened to have booked onto the same course – is becoming real.

Scarlett trusts us. Trusts me.

She looks to Manchester, to the men, with suspicion.

Not here, amongst the milky lattes and the wedges of chocolate cake and the endless, endless packets of wet wipes. Bad things could never happen among the wet wipes.

Sometimes, as we budge up closer, I feel bad – even a little sick sometimes – about what I've done.

But now, it's too late anyway.

Also, what about what she's done to me? That's far worse, surely. I remind myself of that whenever the nausea comes.

12

Scarlett

15 May

As Poppy naps, an email pings in from the website operator confirming they have taken the video down.

I sit back on the sofa and wait for the relief to flood me.

Nothing happens.

I read it again.

Nothing.

Anticlimax, perhaps, after all of the emails, all of the chasing.

Or just the knowledge that though the video is down, it is still out there.

So how much difference can this make?

I message Ed and he at least is euphoric; gives the response that I seem to be missing.

I sit, waiting for the same mood to wash over me.

It never comes.

Poppy wakes up and I pick her up to head to Asha's, where we are meeting for a playdate. I ignore my ringing phone. Flick. It's no good talking now; the decision is made.

'It's insane how fast it's going,' says Asha as she hands me a Pantone mug. Is her hand shaking a little? I think of the last time I saw her, speaking to the man who looked like Mitch. 'I can't believe I'm back at work in a month. Even the four days a week feels like such a lot.'

She is holding another Pantone mug, in a different shade. This is perhaps the best way to describe Asha: she is a woman who has throughout her life successfully kept hold of identical sets of mugs. In her late twenties but more grown-up than me, by far.

This is perhaps the best way to describe me: I have random and disparate and sometimes entirely unknown mugs that have somehow been acquired through life.

I see Flick calling again. Ignore.

'It is.' I nod sagely, sipping from my mug with its just right blend of blue-green. '*Insane.*'

This is approximately the 177th time I have had this conversation about how fast my daughter's childhood is going.

My phone beeps. Flick. Ignore.

While the small talk would normally have me climbing the walls to look over the top for some dark humour and spark, today it's comforting. It's the conversational equivalent of putting one foot in front of the other. We're back to the basics and the basics are what I need. I think I'm acclimatising to the basics.

'Are you okay?' asks Asha, frowning. 'You seem distracted.'

I nod.

'You should write about that on the blog,' she says, back to her topic. 'The weirdness of time when you have kids.'

'Yeah, I'll have a think,' I say. 'Hey, who was that guy I saw you talking to in the village the other day?' I ask, spontaneous, just in case, because something has to give, something has to move forward. 'I couldn't cross the road in time to say hi.'

Asha looks caught out.

'Guy?' she says. Slightly pink? 'Oh yeah, I was giving him directions.'

'To where?' I ask and she tells me the pub but Sowerton is small. Who needs directions to our village's only pub, that cosy old-school hub where the locals turn when you walk in and the gravy comes in slices?

You can see it from wherever you are. It's tiny, Sowerton, thirty minutes outside Manchester. We have one coffee shop that doubles as a bar. There is a post office, doctor's surgery, one of those high-end boutiques only frequented by WAGs and rich retired women who have blow-dries every week and need an outfit for their son's wedding. And that's our lot.

Zoom out from there and it is fields, houses, a small village school. You can climb over a stile and walk for an hour without coming to a road. You don't nip to the post office without having five conversations with people you know; the doctor's receptionist, your neighbour three doors down, that octogenarian you don't remember meeting but who says hello to Poppy by name every time you see her. Friendly, people say. *Stifling*, I mutter quietly as I scurry away.

I pass Poppy a Lego brick.

Sit back on the sofa.

Sip my peppermint tea.

I think about how I move quickly in Manchester. How it fuels me. And how I move slowly here, like the countryside depletes me. I don't know. It's an odd thing because I'm in my thirties with a child and I'm supposed to spend my life muttering about how glad I am to be out of the city and instead, I pine like I've left a hot, wild lover who wore me out but I could never tire of.

I look at Asha and she seems on edge, twitchier even than her normal anxious state, tidying up around the kids.

Was she lying to me? And if so, why?

I come back to the now and look around at Asha's house, painfully tidy. I glance at her bookshelves, perfectly filed; the rows of framed pictures, of Ananya, minutes old, weeks old, months old. Of Asha in Delhi with her grandparents as a teenager, with Aidan on their wedding day, my friend a doll in her exquisite sari. The pictures line up neatly in matching frames.

'I swear my hair is still falling out after having Ananya,' Asha says, looking in the mirror above her fireplace and smoothing down her already perfectly smooth black hair. 'Surely that should have stopped by now.'

I look up. 'Sorry, what?'

I have drifted off, I realise, to thinking about Ollie, sipping his coffee. About Joshua, holding my elbows. About my disintegrating marriage. About that man who looked like Mitch. About Asha, and how she could possibly fit into this.

'My hair,' she says, looking at me strangely. She ducks her head. 'Just saying it's still coming out in clumps in the shower.'

I stare at her and go into a trance. When I wake up, I panic. Where's Poppy? But she is there on the floor throwing a ball. I lean across and smooth down a bit of her hair that's sticking up. She giggles because it tickles and I tickle her properly so that she shrieks and claps her hands together in pure joy. And I laugh then too, genuinely.

'Are you okay?' asks Asha from above when I come back up.

'Oh yeah, yeah. Sorry.'

I feel stupid. Obviously it was just a guy. Not Mitch. How could it be Mitch? We sit in silence for a while and Asha breaks it.

'So what happened with work then?'

'I just decided to take more time off,' I lie. 'It's going so fast, like you say.'

'Wow, that's generous of them!' she says, and I detect envy. 'You must have a decent boss.'

I think of Flick and want to cry. 'I do,' I say.

I reach down, human yoyo, to pass Poppy her Lego brick.

The doorbell rings. I nip out to the hall to answer it as I'm closest and Asha shouts, 'Sorry to be a pain but . . .' as she charges urgently towards us, anxiety etched across her thick foundation.

'It's okay,' says Emma, holding her hand up to Asha as she puts Seth down on the floor with the others. She yanks off her ballet pumps, knows Asha's urgency is about the fear of shoes on her cream carpet.

Emma puts her car keys in her bag and pads across the cream carpet in the living room in her bare feet. She lives in the next village as opposed to the rest of us who are, if we're not feeling the impossibility of putting one foot in front of the other from sleep deprivation, in walking distance.

I look around. Asha's right though, I think, about the footwear. There is too much neatness here for something as risky as pavement grub. Outdoor shoes bring disorder. Then again, toddlers aren't that neat either. And they're a little more resistant to being lined up neatly by the door.

Seth crawls in to join his mates. The toddlers sit alongside each other, some semblance of company for one another but barely interacting.

We say mates; we just push these one-year-olds together, their friendships as forced as ours were at first. When we used to function simply as something mum-shaped that escorted our babies to sit and play with other babies.

I think of Flick, Martha, the others. The friends who came for the initial post-birth visit clutching expensive baby leggings and overpriced biscuits and then disappeared back to Manchester and their real lives. With them the baby was the add-on, not me.

Where are they now though? I was too much effort for them. Consumed in Poppy, to be fair, I didn't make much effort myself either.

My NCT friends are present. I feel a swell of love for them. How fast that's happened.

My phone pings and this time, I check it. I can't keep ignoring it, not when there are so many things to check for now.

Just Ed.

Gym tonight. Going to do a big session. Not back until late.

I suspect he will do anything to avoid our home and discussions about the video.

A few seconds later, another pings in.

Love you x

Guilt?

On the sofa, Asha heaves Ananya across her and feeds her, her eyes drooping as she settles back against a cushion.

Cora turns up a minute later, raising an extremely dark groomed eyebrow at me and giving half a glance in Asha's direction. I know she means '*Daytime breast-feeds? Still?*'

I raise my own slightly overgrown eyebrow back.

With Asha back at work soon too, this will be one of the last chances in a while for this unlikely foursome of ours to get together on a weekday.

Outside, Cora's Range Rover with its personalised number plate is parked in Asha's drive, dwarfing Asha's red Corsa. On the side is the branding for Cora's Cupcakes.

Cora only lives a ten-minute walk away from here but she likes to remind us that she has a fancy car plus her limit for walking in the heels that are on her feet so frequently she totters with an upward arch around her own house in her slippers, is from car to fancy restaurant and back again.

'Is it okay to park there?' she asks, gesturing to the driveway from the door. Her WAG-worthy engagement ring catches my eye. I look at her forehead and think: more Botox.

'No problem,' answers Asha, as she scoops up a pile of toys and casts her eyes anxiously towards Cora's feet. Cora yanks off a spike-heeled ankle boot. Her own WAG-style mansion has so much white that while she isn't a natural clean freak, she sometimes imposes these kinds of rules too. The difference though is that if she doesn't, there is a twice-weekly cleaner who will come and make things good as new immediately anyway. That's a luxury Asha doesn't have.

Cora slips in wearing something I think are called pop socks most often found in the Eighties and sits down, plonking Penelope on the floor. Penelope's outfit probably cost more than mine. Penelope has just turned one.

Emma hangs back, twirls her fingers in her hair nervously. As usual she looks like a teenager who's just grown an adult body. Like her five-eight frame is a surprise to her; like she's uncomfortable in its newness.

'Tell them your news!' Cora says to her from the armchair. She glances at her manicure – you'd think they'd file more off for a woman who shoved her hands in cake mix for a living, I think. Told you, zero-hours workers.

Cora doesn't look up again when she speaks next. 'Go on, hon, go on.'

Emma shifts from one foot to the other, and yanks down her top to cover the bum of her leggings. She gives a quick checking-in glance to Seth, who is cruising along Asha's freshly vacuumed and plumped sofa with a string of dribble exiting his mouth.

Emma looks like she might want to scoop Seth up and leave, rather than reveal to the group whatever she has just told Cora on their drive here.

'I had Slimming World,' says Emma, who's probably a size sixteen, in her faded Welsh accent. Yanks the leggings this time, upwards over her tummy. Her clothes – perhaps a throwback to a pre-baby bygone era – are more like a fourteen. She looks irritated by them. 'And I'd lost three pounds.'

'That's amazing,' says Asha warmly, glancing over her shoulder at Ananya who is waving a toy car around her head. She turns back to grin at Emma and places a tiny doll hand on her arm. I suspect Asha could lose three pounds with a half-hour sweep of this house – her tiny four-eleven body moves like a kitten when she tidies. 'Well done you.'

It's distracted but sincere.

I glaze over as Emma talks now, staring at her hand, in its usual place over her mouth. Is it her teeth she's covering up? They aren't the whitest or straightest but I don't know if it's as conscious as that. More that Emma tries to cover everything about her body; to shut it up and stop it trying to show her up.

'Thanks, babe,' she says. 'I might even let myself have a cheeky wine and a slice of pizza this weekend.'

I look down and roll my eyes. Emma is a sweet person. But if I have to hear her talk about cheeky drinks or naughty biscuits as though they are massive piles of drugs one more time, I will reach down her throat and pull out the clichés.

Emma takes a hesitant step forward and finally makes it into the room properly.

Momentarily, I remember where I should be now and I'm transported to the office. Creative brainstorms on the beanbags, strong eyeliner and expensed pizza lunches. It hurtles back into my brain, what happened. Why I'm not there. God, I miss that feeling of being good at something.

I wonder fleetingly if I can build myself another work world I love from blogging.

I make excuses and go to the toilet to check likes on my last Cheshire Mama Instagram post.

I sit in Asha's downstairs loo for five minutes, in front of a Tracey Emin print. Inhaling a scent from a plug-in that I am convinced is getting stuck in my lungs.

And suddenly I realise that I can't move. Can't face leaving this tiny room. Taking my eyes away from my phone. Living back in the real world.

It's happening again.

The panic increases and I realise how small the room is but still it's worse to leave it and face people and so I gasp and I stay in the toilet for enough minutes that one of the girls knocks on the door, concerned, and I have to feign a bad stomach.

Soon after, I gather up Poppy and leave, knowing I am coming across as rude but deciding it's better than coming across as weak.

Anon

'Are you okay, Scarlett?' we ask, as she hides from us in the toilet. 'Need anything? Can we get you some water?'

We think she is ill. Or do we?

Someone mutters that she is probably in there checking her Instagram likes 'while we look after your kid.'

That gets a laugh. Partly because we suspect it's true. It does often feel like Scarlett has her head somewhere else and prefers to inhabit a world on her phone while we man – woman – her real life. Slipping Poppy some toast, wiping the butter from her tiny chin.

When we share the news that matters to us, she is distracted. When we talk about our jobs, she glazes over. She is attached to her phone, more and more as time goes on.

It makes me feel better about what I've done though, when she behaves that way.

Far easier than on the days when she passes me a nappy I need from my changing bag or orders a drink she know I will be desperate for so that it is waiting for me, with a slice of cake on the side and a kind smile.

How *can* you be kind to me? I think, in those moments. How can you be kind to me when you've done what you've done? To my family.

At home, I am consumed by her. I click on her blog twenty, twenty-five times a day. Stare. Scroll. Feel my body flare up like it is being attacked. I can't cope with the perfection. That must, I think, be what he sees when he looks at her. I am ferocious with envy. The joy. The radiance. The grooming.

And of course the main thing. I am envious of her, sleeping with him, just after he sleeps with me.

When I see her after one of my binging sessions on her blog, I get these urges to punch her in her neat little nose, like a teenage boy having a fight in the playground, scuff marks on his knees, knowing he will be in detention later but believing that it's worth it, in that moment, as long as he can deliver that hard, targeted blow. And I know that at some point, when it is time, I will deliver that blow myself, even if it takes a slightly different form. I just have to be patient.

13

Scarlett

18 May

'Still on for this weekend?' asks Asha, as we wrestle the babies into their coats after our baby rhyme group.

I see a massive hardback on the bottom of her pram; one of those people wade through like treacle.

'I hope we are,' she adds, anxious, before I can answer. 'I've booked a hair appointment.'

She sees me looking at the book.

'Should get through another chapter of that then too,' she says, animated. 'One of the hardest things having kids isn't it? How little you get to read.'

I duck my head in embarrassment.

I'm not a reader, though it's a thing I don't like to admit.

Asha is smart, arty; I want her to think I'm smart too, in that way you need to provide signposts for new friends to know who you are, what you stand for.

I think of the panic attack I had at her house last week. I wonder if she and the others suspected, wondered why I was in the toilet for so long. We've never spoken about it.

'Mmm hmm,' I mutter. 'Really hard.'

Asha passes Ananya a rice cake. She touches her own smooth black hair, halfway down her back.

A hair appointment? The most this girls' night was getting from me was a clean bra.

'I've been pumping like crazy but I'm still short,' says Asha, anxious as she slips Ananya into her sling on her front. 'Going to get as much as I can tonight.'

I see the hint of a sigh from Cora.

'Can't she just give that child a Cow & Gate and stop with the drama?' she asked me a few weeks ago, after a similar conversation. '*All this bloody pumping*. She's one. She could have a carton of milk from M&S. Talk about building up your part.'

So, there are some things I am clear on. We might not have each other's job titles down, but we know each other's judgements.

Just before we leave the community hall, my phone beeps and I am rummaging in the depths of my changing bag with stuff spilling everywhere to find it when a woman I vaguely recognise comes over to me.

'Scarlett,' she says, as I pull out nappy after nappy. 'I wanted to check something. I don't like pictures of my baby going online. I saw you posted some of all the babies on Instagram last week. Can you take them down?'

I raise a distracted eyebrow as she removes a child from her leg and picks some glitter off her arm. Where the hell is my phone?

'Is it important?' I say. Poppy starts crying for lunch. 'I have a lot on and that post did well.'

Her face clouds over.

'No disrespect, Scarlett, but you have no clue why I'm concerned about privacy; what may have happened in our lives to make me ask,' she says, thunderous. 'So yes. It is *important*.'

I go to answer back but don't get chance.

'And FYI, there could be a million reasons that a parent wants their child's picture offline so maybe in future you should check before you post, especially as an *influencer*,' she rants.

'Okay,' I say, chastened and in shock. 'Sorry it upset you.'

But before I can emphasise my apology, Cora has waded in.

'Hon, most parents *want* to show their children off,' she says, haughty, on my shoulder. 'Most parents are *proud* of their children. And you should be happy he's on Cheshire Mama's Insta. It's kind of a big deal.'

I flush pink.

'Is she serious?' says this woman, gesturing to Cora as though she is my child and I am responsible for her. 'Are you insinuating I'm not proud of my baby just because I don't want him plastered on the internet like a trophy?'

This is escalating fast and I'm on edge. I don't want a confrontation. I don't want another enemy. I feel the panic that engulfed me at Asha's coming back. I need to get out of here.

I usher Cora away and I see the woman ranting, furious, at her friend and I look around suddenly, on high alert. Do they know about the video? Is that why she wants it taken down, really? Does she not want her child associated with my blog when she knows that about me? Am I not safe here now?

Poppy isn't strapped into her buggy, isn't even wearing a sun hat despite the hot spring day when I bolt out of the door as fast as my heart is pounding.

I consider stopping at the local but then I remember: someone would see me, it would fly around, I would be a daytime drinking unfit mum. *This claustrophobic place.*

14

Scarlett

22 May

Mundane chart music that doesn't make you feel anything booms around a bar that has no defining characteristics. There is a cocktail list that contains every obligatory cocktail choice and nothing unique. Men drink pints. Women snap pouting selfies.

'You hate it, don't you?' asks Asha, next to me, anxious.

'Of course I don't *hate* it,' I say, but I feel myself grimace.

Cora gives me a strange look.

She chose this place for tonight; booked the table.

Asha blushes.

Emma reaches over us for a chip. 'Oh, babe, the points,' she groans, singsong in that hint of a Welsh accent. 'Nau-ghty.'

And I roll my eyes but it's fond now; part of me thinks she's playing up to her role.

I drink my cheeky glass of wine. Eat a naughty chip. Post a #mumsonthewine picture of all of us on my Instagram and then pretend to need the toilet so I can sit in there for a few minutes and watch the likes roll in.

When I come out an ice bucket of champagne lands on the table.

'Babe, you didn't!' squeals Emma, mouth full of a chip, to Cora.

'Emma, I did,' says Cora, mock serious, unscrewing a cork

with a delicate hand that is heaving under the pressure of its jewellery and violent nails.

The cork pops.

'You're so generous,' I say warmly to Cora, as I place a hand on her arm.

She pours me a glass.

'Not at all,' she responds. 'Just a little something.'

Emma is looking at her phone.

'Does anyone know how many points are in champagne?' she asks. 'Is it more than a gin and slim?'

On a whim, I take her phone out of her hand.

'I have looked it up,' I declare. 'And there are, officially, one hundred fun points in a glass of champagne.'

Emma laughs at herself as she rummages in her bag and pulls out a hair bobble, tying hair back in a ponytail that is frizzing in the humidity of the bar.

I down my own drink. Pop her phone back in her bag.

They all look surprised. They don't think I'm fun because I'm often not, I suppose, distracted by my daughter or my sex tape or my blog. Dismissing the bar, cringing at the locals.

I down the gin that was sitting next to me before the champagne arrived and then I drag Emma with me to the dance floor. Through a slight tipsy fog and in dim lighting, I still see Emma flush with pride.

'The Welsh one has a girl crush on you,' Ed said with a laugh a few weeks ago, when I told him a story about my mum friends. 'It's obvious.'

'She's not Welsh, just lived there when she was little,' I had said but it didn't matter, he had taken a couple of characteristics of each of them and scribbled out a picture. Emma with only her hint of a childhood accent was Welsh, overweight, in awe. And where had he built that picture from really, barely having seen them since NCT classes over a year ago? From me and how I painted her.

'What I don't get is what *you* get from *her*,' he added.

I had looked at his head then, turned away from me, knowing that what I got from Emma – and Cora and Asha – would be impossible to describe to him, unemotional as he is.

They bring comfort; support. Not the sharp humour I have sought from friendships before, no. Not the podcast recommendations or the gallery tips or the acerbic political commentary. But I sink into them like they're my own bed after a newborn night feed. I trust them to hold my baby while I pay. I know that when I meet them, somebody will bring me a cup of coffee. These things sound low-level but right now, in my life, they are the top of the mountain. We're so busy looking after our babies but in between, we look after each other too.

We have become closer, in ways, than most friends do. We talked about our fears of having our vaginas ripped open as we practised putting nappies on in antenatal class. Then the babies came and we helped each other position our breasts into our children's mouths and fed each other toast, desperate for the carbs but unable to free a hand.

We have sat with each other while we wept, not sure why, checking in to see if it's exhaustion or something more. In the odd moment when we have had something to give, having had an extra hour's sleep or with our own baby napping, we've snuggled in the other's child, given the gift of a two-minute break with a still-hot tea.

We have discussed, in detail, the way we bled until simply standing up was torture in the weeks after childbirth. We have relayed the hours that we spent pushing or having our babies cut from us, of the emergency button that was pressed or the forceps that came, gunning for us.

We have talked when we couldn't talk to anyone else about the loneliness of those days home alone with what is technically another human but one that is unable yet to provide any company. About the oddness of that unique time: how special, how scary, how quiet.

We have sighed with relief when we've walked into a baby group and seen each other because that means that we can hand our baby over when we go to the toilet, instead of passing them to a stranger and spending the 10 second duration of our wee convinced that they are at that moment being kidnapped.

I look at the table and see Cora's eyes on us. I grin and motion to her to join but she shakes her head, looks at her phone.

The alcohol hits me then; my drinking stamina isn't back to its former glories, post Poppy.

Emma leans forward and shouts into my ear over the music.

'My sister-in-law told me about the row you had over the photo of her little boy,' she yells, and I go cold.

While it may have been overshadowed lately by my own online dramas, that row had kept me awake at night. Because that woman had been right. And I *should* understand how having your privacy breached online feels.

That was her child and her decision and I had belittled it and I wanted to say sorry to her, but I felt too embarrassed now, ashamed by my response.

'Your sister-in-law?' My voice sounds sharp.

Emma nods. 'Oh, you didn't know?' she says, leaning right in. 'Yeah she's married to my brother, babe.'

I shake my head. All I can think is how I love these women but the rest of it? I am sick, sick, sick of this parochial village. I hate that I put make-up on to walk the five minutes from my house to the post box because it's almost impossible to get there without seeing someone I know. That I have to spend £10 minimum to pay on card at the pub. That I used to stare at the sky and think it was lovely, unobscured by Seventies office buildings, and now it feels like it's closing in on me, and it's darker than before, gloomier. That everyone here wears jeans, walking boots, sensible coats and how they all seem content, as they let you pass on the narrow part of the village where there is no pavement. That I envy that contentment, as I long for eccentricity and colour and even misery and extremes, but there is none, ever; there is just someone wishing me a good afternoon, as they pull a beanie hat down over their ears.

I think of how much I miss the anonymity of the city. How creepy it is that everyone here is related and linked and known.

I look at the walls of the bar with their IKEA art and beer stains, and they feel like they're inching closer too.

It's breeding paranoia, this feeling.

If the men were telling the truth, then it's someone else rather than Ollie or Mitch who posted the video. Someone, somehow, however impossible that seems, got hold of it. Is it weird altercations like the one with Emma's sister-in-law that I need to be looking out for? Is the person who did this a stalker? Someone close?

'Are you okay?' shouts Emma over the music, panicking, I can see, that she has upset me but her face is blurring at the edges.

My heart is beating at a rate that would score off the chart on a blood pressure test.

It's like I have a migraine. Or am having a bad trip.

I need to get out of here.

I stumble as I head back to the table for my bag.

'Drunk too much,' I shout back to Emma, then I signal to the door and flee without goodbyes. Knowing I appear rude again, to these friends that do so much for me.

Outside, I flag a cab. Oh, I mean I call a cab and wait forty-five minutes for it and when it arrives, it is inexplicably a minibus because that's what happens in the countryside.

I look into the darkness out of the window and it seems, still, so alien and I think about how Ed and I ended up here.

We decided on it when we were engaged. I had taken some persuading but Ed had painted a tempting picture.

121

'Hot toddies in the local,' he said, dreamy as we lounged, legs on top of each other, on our tiny sofa in the Chorlton flat we had been renting together for a year. 'We can get a dog, buy wellies. Do our house up like something off Instagram.'

My head snapped up, like he knew it would. I did a lot of social media in my job and I had aspirations of becoming some sort of influencer then. I had been thinking about a direction I could go. Home renovations? With our salaries we could get something pretty big to do up in the countryside. Still.

'We can't move so I can get a better Insta grid.' I smiled. I jumped on top of him, eyes wide. 'CAN WE?'

'Out near my mum and dad, near my brother,' he laughed as he kissed me.

Where he grew up, in other words. A fancy village, near to the other fancy village he grew up in.

'You always say it's lovely when we visit,' he pushed. 'When we have our own children, they'd have cousins nearby . . .'

We wanted kids, and he was right. Maybe it was time to accept that life would change; that Manchester might not be right for us in this next phase.

It took drives through idyllic Cheshire villages, the odd overnight bag packed for a stay in a country hotel. It took mustardy roast beef next to wood burners with a Malbec in my hand. It took a parcel arriving containing fancy wellies real countryside people would never buy anyway with a note from Ed that said '*Go on*'. It took practical things like train timetables pored over to make sure I could still get to work, and RightMove searches, and questions like 'When was the boiler put in?' and mortgage evaluations and then suddenly, as we stood inside the beautiful, four-bedroomed eighteenth-century listed cottage that was now ours, we had crept across the finish line and made the decision.

And when we drove behind the removal van to Sowerton just over two years ago, me, my wellies and my Instagram were more than excited.

We got the keys to the cottage and we drank our champagne in bed that night because we hadn't figured out how to work the heating yet.

'There you go,' said Ed, placing a hot water bottle on my feet. 'I just ordered us a curry too. We might have to get out of bed for that though.'

I'd laughed. The tumbling anxiety I'd had about the move was fading with the crazy, fun newness of it all. We were married now and I was high on the novelty of being a wife and an owner of this fancy house and – as we tried for a baby then too – anticipating other firsts.

Smug could have described it if you disliked me; happy would have done if you didn't.

A month later I was pregnant and then I had Poppy and went on maternity leave and life got busier and my boobs got leakier and friends got more distant and I started Cheshire Mama and I went back to the office to introduce Poppy but it was hard to merge my two worlds. I had thought Sowerton in all of its sleepiness was an extra life, a little bonus. I didn't realise my Manchester one wouldn't be there waiting forever.

But I like having friends. I like being popular. And so I found my mum crew.

My old friends picture my world now, I know, as me spending three weeks designing Poppy's homemade birthday cake and making a Pinterest board for themes for the Christmas tree. I'm the first of our crowd to have a child and I get paranoid that they have written me off as having retreated to the insular world of the parent, with their craft boxes and their playdate schedule and their complete lack of a clue about current affairs or fashion or what's happening in the world outside their bubble.

But I look into the gloom of the countryside from my taxi now and my skin prickles. Too quiet. Too dark. Not enough everything else. I laugh, now, at how I romanticised it. Sometimes I want to take a pin to the bubble and clamber out.

'Good night?' asks the driver and I nod but say nothing.

I lean my head back against the seat, feeling my body shake all over. I have no idea whether it's from standing outside on an evening when the temperature has suddenly dipped and it's far cooler than May should be or from the conversation with Emma or whether it's just from everything that the last two weeks have brought.

Wanting to take up room in my brain so I can't feel, I open up my Instagram.

And then, something happens.

In the comments, right there on my beautiful, filtered, parenting page, people are talking about my sex tape.

I feel the tickle of sweat in my armpits.

Word has spread. Worlds have collided.

One offers a 'rerun'. Another compliments my naked body, as though it were public property. Coarse. Terrifying.

Who has seen this? I think. When was it posted? Who would be looking?

I delete and block as fast as I can, but they are from multiple accounts, these messages, and they keep coming. Someone is doing this to me this second.

I hug my own body and the shaking intensifies.

Help me, somebody, help me.

'You all right, love?' asks the driver.

I must have emitted a gasp.

I nod, tell him I had too much to drink. Dip my head low into my phone. Keep deleting.

I have tried so hard to contain it, but my workmates, my family, friends, then the clients, now this. The reality, I realise, sadly, is that whether the website operator removed it or not, I can't contain it. *That's* why that email was such an anticlimax. The video is a hurricane, far more powerful than me, blasting through my makeshift walls. I consider the word viral; how perfect it is to describe what is happening to me.

I have gone viral and it is a rotten, unwanted illness. The world is exposed and unvaccinated. There are no limits to what this thing can do and while it keeps coming and coming and coming, I can't even attempt to recover.

It can kill me, I think, suddenly lucid. The thing is viral and it can kill me.

Tears stream down my face when I think, for a split second, that that could be a relief.

'You sure you're okay, love?' says the taxi driver, brow furrowed in the mirror.

I nod again. Hide my face in my phone.

When I get in, Ed is in bed for an early start at work, which means that I don't tell him what's happened. But gradually, seeing Ed's face has not been the comfort it usually is when I'm nervous, looking up the aisle at him on our wedding day, or in those terrifying seconds when we waited for the nurse to find a heartbeat at Poppy's scan as he squeezed my hand tight. Now, it would just add to my shame. I lie in bed, missing him, missing myself, missing a clear mind and now I've left them, missing the friends who would have hugged me goodbye, told me they loved me, clambered into the taxi with me, held my hand and listened, if I ever decided that I could speak to them about all of this; if I decide one day that actually, I need to.

15

Scarlett

23 May

Scarlett, the message says. *Please answer my calls. I do need to speak to you, urgently x PS: I can also help you find something else work-wise. I know you must be climbing the walls in Mum Land!*

Flick. It's the anchor I need.

But I'm irritated too. *Mum Land* feels patronising. Flick doesn't know what a support the women of *Mum Land* have been.

I delete the message without reply. No good can come anyway from talking about a life that doesn't exist any more, to someone I can no longer look in the eye. I can't bear the shame; the pity.

And for all my thoughts the other day about telling them, I'm relieved that my mum friends don't seem to have seen the comments on the blog. That they still don't know. That being with them is respite.

Flick sends me another message afterwards.

We've all been young, Scarlett. No one is judging you xx

And I laugh. Because everyone is judging me every day, everyone is judging everyone every day. What they're posting, what they're wearing, what they're ordering, where they're going. What their job is, who they're married to, what car they drive, what make their bag is.

Sling a sex tape into the mix though and you up the stakes.

Everyone has to judge me so that they think I'm different to them. In another bracket. Way more sexually out there. Way more promiscuous. Way less careful. Otherwise it could have been them, and nobody likes thinking it could have been them.

No one is judging you? Ha.

As I sit looking at that text though, I feel something shift. The floundering, the sadness, it's being replaced with a fury and a desire to scream at somebody for what they have done to me. I loved New Social. Ed and I would have been thinking about a second child soon, I'm sure. Now neither of us have mentioned it because it comes under an umbrella of 'future' that no one wants to put their cash on.

Somebody has reached into my life and shifted everything around so that I jiggle, loose, without form now.

But who?

Anon

You see, *nothing* about this place is good enough for Scarlett.

Not our bars. Not our drinks.

Seems our men are fine, though.

I watch Scarlett leave the bar that night.

In an upstairs room, unused as there is no private function, I climb over a rope and look at her from a window as she waits for her taxi. She paces, infuriated at having to wait, calling the taxi company – I presume that's who she is calling – over and over. Scarlett doesn't like to wait for things. Some of us have more patience; have become accustomed to biding our time.

When it finally comes, she steps in wearing her biker boots, looking less drunk than she claimed to be, only minutes ago.

I wish I could see the moment that she reads the messages I posted earlier as I hid in the toilet cubicle, from my multiple fake accounts. But that must happen in the taxi.

I wish I could watch Scarlett's face as her worlds – so far kept neat and separate as though they were in an office storage system – start to become muddled.

The taxi pulls away. I check, and the messages are already gone. I add some more, flicking between accounts, then I head back downstairs, pick up my drink and make a toast.

'To Scarlett!' I say. 'So drunk she had to go home. That's

got to be a sign that she's had a good night, right? Even if she did seem to *kind of* hate the bar.'

We laugh. Because of course Scarlett would hate the bar.

'To good friends,' one of the other girls says.

'To *such good friends*,' I echo.

16

Scarlett

25 May

I put my key in the door and place three large shopping bags and one small person on the floor.

Like often lately, I need coffee. Being ashamed is exhausting; nobody mentions that.

Next to the kettle is a piece of paper.

It strikes me then how rarely I see Ed's handwriting. Cards. And now notes, telling me he's leaving me.

It's short, Ed's note.

Staying with my parents for a few days. I think we need some space after the pressure of the last month. Let's talk later. Ed x

A little life holiday. How I wish I could book myself one of those. Thanks for the support, Ed.

It's been ticking away in the back of my mind, the question of whether he is cheating, and it comes back now. Is that where my husband Ed has really gone?

And where does our child come into this, I think, as the kettle boils? Could I just leave, no matter how angry or hurt I was? Of course I couldn't.

I make my coffee strong. Message Ed a picture of the note asking what the hell he's doing and realise that I'm not sad, but furious.

Shaking, now, with rage.

Shaking with rage at Ed, at a skewed world that means I can't sashay out of our home and our responsibilities but my husband can. It's hard to do dramatic sashays when you have to make fifteen phone calls to sort childcare and pack a Peppa Pig rucksack first.

But mostly I'm shaking with rage at whoever has done this to me and started the Jenga bricks of my life toppling over. I had it all, I think. Now look at me.

I lean back against the kitchen island with my coffee in two hands and sigh. If not Ollie – and how can I think anything else, really – is Mitch the only credible option?

I can't imagine he ever thought about me or cared enough to have done this. But he did film it; that's pretty damning. And then there was the oddness of thinking I saw him that day. Too much to be a coincidence?

I can't think straight.

I message the girls to see what they're up to because I need human contact. Adults.

Emma replies.

Bumped into Cora at a baby class so came back to hers, she says. *Asha too. Come!*

I down my drink and grab my keys and strap Poppy in to the pram to walk the ten minutes round to Cora's.

'Coffee?' Emma asks as I walk in and I nod, mute.

Emma puts Cora's coffee machine on and does mine, then places her already used mug back underneath it. There are at least three very expensive candles vying for aromatic prominence around the house and making me struggle with the urge to gag.

There are kisses and hugs. I am sweating.

Emma turns to the girls. I see them all exchange looks. I realise I have barely said a word since I got here. That I may look a bit odd.

'Scarlett, are you . . . all right?' asks Asha, soft.

I stare at her and cannot remember how to lie. I wonder if they think it's odd, me having this extra time off work when

I regularly bemoan the size of our mortgage. And all of a sudden something is obvious: my mind has run out of space for all of this secrecy. My lies and evasions are pushing at the seams of my mind; they need out.

I sit down at the table and stare at the 'Live. Laugh. Love' sign on Cora's wall. Out of the corner of my eye, I see my friends look at each other. I start to cry.

'Scarlett?' says Emma.

Put your seatbelts on, friends: I'm about to go off-message. This is nothing to do with sleep deprivation or weaning methods. We are truly friends now, so this is what you get.

'Everything is a mess,' I say, relief in admission. In not swerving and dodging.

Asha glances nervously at Cora. Emma goes to check on the babies and then loiters from her mid position at the door, the nearest thing to childcare that we are going to have for the next half hour while everyone prioritises the gossip of my life over the safety of their children.

'Ed and I are having some problems,' I say. 'He's moved out for a while.'

I know, already, that the girls are thinking of a spark, diminished after having a small child, not an awkwardness that's come from me making a sex tape.

So I go with that, let them assume. It's a version of the truth, which is always easier than an outright lie, and it means I have to speak less. It's like letting a little air out of a balloon, just to stop it popping.

'Things haven't been great,' I start, but after that I don't need to decide which way to go because they fill in the gaps for themselves.

And suddenly, the story of Ed and I is forgotten. No one cares. Everyone has seized it and taken it as an excuse to say what they wanted to say, like people do.

Everyone wants this to be a mirror.

'We were at each other's throats all of last week, babe,' says Emma, eager, as she sticks her head around the door to check on the babies. She looks back at us. 'Always bad on my period.'

Then she goes into the living room to check which one of our children has a nappy that is laughing in the face of the myriad scented candles.

'Cora, it's you,' she says as she re-emerges, then looks sheepish. 'I mean, it's Penelope.'

'Penelope,' mutters Cora darkly under her breath as she stomps off in her designer slippers, because this is just the opener she needs to unleash about her marriage and she's missing her window. Bloody Penelope.

We all know that Cora is dismissive of her husband, despite the approximately forty-five pictures around the house of their stunning, expensive wedding involving about a hundred guests in the Caribbean. There's her other man, Hunter, of course. He's a key sign.

Cora is back in the room, clutching a bag of poo as far as she can away from her vest top and her prominent fake boobs.

'What did I miss?'

I watch her drop it in the bin.

Cora goes to the fridge and pours a glass of rosé then puts it in front of me.

'No I'm okay,' I say, but she holds a hand up.

Glasses arrive all around me along with a tray of pretty gross mint chocolate cupcakes that Cora is 'trying out' and suddenly everyone has one or the other or both in their hand and is speaking over each other, with vents about their marriages masquerading as wisdom.

And yet halfway through that glass of too-sweet wine, with a group of women I have known for only just over a year, I feel the nearest to comforted I have been in a long time.

'You know what we need?' says Asha, gently. 'A night away. A spa?'

'I could ask my mum to have Seth,' says Emma, nodding. 'She'd just be glad to see him. Glad I got in touch.'

I know things between Emma and her mum – between Emma and her whole family – are strained because they don't get on with her husband. It's not even an option that he would stay home alone with his own son. We all know that by now, as we know a lot of things by now.

'I've got a decent amount of milk in the freezer after the pumpathon.' Asha smiles.

An almost token eye-roll from Cora.

A weekend of space from Ed and this nightmare sounds idyllic. Glorious. That's if he's even at home anyway. Depends how long this life holiday goes on for. I am crying again, suddenly, as the content of Ed's note hits and I don't know whether it's the afternoon wine or the fact that Emma is holding Poppy on her hip and taking some of the weight of life, but I am appreciative of everything they do for me and of their role: new, odd, intense. Crucial.

So what if we have barely anything in common? We're building something here, something long-term. It takes a village, and all that.

I look at Emma, jiggling a sleepy Poppy whose eyes are drooping. She rubs at them and leans into Emma. I glance at Cora, holding my hand with her silky smooth manicured one and still suggesting, every now and then, that an affair with a beautiful bendy man can do *wonders*.

I look at Asha, tipping a bag of Waitrose crisps into a bowl and pushing it in front of my face. I think I would like to have an affair, if we could leave out the other parts and it could just involve someone holding my hand and decanting my crisps.

These women are a team, I think, as I look around at them. And a team is what I've been missing.

'I'm up for a trip,' I say, as Emma nervously passes me a tissue. 'I'm absolutely up for a trip.'

Anon

'You have no idea how much I need a girls' weekend,' I say to my friend Scarlett.

And I mean it.

What could possibly be bad about a trip away with Scarlett?

An opportunity to see her up close, twenty-four hours a day.

To observe her, even more than I do the rest of the time, in her pyjamas, as she wipes her make-up off her face, side by side as we brush our teeth.

To see what he sees. Her, then me. Alongside each other.

To see who she really is, this woman whose life is tripping over mine.

To see how she could have done this to me.

Oh, it means putting up with the other stuff, of course. The self-obsession. The drama. My blog! My marriage crisis!

Just let someone else speak, Scarlett, *for once*.

But it will be worth it.

How could I do that to a friend? Maybe the question needs to be rephrased: how could I do that to somebody who was becoming, even when she didn't know it, my worst, my closest, enemy? How could I do that to somebody who had, when it came to it, done far worse to me?

I count down the hours to that weekend.

Apart from anything, it means I will know where she is all the time too. That I won't have to torture myself with wondering if she has her hands, with their elegant long fingers, all over him again.

17

Scarlett

29 May

It's been months since I went on a night out, and now a second is following closely after the first. Which is especially odd since I hated that one and bolted from it.

Ed is back from his parents', but stays out a lot. Gym sessions have got longer.

'What was that about?' I asked, when he came home but he answered in one-word responses and I was too angry to make any effort.

Instead of living together as a couple and a family, at the moment we coexist and speak in instructions and questions. Things have deteriorated fast.

'Has Poppy had lunch?'

'Any updates on the lawyer?'

'Can you pick up some nappies?'

'There are clean vests in the washing basket.'

It crosses over, too, to critique.

'She isn't having more biscuits.'

'You've drunk all that wine?'

I don't know how this happened to us but we have become that couple who have nothing else to say to each other, except we have so much to say: we just can't manage it.

I don't completely blame Ed. He's reverted to what he knows; the way the men that created him do it.

Ignore it, shelve it, pour giant bucketfuls of sand over the place in your brain where it lives and move on with an air of tension around you wherever you go because you are so desperately trying not to let that sand dune shift. Drink a beer. Talk about that 3–0 win.

Ed is now so thickly covered over that I can't dig through, whatever I try.

It's your birthday this week, right Em? I type to the group. *We should go out! Last time was so fun.*

I lie so often now that I have started not to notice or to be confused about when I am lying and when I am not. I just need company. People. A hug. To laugh.

Besides, it's all relative isn't it? Compared to the awkwardness and shame that is being at home with Ed, or the pain of those final days in work, or talking about my sex tape with my dad, that night out, being drunk, *was* fun.

Or blurrier, at least.

I have to get on top of the ironing, messages Asha, who may be the only person of our generation who would actually get out an ironing board for anything other than a wedding.

But she's making this sound more wifey than it will be. I know Asha and her multitasking. There will be an epic novel propped up next to her, or a mental health podcast – Asha works for a mental health charity – as her soundtrack. *Sorry, ladies.*

Emma comes; it's her birthday. Cora says yes because she loves drinking.

At the coffee shop bar, Emma double checks her tonic is slimline; asks if I'm sure her dress isn't mumsy (it's the epitome of mumsy and she's wearing tights despite it being late May but bless her, who could tell her that and see that face fall?)

Cora complains loudly that her glass of Veuve Clicquot isn't cold enough and whips out a Chanel compact from her Louis

Vuitton bag every ten minutes. She is not subtle about her money, Cora. Nor does she have any desire to be.

'I am just not made for average things,' she will tell me frequently, glint in her eye with a big belly laugh. She can joke about herself, Cheshire set personified, at least.

And then there's me, sitting somewhere in between in a Zara jumpsuit I used to wear to work, the red lipstick marks on my wine glass surprising me every time I spot them because I have forgotten that I have make-up on. It's a rarity these days.

We make an odd crew.

I swig long from the large glass of house red and wish it were neat vodka. But I'm no longer a vodka person, I remind myself. Like I'm no longer a threesome person. Except I am, aren't I, it turns out. Even if you were only a threesome person once over a decade ago, on the internet you're always a threesome person. And the internet won't be posting context or reason or the grief you were consumed by at the time, either. You're just a threesome person, simple, done, gross, cancelled.

On a whim, I order three straight vodkas with my next round.

'Don't worry, Emma,' I reassure her, as I pass them around. 'There are virtually no calories in a shot of vodka.'

That's enough to persuade her and she necks it. Cora has her head in her phone and nods distractedly.

'Vodka shots,' grins the waiter. 'Impressive.'

'You ordered shots?' asks Cora, head snapping up from whatever message she was furiously typing. 'God he's a shit,' she mutters, about her husband I presume, and then reaches out and necks the shot without looking at it.

'See, I knew you needed a vodka,' I tell her. My old pushy self coming out. Persuade other people to drink as much as you and you'll never feel paranoid the next day. It's all coming back to me now.

The barman looks at me for a second longer than he needs to. Holds my gaze.

Hot, I think, because old me has taken over my brain now. She's single. She's drunk. She notices beautiful men.

'How have I not noticed how good-looking he is before?' I ask them as he walks away.

'Because you're usually in here with Poppy picking up bits of cucumber off the floor or wiping shit off your hand and trying to neck your coffee before it's ice cold,' says Cora, deadpan, putting her phone away in her bag.

Fair point.

'Oh and also, because you're pissed.'

I laugh. Another good point.

Cora signals to the retreating barman to bring us another round of shots.

I glance at him. Early thirties, maybe. Comfortable in his own skin. I think about his hipster beard, hanging out here in the countryside. He doesn't have the known quality of the locals either. I suspect that no one is friends with his sister; no one lives next door to his nan. Interesting.

But Cora brings the attention back to her, as Cora likes to do, giving us an update on Hunter and their fling.

Then she looks at me, and at the barman who is passing again, and who my eyes are following.

'So,' she says, downing the rest of her champagne and sitting back to stare at me. 'If you are seriously thinking about prop-ositioning that waiter, no judgement here.'

Is that why she told us the other day about her affair with Hunter? So that if I do anything with the waiter, I will tell her too?

'Oh come on!' she exclaims. 'You two have been checking each other out all night.'

Emma's eyes go wide. While Cora is looking for it in others now, Emma is utterly naive to flirting. If she noticed my eyes following the waiter across the room, she would have thought I was debating whether to ask him for some nachos but fighting

140

my concerns that the melted cheese would make me feel guilty tomorrow.

Would I regret *that* tomorrow? I think.

I stare at him again then turn to Cora.

'He is shaggable,' I concede and I see her eyes widen because I don't speak like this any more, not normally. I temper my language now. Mute myself often. Think about what I say before I say it. Try to be a little less Old Scarlett.

'But no,' I confirm. 'I'm not in the market for an affair. Too much effort.'

She nods, sagely.

'It's true. I'm on the Brazilians again every four weeks since I started seeing Hunter. Leg hair no longer plaitable. It's not easy. But worth it.'

I glance again at the barman.

'Joseph,' says Cora, following my eyes. 'I can find out his surname for you if you want. Say, in case you fancied adding him on Insta.'

I down the latest vodka shot. I can't remember who ordered it. Or if anybody did. Did *Joseph* bring it over? The tiny shot glass in front of my eyes is spinning.

Emma and Cora pick up their bags to leave and I realise everyone else in the bar has gone now too. I make a decision.

'Head off without me,' I say with a glance in Joseph's direction, and my voice slurs. 'I need to . . . nip to the loo.'

He's the last person working.

Cora squeals and squeezes my hand and Emma opens her eyes, make-up free like the rest of her face as always, as wide as they will go.

'Scarlett, are you . . . sure?' Emma asks. 'Ed is . . .'

I roll my own eyes. Ed is . . . what? Ignoring me? Ashamed of me? Showing no desire to sleep with me? Possibly sleeping with somebody else instead? Starting to feel, really, like a stranger?

'About going to the toilet, Emma?' I feign a serious face.

She barely knows Ed. 'Yes, I think I am. The last thing I need is a UTI.'

Cora squeals again and I feel even more warmth for her than usual. I hug her enthusiastically but she pulls out of it quickly.

'Don't let us keep you from . . . the loo,' she says with a conspiratorial wink.

Then she drags Emma by the hand towards the door.

'Leave her to it,' Cora instructs loudly as Emma looks tortured. 'She's a grown woman. And you only get one bloody life.'

Then she mouths '*message me*' over Emma's head as they pull the door shut behind them and I head over to get to know Joseph.

Six hours later I wake up from a dream about blackcurrant squash. All I can feel is thirst, layered with panic. Poppy is shouting me from her room, Ed asleep next to me. Worlds are converging as I have a hangover of my twenties and the responsibilities of my thirties. I'm disorientated. Nauseous.

'I'll get her,' he says. 'You could probably do with the sleep.'

I nod and roll over, but I am wide awake now.

The last thing I remember is leaning in closely at a table alone with Joseph, saying cheers with another vodka. The memories are more like pictures than moving action. Joseph, brushing back his semi-long curls with his hand. Hand to his beard. Me, stumbling. Joseph, reaching out to help me. Me, laughing. Joseph, holding my hand. Us, walking down the street together. And then what? I can't remember any of the later part. Did he walk me home? Through our gate, down our little path, up to the front door of my picture-postcard family home?

'DADADA!' shouts Poppy from downstairs.

I dive under the covers and try to make sense of this.

I would know, wouldn't I, if something had happened? We couldn't have had sex but a kiss. Could a kiss have happened without a memory? It did often enough, back in the day.

How am I here?

My phone beeps on the bedside table and I lunge for it, like Ed could read the message from downstairs.

It's Cora. With just one line of *????*

I ignore it and get back under the duvet.

I would know. I would know. And I can't *picture* a kiss. Surely I'd have retained that image.

I get up and choose Poppy's clothes for the day, her bright red tights and her little tartan skirt and her jumper, and have a hot shower.

'I love you,' I tell Ed as I walk into the kitchen in my slippers and he glances at me and frowns. It's been a while since I said that. I can hear desperation in my tone.

'Are you okay?' is his reply.

I load the dishwasher. I put a dark wash on. I wipe the worktops and get some chicken out of the freezer for dinner. Ed goes for his usual Saturday morning run.

And it's okay. It's okay.

It's the twenty-first century. As long as everything looks how you want it to, it doesn't matter if inside you're falling away from your own skin, if nothing is solid any more and if you do not have a clue who you are, what you did, if you kissed the hipster waiter and what the hell you are going to do next.

Anon

Oh, we all know about the thing with Joseph, after that night. The ongoing flirtation. The blurring of the boundaries. The fact that Scarlett fancies him, and him her, and her marriage – I allow myself a moment of congratulations here, as I am almost solely responsible – seems done anyway.

It makes me angry though, how greedy she is.

Because it reminds me of how all this started in the first place.

Of how, most likely, she doesn't even want that man we are both sleeping with. When I do, so desperately.

And the morals! So superior and judgemental to everybody else but then all it takes is a few vodka slammers to send her to lock-ins with the local hipster.

But Scarlett is, always, *obsessed* with men wanting her. With everyone actually, being interested in her, and impressed by her, and coveting her things and envying that beautiful face and clicking on her blog.

How can model-like Ed not be enough for you? How can you want *more*?

Often I am speaking and I glance at Scarlett and see her, staring past me across the room to see if anything else is going on, who else is there. I get it, Scarlett. You are too good for me. Making do.

That makes me feel so stupid that it pinches.

The worst thing is that she thinks we are all so oblivious. That we don't realise her head is elsewhere. That instead we are *just so grateful* to have a fancy new friend like Scarlett that we'll take whatever she wants to throw our way.

Except, she isn't that fancy, not really.

Po-faced and pristine sometimes, but then very quickly she becomes drunk and vulgar, swearing like she is in an eighteen movie with lots of guns and not much plot.

At least I know who I am, even if it's someone you often scoff at, Scarlett.

Do you know who you are really: the blogger, the city girl, the high-flyer, the country mum with her wellies on, the loyal wife, the hot flirt, with your working-class accent when it suits and your clipped one when it doesn't?

No. Didn't think so.

Your friend. How could I be your friend, when you've committed the ultimate betrayal towards me, and then sit with me, looking me in the eye and never speaking of it?

And when I think of it like that, I don't feel bad about what I did at all. Or about what I am about to do to up, up, up the ante.

18

Scarlett

3 June

I hear Ed's key in the door as I am checking for an email from
Jonathan White. I leap from my phone, guilty when he walks
in, and I have no idea why. I am supposed to be keeping in
touch with the lawyer; that's the idea. But somehow everything
connected to this whole thing makes me feel guilty, sheepish,
part of a grubby cover-up.

My husband and I stare at each other.

'Hey,' he says, then walks over to kiss Poppy.

I can't bring myself to reply.

I wipe down a table where we used to lose hours talking
about friends and the news and how good the tagliatelle tasted.
I look at photos framed on the window ledge that are looking
less and less like us; these people squishing their faces up against
each other to get closer. This naturally uptight Ed who had
softened with that first fun wave of love. Who couldn't be in a
picture with me without kissing me. Who could hardly be *near*
me without kissing me. We loved long weekends in European
cities, taking our running kits and beating our times along the
Seine, around big Madrid parks. We loved having no guilt about
the oily prawns or the sticky cheese board we would eat afterwards. We loved falling into bed later, limbs falling into each
other whenever we stirred. We loved, if we're honest, always

being the hot couple at whatever wedding we went to, the statuesque model-like pair, everyone telling us we looked like celebrities. It's probably why we got a kick out of the blog.

The new us moves around each other oddly, like losing track of each other's minds means we no longer know the shape of each other's bodies either.

I wonder why again. Is it just the video? Or are his limbs touching somebody else's now?

Knowing how it used to be makes it so much worse.

Without comparison we have no idea what's good, what's bad. We used to stick together, now we float around miles and miles apart.

'Do you have any plans this weekend?' asks Ed, tentative, like we are on a second date and he is nervously suggesting a third.

Do *you* have any plans? It used to be *we*. Now we exist on separate planes, our plans and weekends presumed to be spent apart. I've seen it happen in divorced couples, friends of my dad's; this is the start of the end. You move away, gradually, until no one has the energy to put their boots on and trudge all that way back.

I look up, holding a mug with our faces on it. A wedding present from my half-sister Josephine, now about to get married herself but at the time too young to enter into the systemic polite-ness of a John Lewis gift list. 'I got you a mug!' she said, so pleased with herself. 'It's got your faces on!' It was one of my favourite presents, to be honest, in a sea of fancy stuff with no feeling.

I think of Asha's matching sets. I'm fond of this mug, though less so since looking at it started to feel like nostalgia for the old Ed and me.

'I don't think so,' I say nervously to Ed now because where is this going? Do I need to steel myself? Is he suggesting couples counselling? A divorce lawyer?

Ed looks emboldened. 'Let's go away,' he says, decisively.

This is a long way from what I was expecting.

'Where are we going?' I say.

'Anywhere,' he replies, almost desperate and I wish I could close the gap and cuddle him tightly. 'Anywhere. We just need to be on our own, Scarlett. Out of these walls. My parents will have Poppy.'

But are we ready for this?

I think of Joseph and the night at the coffee shop – a place I have had to steadfastly avoid in the weeks since – and I cringe.

Alone. Away from home. With nothing to do except talk. Can we do that? I'm so angry with him for leaving me alone through this. For that life holiday at his parents'. Do I even *want* to do that?

I am still holding the mug and I look at it now. At our faces in the grainy picture on the side: happy, naive, sure. Split up? Not them. Not those people.

'Yes,' I say. Don't give in, Scarlett. Don't give in. 'Let's book something.'

And miraculously, I can feel something that is not dread.

Forty-eight hours later we are dropping Poppy and her sixteen bags at Ed's parents' amidst promises of Peppa Pig marathons and strawberry ice cream.

I take a deep breath before we walk into their huge modern house to drop her off. It's the first time I've seen them since the video – both parties, I suspect, as keen to avoid each other so that Ed has done every drop-off with Poppy. Whole-family visits – with Ed and I barely speaking – have been off the table anyway. Ed and Poppy head off together while I run or sleep or cry.

'Scarlett,' says Phillip, as red-faced as a drinker. 'Good to see you.'

Nancy, in her cashmere cardigan and thick glasses, gives me a hug in which she manages to barely touch me. Fingertips float just above my skin.

I look down at the floor.

I wouldn't say we'd ever been close.

But there are nations and continents and time zones between us now and I am not sure we'll ever stumble back over to sit in the same country, let alone the same sofa.

148

We stay only long enough to settle Poppy in and then Ed and I and our two tiny bags are dispatched to our country house twenty miles away amidst promises of happy hour mojitos and stomps in the forest.

I don't connect to the Wi-Fi. My marriage has my undivided attention. If I want this relationship to work, I need to put effort in.

Ed and I sit at a table outside. I kick my sandals off and tilt my face up to the sun. I exhale, and it feels like I've been holding my breath for a month.

'What can I get you?' says a slightly sweaty waiter.

It's one of those moments that so rarely combine to mean you're outside in an idyllic setting when it's actually hot in England and it seems a sign. It's helping us be fun us. The grass is cut neatly like a lawn at Wimbledon, the flowers are bright and we are the only ones here. It's like we've got our own mansion with our own sprawling gardens.

I smile, lady of the manor.

I order a Prosecco cocktail, and I am getting into this now.

Maybe we'll be okay. Maybe we can spend tonight clawing it back.

I smile, take my sunglasses out of my bag.

But as I look up, eyes shaded now, I see a flicker of something cross Ed's face.

'Just a beer for me,' he says, snippier than anyone in this image should be.

Am I being paranoid or is Ed letting me know that I shouldn't be so flash as to order a cocktail when my sexually deviant past has resulted in me leaving my job and us being short of money?

I try to let it go but all I can think of is the thing I am trying to let go and I know it will come out in the end so I might as well speed on to the inevitable and get it out of the way. Eventually, it bursts out of my seams.

'Should I not have ordered the cocktail?' I ask. I've already downed half of it.

Ed looks at my glass and laughs. 'Bit late now.'

I pause. 'I'll watch my spending,' I say, chastised. 'I know it's my fault we've lost an income.'

He rolls his eyes. 'There's no need to be a martyr, that's not what I was saying,' he says. 'Jesus, we're supposed to be getting away. Does everything have to come back to *that*?'

But you did it, I think. You did it!

We sit in silence for a minute before I change the subject.

There is a certain type of misery you can only feel when you are in a setting so beautiful, and you can almost touch the joy you could or should feel there, if only you weren't in a slump.

I look around. Across from us there is a hammock between two trees.

'Swing?' I say, trying.

'My allergies are playing up,' he sniffs. 'Being in the trees won't help.'

I'm embarrassed at how juxtaposed Ed and I are to the indulgent happiness of our setting. This garden needs honeymooners and dirty weekends and kissing in the hammock with one last G&T you'll regret in the morning. It needs sunburnt shoulders and too many Aperol Spritzes and scallop starters and holding hands in the gazebo. It needs proposals and flings. Instead it has us. Wonky, unright us.

Stroppy, I walk over to the hammock and swing alone, still nursing the first cocktail while desperate to order the indulgent second that I don't deserve. This weekend would be better with my friends, I think, than my own husband. Cora would have ordered champagne, everyone would be piled into the hammock, I wouldn't have a knot in my stomach like the one I have now. What does this say about my marriage?

I feel petulant. Why come here if he was going to be like this? Across the lawn, Ed scrolls on his phone with his humble beer by his side. I slap on a smile and take a selfie for my Instagram. If I'm going to grow the numbers, I need content, whatever the mood. The equivalent of dragging yourself to work on a bad day.

I see the waiter look between us at this picture and register its anomalies.

Eventually Ed heads over (*braving the trees*) and mutters that the waiter has told him our room is ready, so I heave myself out of the hammock – no hand reaches out to help me – and we go to check in.

The heavy wooden door slams behind us and we are alone again, face to face.

Ed sits down on the bed, rumpling the bedspread as his own face does something similar and crumples.

'I'm sorry,' he says, real Ed for a moment and I am caught off guard, realising that for all of his stoic appearance, he's in pain too. I'm torn, like so often, between wanting to hug him and wanting to slap him.

I remember when he proposed to me, in a similar setting to this one but in the Highlands. Frost not heatwave, hot toddies not Prosecco but the countryside was pretty; the hotel fancy.

I came back from the toilet to find a piano playing and Ed on one knee in the middle of the restaurant looking so like something out of *Gone With The Wind* that I stood there and stared at him for a good five seconds before I remembered he needed a reply.

'Yes,' I replied. 'I forgot to say that bit. But yes.'

And we kissed more than was appropriate for a restaurant and then skipped dessert and moved the kissing to a more appropriate bedroom that looked similar to this one. Oak beams, sheets that felt brand new and this beautiful man with his big eyes standing in front of me, then, now.

And now I make a split-second decision and I kiss him. It's hard to say I want to kiss him because he's irritated the hell out of me today but I want to want to kiss him and I think that's enough. I want my marriage to work. I don't want to cheat with Joseph. I want us to stick together. I want Poppy's family to be in one place. But if I'm Sheryl Sandberg leaning in to the kiss, Ed is physically leaning out. His whole body is reacting on autopilot to pull away from me, even as his lips touch mine. His arms are flailing awkwardly out to the sides.

I pull away and look at him and suddenly I get it.

'Oh,' I say, flat and lucid. 'I'm repugnant to you.'

When I made that video, I had never met Ed. I didn't cheat on him but I may as well have. We are that couple. We want to get it back and we are making the effort but. But.

'You're not *repugnant* to me,' says Ed, exasperated. 'Do you have to be so dramatic? It's not easy. All I can think of is you with them.'

All he can picture when he thinks of me naked is me having sex with somebody else. All he can feel about my body is shame. I slept with somebody else – some other people – in a different lifetime but it might as well have been behind his back last week.

My insides collapse. Because how do you come back from that?

He lies back on the bed.

I take a deep breath.

'I realise it's not easy,' I say. 'But it's also not easy for me. In fact, having your whole life blown apart and your body splashed on the internet and your career taken away and your husband disappearing on you and not wanting to touch you is *fucking hard*.'

I tell Ed to stay at the hotel alone because we have paid for it and we could do with the space and I drive home at 4 p.m., leaving Poppy at her grandparents' house anyway and thinking that it's a good job I didn't get Joseph's phone number. Tonight I would have used it.

I go to sleep late, sad, wishing I could tell my mum friends what just happened; wishing they knew the whole story. With our marriage in such a mess now, I am aching to talk without omission to people who love me.

19

Scarlett

6 June

When Ed gets home the next morning, Poppy is still at his parents'. I couldn't face explaining to them what had happened. Left the plans in place instead. We aren't due to collect her until lunchtime.

Ed stands in the doorway to the living room.

I wipe away the flakes of black mascara that I know must be beneath my eyes. There were a lot of tears last night, as I sat here alone, Ed at the hotel, working out if my marriage could be saved. If I even wanted to save it. I still don't have the answer.

Ed unframes himself and comes in. Plonks down on the sofa. I stay at the other end. A bit of space was good for us; a bit less space might be even better. Kiss me, Ed, I think. Touch my forehead. Put your arms around me. I am so tired. Make it simple again.

'I'm sorry,' he says. He sounds exhausted. I suspect he had no sleep either.

Then my husband slams the sofa in frustration.

'I just . . . I need this video thing to be resolved. Then I can try to move on.'

I nod. I. I.

'It has to be one of them,' he seethes. 'One of them is lying, clearly.'

I tilt my head back into the cushions. So tired. So tired.

'I don't know, Ed. They say they didn't do it. I don't know.'

I look at him then, so far away, like we have never been the people in this same spot with their legs draped over each other sharing salt and vinegar crisps and arguing over who is going to put the kettle on.

'But did you push them on it?' he says, looking irritated. 'They're going to *say* it's not them, aren't they? That's obvious.'

I bristle at the implication of my stupidity.

'Well not really,' I say. 'If they wanted to blackmail me why wouldn't they say it's them?'

Ed stares at me.

'Unless he has another motive,' Ed says. 'Stalking you, wants to sleep with you again, wants to break us up?'

We both look away, talk of a break-up too close to the bone.

'Or wants to ruin your life,' says Ed. 'Bitter?'

I shrug. 'Nothing gave that impression,' I say. 'They were both all right, not mean, not cruel.'

We are silent then. Nowhere to go.

'Well, last night was a waste of time then,' Ed says, finally. 'I missed George's birthday drinks for nothing.'

And there was me thinking I couldn't confront any more.

I'm not tired, suddenly. I'm enraged.

'God forbid that you shouldn't go to every single event that's ever on, Ed,' I say. 'That a night away to try and save our marriage was a waste of your time. I have had to leave my job – which I love, incidentally – *for good* through all of this and you haven't once asked how I feel about that.'

He looks like he might interrupt me but I can't let him. I need to get all of this out.

'Instead, I'm supposed to snap straight into my natural role as a stay-at-home mum who sits around drinking coffee all day with people I barely know . . .'

This time he manages it.

'Barely know?' scoffs Ed. 'Oh come on. What about the ones you go boozing with at any opportunity?'

We stare at each other. Who will break?

I want to tell him how complicated it is. How much I need my NCT friends, how much I depend on them. How close we are in some specific ways; how much we are still working each other out in others. How I *do* barely know even them when it comes to their pasts, their depths, their non-mum selves, but then how still, in other zones, they are everything.

'Did you not make any mistakes, Ed?' I ask, quiet. 'Not even when you were young?'

He doesn't answer. Perhaps because there is no time before I am off again.

It's been stored up.

'I'm sorry about all of this, Ed,' I say. 'And I'm sorry that I've been getting too drunk sometimes lately.'

'Sometimes . . .' he mutters.

'Yes, sometimes. Sometimes too often, sometimes too much, but sometimes. I'm here, I'm a good mum to Poppy, I love you and, sometimes, I balls up. But you know the video? That actually wasn't my fault, Ed.'

Ed doesn't reply and we stand there in our hall where we have yanked muddy boots off each other's legs after long walks and opened the door for hot pizza in our pyjamas and now we are here, with nothing left to say and nothing left to do.

Our home, I think, and I realise that I am starting to hate it here now, in what was supposed to be, as we drove towards it behind the removal van that day, our countryside idyll.

Ed goes to collect Poppy and we spend the rest of the day playing with her, ignoring each other.

When she goes to bed, I can't take any more.

'I need some air,' I tell him, as he stares at the TV. 'I'm going for a walk.'

Pushing my feet into trainers, I walk out into the night

without my phone and I don't stop for hours even though there is nowhere to go.

I stare up an eerily quiet road with five or six dark houses and this does not feel, I realise, like where I live.

I have no idea how I got here or, as I walk, here or here or here or here and by the time I walk through the door it is the blackest, harshest part of the night and Ed is in bed and this building doesn't feel like home any more either. I am at the dead end; the end of the road, again.

20

Scarlett

9 June

The next day, Poppy, newly on her feet, stumbles into the corner of a table and shrieks so loudly that it makes the hairs on my arms stand up as I run towards her and my insides go into shock. Another thing that's been a victim of Ed and me not communicating: a proper plan to childproof our house ready for the toddler years.

I scream.

Poppy screams.

I'm distraught. How could we have neglected our girl like this?

Emma happens to be at our house, staying for a cup of tea as she has come round to borrow a travel cot. Emma doesn't scream. In fact she is disconcertingly calm.

She takes Poppy from me and pushes her hair to one side, looking at her head closely.

'Frozen peas?' she asks and I run to the freezer. Wrap them in a tea towel.

'Hold them on there,' she says to me, with about sixty times the authority I've ever heard her demonstrate. 'She's going to be fine. But it is her head and it was a real whack so we do need to get her checked. We're taking her to hospital.'

I freeze, in a rare north of England twenty-five-degree

heatwave that's rolled on since Ed and I were at the hotel. Not hospital. Never hospital.

'I'll call Ed,' I say. 'You don't need to take us. Pop's car seat won't fit in your car anyway. Don't worry. Ed will be here. Ed will come home from work. Ed . . .'

I take Poppy back from her; my baby is short of breath in panic and I know I can't be helping. I try to breathe deeply myself.

'Shhh, my love,' I whisper. 'It's all okay.'

Is it? I stare at her head, a giant lump coming up by her temple.

'Ed works in Warrington, right?' says Emma. 'You don't want to be sitting here worrying while you wait for him to get back. I can strap the car seat in to my car – it's not a problem.'

We walk outside together. She takes Poppy from me and puts her in the car seat.

I've never seen her so decisive. Emma leading things, me following. It's not the natural order.

Emma sees me notice the difference and ducks her head. That's more like it: more her usual body language.

Then she looks up.

'If it reassures you at all,' she says as she straps Poppy in. 'I work at the walk-in centre.'

Is she serious? She's a doctor? How could I not have known this?

'Not a GP,' she clarifies. 'On reception.'

I think then of messages she's sent at strange times when I presumed she was up with Seth. How she can meet up often some weeks but never on others. When we talked about Ronnie and she said how great it was that she accommodated odd hours. Shifts, I guess, but no one's ever asked or mentioned it, though Cora must know. Everyone's just talked over Emma more loudly, or more urgently, or veered off to Cora's affair or dairy allergies or that baby cinema that's started that does the good snacks.

Not our fault, I think, defensive – Emma should have spoken up more. That's what I tell myself, anyway, when I think how awful it is that I've never asked.

It's pushed out of my head anyway as Emma is moving me towards the door and Poppy is screaming again, in pain. She sits in the back with Seth, me wedged in the middle of them so I can hold her hand.

'It's okay, Pops,' I mutter, holding her pudgy fingers as she stares wide-eyed, not understanding the pain. 'Emma's coming now.'

My heart races.

Of all the saviours I thought we would have in life, this one, with her cheeky wines and her Slimming World points, was not it.

I talk to Poppy all the way to the hospital while she cries, even though I am on the brink of a panic attack.

Because my baby is hurt and I am going back to hospital.

Poppy still screams.

'It's okay, it's okay, it's okay.'

I touch the lump on her head and feel my breath get shorter.

In the hospital waiting room I shrink from the other people who want to make small talk and clutch Poppy to my chest as she whimpers.

How can these people chat about their dogs and the weather and that ticket machine that isn't working? How can they breathe? I bury my head in Poppy's soft brown hair as she burrows into my lap, screaming abated now but not herself, sad.

Ten minutes later we are in the triage room and I'm reminding myself that it's not the same hospital, not the same hospital, not the one where I left her behind but it's hard to remember it because of the smell, the sounds and because it's another baby girl, vulnerable.

'Looks worse than it is,' says a nurse, as I struggle to breathe. 'You're right to come in but it's just a bad bump. Scares you when they're little, I know.'

'So we can go?' I ask.

'Not quite so fast.' The nurse laughs, as I am already picking my bag up. Emma is in the waiting room with Seth.

I look up at him. What?

'You still need to see a doctor,' he says. 'Just to get a proper check.'

My heart is hammering.

I am burning up, suddenly, and the nurse looks concerned.

'Sit down for a second,' he says. 'I think you need to calm down. Let me get your friend. She can wait with you right?'

And he nips out to the waiting room to speak to Emma, then comes back to take me out to her.

It was summer then too, with the same sweat that's a constant in this heatwave, the same sterility. It's too much. The feeling that I will be sick, and it will keep coming and I won't be able to stop it.

'What's going on, babe?' Emma asks gently as I sit back down next to her holding Poppy and the room starts to spin again.

And after years of trying to keep myself closed, it's like I'm losing the battle. It's like I'm breaking open, and the world is exposing me with its online videos and its threats and its panic attacks and its tears, which are streaming now, so fast down my face that they bounce onto my chest.

It's happening again.

Emma holds my hand in her palm and I try to take deep breaths, over and over, until finally I manage it and I start to calm.

It's hospital and all it reminds me of, yes. But it's also an inability, since the trauma of the video, to deal with any type of stress without freaking out, jumping to the worst-case scenario, my body hammering and convulsing and gasping, showing me clearly, visibly, that things are not okay.

'We're going to be here for a while,' says Emma, Poppy and

160

Seth playing now with the hospital toys on the floor below us. The scratchy sleeve of her jumper itches my arm and it strikes me then how she is always covered, as much of her as possible, even though it's the hottest day of the year and the nylon must be torturous.

'If you want to talk, it's not a bad time to do it?' she continues, hesitant, watching my heaving breath slow, feeling my whole body tremble gently. She looks shocked. I try not to show this side of me.

How lovely it feels to have somebody squeeze my hand.

I blink away a new onslaught of tears.

I don't deserve this kindness. All the ways I've judged you, Em.

She is right. It is a good time to talk. But I can't bear the pity and just in time, a second pair of arms is around Poppy and Ed is here.

'Oh thank God,' I say as he scoops her up, looks at her head, cuddles her. Despite everything, seeing him here brings a swell of relief.

'How are you, sweetheart?' he asks Poppy. She chomps on her dummy.

Then he turns to me, still holding her.

'It's not the same, Scarlett,' he says, sitting down next to me with Poppy cuddled up in his lap and I am grateful that he knows without me saying it. I fall into him. 'You're okay. You're safe. I'm here.'

Ed knows how I am with hospitals, even if we don't talk much about why. He saw me hyperventilate at every scan appointment we had when I was pregnant with Poppy. He saw my eyes wide with panic even through the agony of labour as we arrived that night on the maternity ward. He saw me beg a doctor to let me go home though it was too soon after Poppy was born because I couldn't cope with the alarms going off; with footsteps moving at speed through corridors.

161

'It's not serious,' I say. 'We just need to get her checked over.'

I am appreciative, at least, that he knows where I have gone. That although he can't feel my sweat and may not have noticed my chest heaving unnaturally under my T-shirt, he knows. That he is acknowledging that this happened to me, which he does rarely. That he still cares, even if he didn't come and find me last night, or ask where I had been until the early hours, alone.

'Breathe, Scarlett,' he says quietly, holding Poppy in the seat next to me. 'All you have to do now is remember to breathe.'

Finally he turns to Emma who is looking the other way, trying to give us space, when a busy hospital waiting room means we only have millimetres.

'I'm glad Emma was with you,' he says, smiling. 'Nice to see you again too, Emma.'

They haven't seen each other since NCT classes over a year ago. He shakes her hand then, as Ed always does and it makes me laugh, like his formality used to.

He kisses me again, and I remember his smell, and inhale it deeply and think if I can just hold on to that smell then it'll be okay.

Later, Ed holds my hand as we sit next to Poppy behind a curtain while a doctor looks her over. We don't mention last night. Something has superseded all of that.

Poppy has stopped being sad and is now finding the whole thing quite the adventure, shrieking and hiding and laughing. Ed and I look like a couple, it strikes me, all of us together look like a unit. We haven't looked like this for a long time.

The doctor turns to us, hands me Poppy.

'You can take her home,' she says. 'All looks fine. It's going to be a nasty bruise but she'll recover. Kids do. It'll knock you harder, probably.'

She looks at me pointedly.

'You okay, Mum?'

And I can't even get irritated by the thing that usually irritates me: someone who is not my child calling me mum.

I nod. Who cares, I think, who cares.

'Yes,' I say, picking up Poppy. 'Thank you.'

Was that a squeeze of my hand from Ed?

Barely palpable but something.

In the car on the way home, Poppy falls asleep and I take a picture of her and post it on Cheshire Mama with a brief story about what happened. And after that there is that peace that parents experience when their child sleeps in the car. Just you two. Nowhere to go. Bit like a date night; the nearest you'll get for a while.

I turn to Ed.

'Poppy is okay,' I say. 'Can we try to focus on that? On her?'

He is silent but a minute later, at a traffic light, he reaches over and holds my hand and I squeeze and hope hard, in a way that is almost like a prayer.

21

Scarlett

10 June

'Are you cheating on me?' asks Ed, as I kick off a bright pink trainer. I've done 6k powered by the giddiness of thinking that my marriage might make it after all. Our perspective has shifted, I thought, powering up a hill. The video seemed like the biggest thing and now it doesn't. Now it seems like the smallest thing, compared to our child and our family.

But now this.

I plummet. 'What?'

I think of how paranoid I have been lately that *he* is cheating with all the gym visits and nights out and how I've wanted to ask the same question but never have.

'Are you cheating on me?' he asks, one leg crossed over the other knee, slipper dangling off his foot. The picture of comfort in our home, as he accuses me.

I sit down in my leggings and marvel at the speed at which you can alter your feelings towards people who mean the most.

Two minutes ago I wanted a long life with Ed. I wanted to hug him, curl up on the sofa with him, run marathons with him. I thought we'd found our route back.

Now, I'm back at the dead end.

I feel violent, like I could walk over to the drinks trolley in the corner of the room, take a bottle of vodka and smash him over the head with it.

At this moment I don't believe that I loved him ten minutes ago. I only believe the emotions charging through me now.

'So what we said last night meant nothing then?' I say.

We had slept in the same bed when often lately, he's been in the spare room. Kissed before we went to sleep.

He sighs.

'Look at this from my perspective,' he says. 'If you're cheating on me, it's not something we can ignore. Whether Poppy bumped her head or not.'

'Why would you think that though?' I rage, sadness that looks like anger. All of these emotions trying on each other's clothes and dressing up as each other.

I tell myself to calm down and remember that Poppy is sleeping. But I can't make myself feel any of the logic.

Ed reaches for the phone next to him and hands it to me.

It's a text message, from an anonymous number, telling him that they have been sleeping with me.

I stare at him.

'If someone sends that, I have to ask,' says Ed. 'It's a simple yes or no, which funnily enough you haven't given yet.'

'You think it's fair,' I say, trying to steady my breathing, again, to ward off another panic attack, another moment where all control is lost. 'To take the word of an anonymous stranger over your wife. Would you have asked if the video hadn't happened?'

Ed wobbles. I see it.

Who is doing this to me? Who hates me this much? Videos, comments, lies to my husband.

'I'm not taking their word over yours,' he says, more gently. 'I'm just trying to get your word in the first place.'

I stand up.

'I'm going for a shower, Ed. But if you really need me to answer, then no. I'm not sleeping with any man. I'm currently battling this living hell with the video and I haven't got the motivation to shave my legs let alone sleep with somebody else.'

I think of Cora and her affair. It's true. Every action needs the impetus to be bothered, first and foremost. I walk out of the room and peel my damp clothes off. I lock the door and step into the shower and look down: I was telling the truth about the leg shaving.

I grab my razor, hack at my calves angrily without changing the blade so that there is blood eventually, quite a lot of it.

I think about the man in the coffee shop, and how he looked at me, and how close I came. I haven't. But I could have, Ed, and you're pushing me closer.

Would I even feel guilty? Ask those changing feelings. It would depend on the day.

I hack more.

I step out of the shower and pull a towel around me, then head straight into the living room, leaving damp footprints in my wake and two trails of blood, trickling down the backs of my calves. I wipe, cursory, every now and again but blood on the carpet no longer seems the disaster it would have a few months ago.

Ed is still sitting, watching golf, phone in his hand.

He glances at the damp marks I am leaving, winces.

'Any other messages?' I ask.

'Yes actually,' he snaps, holding up his phone. If I was expecting reticent, I'm not getting it. 'Same guy.'

He leans his head backwards. Puts his hands behind it.

'Scarlett, I'm not trying to be a dick here, but what do you expect me to do? Ignore it?'

I laugh one of those mean, horrible laughs that shouldn't be called laughs at all. We should get a different word for those.

I don't have an answer, to any of it. I want to erase and wipe and travel back in time. I think again about deleting the blog after what Mitch said, how maybe that would make me less of a target. But it's too late. Any damage it's caused has been done. And I feel petulant too. Whoever this is has taken everything else, my job, my confidence, my happy marriage. Cheshire Mama was one thing for me. Why should I let them have that too?

'Sleep in the spare room tonight, Ed,' I say, weary, as I walk out of the room to bed.

I think about the feelings I had last night as we sat alongside each other, the only people in the world who understand that Poppy is the centre of the world's axis.

United, like we had been when she arrived, gloopy and noisy and spindly.

I lie in bed for hours before sleep comes, going over my conversations with Ollie, with Mitch. Is there *anyone* else who could have done this? Any other answer? Bring me evidence, said the lawyer, and I vow to myself that somehow, some way I will. I can't let life keep continuing to slide away from me like this. Ten minutes later, I hear Ed slowly close the spare room door. Eventually, sleep comes.

Anon

When I weep for a man who is slipping away from me, Scarlett holds on to hers. And that seems so bloody unfair.

I think she and her husband might *even* be getting back on track; she sent a message to the group the morning after Poppy came out of hospital saying things were good between them, that she thought they would be ok.

Greedy Scarlett, breezing around getting what she wants. Even now, after what I have done to her.

So I take matters into my own hands.

Ed's number, I have, from a dormant NCT group chat we had set up, never used. Instead, the all-female one became the constant for questions, reassurance, pictures of your nipple up close in your baby's mouth.

But his number comes in handy now. From my other phone of course; the pay-as-you-go one.

Hey, mate, I write, getting into my new laddish persona. What next? A chat to Ed about the footy scores? Oh wait, no. He's a golf man. I'd need to do quite a bit of research to be up to speed on that; not my natural territory. *Man to man, I thought you'd like to know that I'm sleeping with your wife.*

He doesn't reply, though I can see it has been read.

I'm kind of irritated. Craving something. Wanting to move things on.

Me again, I say, ten minutes later. *If it helps you piece the dates together, we were together while you were away for work last Tuesday. She invited me round to your place.*

Handily, I'm in the know on Ed's schedules. A quick scan back through messages from Scarlett gifts an easy timetable. We share *a lot* of minutiae.

I nearly start to tell him things I know about his house – of course I'd spent enough time there – but stop. I don't want Scarlett getting close to the truth by working out who *has* been to her house lately.

So I sit back.

Wait.

Told you I'm a lot more patient than Scarlett.

22

Scarlett

13 June

The house, in the middle of nowhere in the Peak District, is messy with clothes and food strewn everywhere, but we don't care. For once, we're not responsible. We're teenagers again. It's someone else's problem.

Emma is shrieking, drunk on a few gin and slims as she is not a big drinker.

'I thought we were going to go to a spa!' she slurs, then giggles. 'What happened to the spaaaaaa?'

I have my long legs propped up on a sofa that is not mine and am in old baggy leggings and bare feet. I have a glass of warm supermarket red wine in my hand. I am on my phone, posting a picture of Poppy I took yesterday, trying to keep up more regular traffic on Cheshire Mama's Instagram.

I laugh at Emma.

'Remember the spa you found was a bit . . . well, shit?' I say, laughing. 'We came here instead. I found it on Airbnb.'

Then, we planned to go walking but bad weather and being shattered made us abandon that too.

'We could get the bus into town?' says Emma, smoothing down frizz at her temple that keeps popping up ten seconds after she does this. It's about the tenth time. 'Have a potter around the shops?'

Everyone ignores her or rolls their eyes. That's what happens to Emma when she suggests things like potters or cheeky pizzas.

There's a Chinese takeaway menu floating around somewhere and Emma, perpetually dieting, is talking romantically about fried noodles.

Beyond that, we're just going to drink and not think about anybody else, and that's the point of being here.

Someone puts a Sonique song on I like on Spotify and I stand up to dance to it and wonder why no one is acknowledging that this is one of my favourite songs but then I remember that no one knows which songs are my favourites, yet. As I dance with my eyes closed, Cora says something about a group shot.

'Yes!' says Asha. 'A group shot. I'll get my phone.'

'I meant tequila,' says Cora, deadpan, and the next minute I am roaring with laughter and downing one tequila then a second from a bottle that I did not know anyone had brought.

After that, my memory gets blurrier.

A third slips down, I think.

I talk a lot. I know that.

Next thing, I'm waking up in a double bed next to Cora and my eyes are sticky with mascara. My mouth is claggy with a lack of water and the remains of a thick, spicy Asian sauce.

The usual thing happens.

Whereas before I might stir gradually, since the video I wake like somebody at war. I am on high alert, grab my phone, check what I've missed, if other disasters have befallen me while I slept. It's worse when I've been drunk and have taken my eye off the ball for longer.

This morning, I grab my phone from this Airbnb's shabby-chic bedside table.

As soon as I've checked my messages to make sure that Poppy is okay, I realise that what I am worried about, today, is not on a phone.

Instead, I think – what did I tell my friends last night? What did I share?

I glance at Cora, gently snoring with an expensive eye mask on and her make-up removed. Next to her on her bedside table sit a messy pile of five tubs of creams I know all cost over £100, two of which have the lids off. She was definitely drinking last night – even steering the shots – but from the evidence, clearly not in the state I was.

I get up and walk down the hall in bare feet on cold wooden floors. I shiver. I open cupboards and drawers and eventually find a chocolate cupcake with half a Crunchie on top of it in a Cora's Cupcakes branded box and I eat that for breakfast in two bites.

I put the kettle on and lean against the work surface.

The thought that buzzes round my brain constantly comes to the surface again. *If not Ollie and Mitch, who?* I have a meeting with the lawyer next week but he has been clear: the website operator has taken it down and it's not appeared anywhere else. Strand one. For strand two, getting whoever did it, the best – the only – way to move this on is to get some evidence, so we can hand that over to police.

As I wait for the kettle to boil, Asha comes in holding two coffees.

She is in leggings and a hoodie and out of breath.

'Went for a walk,' she says. 'The only way I could think of to shift the hangover.'

She nods towards her coffee cup.

'Wish I'd got up in time to get my order in,' I mutter, opening cupboards to locate a pot of instant.

'Good news,' she says. 'It's yours. Got an extra one, for whoever was up first.'

I want to kiss her.

'Was I . . . embarrassing last night?' I say, taking the cup from her hand, sipping even though it burns.

Asha heads across to the sofa. 'We were all drunk,' she says. 'Don't worry about it.'

But I have more to fear, I think, more to share. That's what she doesn't realise.

I drink my coffee with Asha in front of a *Friends* repeat and then I head back to the bedroom, passing Cora on the way.

'Just going for a shower,' she says. Smirks. 'Bloody hell, I bet you're feeling rough.'

And I feel disproportionately angry. Just one day, I think. Just one day where I don't feel shamed would be nice.

I fight the urge to tell her that her cupcake tasted of zero-hours contracts.

Is the key in drinking? Do I need to stop? Or is it too late for me? Am I destined to have an aptly scarlet letter across my chest forever?

I lie on the bed on my front like a teenager in a hungover sulk and scroll through my phone. Pictures, on Facebook and Instagram, from last night, in which I look like a mess. In which my eyes don't focus.

And then worse.

I open my email and see a message from the website provider. After they agreed to take the video down, Jonathan told me they could potentially give me information about who posted the video. I asked.

And finally, they have something for me.

'We have been able to pin down the area that the video was sent from,' it says. 'Hopefully this will be of some use to you.'

Cora comes into the room.

'Want some toast?' she asks.

'Just give me a second,' I say, angling my phone away from her, my heart thumping hard.

'You okay, hon?' she asks.

I nod, distracted. 'Uh-huh.'

She stands there, waiting for more.

I look at her. 'Just got to deal with something at home. I'll be out in a bit.'

But I have taken it in, even as she stands there. What the next line says. What this means.

Because the area that the video was sent from is not Manchester where Mitch is.

It's not the Midlands near Ollie.

The video was posted from a place closer to home.

My hands shake now, as Cora walks away.

I shove my things in a bag and tell the girls my hangover is too bad to stay for the rest of the day for a pub Sunday lunch as planned and I head home early. My mind is buzzing about who could have done this, who wants to hurt me so much that they sat in their home in a sleepy, leafy, boring village and posted a video of me having sex with two men.

Because the video was posted in Cheshire.

In the car home, I look around at those fields, those country pubs, that farm shop that sells the good brownies and it feels like they are edging closer to me, surrounding me, so I can't escape this place now.

Cheshire.

It is too much to be a coincidence.

Someone from the inside of my life is out to get me.

Now I just need to figure out who it is; who I can no longer trust.

Anon

'Girls, I'm going to have to head off too,' I say, as soon as Scarlett leaves. 'I'm feeling rough as well. Bad noodles?'

The other girls laugh.

'Sure, sure, the old "it was the takeaway." Not the eighteen wines.'

In truth, my stomach *has* been edgy since Scarlett went. Nothing to do with noodles though, or even wine. I know she has figured something out.

She was different suddenly. Her eyes were alert, bright, and they didn't look at us properly.

She was edgy. Not like the night before when she had danced barefoot with her hands in her own hair like she found herself irresistible, lids drooping.

I looked at her then and felt any latent guilt shift – well, it didn't hurt you too much, did it, this video? And you clearly don't feel bad about what you did to me. Even if you don't realise I know about it.

She buried her hands in her hair, sang along quietly.

I stared at Scarlett in those minutes and imagined having that self-belief, imagined having that body.

I remembered *seeing* that body – all of it – just before I had clicked send. Watching the video again and again. Imagining the hurt it could cause. The adrenalin rush. Send. The panic. The buzz. The sense of righting a wrong. The nausea. The horror. The pride. The euphoria.

I had sat quietly that weekend we were away together in the Peak District as she posted pictures of her daughter on her blog *again*. Saw her smiling to herself across a room as she was self-effacing in her replies to all the hundreds of comments online that told her how pretty she is, even though she *knows* that, that's why she posted it, that's why she is always posting, posting, posting.

And in those moments, I had realised something.

The video hadn't been enough to ruin her.

Even my messages to Ed hadn't been enough to ruin her.

But that didn't matter. Because there was more, Scarlett, still to come.

I drive home wondering what she knew and how.

And think about whether that means I have to speed things up. To deliver the next blow sooner than planned. Imminently.

23

Scarlett

16 June

Another evening, another split into separate rooms of the house.

Does it all come down to the furniture really? Share a bed, a sofa, a dining table and you'll be all right. Start dividing off and where you divide next, right through the centre of your feelings for each other, is inevitable.

I am in the bath long after it has become tepid because it is still less chilly than being in a room with my husband.

Cheshire. The video was posted in Cheshire. What the hell does that mean? How close has this come from? I glance at the door. Ed is in the living room watching something on his iPad with his headphones on. I think again of all of those nights out he's been on lately, of my suspicions that he's cheating. Would a woman who wants me out of the picture do this to me? And could she be here, just out of touching distance buying new underwear to show to my husband behind a pretty moneyed door in Cheshire?

The door is locked and I have taken my phone in with me; I need short, sharp hits of distraction. It feels the same as the Haribo. I scroll old pictures on my blog of Ed, Poppy and me looking happy and content. Looking like people you would want to be. The comparison is almost unbearable.

I file the email from the website provider in case I need it as evidence, in a trial I can't imagine being brave enough for, to speak up about things I never want to speak up about. That's how they get my silence, isn't it? With my own shame. I remember Asha talking about the theory of the greater good; risking your own self for the bigger picture, in case this happens to somebody else. But I'm not strong enough. I'm not.

Without realising, I've opened Facebook. New friend request. Joseph Jacobson. It takes me a second but a look at the picture and my familiar response to his face confirms it: he's the guy from the coffee shop. I glance at the bathroom door, guilty. Something happens that feels nostalgic. The way you feel at the beginning. The way you feel about potential.

I accept his request and a message pops in. It's incongruous to my social media presence with its family life and its cute baby.

I don't bite, it says. *Never feel like you can't stop in for coffee. Nothing happened between us, after all. We can still be mates.*

I exhale. I had been fairly sure there had been no kiss but still; it's good to hear him confirm.

If he'd left it there it might have been okay. But he's typing, typing. Don't do it, I think, but at the same time I think, *do.*

You look beautiful in that profile picture. Ridiculously beautiful.

I need to distance myself from this because my physical response to it screams danger.

I look at his picture. *Ridiculously beautiful.*

Could he be something to do with the video, with the threats? A man who fancies me, and lives and works in Cheshire? There are more unlikely scenarios.

Immediately my phone pings with a text and I think, *Joseph.* But three words give a different reveal.

Scarlett, Scarlett, Scarlett, it says. Ollie. *I liked seeing you. Can I see you again?*

I sit bolt upright, water splashing over the side of the over-filled bath.

Jesus.

I've pictured it, haven't I, even when things have been good with Ed, being back with Ollie.

I've pictured the reunion and felt the kiss and known the squeeze of emotion through my whole body and I've wondered: do other people feel this way? Is this just first love? Perhaps it even happens if you didn't care that much; it's just something your brain does; a chemical response when it remembers how powerful everything was first time around.

I glance at the door to check it's locked.

I read it again.

Scarlett, Scarlett, Scarlett.

Joseph is forgotten.

Could Ollie be contacting me for any other reason than the one I'm thinking of?

But really, what he is saying is simple. What Ollie is asking is whether I will meet him in a pub again, with no practical reason this time. He wants to meet me in a pub when we are both married and despite us sharing an obscene attraction and a lot of love, whether it's past or present.

The answer is obvious, and I start typing.

24

Scarlett

16 June

Ollie and I are in a club; we drink vodka tonics. We're older than most of the people around us, sure, but we're better dancers, and we know dance classics like they were written on our bones.

This laughs in the face of a baby exercise class, and we sweat and it's beautiful and Ollie kisses me. We've aged, yes, but the kisses have not.

I wear a short dress and trainers and from a distance, in the flattering night-time, I am twenty-two.

We kiss on the dance floor and then we kiss in the taxi home but this time it's not home, as there are husbands there, and wives, and children. We realise occasionally that we are grown-ups with our own recycling bins and the memory is funny. The weight of responsibility has lifted for this brief moment and we revel in it. Can barely remember those people we are on Mondays, on Tuesdays, on all the days.

We go to a hotel and it's not grubby because he is my first love and this is romance. Sex with him is different but the power of it and the strength of my adoration for him is the same.

The next morning we order room service brunch and I laugh that Ollie is happily eating eggs after years of being suspicious of them and their odd chameleonic ways. He smirks when I order a green juice when healthy drinks used to mean Diet

Coke. We raise an eyebrow at our new funny habits; our millennial leanings.

Next we take a long bath together – as we used to do but this is a far superior bath tub than any our skint youth ever brought us – and we plan to leave and start over. We're glad we've lost those years because of our children and we're relieved that we have that caveat because otherwise the pain of that loss and that waste would be too much to deal with.

I picture it over and over, this scene.

But it's not real.

It does not happen because my answer to Ollie is no. It has to be a no, doesn't it, if I am giving my marriage even a fighting chance. Currently it clings to the rafters, bloody of lip with a clump of hair yanked out of its skull. It needs all the help it can get. But I am doing it for past me, who used to stare at Ed in bed and think I'd never seen a man so beautiful. Who used to look at our life and our family and our home that looked like a Pinterest board and think this, *this* is the stuff of fantasy. I wasn't the only one who thought that either; why d'you think Cheshire Mama is so successful?

We made small talk at first, Ed and I, when we met at the agency and then one day he asked me for a drink. We had this physical chemistry that meant I slept with him after two dates, and that felt like I had waited a year. Something about us clicked into place and I was excited too, about being part of his close family and its big, fancy gated mansion in the country and their annual Salloway Sports Day and their four-course meals and their poshness. I made him laugh until he roared, I knew, and he used to stare at me regularly. 'I've never seen a face I like so much,' he said, a month or two in. 'Never take this face away.'

So I tell Ollie no, for that Ed and that me, and then I lie there and carry on imagining that other world, where I had said yes and Ollie and I picked up where we left off, the new us, and found out exactly how that worked.

I dip back down under water.

You wanted respectable, Scarlett, then this is the sort of sacrifice respectable people make. You think respectable people aren't tempted? Hardly. They just learn to say no, over and over, to the late night and the single-use plastic and the chips for dinner and the fourth gin and the affair. Definitely to the affair.

But *Ollie*.

My phone beeps and it's one word in response to my negative. *Shame*.

I tilt my head back against the tub and groan.

My phone beeps again.

Any luck with Mitch?

It's no harm to tell him about that, surely, to keep the line of communication open to pass on this information. It concerns him too, after all.

He says he didn't do it, I say. *I met him for a drink*.

I should have messaged and told him that, I realise. It impacts him as well.

Sorry I didn't tell you, my brain is all over the place, I write.

And what do you think?

My gut instinct was that he was telling the truth.

Ollie is typing. Like we're friends now and I don't know why but I'm glad. *But if not him, who? Who would have had access to his phone?*

I sit back. Don't reply as I don't know, and I feel stupid for not knowing. I should be able to solve this; it should be intuitive.

Website operator says the video was posted in Cheshire, I tell him. He's in my team now; there's going to have to be some trust.

I have no idea how they would have got hold of the video, but any exes bitter when you left them and based there? he says. *I know how much being dumped by Scarlett can hurt*.

A few months after we had the night with Mitch, things had completely unravelled in my brain. I was struggling, and booze and nights out were making it worse.

When a friend told me she wanted to get off the party circuit and was looking for a buddy to go travelling with, I took out a credit card and said yes because I had been waiting for something like this to break the cycle and I ended it with Ollie abruptly, like a coward. A phone call, the night before I got on a plane, after all that we had been through.

'Is this because of what happened with Mitch?' he asked me that night, speaking into the last days of the landline.

I was silent. In a way, I thought. Kind of.

'I regret it,' he carried on, crying. 'It's taken something away from us, I know, an intimacy, but we can get it back, Scarlett. We have a lifetime to get it back. We can have another baby. A family. Don't end this.'

I sounded cold in my effort not to cry but I promised to call him when I got back from my trip. I went away for three months. We never spoke again, until this.

I am an in or out person, always have been. I got rid of my phone and picked up a pay-as-you-go for the trip, and it was easy to disappear when you left the country back then. You didn't update social media, you only paid the obscene prices to message if it were an emergency.

When I got home, I moved in to my dad's house and saved up some money.

I had started to get into the advent of social media and I got work experience at a digital marketing agency and I applied myself to it with as much dedication as I used to dedicate myself to getting off my face. I needed this; my life had to change. I was offered a junior position in the social media team and started to climb, being promoted and doing better than I had ever done at anything. It was a buzz like the ones I got on the dance floor, albeit a little more muted.

Eventually I moved out of my dad's house and into a shared flat with a couple of girls in Chorlton, where you went out on Sunday mornings for eggs benedict, not Friday nights for lines of coke.

I got a two glasses of red wine habit instead of a vodka one. I wore heels. I dyed my cheap blonde highlights back to my original dark brown and when I could afford it, put a glossy sheen from a fancy salon on top.

I became addicted to it all too, and what it brought, and with every new choice I added to the new me, with her sharp bob and her pension and, six years after she left party-boy Ollie, her new boyfriend, posh Ed, the financial controller from work, who became her husband in an expensive wedding where we served good wine and rare beef. We celebrated with smart, successful friends.

It's a path that my mind has taken me down many times in the last two months. How far things have fallen back, back, back.

Any exes bitter when you left them?

I think, over and over.

After Ollie, there was no one serious until Ed. But there *were* flings, love stories in miniature.

I think carefully about each one now. How things were left and if, somehow, those people could have had access to the video. I don't come up with anything.

If you change your mind, I'm up for a drink, says Ollie from my phone at the side of the bath, from the past.

I pull the plug out, grab a towel then head to bed. But I leave my phone behind to make sure that I don't message back and dive into that past because the present is so very, very bleak.

25

Scarlett

18 June

'Forgot my phone,' I say, putting my key in the door. 'Got all the way to the gym before I realised and no way can I do the treadmill without music.'

Ed is sitting on the sofa, holding it. He brandishes it at me. Again.

'What now?'

And my husband looks at me with such disdain that I think if it weren't for Poppy, I would give up on us for good because who can take a life like this? Who can take a face that looks at them like this?

'You've been messaging Ollie,' he says.

I exhale. That's all.

'Well he's involved in this too,' I said. 'It seems fair to update him.'

There's a beat.

'But that's not what happened,' Ed says. 'He asked you for a drink. You only told him about Mitch and the Cheshire thing – which incidentally you've never told me – later.'

Why had I never told Ed that I knew the video came from Cheshire? Because somewhere, deep down, I wondered if it could be a woman Ed is seeing who did this to me. And the Cheshire link seemed to increase the possibility of that.

I shiver.

'You looked at my phone.'

For the first time, he makes eye contact.

'You say that as though these are normal circumstances, Scarlett,' he says. 'I haven't looked at your phone in the five years we have been together. I've had no need to. I trusted you. But we're not in normal times here.

'You're in a sex video online. Men are contacting me to say they're sleeping with you.'

I sit down on the floor.

'So,' he says, swimming out of my vision. Everything is blurry. It's exhaustion mixed with endorphins mixed with thirst mixed with anger mixed with sadness.

But then he appears again.

'So. I'll ask you once. Why are you messaging Ollie? Why are you flirting with him?'

Hearing him say Ollie's name makes me start to shake. It's the two versions of me overlapping and blurring. It's lives, squishing together. It's naivety and fun and it's electricity bills and raincoats.

I look at Ed, lucid for a second.

'You mean the messages to Ollie that I wrote saying no to a drink?' I say, anger building. 'Those messages? The ones where I stay loyal to you despite temptation?'

It's out before I can think.

He nods, matter-of-fact.

'Tempted then,' he says, martyr. 'Nice to know.'

I lean my head back against the wall, try to unload some of the weight.

'Of course I was tempted, Ed,' I say, quiet now. 'Don't tell me there isn't someone out there who could tempt you, if they got you at the right moment. Which let's face it, for us is definitely now.'

I pause.

'We aren't even sharing a bed.'

Ed bows his head, shamed briefly too, thinking of the old us that would have felt starved by this lack of touch.

'Are you sure it's not him?' he says. 'If it seems like he fancies you now too, it could be part of some weird way to get back in touch, make you need him . . .'

I hesitate.

It seems odd to be affirmative to Ed. To acknowledge how well I know another man. How much I trust another man. I redden.

And also, he has a point.

'Fucking hell, Ed, reading my messages. Come on.'

I lie down now, supine on the floor.

And from there, when I can't look at him, I ask.

'Ed,' I say quietly. A last throw of the dice. 'Can you hug me?'

I stay there on the floor so that I can't see his response but when I finally sit up, minutes later, he is gone.

I hear him moving around upstairs. Shutting the door. No gap, no opening. Goodnight then, Ed. And I cry the silent tears that you do especially so that no one hears and no one has to deal with the hassle of comforting you.

And when I'm done with crying and I am done with being in this room with just me, me, me, I message my friends and I ask if anyone wants to go to the pub because I am having, I can't think of a less dramatic way to describe it even though I know what a stir it will cause, a marriage crisis.

My mum friends don't normally do impromptu drinks but the words 'marriage crisis' get people slapping some mascara on and heading for the door.

I slam my own without a word and I walk to the pub wishing that I knew how to bring this back and turn it so that we faced the right way. But it is so far gone, isn't it. It is so very, very far gone.

You think when you have been through big things like childbirth together that it means you're right with each other, always. But sometimes you're still wrong with each other, at a certain point.

Sometimes shared experience isn't enough.

Sometimes, one type of shared experience bonds you and another yanks you apart, and you have no way of knowing which one is which except maybe, somehow, it's to do with blame. When there is blame to level, teams stop being teams, couples stop being couples.

An hour later my friends and I are in our local and I am drinking fast and slurring, and I know I will regret this but I cannot stop it now it is in motion. I'm tired of hiding and lying and spinning. Take it all, know it all.

Emma, her lime and soda next to my Malbec – she's driving – is holding my hand and I look down and see my rounded nails, manicured once but now, bitten down.

'Has he strayed, babe?' says Emma in a stage whisper, clinging to my hand so that we have become sweaty together. '*A lot* of men do it. It doesn't mean you can't move on from it.'

She speaks like she has some unique wisdom. I roll my eyes.

'No he hasn't *strayed*,' I mutter but then, the gym visits, the drinks, the distance, the coldness. *Has* he strayed? Maybe, Em, maybe he has bloody *strayed*.

I look up and realise I'm missing Emma's hand. It felt nice to be touched.

I think.

Strayed.

Would it be easier if that were what had happened? A linear problem. A well-trodden path. Rage, fury and then a balance of what would be lost versus what would be gained from leaving. We'd batten down the hatches, talk, leave it behind. Maybe book a fancy holiday. See a relationship therapist. Paint the house. Regroup.

I let Emma, who clearly has no gauge of the right amount of personal space but I am currently pathetically grateful of that fact, put her arm around me as I begin to cry again.

Asha thinks we should eat, and goes to order bar food.

'What have I missed?' bellows Cora, walking as fast as her heels can carry her across the pub towards us and sporting what I can see even for her are incredibly dark eyebrows. 'If he is cheating, you've got Joseph there waiting. You could get your own back like *that.*'

She clicks her fingers.

I stare at her face. It looks odd.

'Yeah I went a bit overboard on the old HD brows,' she says, finger to her face. She shrugs. 'Ah, well. It'll fade. So, hot hipster or not?'

I look at Cora then and feel a swell of admiration.

Would she care, that I have a sex tape online? Would she laugh, shrug, tell me to move on and forget it? Ask to see it then tell me I had 'great tits, hon' and dilute the whole thing for me?

I open my mouth and I am so close to telling them, but then I see the receptionist from our doctor's walk past to leave the pub, putting up a hand in greeting, and I close my mouth again, wipe my eyes and wave back.

Cora goes to the bar and our chips arrive, some hummus and dips, mini burgers, and Asha and I don't touch them while Emma talks to herself quietly, totting up calories each time she dives in. She is still holding my hand.

Then Cora sits down, glass of Prosecco in front of her now.

'Best they had.' She grimaces. 'Right, I've got the nanny to stay on an extra few hours for this one.'

She leans forward on the table. Eats a chip.

'Shit's hit the fan? Talk me through it.'

And I go to make a joke, to be acerbic about it, or light, to do what I'm supposed to do in this situation so that I don't make anybody feel uncomfortable but I can't manage it.

Instead, I break down and sob tears that sting my eyes like I have rubbed vodka into the corners.

I can't keep this in. Without Ed to speak to about it, it's bursting from my seams. My dad talks in code. I'm too ashamed to thrash this out with my little sister. Ollie is now off-limits.

'There is a video of me,' I say, quietly. 'It's online. I'm having sex in it, a long time ago, and it's been sent to all of my friends and family. Except you lot: whoever did it obviously doesn't know you are in my lives yet because that's recent.'

No one says a word. But I'm used to shocking people into silence.

'I'm not having a longer maternity leave, I've left work for good. It was too embarrassing that my colleagues had seen it, and clients felt weird about working with me,' I continue. I still cringe at the memory of overhearing Flick, something I've never told her about. She's the last person I want feeling guilty. 'I'm trying to find out who posted the video but neither of the men . . .'

I see eyebrows shoot up.

'Oh yes, there are two men. Neither will admit to posting it. I met up with them both. So I don't know if it's got into someone else's hands somehow, or if they're lying.'

I pause, to more silence. It's weird seeing Cora without hearing her voice.

'Sometimes . . .' I whisper, heaving breaths. The relief of this. The pain of it. 'Sometimes . . . it . . . feels like being tortured. Sometimes I've wanted to be dead, just for the peace. To quiet my brain.'

No one says anything but Cora walks round to stand at my shoulder and hug me into her soft expensive neon pink cashmere from above, my face inhaling what must be half a bottle of Chanel. My breath shakes.

Asha reaches across to do small rhythmic strokes on my arm. Emma tightens her grip around me, clutching on to both of my palms with small, chapped hands. Her arm feels skinnier, I notice. A lot skinnier. I look up and realise that's the case all over. I've been so consumed by what's happening to me that I haven't noticed that Emma's gym trips have paid off. She must have lost two stone. She looks lovely.

I look down at their hands then up, at their faces.

I am encased from all sides and whether they are the same as me or different, whether they are 'mum friends' or whether we will know each other in ten years' time or not, this is something meaningful. I lean back into them, hold their hands tighter.

'One other thing,' I say, quietly now. 'The website operators told me where the video was posted from.'

I look up at their faces.

'It was round here; it was sent from Cheshire.'

I see my friends exchange a look.

'I know,' I say. 'Someone so close. I think that might be the creepiest thing of all.'

26

Scarlett

19 June

I wake up next to somebody I shouldn't. Someone I've only slept next to once before, away from home.

We headed back to theirs after the pub and I stayed over.

Shit, shit, shit.

I reach down to the floor and pick up my bag.

See my phone, on silent, showing sixteen missed calls from Ed.

It's 5 a.m.

I message quickly.

Shit.

All fine, stayed at Cora's, too much to drink, sorry, I type.

This is like being nineteen. How has my life taken this turn? I might miss the music and the highs sometimes but I do not miss this paranoia, this emergency alarm of a wake-up. I think of Poppy at home, warm in her bed.

Cora rolls over.

'Can you be quiet?' she mutters. 'If anyone but a baby wakes me up before 7 a.m., I do not deal well. In fact even when it's a baby, I do not deal well.'

She turns back away from me and I lie there, still, as though this is a one-night stand and I'm running on awkward adrenalin.

I try not to move and I stare at Cora.

Silk sheets pulled around her waist, silk pyjamas and eye mask on. The bedside table similar to when we were away but messier; piles and piles of fancy pots, face masks, hefty glossy magazines, junk.

Just like the last time I woke up with her, she can't have been as drunk as me last night. I can't remember a thing. I wouldn't have been capable of finding my pyjamas even if I'd been in the same house as them.

What the hell was I thinking, staying at Cora's?

My phone beeps. Ed.

You can't do that, Scarlett. I've been up all night freaking out.

Didn't know where the hell you were. Jesus, we have a child here. I nearly called the police.

But you didn't, I think. What's the point of nearly? Would nearly have found me if I was in trouble?

It's irrational to be angry about something that didn't happen but nothing is rational now.

I sit up in bed, try to move stealthily but even expensive silk sheets aren't silent. Cora grumbles.

'Look, before you go, you should know something,' she murmurs and my body is on its hind legs again, primed. 'I've seen mention of stuff online about a mum blogger and a sex tape. All anon, and obviously I had no idea it was relevant . . . until last night. But someone might have connected the dots, hon. And the press are gunning for influencers at the moment. If you don't want to be on the front page of MailOnline, I'd think about deleting the blog. Going quiet. For a while at least. And delete social media too, Scarlett. Seriously. You need to make yourself uninteresting.'

Her head is still on her pillow; her voice muffled but her message clear.

My stomach makes an odd noise. My insides flare with a mix of terror and last night's wine.

Every time I think I can't take another hit, it comes.

I mutter yes, I will, and thanks for telling me and then I slope out, Cora muttering instructions for the door and the intimidating security gate as I go.

'Lock and put the key back through, hon,' she mutters, a soft foot with bright red nails sticking out of the duvet as I walk past. 'And meet me at the coffee shop at ten. I'll message the girls. We'll all need coffee and sugar this morning.

I let myself out and tremble as I walk home, terrified of being even more exposed than I already am, running eventually because I just need to move fast, do something.

I told Asha, Cora and Emma about the video. The last remaining people in my life who didn't know, and now they do. It's out. It's staying out.

When my key opens the door, all I get is stony silence. Ed is up and dressed, despite the fact it's before 6 a.m., and he stalks around the house.

'I'm sorry,' I say again as he walks past me in the kitchen without a word. 'I got drunk with the girls.'

He looks at me.

'Not a problem. Not like you have responsibilities.'

And I snap then. 'Like you did when you left me?'

He says nothing but his eyes are still on mine. It's unnerving. Eventually I walk away. How am I going to tell him that there's no money to be made from the blog now, either? That I'm about to walk out of this room and shut everything to do with Cheshire Mama down.

'Whatever this is . . .' Ed says then, eyes on the clothes I have slept in and the usually smooth hair that is sticking up at angles that someone else's silk sheets apparently create. I smooth it down. Try to.

'Whatever this is,' he begins again, as his voice catches. 'A midlife crisis, an affair, the video or just a reaction to being a mum. Please, Scarlett. Please just grow up.'

And then he leaves the house and I have no idea where he

is going. But I suppose it's his turn. We tag-team our life now. You take possession of it for a while; I'll be over there living another unknown one.

I crawl back into bed and hope desperately that Poppy sleeps later than usual. And then, one by one, I delete Cheshire Mama's Instagram, Facebook and finally the blog itself. Another part of my life gone. Another slice of me deleted. But I am matter-of-fact about it, feeling numb. I've shut myself down too.

At six thirty on the dot Poppy wakes and I exercise the skill I've learnt since being a parent of snapping into a different tempo immediately.

'Breakfast time!' I chirrup and I carry her downstairs kissing her skin all over as I go.

I serve up porridge for Poppy and down two cups of instant coffee and then I find some crisps in the cupboard and I think yes, that's what I could eat for breakfast so I have a packet of salt and vinegar chipsticks to ease the hangover like a teenager.

For the next couple of hours, I let Poppy watch far too much kids' TV before I eventually drag myself to the shower. I have had no contact with anybody to confirm that we are still meeting up but I'm holding on to Cora's early morning words. I need coffee. I need my friends. So Poppy and I leave to go to the coffee shop.

I calculate who will be here today with their complicated schedules of work and childcare. Of the shifts that I know now Emma is juggling. But she isn't in work today because suddenly Emma is behind me, Seth in the pram, and she shouts my name, out of breath.

Seth giggles at Poppy from his buggy and Emma and I smile down at them. I stop briefly to take a picture for Instagram then remember I'm not Cheshire Mama any more. I'm just Scarlett. We walk alongside each other, Poppy's buggy colliding occasionally with Emma's large feet as there isn't quite enough room on the pavement.

'How are you, babe?' she says, hand on my arm.

'Hungover and desperate for bacon,' I say, fake laugh. I can't bear being seen as a victim. 'You?'

'Oh not too bad. Don't think I was quite as drunk as someone.' I give a half-smile.

'Yeah I was shitfaced,' I say, stopping to pass Poppy the teddy she just dropped on the pavement. Dusting it off. 'Sorry to drop all of that on you last night.'

Emma stops now.

'Do not say sorry!' she gasps and she's so earnest it hurts. 'I was *happy* we could be there for you. I hate the idea of you going through this alone.'

'Well I wasn't *alone*,' I say, defensive because let's face it, I was alone.

Emma dips her head.

'Sorry, I didn't mean. You know, just because you and Ed are . . .'

'We're fine,' I sigh. 'It's just not the easiest time. It's a lot for him to deal with.'

At the café, Cora is waiting with a large Americano and long shellacked fingernails clacking on her phone.

'Just sexting Hunter!' she says, as we walk in. 'But I'll stop now. You have my undivided attention.'

She puts her phone down; recalibrates. Necks the end of her Americano and signals to the waiter to order another. As he comes over, I tell him to make it two.

'Right, let's talk about this sex video,' she says, loud enough that the pensioner nursing a pot of tea on the next table swivels round with wide eyes.

'Cora!' I hiss as I sit down.

But I think about what would have happened if I'd not talked to them. If Cora hadn't told me about the whispers online. If she hadn't helped me avoid becoming the next big influencer scandal. I shudder.

My hands are shaking. It's been too long since my last caffeine hit. Coffee used to be an occasional treat, in between the turmeric lattes and the fresh mint tea. Slowly, in recent weeks, it's taking over. Occasionally, I remember not to drink it like water. Notice that it makes me tremble harder, those bad thoughts in my mind whirl faster.

As I think this, I see him out of the corner of my eye: Joseph, making me coffee. I picture him bringing it to me in bed, with a croissant. He meets my gaze. Holds it.

Since he messaged me, I have managed to avoid Joseph entirely. He's helped by ignoring me and not serving me and I am relieved.

Today though Joseph comes over with our coffees but he pointedly doesn't look at me. I see Cora pull her stomach in, like she does whenever a man is around.

She steals a glance at him.

'Man, that is one bitter rejected guy.' She smirks as he walks away.

'Oh behave,' I say, but I am sheepish. 'I doubt I'm top of his agenda. He's a single man. I'm sure he flirts with customers every bloody day. Customers who are far younger and more glam than me.'

I glance in his direction anyway. I'm sober now but yes: he's still beautiful.

Cora leans in, conspiratorial.

'Could it have been him?' she says, Jack Bauer suddenly, Jimmy McNulty. 'Guy's got a crush. Guy gets the knockback. Guy takes revenge. Wouldn't be the first time.'

I laugh at her.

'Except for the fact that the video predates all of that,' I say. 'Which slightly scuppers your theory.'

She's unfazed. 'Sure, it predates it for *you*. But he knew you before the video got posted. Saw you around, in here. How do you know he hasn't been obsessed with you for a long time?'

We all fall silent as Joseph's colleague puts my bacon sandwich in front of me.

'Cheers,' I mutter. We wait until he's at a safe distance.

I look at Cora. Emma is sitting quietly, wide-eyed.

'One other problem,' I say. 'How is he supposed to have got hold of the video?'

Cora shrugs. 'Isn't that the case for anybody? Other than the two guys, I mean. For anyone else to have it is weird. It's what makes the whole thing so completely fucked up.'

Cora ploughs on. 'And,' she says. 'AND. I heard him joke about hacking his friend's phone the other day. So he can, you know, *hack*.'

Now I'm laughing, despite myself. 'Well he's a millennial,' I mock. 'They can all, you know, *hack*.'

Cora looks triumphant. 'A millennial! Barely. He's only a couple of years younger than us. Wait, are we millennials? And get this. His mate over there told me he does coding work in between café shifts,' she says. 'And you can't say that all millennials can code.'

I raise my eyebrows at her.

'You can actually,' I say. 'You absolutely can.'

But suddenly Emma looks animated. She's into this. 'I know who!' she explodes. 'My sister-in law! The one you fell out with when you posted those pictures.'

I sit back, wait for this. 'Do you really think so? Is that her style?'

Emma looks doubtful suddenly.

'I don't think she cared enough to ruin my life,' I say. 'Plus how on earth would she have got it?'

Which brings us back then to Mitch, to Ollie. But they were both so *genuine*.

Emma's still on her sister-in-law, who I presume she mustn't like a lot. 'Isn't it the ultimate punishment?' she asks. 'You betray my privacy online; I'll give you the opposite of privacy online?'

Cora laughs. 'That's a bit of a leap, Miss Marple, but also, the link was sent before we had that conversation,' she says, rolling her eyes at me as though Emma can't see us.

Emma's face darkens. 'It made more sense than your theory,' she mutters and then she shuffles in her boots to the toilet and Cora laughs at her and I join in because it's awkward not to.

I am still laughing when I look up and see Asha, standing above us, having managed to glide into the building without anyone noticing. This is a very Asha quality. Fuck. Did she hear us laughing at Emma? I feel awful. Bitchy. My face flushes pink.

I look down at Ananya, smiling in the pram in a Peter Pan collar. They float, the pair of them, while at the moment I career around the place.

I stand up to kiss her and I wave at Ananya.

'Handy that it's your day off today, hon,' says Cora.

'Well, I wouldn't have been drinking that much last night if it wasn't,' she says. She does look a little nauseous.

Asha's eyes ask me how I'm doing over Cora's head. I nod, a tiny movement.

The waiter takes Asha's order of green tea and an avocado and egg protein bowl and I ask for a blueberry muffin and another coffee. I feel my jeans pull on my waist a little; promise myself that I'll ease back on the sugar, the booze, the processed meat, the caffeine, soon. Not now. But soon.

'I'm sorry,' says Asha gently and she is so genuine and warm that I want to hug her but I resist. Even with a hangover, her black shirt looks beautifully ironed, her black hair perfectly straightened; I don't want her creased and tainted and smudged by my misery. 'But touch wood, fingers crossed this is the worst of it and it'll go away now, right?'

I don't know anyone as superstitious as Asha, who took her pram onto a fairly dicey road the other day to avoid walking under a ladder and caveats most positive statements with concerns about jinxing things.

Asha looks thoughtful. 'I tell you what I wondered though,' she says. 'And tell me if I'm speaking out of turn.'

She looks up and I shake my head no no, do go on.

'I wondered about your blog,' she says hesitantly and I glance at Cora, who raises her eyebrow at me. I give Cora a hint of a nod. It's done. Gone.

Asha carries on. 'About what information you've put on there, and how that could have something to do with it,' she says. 'Since the whole thing would have coincided with you having more of an online presence?'

I nod, thinking about Mitch making the same point.

'Yes,' I agree. 'I've actually shut Cheshire Mama down for that reason.'

'No!' says Cora. 'That's gutting!'

And I look up, confused, before I realise she is acting.

Anon

Have you *ever* asked a question about me, I think, in the whole time we have been friends? And yet I drop everything and sit through emergency summits like this one and the one last night in the pub, to try and fix your whole broken life.

I mean, technically I was the one who broke it. But still.

Finally, Scarlett has 'told' us about the video.

I had wondered how long she could hold out, and she impressed me to be honest.

After all, we are such good friends. The closest. She had to confide in us in the end. Who else *is* there to talk to now? Those old friends are long gone. Ed is in the spare room.

Even now though, as we sit in the coffee shop and try to help, she sneers at our opinions. At our verdicts. At our theories.

Like you've done any better, Scarlett, I think. Like your judgement isn't the worst in the fucking world.

Surely you'd have shut down the blog at the very start anyway? As soon as this happened. But not when you're Scarlett. Scarlett couldn't relinquish the likes. Couldn't relinquish that semi-celebrity identity she felt like she had when she posted. When a free pair of baby leggings came her way.

I've thought so many times about how I could use Cheshire Mama against Scarlett. It felt like an opportunity.

But I couldn't post the video on there without her approving it.

If I added it to my comments on Cheshire Mama's Instagram, she would delete it straight away. Could my accounts be traced for posting graphic content?

Now though, everything to do with that awful blog has gone. Someone from Cheshire.

Scarlett shocks me when she tells that.

I had no idea she *could* know that; that anyone could get that information. What can I say? I'm a novice. Learning on the job. What I lack in experience though, I make up for in utter fucking hatred.

I feel my face contract. Snap back into Good Friend mode quickly.

Horrific, Scarlett. So close. Who could it be? Why would they do that?

There is satisfaction in seeing her now, exposed, weakened. I sit back to assess her, now she isn't hiding.

When I do see glimpses of change, I bathe in them.

Scarlett *is* a little fatter, a little more bedraggled, a little less confident.

She no longer has the celebrity status that Cheshire Mama gave her.

That spurs me on. Because it means that she is less likely to hurt me again. That *he* is less likely to want her. And that, of course, is the reason I've done this to her in the first place.

27

Scarlett

26 June

I'm not used to seeing Asha without her having one boob hanging out, so the solidity of a sports bra is quite the departure.

'Shimmy!' orders the instructor and we try to follow as our babies career around the middle of the room on some mats. I hear Asha breathe heavily next to me. 'Shake! It!'

I do what I'm told.

Asha's boobs, I notice admiringly, as I glance to the side, look pretty good given that someone has been gnawing on them multiple times a day for the last year. Probably because they'd barely need a B cup versus my own Ds.

Sweat drips down my back. I used to run half-marathons before I had Poppy and I was running again, 5k here, 6k there. Since the video though, it's rare.

'Come to this class with me,' messaged Asha a few days after they found out about the video. 'I think you need to stay as busy as you can. Grab loads of time with Poppy. Take the pluses; all of that bonding.'

When we've stretched it out, most of the women grab their babies and disperse.

I look at Asha. She is frowning as she checks her phone, Ananya roaming around the room.

I am distracted by my own phone; another message from Ed

telling me he needs to be away overnight next week. The niggling feeling of an affair, of *that* being the story behind the video, sent from Cheshire, keeps coming.

'You exercised a lot before, right?' says Asha, still Christmas stocking red up to her hairline.

'Before' and 'after' are words enough in their own right; we know what they mean. Those positive pregnancy tests may as well have been made of lead, crashing down the middle of our lives to saw them in half. The oddest part, I think, is that Asha and the others didn't see the first half. It's floating around somewhere unanchored to this one and unknown to them.

I nod. 'Yeah I did sometimes,' I say. 'In Manchester. Not since.'

'Since' is another of those words.

'Did you enjoy today?'

I nod again. I didn't enjoy it at all, it was torturous, but do you enjoy anything when you're in the middle of it, other than, you know, burgers or a large red or lying on the sofa watching Netflix? The rest is to enjoy afterwards or before. The knowledge that you *will* do it, or that you have completed it. Not the faffy in between bit.

Asha wipes sweat off her brow. I mirror.

'Fancy a drink?' she says and I indicate the perspiration and the Lycra.

But I still go.

I think about my bottom as I stand at the bar while Asha entertains our babies in their highchairs and I wonder if anyone is looking at it, thirty-five years old, motherly, unexercised and flaunting itself in Lycra. Who does it think it is, this arse?

I order a wine even though it's 2 p.m.

I head back to the table and hand Asha a fizzy water. She glances quickly at my Malbec. Looks away. I start rambling, embarrassed, about baby gates and child locks.

'It's genuinely astonishing that other people from the group didn't want to come with us.' I smile. 'When my chat is this good.'

Asha laughs. But now the beat and the moving of the class have stopped, my mind is whirring again. I have a meeting with the lawyer in a few days and barely anything to update him on. I've reached a dead end and the idea of standing still there is terrifying.

I take a large gulp of wine.

'Are you okay?' Asha asks.

'Yeah, you know,' I sigh. 'Just fighting with Ed about the whole video thing.'

'Want to talk about it?'

Yeah sure, I think, more chat about my sex tape side gig. My terror of the future. Being ashamed of myself, every second. Not being able to look my dad in the eye any more. Drifting from my sister. Career in ruins. My crumbling marriage.

Too much. Too awful.

'No,' I say, and then I think I sounded a little snippy.

But I was desperate to talk and then I was sick of talking and that's just how it is.

'Well if you ever do, I'm here,' she says quietly, sipping her water. I don't *think* she looks annoyed.

I nod, down the rest of my house red and flee.

And it's on the walk home that I check my phone.

It's not a surprise but that doesn't mean it doesn't puncture me in the lungs, pummel me in the gut.

It's what I've feared.

Through all of this – which it strikes me now may just have been a warm-up – it's what I've feared the most.

'*So you've quit your job as an influencer?*' it says. '*Not planning to go back to the job you used to do back in the day, are you? That's what everyone will find out next. Unless you leave him alone.*'

I stand in the street, next to a tree, as a dog runs past me and children shriek and thwack footballs in the playground of a nearby school and I feel my whole body tremble and reality and normal life drift, drift, drift further away.

I knew it was coming. Knew Mitch, Ollie and me was just the starting move.

That if somebody really wanted to wipe out my life – maybe not the breath but the joy, the pride, the self-worth – this is where they would go. It's the picture that keeps me awake. Short skirts, long nights. The penthouse.

One part is confusing though: leave who alone? It sounds as though I'm supposed to know but I'm blank. Joseph? Ollie?

I am about to reply but I know I can't.

I email Jonathan instead, as I've been told to do whenever anything happens.

Firstly, I say. *This part of things must remain completely confidential from my husband. But there is something new.*

And then I fill him in. On the truly murkiest part of my past, the one there is no way Ed would stick around if he knew about. The one I have to bury, if I have any chance of keeping this life, of still being respectable Scarlett, of not falling apart entirely.

Anon

And then, he dumps me.

I sit on the floor and grip onto his shin as hc walks out of the door. It's a basic fact that I beg, rather than anything I am ashamed of. I would beg again, a thousand times.

I love him.

He shakes me off, though, like a minor cold.

Tells me I am a despicable person.

I sit there on the floor after he's gone, alone, and take out my other phone.

I know something else about Scarlett now and I have nothing to lose. Despicable people don't.

I suppose Scarlett thought it was all well hidden, buried deep in Manchester from long ago in a different life. But she must know from the video that it's not that hard to shift a bit of soil and expose what's in the ground.

An *escort*. Add your own inverted commas. I do.

What a gift it is, this information. Because so far nothing has utterly broken Scarlett but this has to. Can you imagine? When she is so superior?

I message Scarlett with what I know and try to picture her when she reads it. Visualise it like the last brick on top of her, the one that will make her collapse under the weight.

This will make her leave him alone.

This will break her.

And then I will be able to live my life out of the shadow of Scarlett Salloway. Out of the shadow of who I could be, who I should be.

After he ends it with me, I weep, lost, for days and during that time, something shifts.

When I started this in spring I had wanted to stay anonymous, to watch from a distance as Scarlett fell apart. To get my revenge that way without anything as high-octane as confrontation, showdowns, exposing myself as the perpetrator.

Once he ends it though, things alter.

Anger does that. Charges through everything, rewrites intention.

Now I want to stand in front of Scarlett and tell her who has done this, and why.

I want to tell her that I know what she has done to *me* as well. That I am not an idiot. That I have known for a long time.

You were wrong to trust me, I want to tell her. You were so very, very wrong to trust me.

I want to see Scarlett's face as she registers what that means. How much she has told me. How much she has leant on me. How few friends she really has. How strong I am. How weak she now feels. How maybe *I* am the fucking alpha, Scarlett, and how do you like that?

I want to tell her: you brought this on yourself, Scarlett. What did you expect?

And I want her to promise me that it will stop, and mean it.

28

Scarlett

30 June

At the lawyer's office, Jonathan frowns at me.

'Are you okay, Scarlett?' he says. 'You're looking anxious.'

I laugh.

'Well, wouldn't you?' I say. 'If this happened to you, d'you think you might not be too chilled out? Silly question really – you're a man, it can't happen to you. If you made a sex tape, no one would care.'

He raises his eyebrows. 'That's a sweeping statement but okay, point taken.'

He looks around the room, like he may have missed someone. 'No Ed?'

'Given the email I sent you I thought that might be best,' I say. I am snippy now. Frustrated. I'm paying him money. And really, what does he do? I do all of the work.

Jonathan nods. Head down.

Ed didn't take much persuasion not to come. It saved him taking the time off work. And from spending it with me, I suspect. We're different people to the ones who came in here that first day. There's no united front. Hands are not held.

I look around at the walls of this office; nothing personal here, so bare that Jonathan could be borrowing it from a colleague. Out of his window into the grey of Manchester. And

I think of looking out of an upper floor somewhere else in this city, years ago. My head is there, resting with its long white blonde hair on a black leather sofa in a slick penthouse apartment in Manchester. The room is stark but even the starkness is expensive. Designer grey paint, wall to wall to wall. The art made up of collector pieces I am too young, too naive to recognise, but he tells me they're impressive. And you can tell, anyway. Everything here is superior. The electronics spread themselves across walls; the gin is special edition.

And there in the picture is me, thin like a pre-teen, jiggling my body and unable to sit still then as I throw my head back and laugh. As my drink is topped up, again, higher. As I touch his knee. As I move in closer.

I look back at Jonathan and suspect more time has passed than it should have in the middle of a conversation while my mind has wandered off.

'So, your email,' he says, leaning forward onto his desk. 'I wish you'd told me that was a possibility earlier on.'

I sigh. 'Well, I didn't know it was,' I reply. 'I mean, obviously I know it happened. But I didn't know that whoever did this knew. That it's something they would come at me for.'

'And now you do?'

'Yes,' I say, cold. 'Now I do.'

Jonathan folds his lips inwards. Types something quickly on his computer.

'I just need to do whatever the hell I can to stop it coming out,' I say. 'To everyone. Including Ed. And my family. Just everyone. I can't weather another thing, and not this. So how do I do that? Stop it? At least this time there is warning.'

Jonathan is firm. 'The same way as we do the other thing. Find whoever sent you the message – and you're confident it's the same person that posted the video, right?'

I nod. I can't have two people who hate me this much. *Surely.*

'Find them, then we take this to the police. That's the only route, Scarlett. *Do not* start engaging with them.'

I am so tempted though. Go direct. Find out who they want me to leave alone. See if we can talk this out. Then I laugh; this person posted a sex tape of me online, emailed it to my friends. Do I really think we'll have a chat over a cup of tea and shake on it?

And I am sitting there, in the lawyer's office, but I am standing there, at that dead end again. Fuck. Where the hell do I go from here?

29

Scarlett

2 July

The white professionally painted walls are closing in on me. Cora's huge modern house – designed at such a monumental cost to be airy – hanging out solo on its country road seems suddenly like the most claustrophobic place there is and I am struggling to breathe.

We are here, my daughter and I, on a playdate.

My head is still in the penthouse.

With the drinks.

The jittery body.

The white blonde hair.

Do I message them back? Ignore what Jonathan said?

I walk out of Cora's living room, leaving Poppy in a playpen with Penelope, Seth and Ananya. The playpen is baby jail; a way to stop them dribbling/ pooing/ wiping slightly gross fingers on the white leather sofa. They spend a lot of time in it at Cora's house.

The only time they don't have to be in the playpen is if they are in the playroom, conceived of by an interior designer who has certainly never met a child.

I walk past it as I go to wash my hands after changing Poppy's nappy and – untouched yet today – it is spotless. Pastel pink walls, more cream carpet, expensive white bookcases that are begging for a felt tip pen to decorate them with unidentifiable murals. Still, I think, it's very Insta friendly. Cora loves it when I post pictures of Poppy and Penelope's playdates and my followers comment on her house. Loved it. Past tense. Goodbye, Cheshire Mama.

I stand at the sink and look around at the crazily expensive soap and the Jo Malone candles and the fancy tiles on the floor and I think: Who is all this for?

Because I might not have Cora's wealth but I do it too, this performance.

It helps me convey a version of myself to other people without having to stand in the middle of rooms and shout it: 'I am good, I am balanced, I am smart, I am cultured, I am on top of life.'

And now, it's fallen apart. Stuff has conned me. In the end, stuff didn't make any difference after all.

When fancy soap runs out now I forget to replace it so Ed picks up a bar of cheap stuff from the supermarket and I no longer care. When towels need washing, I let it go a week longer, two before I bother and they smell. Washing up lines the surfaces; deli cakes are replaced with stale biscuits.

My narrative is unravelling.

It can't come out. Not another thing. Not the worst thing.

I tilt my head back against the pristine cistern. Gear myself up to going back into the living room.

My brain swims with thoughts of the penthouse.

Just then Emma bundles in, flinging cupboards open and grabbing a roll of cloths.

'Don't forget the Vanish!' yells Cora.

I hear a baby crying and hurry into the living room.

I look at Cora whose face is doing what it would do if you served her champagne lukewarm. Ananya, no nappy on, grins with just two teeth.

A smell drifts upwards from the cream carpet.

'Oh!' I exclaim, realising. Relieved, if I'm honest, that it wasn't Poppy.

'How did she get out of the playpen?' asks Emma, coming back in and gingerly picking it up with a cloth.

'Not now, Emma,' hisses Cora, pushing past Asha to pick up Ananya.

'No, Ananya! Not on the carpet!' she says, stern.

Then she shoves her at Asha, holding her like a dumbbell. Ananya starts to cry.

I draw a sharp intake of breath at how physical she is with her, when she isn't her own. When she is a baby.

'Maybe it's an idea to take her home,' Cora says deadpan as Emma scrubs furiously at the carpet.

I try to read Asha's face as she scoops her up and does exactly that, muttering an apology. I look at her and wonder how she isn't screaming at Cora. I would be. Somebody else's child!

I know for a fact that Martha, Flick and the rest of my old friends would never have done that to Poppy. But, it seems, Cora would have.

I think of Cora sleeping with her yoga teacher and her private number plate and her Botox and her bright pink Cora's Cupcakes branding and I think for the hundredth time how different we all are. Of what an odd trajectory these intense but distracted friendships have taken.

Suddenly, I feel edgy. Was it an error, telling them about the video, about my marriage? What's just happened has thrown me.

Maybe I should have taken more time before I shared so much.

The panic starts to submerge me again.

I grab Poppy from the playpen.

She protests and wriggles away from me but I insist, though my forearms shake.

Everyone looks at me. Can they tell, I wonder, what's going on in my insides? It feels so huge that it would be impossible for them not to, but maybe that's just how it is for me. Perhaps everyone else is thinking about their own insides instead.

'We're going to leave as well,' I say as Asha bundles Ananya into her clothes and her face burns with embarrassment or rage or both.

Cora looks up at me, questioning. She has no idea I think that what she did was so inappropriate. Ananya's mum was *right there*. But the last thing I want is a confrontation, especially on somebody else's behalf.

I throw Poppy into the buggy and head off quickly down the road with minimal goodbyes.

At home as Poppy sleeps in the buggy, I go to log on to Cheshire Mama, to consume myself with something practical. To stop thinking about the penthouse. To stop me from messaging that number back. Then I remember. Cheshire Mama doesn't exist any more, like all the other things that don't exist any more. Fuck, my world is small.

Instead, I message Flick.

Could we meet up? I write. *Maybe outside of the office to talk without me worrying about everyone watching?*

I hate how pathetic I sound when we used to be equals. When I used to pitch to clients and Felicity would walk past the room and see them smiling and catch my eye. When I knew that if she trusted anyone to pull together a strong proposal, I was that person.

I reread the message and delete the last part; I don't need to spell out why I'm avoiding the office. Plus, we have a friendship that transcends work; it's not unreasonable for me to suggest that we try and hold on to that even while our working relationship is struggling.

Although really, what is the point of Felicity's friendship and all of my other old friendships – also limping on with only the odd message linking us now?

I delete the message. Instead, I message the person who texted me. The person who hates me. Yes, I know, Jonathan. But something has to give.

Who am I meant to leave alone? I write.

You know, comes the reply.

I really don't, I type, then: *Why are you doing this to me?*

But they don't reply, other than one line telling me not to bother trying to trace the phone, as it's pay-as-you-go anyway.

Anon

It looks to everybody else like my life is normal.

I turn up for the playdate; I drink the coffee. I go through the motions. I smile at her, at the same time I think about how I would like her to be dead.

Over and over, it hits me what's happened to me, to my life, and I hold on to a surface to stay upright. Carrying on doesn't seem possible.

Then I regroup and plough on.

The reply Scarlett sends gives me a boost. An adrenalin rush. You can't trace me, I remind her, then I whisper into my phone, 'Hey. It's me,' and grin and love my secret. I've never had one this big. Life's never been this exciting. I'm getting into this. It's why I don't want to confront her on a text message. It's a waste. No. I've decided now. We will do this in person when I can see her eyes avoid contact and her cheeks flush red and then I will know, absolutely. And once I do, I will break her. Just like she has broken me.

30

Scarlett

11 July

'I couldn't be prouder of you,' says my dad. Not to me, obviously, I'm the daughter whose breasts are splashed across the worldwide web. God no. He's speaking to a different daughter.

My half-sister Josephine, next to him, is other-worldly. Straight-without-electricals brown hair that goes all the way down her long back adorned with a flower headdress that says 'beach in the Caribbean and no shoes' but is actually being paired with a buffet in Greater Manchester, late summer drizzle and some heels from the Selfridges sale. Still.

She's young, Josephine, all peachy-cheeked and innocent like brides used to be. Twenty-six, now I think about it, but she seems younger. Her husband Rafe, grey around the temples, is older by what looks like a decade and a half and I suspect wanted to lock this down before his luck ran out. He's fine, Rafe, but my sister is a goddess.

I smile at her, even though she isn't looking at me, and I soak her in. Josephine deserves happiness and kindness and love.

Her and Rafe's set-up is old-school: Rafe earns the cash; Josephine 'has a little hobby' according to him even though her greetings card business is growing into a lucrative operation.

'And,' says my dad's voice, cutting into my thoughts and staring, like me, at this goddess, 'anyone would be utterly lucky and blessed to have you in their life. You can put that in one of your greetings cards, if you like, Jos. Ha!'

He raises his glass. 'To Jos and Rafe!'

I raise my champagne and neck it quickly as my dad looks around the room and we make eye contact over the top of our glassware. I look away before he can; the contrast between pure Josephine and sullied me too much to acknowledge today.

'She looks beautiful, doesn't she?' says Aunt Denise, interrupting my thoughts. She is a distant aunt, only seen at weddings and funerals. There are a lot of cheeks suddenly and kisses and pleasantries. And then.

'So, how *are* you?' she asks, head on the side, hand on my arm. Why the wrong emphasis?

But I look at her eyes, which are searching.

She's seen the video.

'Good, thanks,' I mutter then show her pictures of Poppy in her flower girl paraphernalia from earlier – Ed's parents have taken her home now while we stay for the evening do – so I don't have to speak any more, or look at her eyes, though she can see my hands are shaking.

I look around the room as she coos over Poppy and try to figure out a way to move away from this woman who has seen me naked. But then, maybe everyone has. I look at each face and they swim in front of me. Have you seen it? Have you? My stomach still isn't used to this feeling. Still rejects it and threatens to vomit.

'And are you back at work now, my love?' says Denise.

The pause presses down on my shoulders.

Huh. Work.

I need to get better at this; it's not going to stop happening.

I cast a glance at Ed but if I am seeking someone to save me, he is not that person. He stares at the floor, at the wall, anywhere. On your own again, Scarlett, I think bitterly, even when your husband is next to you.

'I decided to take more time off,' I say, quietly.

Ed mutters his excuses and heads to the toilet.

I brace, ready for Aunt Denise to ask about the video, but she doesn't need to.

'Probably best,' she murmurs.

Then she scoops up the bottom of her dress and heads off to the bar for another G&T and I wish it wasn't Josephine's wedding day with all of its obligations and mingling so that my sister or my dad could put their arm around me, or even just stop and be kind to me next to the cake. I've stopped expecting Ed to take on that role.

I sit alone at a table and think about how other people experience their sister's wedding day, in a huddle of love and salmon mains and dancing. Not a moment unaccompanied. A day full of 'I've got to speak to . . .' and cramming people in. I drink the remnants of the last bottle of red that's been abandoned on the table, as everybody else has gone to find friends or to dance, now that Rafe and Josephine have kicked things off with The Beach Boys.

I stare, missing her. It's too clear to ignore now: Josephine and I have drifted too, because of the video, because I'm embarrassed. There is barely an area of my life that this video hasn't driven a bulldozer through.

'I'm presuming you've got enough on your plate to not want the hassle of being my bridesmaid?' Josephine had said when she announced her engagement and we met up for a celebratory lunch nearly two years ago, when we were still very close. I was pregnant. 'But it's totally up to you.'

I had nodded sagely. I was a responsible adult woman. I couldn't be organising hen dos and ordering straws in the shape of penises and flouncing around in tulle. I was going to have *parenting* to do. Now I wish I was side by side with Josephine, flouncing around in some tulle. Oh, to take a day off from adulting to flounce around in some tulle.

'Want to dance?'

It is not a voice I expect. My husband.

I stare at him.

We are staying in a hotel tonight. We have the freedom to stay up late and drink and dance and nothing is restricting us. Why does that feel terrifying? Restrictions, over time perhaps, become excuses. But if I want my marriage to work, I need to take the moments.

'Sure,' I say, and we hold hands as we head to the dance floor. I try to remember our wedding day but I feel coated in a hefty smear of everything that has happened since. My hand is clammy. It hits me again; whatever our palms are doing, we are no longer hand-holders.

'Sit down for a bit?' Ed says, flat.

I nod.

We are back at our table, alone. He gets up again immediately to order drinks. I look over at him. At the bar, he is typing as quickly as he can, a smile on his face that I don't elicit any more. I watch with an oddly removed interest.

Whatever he is writing, it's intent.

I think of me, with my secrets. With my confidential emails to the lawyer who agreed to keep my counsel; I am the client, after all.

And so now the lawyer knows things about me that Ed does not and – unless I'm exposed again – won't ever know.

Look at us, Ed, I think sadly, what a mess.

'Everything okay?' I ask, when he comes back.

'Yep,' he says casually. 'They didn't have Fever-Tree. Got you normal tonic.'

It's a non-event.

He could have been typing to a friend. To the plumber, about something boring but urgent we need to sort out in the bathroom. To work, not telling me because he knows I'd be mad at him for focusing on that when we are at my sister's wedding. But that smile.

At 5 a.m. the next morning, when I am wide awake with that brutal combination of a hangover and anxiety about my child being asleep in someone else's home, that image of the focus on Ed's face as he typed is flashing over and over. What did that focus mean? Was he typing to someone who matters, about something that matters? To someone whose hand he'd grip, tight?

I've wondered, haven't I, for a long time now.

Now, Ed is in a deep sleep next to me. His gentle snore exhales beer. I raise myself up slowly in bed. My heart speeds up because I know now that I'm going to do it, and I've never done it before. Well, you started it, Ed, I think. How many times have you brandished my phone at me lately?

I slip out of bed and walk around to his side, pick it up. I enter the passcode that I know he has had for years.

It doesn't work.

I try a couple of other numbers – Poppy's date of birth, mine – but neither of them let me in. Eventually I skulk back to my side.

Why do people change their passcodes?

I stare at his sleeping face.

I think of him, furiously typing. I think of him typing to a woman who, were she to be wearing nothing next to him as I am now, he would want to touch. I think of her falling for him.

I think of her hating me. I think, skipping step after step, about where that could lead. About quite how much a love rival might want to hurt me.

I message Cora, desperate to talk.

Do you think Ed could be sleeping with someone else and SHE posted the video?

I lie back against my pillow. Is this now my life, suspecting everybody and even inventing new people to suspect?

But again I come back to the biggest mystery of all: how

anybody but Ollie and Mitch could have got access to that video. I think of who knew what had happened back then: Suki and Felix, our flatmates at the time, a few friends we were out with that night, I suppose. Zoe, the girl I went travelling with and talked to about it, on a long bus journey down the coast of Eastern Australia. Even if they knew though, I don't think any of them were close enough to Mitch to have access to his phone. I don't *think* Mitch ever sent it to my phone. None of this makes sense.

Cora replies.

Do you not remember what I told you about people who wake me up early? her message says.

Then another.

But it doesn't sound like the most unlikely scenario. Let's talk when I see you xxx

I squeeze my eyes closed, try to bury my head under the duvet and grasp at sleep again.

This is torturous.

As I drift off, somewhere in between sleep and awake, I think about Josephine, lovely Josephine in her dress, and how I wish wish wish I could be Josephine and go back to the beginning, start again, with all of my fuck-ups still to make.

'Scarlett,' says Ed suddenly. I bolt upright. What? Sleep had come, at some point, or a semblance of it. 'We need to get up. We're supposed to be picking Poppy up in half an hour.'

My mind feels like it's sparking. I jump in the shower and lock the door behind me and I'm relieved there is no time for breakfast. Relieved there is no time to talk. Relieved that there is no time to spend with a husband who I realise then, I no longer trust.

31

Scarlett

15 July

I glance behind me to check on the girls and see Emma bouncing inelegantly with Seth asleep in the buggy ('His dad's out, needs must').

We are out running. Emma has come for the negating of SlimmingWorld points against a cheeky curry that will be consumed when she gets in. Her face is the colour of a livid pimple.

'I've been going to the gym too!' she yells. 'I thought my fitness would have improved.'

'Doesn't work if you just spend it in the Jacuzzi then eat a cake in the café, hon,' Cora shouts back, deadpan but we know she's joking, Emma looks slim, toned.

Asha jogs alongside me, childlike and spindly in Lycra. Cora lags back, looking utterly unlike herself in her trainers and designer leggings, her exercise normally done behind the closed doors of yoga studios. Or hotel bedrooms. But Cora hates being left out.

'FOMO, Scarlett,' she sighs to me regularly, phone sellotaped to her palm. 'I'm a slave to it.'

For me, it was the air of awkwardness that inhabits our house; my overwhelming desire to escape it that got me out running tonight. And then there is the need to outrun what's next. What I fear is coming for me. Of the penthouse.

'Is that . . .' says Asha, but I concur before she can finish.

Yes. It's Joseph. Standing across the street, ignoring the advance of autumn in a T-shirt. Pausing as he clears tables. Watching me as we run by with an empty coffee cup in his hand.

Is it him I'm meant to leave alone?

My skin prickles. He's too close to me, too tempting.

But when I suspect that Ed is doing something far worse than any small flirtation I've had with Joseph, should I care?

'Well I tell you what,' Cora shouts from behind. 'I'd be tempted. That's one beautiful man.'

I ignore her and speed up. Asha keeps pace.

'You okay about what happened with Cora the other week?' I say, a quick glance at Asha.

She laughs.

'Bit pissed off at the time,' she says. 'But it's just her isn't it? That's her way. I don't think she meant any harm.'

We run in silence as I think how much I'd have stewed on this. Perhaps Asha doesn't hold grudges like I do.

'Do you think Ed could be cheating on me?' I ask Asha suddenly too, out of nowhere.

Asha turns as she runs, a half-second glance, and then looks ahead again.

We are silent for a minute or two except for the thwack of pavement beneath our trainers. I know I've made her feel awkward.

'Well I only ever met Ed at NCT classes and don't know him well,' she says eventually. Thud, thud, thud. 'So I'd say your judgement will be better on this one than mine.'

She gives me another mid-run look.

'I was just thinking that could be something to do with the video?' I lead her. 'If he's shagging somebody else, they could have reason to want to hurt me?'

Some of my past runs have settled in my bones so that I can keep going at a decent pace even when I'm at my least fit but I am still struggling to speak at the same time.

'Do you have any evidence?' Asha says and Cora yells to us to wait for them.

'I want to join in the gossip!' she yells and I flinch. This is my fucking life.

Asha turns to me.

'Sorry,' she says, short of breath. 'That sounded a bit dramatic.'

I raise an eyebrow, which is about the most I can do with the energy I have left while I run.

Let's face it: everything about me since I hit the internet naked is dramatic. And it makes for a relentless paranoia.

I stand in the queue at the doctor's and wonder if the man behind me, coughing without covering his mouth, knows.

I go to get my hair cut and I look in the mirror and see the face of this young, happy blonde girl holding her scissors and the first thing I think is 'Do you know?'

And you, and you, and you. It's incessant.

And still, it's not even *close* to how it would have been if I'd been exposed as the mum blogger with the sex tape. I shudder.

'Why have you deleted Cheshire Mama?' the odd acquaintance asks. And I tell them I have been concerned about privacy. Concerned about sharing, as Poppy gets older, becomes a little person. They nod, understanding, then tell me it's a shame, it was doing well. I know, I think. We were almost at eight thousand. Now, gone.

We run in silence for a few minutes.

I keep going, going. I know how to get in the zone, to focus on the heavy pad of good trainers on hard pavement and to block out everything else but the next step.

Plus I have a lot of rage that needs an outlet. In the absence of a punch bag, the pavement can take the pounding.

'It's probably not what you want to hear . . .' Asha says over the noise. It's nice having someone running alongside me. 'But yeah. It doesn't sound like the most unlikely scenario. Who wants to screw you over in life? Love rivals are up there, right? I mean if this were a BBC drama, it would be a love rival.'

We laugh. But Asha's right. It's logical.

If my life has been ruined because Ed is fucking about though, I think, running, running, running harder, I will lose it. If Ed is fucking about while implying that all of this has happened because I had sex, when it's because *he* had sex, worse sex, sex that betrays, I will lose it, lose it, lose it.

Slam, slam, slam.

'Scarlett, I can't go that fast,' says Asha, over the noise of my trainers as she falls behind me. The air is charred, smoky with a nearby barbecue. I hear the others complain too but I can't slow down.

I need to keep running because I can feel my head spinning off somewhere bleak. Is it coming for me? I think. Is the next thing coming? The biggest secret of all? They could email it again; they have the addresses. They could message Ed; they have his number. I imagine his face; my dad's. I can't take another hit.

When Asha catches up with me I am bent double, resting my hands on my knees, gasping for breath and I am sobbing, hard and louder than I am ever allowed to at home, terrified that I have lost control.

32

Scarlett

24 July

Ed is away on a boys' trip for two nights and I am suspicious. Two nights in a hotel is a convenient thing to have in the calendar if you're sleeping with somebody else.

I haven't asked him because my brain needs wiping like dirty glasses at the moment and can't be trusted to judge things. Am I trying to get myself off the hook? Shift the blame to him? The worst thing each and every time I lose myself in life is that I can't trust my own thoughts. And isn't that the most terrifying thing of all.

But then, I get a message from Flick.

You around for brunch today by any chance?

Flick names an edgy place in the Northern Quarter and I try on five different tops.

It happens so quickly when you move out of a city. One minute it's instinctive, the vibe, the style, the mood. And then it's like a language you don't speak.

I drop Poppy at Ed's parents', where we make small talk with no eye contact, and head into town to meet her.

I walk in to the restaurant wearing jeans and trainers. Is it worth trying to impress people now, given what they know?

Flick is in her Pilates clothes, straight from a class with her hair scraped back and I remember that: the coolest thing you can do in a city at brunch is give zero fucks.

She sips a green juice and looks young without her heels and her make-up, so that her wedding ring seems incongruous. I, on the other hand, feel weathered.

As I say hello, she slurps from a straw.

'It's good to see you,' she says, putting her drink down and standing up to kiss me. 'Sorry it took me so long to reply.'

From then on though, the conversation is stilted and that makes me sad. Like a relationship, can you pull back a friendship once awkwardness kicks in?

We order: eggs and smoked salmon for her, a bacon sandwich for my hangover, more juice for Flick and strong coffee for me.

I chew fast so that I can finish and say something and fill the silence, because it isn't comfortable like it used to be.

And then when the food has gone away and only the dregs of our drinks are left, Flick looks up at me and the expression on her face makes me feel sick.

'You know I said a while ago I needed to speak to you urgently?' she says.

I nod. Sure.

'I wasn't up to it.'

'It wasn't about the video, Scarlett,' she says. 'It was about Ed.'

I think about the other messages I had from her afterwards, the missed calls. All ignored. Thinking she wanted to talk to me about work when really, it was this.

I've known, anyway, haven't I?

Those nights away. The texts at Josephine's wedding. His distance to me and how sometimes I have an instinct that this video has been a gift, to let him pull back from us and our marriage. To give him an excuse to blame me, when it comes to it. And it will come to it, I know.

I look up. Wait.

'I changed my mind about telling you because I didn't know anything for certain, Scarlett, and I decided that wasn't fair,' she says. 'I wanted to have something more solid to give you.'

I put my head face down then, looking at the menu on the place mat: *avocado, scrambled eggs, hot sauce, Nutella pancakes*.

'I had heard rumours that Ed had been cheating. And now, I've heard them from other people too. People I trust.'

I keep staring. *Fried potatoes, banana and honey, homemade granola, steaming porridge.*

'Scarlett?' she says. 'Scarlett, are you okay?'

Déjà vu, I think, of her offering to call medical the last time I was shamed in front of her and she had to take care of me. Not again. Not again.

'Who is it?' I say, quietly.

Crispy chorizo, streaky bacon, chilli halloumi.

Flick pauses, and sounds pained when she speaks. 'I don't know. Jared was drunk at the summer party and heavily hinted. And then, this week Martha told she heard it at her place too.'

I reach slowly into my bag and take out some cash; hand it to Flick who waves me away.

'I'll get this,' she says. 'It's the least I can do.'

'Why?' I say, looking up and laughing. 'None of it's your fault. Not my sex tape. Not my husband's affair. None of it. It's not your fault, Flick. It's nobody else's fault.'

I put the cash on the table and walk out, to that city buzz and that throng of people that I've craved but I can't feel anything any more.

Later that night, Poppy back home and in bed, I have a chance to think.

I've had some evidence Ed is cheating, I tell Asha, Cora and Emma on our group chat.

I go to check on Poppy. Stare at her tiny chest rising and falling.

I wanted to be good at this, I think. I wanted to be the mum

I wish I'd known into my school years and adulthood. To be perfect; part of a perfect family. Though I am starting to think that perfect is the most dangerous word there is.

I lean over the cot and stroke Poppy's head. I sit on the floor with my head on the bars. By the time I sit up the bars are wet.

What now, for your family, Poppy?

Are you okay, sweets? asks Emma. *Do you need someone with you?*

You've got this, hon, says Cora with about fifteen emojis.

As I sit there, I picture where their messages are coming from. From cosy evenings in front of Netflix binges. Freshly showered, in pyjamas. With pappardelle on their laps, or wine in their hands alongside still-awake toddlers or home from work husbands. I light my imagined pictures with Tiffany lamps and fancy candles and I scent them with homemade biscuits and expensive perfumes.

The lamp bulb is gone in our living room and nobody can be bothered to replace it. We don't tend to our home now.

I sit, harshly lit and shivery and I'm jealous of all of it. Of things that may not exist and scenes that I've invented myself.

If we can do anything, babe, just let us know, says Emma. *Here for you.*

I scroll through my phone absent-mindedly and end up at pictures of Poppy taken when she was weeks old. Ed and I, finding our feet.

When life was simple.

Then was simple. *Then* was perfect. *Then* was the easy part.

But all of them have got the behind-the-scenes version.

Then, really?

Then was so exhausting I thought the tiredness would make me ill. Then was terrifying. Then was lonely, without a mother of my own to learn motherhood from. Then was emotional, now there was a baby, because so often I would stare at her and wonder about the baby who came before.

Then was unsettling, when my identity felt lost and altered and unknown. Then was guilty, because some people didn't have this and I did, and when I knew sadness and grief existed in the world, how could I walk around the place being so smug in my joy? Because then was joy. Joy at Poppy's existence. Joy at being loved. Joy at being part of a team.

All of this makes so much more sense if my husband is sleeping with somebody else. It makes the parts fit together. If I figure out who that is, I am pretty sure I have figured out who sent the video too. That doesn't make it any less sad though, as a family combusts, and I lie on our sofa, in our home, for most of the evening and weep.

33

Scarlett

24 July

It comes late at night, as all the dark things do.

It comes into my home, because that used to be the safest place but these days it's the worst, with its Wi-Fi and its iPad and its phone, all snuggling in with me on the sofa.

I reach for the glass of red I have been nursing.

My phone beeps. The dopamine hits.

Since the internet became the worst place for me, it's the place I've gone to the most. A form of self-harm? I don't pick up a razor, but somehow I've always got the impetus to pick up my iPhone.

What am I hoping for, I wonder, as I reach for it? For Ollie, again? I have told him I'll update him with anything new on the video; beyond that we don't speak. I am scared now anyway. Is it him I am meant to leave alone?

Am I hoping for Joseph? For Ed, perhaps, to prove me wrong? To tell me there isn't anybody else, that Jared was drunk and nonsensical; Martha was thinking of someone else.

I will anything that might be enough to pull me out of this bleak place.

Because make no mistake, I think, this is the kind of bleak place people go to just before they opt out.

I longed, when I was younger, to live a sizzling life. Lukewarm seemed like the worst option. Now I long for it.

I can't see a way back.

I can't feel the joy.

I can't remember who I am.

And I am terrified of what's next.

I take a sip of wine. Then I read the message.

Be kind, I tell Poppy, over and over when she pushes Seth over or pulls Ananya's hair. *Be kind*. I say it because it is the best advice I can give; the simplest rule for life, even if I sometimes don't manage to follow it myself. This message isn't kind, is the first thing I know.

You think you are so perfect!!! You think u are better than the rest of us. I dot. You deserve this, Im glad I shared the video.

From the same pay-as-you-go phone as before.

Someone that has my number but that doesn't narrow it down. As Mitch and Asha both pointed out, I am public property, with contact details that until recently were easily available online. And anyone can pick up a spare pay-as-you-go phone.

I look at the spelling errors. Possibly drunk.

I check the large clock above the fireplace: after eleven.

My heart drums in my chest because I tell you what else happens when Ed is not here, and I know somebody is trying to harm me: I get frightened.

I glance towards the living room door.

And then, when I realise that the person in the house who is supposed to get frightened is dependent on me *not* to be frightened, I get more frightened.

Because here's the reality that has made my body unable to stay still lately, like it refused to so often when I was young, foot tapping, hand twitching. If they'll come at me online, they will come for me in real life too. They know, most likely, where I live. They may have been deleted now but they were up there for long enough – the many, many pictures of my home, my view,

234

in such a tiny village make it easy to find. And there are expensive things in this house, for someone in the mood for blackmail.

This person knows things about me, my life and maybe my finances. They know what I used to do, about that penthouse apartment in Manchester. My hand twitches faster.

I go to get a second glass of wine but stop because she needs me to be alert, Poppy, doesn't she? See, Ed, I think. Not such a lush after all.

Instead I stalk the house, flinging open cupboard doors, bursting into rooms. I crouch down and peer under the dining table. I spirit in and check Poppy's wardrobe. I sit on the plush carpet of her bedroom and I reach through the bars of her cot and stroke her face. Then I stay there on the floor again.

I feel the dull sensation of tears but even I can't bear to cry again and I stop, angry, and then I pull the door to her room closed and go back downstairs.

Something has just occurred to me about that message.

I pick up my phone, to reread it and check.

But it's been deleted.

And she would delete it, wouldn't she?

Because suddenly I know. It has to be a she. Outside of Ed, I only belong in an 'us' with groups of women. I'm certainly not an us with Ollie; with Mitch. Neither would think I thought I was better than them.

That's why I shared it.

Us. Us. Us.

Whoever is out to get me is firmly in the present, on the inside of my life. Known.

And there aren't that many people in the present, on the inside of my life. Known.

Particularly in Cheshire.

Who do I even speak to really? I make small talk with my sister-in-law Jaclyn, or I did before this happened and she stopped inviting us round, preferring to see Ed and Poppy on their own now, or maybe that's just what Ed wants. I pass those people in the village and swap generics on the weather, the upcoming season, back and forth. I flirt a little as I order coffee from Joseph. I make faux pas to Emma's sister-in-law. I am too distant from the playgroup floor chat to make friends. I no longer have any reason to see Ronnie.

You think you're better than the rest of us.

Who has welcomed me and ruined me at the same time?

Us. Us.

I feel my stomach flip.

It couldn't be, could it?

Because it occurs to me then that there is only one group of 'us' that I am truly part of here, in Cheshire.

I look at our group chat, at the obscene amounts of information shared in there. Emotions, plans, personal details. I think of how I sent a close-up of my nipple to people I had known, at the time, for three months. Of everything I have shared.

I pace around the house, body twitching more now, deeper, unable to stay still.

I walk into the kitchen and pour a glass of water. Try to breathe.

My stomach lurches as I realise that all of my mum friends could believe I thought I was better than them, rolling my eyes, drifting off, posing for selfies for Cheshire Mama while they hold my coffee.

These women have seen a version of me that did look haughty.

That, lost in the countryside, at first cringed and viewed them as too local, too limited, too clichéd, too middle-aged, too WAG, too uncultured, too unaware, too stupid, too unfit, too aggressive, too too too.

The rest of us.

I see myself through their eyes and it's horrifying.

Could Emma be this angry with me, resentful that our relationship is like the seesaw we put the babies on but always swung up my way? As she asks me questions and gives me compliments and arranges to see me and I struggle to concentrate when she tells me stories or to remember what's going on in her life?

I pad back to the living room, my bare feet cold on the wooden floor that surrounds the rug in front of the wood burner. I don't have the energy to locate socks.

There's what I think of Asha, my brain grimacing at her attachment parenting. I judge Asha for the fussiness we'd have called OCD before we knew what OCD really was and that using it to point at someone who likes to plump cushions is pretty awful.

'I have to wear contacts,' she told me once, genuinely traumatised. 'Because it stresses me out how much babies put smudge marks all over glasses. I can't cope with it.'

I cringe at Emma's clichés, at her constant diets, her relationship. If you're that miserable, just leave, I think regularly. Like it's that simple. Like I'm not now in an identical situation anyway and what do you know: not left yet.

Then there's Cora, with her nails like knives, an engagement ring designed for Instagram and a made for Mills and Boon yoga teacher lover. I've judged her too, even as I've laughed with her, slept next to her, kept her secrets.

You think you are so perfect.

Of course someone would come to that conclusion, I realise with a crash, when the picture I am trying to present is so fraudulent.

When I've wiped out my past, my grime, my pain. When I kept my sadness inside. I thought it was better not to expose everything. I thought presenting a strong, cohesive, respectable package was the best thing. But perhaps the world needed to see my weakness to not hate me. And perhaps *I* needed to expose it, to make real friends; for Scarlett 3.0 to be fully formed.

I shiver, deep in my insides.

Here's the real picture, I think, sitting now paranoid on the sofa in tracksuit bottoms in a starkly lit living room strewn with toys. Not a perfect mum. No longer a blogger. Not someone who commutes into town to do a cool job in an on-trend midi. Barely, these days, a wife. A friend? I thought so. I don't any more.

Suddenly, I feel lucid.

Cora. Asha. Emma.

I don't know them.

I wanted to have real friends, to belong, so I fast-tracked it, emulated closeness that really should take years to build. One minute they were the add-ons, the next I was replacing my husband with them when I needed someone to talk to.

The rest of us.

I let them in, close, without vetting, without time.

I let them in and I shared too much with no idea who any of them were.

On the sofa, I try to breathe and I try out both theories.

The person who has broken me is one of my mum friends.

The person who has broken me is sleeping with Ed.

It feels like my own mind needs a glasses wipe. I see very different things there, minute to minute, like I am at the optician's. *Which is clearer*, I'm asked, as the lens is swapped, *A or B?*

But what if there is option C?

And my body feels flooded with the adrenalin that tells me I am right, I am right, this is it, finally.

Option C: the person who has broken me is one of my mum friends. *And* the person who has broken me is sleeping with Ed.

The person they want me to leave alone? My own husband.

My fingers slip away, then, from the cliff they've been clinging on to.

I feel stupid and sad and livid and in pain.

I feel desperate.

Sweat oozes through my top.

And I pace, like Ed the first day, at our emergency summit in my kitchen.

Asha is beautiful, young; Ed would fancy her. Emma has been going to a gym, possibly Ed's, and is looking lovely for it. I know Cora has no issue with cheating.

New messages are there even now from them, in our group chat, as they are every day, almost every hour.

Bring me evidence, said Jonathan though, and what version of that do I have?

Think, Scarlett, think.

Tomorrow, a Saturday morning meet-up arranged, I will sit in the coffee shop with Asha, Cora and Emma.

Whoever has derailed my life will be waiting for me. Asking if I want to share a piece of ginger cake. Holding my hand if I cry. Taking care of my baby. Passing me the wet wipes. Being my friend. Ruining my life at the same time.

The circle has shrunk.

And only my mum friends are left in it.

Anon

Bloody wine. I never would have slipped up, if it hadn't been for wine.

Is it a big enough thing, I think, the *us*?

Scarlett is sharp. But Scarlett is distracted lately, weighed down, more and more broken. I think of her face when she left the playdate the other day, haunted, hunted.

I delete the message straight away, hope for the best and walk through my silent, empty house to find more wine.

But then, flopping back down onto my sofa with a topped-up glass, I think. Maybe it's not such a bad thing if she knows. Maybe this is where this is going, inevitably. Maybe I subconsciously wrote the *us* because I want her to know.

That wasn't what I wanted at first. I just wanted to watch from afar as she was ruined; as she fell apart.

But now he has ended things, the goalposts have moved.

I can't take it, him going back to her.

Not when I have lost him.

I start picking up toys from the floor but I need an outlet; a punchbag and I throw them one at a time at the wall. Some break, some begin playing songs that could drive you insane, even on a good day.

This isn't a good day. I can't imagine having a good day again. I need more.

I stagger back to the kitchen for more wine.

I need to stand face to face with Scarlett, and tell her what she has done to me.

And then I need to make sure she never goes near him again. Is incapable of going near him again. Ruin her.

I lie there on my sofa and fantastise about telling her.

It was me, Scarlett, *it was me*.

Gobbling up her shock. Watching her shrink, shrink, right down in front of me. Who's the alpha now, Scarlett, who's the alpha now?

34

Scarlett

25 July

And so I walk in to 'our' coffee shop the next day, feeling the tickle of sweat. Outside it is chilly for July but in here there are bodies and steaming tea. And fear.

I sweat with the belief that one of these women could have betrayed me. I smell the coffee beans as I park the pram up in the corner of the café and they make me feel nauseous like I am eight weeks pregnant.

I look across the room, register their familiar faces in profile. My friends.

There's a film over this setting now and it's been turned twenty degrees, thirty.

I walk slowly to Cora and Emma, at our usual table.

'No Asha?' I say, quiet, but if my voice sounds different to me, they don't notice.

Cheshire.

Us.

I sit Poppy in her highchair next to Penelope, across from Seth.

I thought it would be a full house. That I could nail this, once and for all, with them all here. That now I suspect, it would be obvious who had done this to me.

Cora doesn't answer though, her nails clacking on her phone and I bristle. On top of everything else, *do not fucking ignore me.*

I'm not the only one being ignored; Penelope blows rasp-berries to try and get her mum to make eye contact.

'Realised she had double-booked. Ananya's got swimming,' fills in Emma. 'Got your drink.'

I take a sip of turmeric latte – thinking how much I could do with a strong coffee – and thank her.

Emma looks at Cora who is still oblivious and back at me, raising an unruly eyebrow with flecks of grey through it.

I look away.

Sharing a wordless grumble about how distracted Cora is, is too much today when I no longer trust these women. When I think somebody is faking being in my camp.

But how difficult it is not to bitch or judge when people bitch and judge and will you along with them. You look pious or awkward. You look po-faced and no fun.

And apparently I do enough of that already.

I stare at my latte. When I look back up, does Emma look irritated?

You think you are better than us.

The Welsh one has a girl crush, said Ed.

What if it was something darker, a fixation?

I take a sip of my drink and watch Emma walk to the counter for a teacake for Seth.

I turn back to Cora, still messaging.

'What?' she scowls, looking up.

When I tell her nothing, she goes straight back to her messages.

If I have judged or criticised these women, I think, then bloody hell I have envied them too. Emma's surety in where she is, where she wants to be forever, while I flail around the countryside, dreaming about the city. Cora's flippancy; her lack of worry about where her affair is leading, what will happen to her marriage. Asha's neatness, the order in her life while mine needs a deep clean.

I think that's how human emotions in their messy, crossover way, work. Yin, yang. Dislike, envy.

I slump forward.

Cheshire. Us.

Ed. Is one of these women sleeping with Ed?

'You okay, hon?' Cora asks, still messaging, and I mutter a vague yes.

I'm not okay.

This was my only respite, I now realise, and the room feels like it's underwater.

These women, odd band of sisters that they are, were my swaddling blankets.

'I have a headache, I'm sorry, I shouldn't have come,' I say, this tiny room shrinking smaller, smaller and I need to get out before I am crushed between its walls.

The glances behind me are worried or fake.

'Message us later, babe.'

'Hope you feel better, hon.'

I battle the urge to retch.

Surely it can't be one of them.

But it's the only thing that makes sense.

'Jesus!'

Someone has stepped in front of me.

'Sorry,' he says. 'Just wanted to help you with the pram.'

Joseph opens the door.

Even now, and with everything that is in my head, I think of my lank hair and my eyes, puffy from a lack of sleep.

I manoeuvre the pram past him and we stand still, outside the door.

'Not spoken to you much since . . .' he starts.

I look down. 'Just busy,' I mutter.

'You back at work now?' he says, trying for small talk, like we are pals. 'How's that going?'

'I put it off until a bit later,' I say. 'Not quite ready to be parted from this buddy of mine.'

I tickle Poppy's chin and she shrieks. And even today, it's

a jab of joy. The only thing that provides them at the moment.

Joseph smiles and I fancy him and then I think: How is there space in my brain for this? Perhaps it's pleased to zone in on something primal, physical, instinctive? Instead of all of this other stuff: complex, unknown, modern.

But should I be suspecting him, as Cora said? Local, interested in me. I look at his face. My brain may combust.

Us though, *us*.

I glance over Joseph's shoulder through the glass door and see Cora watching me. She looks away quickly, goes back to her phone. Emma rescues pieces of teacake, over and over, from the floor to feed to Seth. Up, down, up, down.

I look at Joseph again, his brow furrowed.

'You sure you're good?' he says. 'You know, if you ever want to talk . . .'

His fingers graze my arm and I pull back because I want him to stay there.

'All good,' I say, moving away. 'Cheers for the drink.'

And I walk away before I am too tempted by touch and words and before I fall open and everything unravels.

35

Scarlett

27 July

'She loves this one,' says a woman with a scarlet smile next to me.

I stare at her. Can't summon the energy for the requisite small talk.

Her smile drains away and she turns to the woman on the other side in the circle instead, moves a barely perceptible centimetre.

I say woman. She is – here – a mum. That's what we all are, solely.

I don't know her name, or her job, or what gives her goose bumps but I know she had a third-degree tear and her daughter has three middle names.

But hey, I can't exactly hang out with my own friends, merrily whistling Head, Shoulders, Knees and Toes with someone I am sure has ruined my life, right now.

Poppy totters back over to me and grins, arms raised ready for me to sing and my insides hurt with how brilliant she is. But even for her, I can't do it today.

I shift uncomfortably on the floor. Notice everyone else has taken their shoes off. I stare at the feet clad in Muppets socks across the circle. The odd socks with the hole in the toe next to them. I remove my trainers and think about how infantilising it is.

Mums have started to be replaced by grans and grandpas and nannies at these baby groups. We are out of the newborn classes now and a lot of the parents have gone back to work.

I listen to the tuneless singing; look at the woman leading the class in her branded T-shirt and her kids' TV presenter dungarees. And I am suddenly filled with a desperate panic.

I loved this when it was temporary, precious, limited.

Now that life stretches before me with no other focus and no idea how the hell I can go back to my job or my entire industry – what if word's spread? – it's terrifying.

What happens when Poppy is older? No job. No friends. No marriage?

The music changes to another generic nursery rhyme and I am observing from outside the community centre windows.

This is it.

No job, I repeat to myself, like a mantra.

No marriage?

No friends.

Whoever posted that video has taken my life away from me, whole. When that night happened it seemed a tiny part but now it's pushed itself into the furthest corners of my life and everything is infested, everything is dying.

And then there is the knowledge: the worst could still come. I picture the penthouse. Taste that expensive gin. Shiver.

At the same time sweat, I realise, is pouring down my back.

I feel dizzy.

It's happening again.

I have got to get out of here.

I grab Poppy and my bag and I almost run to the door as I mutter about a migraine.

'It's okay, it's okay,' I murmur to a one-year-old who is mad at me for ending her class prematurely. 'I'm sorry.'

And I am.

I'm sorry I can't sit back and enjoy this bonus extra time with her.

I'm sorry that when I take her out, in this dreamy village to its traditional classes, that I scour the room for evidence, feel my mind drift off, instead of drinking up that time with my daughter.

Later when Poppy is in bed, I am the worst combination to message my boss – morose, self-pitying, drunk – but that is what I do.

I need my job back, Flick, it says. *I know I'm an idiot for only realising this now but I do. I need it.* Especially *if Ed is fucking about. I need to be me again x PS: If it's already gone to somebody else, can't you just kick out that useless shit Carl and give me his job instead? HA!*

I need to extricate myself from Cheshire, and whatever the hell is going on here. I convince myself that if I can just claw my way back to Manchester, to Scarlett 2.0, it will all be okay. If Ed is cheating, I will leave him, get an apartment, register Poppy with a nursery near work. This is manageable. Breathe, I think, breathe.

At 4 a.m. the next morning, I wake up on the sofa with a gasp from a nightmare. I get out of bed and look down the stairs and I can see Ed's shoes by the door. I didn't hear him come in, late again. Have barely seen him since he got back from his weekend away. He is in the spare room, I presume. I think about going in there and confronting him. Are you sleeping with one of my friends, Ed? But treat this like Jonathan would treat it, I think. Get your evidence first. Then act.

I remember the text to Flick then. Groan.

It had seemed like the perfect tone at the time. Felicity is my friend. Felicity hates Carl too. But now, from the outside, when Felicity is Carl's boss, it's awful. I am not being the grown-up.

There is no reply.

By mid afternoon, trapped home alone with nowhere to go and no one to see. I send a follow-on.

Sorry about that message, it says. *Bit too much wine! But it would be great to talk, if you get a chance. Sx*

Still nothing, and my shame, already meandering around parts of my skin, speeds up, spreads out and multiplies until it covers me like a onesie.

Ed comes down, dressed, kisses Poppy, says a cursory hello to me and heads out. Poppy plays on the living room floor. Brings me books and toys that she wants me to read and play with. I say no, I can't. Feel shame at that too.

I keep the curtains closed, even though no one walks past. Poppy's getting used to playing without daylight.

This village is small and I am convinced my only friends here are involved in this. I am convinced too that everyone knows that I am the woman in the video, the glassy-eyed mum who runs out of playgroups or the one who gets drunk and flirts with waiters. All these versions of me, and all of them the bad kind.

If they feel like you are good gossip here, in Sowerton, they will detect you like metal, and they will wrestle you out of your sensible mum coat and make you expose your soul so they can pass it on at their next coffee date with the girls like the baton at primary school sports day.

I can't face that. Can't cope with being exposed any further.

So when I have to go out, I choose paths that are off the beaten track; the unadopted roads. I keep my head low. I walk like I am nineteen and scared, being followed from the night bus by a big, leering man. Instead of thirty-five and being followed around the internet by someone without height, breadth, without any physicality.

Could it really be them?

And why?

How?

I long for Manchester and its grime and the smell of eighteen different types of food cooking as you walk along the street and see a fox just stroll by like it's on its way home from the pub at closing time. I long for its refusal to go slow.

When I leave my unhappy home, I want to fall into the sea of a city. Swim deep into it. Float around, alone, while I get my head clear. But here, there is nowhere to go.

Poppy sleeps and I stop in the middle of a field and sit next to her pram. Poppy is protected with a rain cover but my trousers soak through as I sit, numb in the rain. Eventually, I go home and as Poppy continues to sleep in her pram, stand under a steaming shower for a long, long time.

In there, I think.

Us. Cheshire.

The water is so hot it stings as I think about them, my mum friends.

Cora, fixated on finding a plan to get a night away with Hunter around childcare.

Emma, juggling shifts, stressing about her late-night chip binge.

Asha, frowning about the wrong number of magpies, pining for her books, frantically trying to wipe her house clean of all traces of the child who is at that second careering through it with buttery fingers and a rogue felt tip pen.

How can I be looking for the person who has ruined my life within this crew of busy, preoccupied women with their young babies and their tunnel vision? Who would have the time, the energy?

And yet, something about it makes sense, in my gut.

I hear Poppy cry and I turn off the shower and step onto the bath mat that's lost all bounce and should have been washed a month ago. I go down to Poppy wrapped in a too-small towel, hair dripping, and I am standing like that next to her pram in the hall when Ed puts his key in the door. He's early.

'Hey,' he says, unstrapping her and picking her up as he looks away from my bare skin. 'Dentist. Working from home this afternoon.'

We stand there in the most painful silence there is; the one in the space where there used to be in-jokes and kindness.

Ask him, I think.

Get your evidence first, I tell myself.

Ed keeps his eyes trained on our daughter even as he speaks to me.

'You remember tonight's the night I'm taking Poppy to Liam's new house for a couple of days?' he says. 'I booked the time off work. Going to help Liam decorate and put furniture together while the kids play with Poppy.'

His brother. Right.

He goes to walk away then turns back, cheeks a little pink.

'Are you drinking more lately?' he says, clearly having rehearsed this. 'We are getting through a lot and I'm not having much and I worry. When you're with Poppy.'

I wonder how much he got through on his 'boys' weekend'.

Fucking hypocrite.

I walk away without answering and a little while later, they head off, leaving me with a house that is so empty, eerily still.

I sit in the silence and think about what happens if we split up. Of shared custody and solitary weekends and of how the hell I am ever going to fill them when I have a life that looks as empty as mine now does.

At 8 p.m., Cora messages.

Want to come round? she says. *Michael's at the pub.*

No, I think. No. I don't want to hang out with any of you until I know, for sure, which one of you has betrayed me.

And yet . . . I am desperate for company; desperate for noise.

And the terrible realisation, there is nowhere else I can go.

Perhaps spending time with Cora, one on one, will elicit some information too. Perhaps this will clear things up, one way or another. Get your evidence, Scarlett, get your evidence.

I walk round to Cora's house and we drink wine quickly, before moving on to her spirits cupboard. If I'm holding back and on edge, she doesn't notice. Too drunk. Too self-absorbed. I look up at the giant picture of her on her own living room wall. A faux fur wrap falls from her shoulder.

'So, we think Ed's not keeping it in his pants, right?' is her opener, as she pours me a large red.

I bristle.

'I don't want to talk about it tonight,' I say. 'Can we just . . . talk about something else?'

She looks offended and we sit in silence for a few seconds.

'God, Emma today,' she starts, eventually. 'Driving me *crazy* about bloody Slimming World points.'

'But you like Emma, don't you?' I say. 'She's your mum bestie.'

If Emma did have some weird obsession with me, would Cora know?

'Oh Emma,' she says with a dismissive tone. 'Well, we just bond over our shitbag husbands. And we've known each other a long time.'

But there's affection in her voice.

'Now,' she says. 'Talk to me about what's happening with this video. We find out who posted it yet?'

I like the *we*. I am always so grateful for a *we*.

I try hard to remember that I suspect her, that I can't relax here but there is alcohol and sugar and a giant faux fur cream throw over my legs and it is difficult. I want this to be real.

'Well, Mitch was the one filming,' I sigh. 'But it makes no sense, why he would. I can't stop thinking it's somehow linked to Ed. To the way Ed is being with me.'

I glance at her for any reaction. The edge of a blush. Eye contact dipping away. But there is nothing.

And then Cora's husband Michael comes through the door and I say my goodbyes.

I walk home, brain mushy with suspicion and unease layered over with amaretto and wine. I collected no clues. Learnt nothing. Surely it's not her, I think. But then.

Turning into my path, I see darkness where there used to be candlelight and early nights and a man who loved me passing me a glass of red and smiling as he listened to tales of my night. Now, there is just an empty house, unlit and unwarmed. I shiver.

I have to claw my marriage back, I think melancholy. I don't want this. I want cosy and candles and a house full of people.

But suddenly there is something to distract me from the future. Out of the corner of my eye, somebody moves, quickly, in the side passage of my house. Too scared to investigate I put my key in the door and slam it behind me, double locking once I'm inside, willing myself to go and investigate. But I can't.

Bury your head in the sand, Scarlett, about this as with everything. I don't sleep until the early hours of the morning when the sun is coming up and I feel almost safe again.

Anon

It's not my style, really, loitering next to wheelie bins, ducking into the shadows just along from the tomato plants and the pergola; honeysuckle rampaging over it.

That, Scarlett, is what you have driven me to.

I have been drinking more these last few weeks. Days are blending into night. At home I watch the video, over and over. Study you. Hate you.

If your intent was to break my life, then it's worked. All I ever wanted, gone. I can't see a way forward. Can't see sky above me.

An existence that was grey when I started this has, as time has gone on, edged darker and darker to black.

And so, I will do the same to yours. What will hurt most, Scarlett? You have already lost your job, your reputation, your pride, your blog. But they have nothing, do they, on what you prize most. Your family. Are you fit to look after Poppy, really? A woman like you? Will you even be *able* to, once this has finished? Ed certainly doesn't think so any more, not after the things I've told him. Where did he say he had taken her this weekend? You sure he was telling the truth, Scarlett?

Now I have nothing to risk. It is all lost. He is gone. I am smashed into pieces. And you did that, Scarlett, you.

But when I see you there, you dart in and put your key in the door faster than I can act, as my heart hammers in my chest, as I think about what I want to do to you, as I hesitate just for that second and the lock is turned, the door bolted.

But it will happen soon, Scarlett.

I think you know that too, really.

Two women. Such good friends. Such bad choices.

It has become inevitable what will happen between us two.

36

Scarlett

28 July

Only a few hours later, I wake up groggy and hungover and drink three coffees, back to back.

I message Ed. I know he'll be up with our early-rising Weetabix fiend of a daughter.

How's Poppy? I write. *Give her a squeeze from me.*

But there's no reply.

My body tenses as I think about what will happen if Ed and I split up.

Weekends will be like this, without Poppy. Nights roaming around the house alone. Nothing to stop the panic coming. The vodka being opened. The bleakness kicking in.

I try Ed again. Nothing.

Maybe there would be bigger changes too.

Would we need to sell the house if Ed moved out?

I think about when we moved in here. Ed's face when Poppy was born. I think about us all on base, barely leaving the house in those weeks after we brought her home as we worked out how to be a family and how to keep her safe here in a sanitised environment before we could consider exposing her to the dangers of the outside world.

I start to cry.

I don't remember how I get there but I am sitting on the

bottom stair, a pile of Ed's coats on my lap. I check his pockets and I don't know what I am searching for because these days nothing is in hard copy anyway and so I stop and I just sit there, buried in coats like I have crawled into a den, sad.

I message Martha.

Flick says you know some stuff about Ed, I say. *Can you tell me everything?*

And she calls me.

'I don't know for certain,' she sighs. I hear it, attuned to it now: pity. 'But I work with this guy who used to work with Ed, when he was at your place. Paul?'

'Yeah, Paul Costello.'

'That's it.'

Ed still sees Paul.

'Paul got a bit loose-lipped at the pub. Says it's . . . the worst-kept secret. That all their mates know what Ed's up to with some woman from the gym.'

'Why didn't you tell me sooner?' I ask. 'You're my friend.'

She sighs again. 'I'm sorry – I am,' she says. 'But it's been hard, Scarlett. You went off radar and you didn't seem in a great place. Or like you wanted to speak to me. I didn't have any proper evidence – I still don't – and I just thought that I couldn't drop that on you with the situation like this. It was only when Flick heard it from Jared too and told me that I thought, well, that seems a bit more conclusive.'

She goes quiet.

'We weren't talking very much either,' she says.

I say goodbye to her and thrust the raincoats and the puffas and the smart suit jackets off me, onto the hall floor.

Alone in my big house in the countryside, I take a large swig of the same cheap brand of vodka that I used to drink, back in the day.

I ignore the beautiful bottles, the drinks brought back from holidays and adventures. Because it is beauty again, the icing of life, and whether it is because I feel I don't deserve to enjoy that or simply can't see it any more, it feels like that part of life is gone for me now.

'Fuck you, Ed,' I mutter to myself.

I may not have made much effort but at least I have *tried* to keep our marriage going. Meanwhile Ed has shamed me, for sex I had with someone else twelve years ago, when he had sex with someone else – what – twelve weeks ago, a few *days* ago?

I think of all those evenings out, nights away – at his brother's, with the boys, staying at his parents. So many opportunities.

Check.

No messages.

No wonder he can no longer touch me.

More vodka.

Cora tries to call me but I don't pick up, knowing that I am more drunk now than anyone is supposed to be at 2 p.m. and that it's not in a socially acceptable way, with friends and oily roast potatoes and shared bottles of Prosecco or a good red. Knowing that it could be her. That I can't trust anybody.

I long for Poppy and look at old pictures and videos of her laughing. Time dawdles.

I try to FaceTime Ed again but he doesn't pick up.

Paranoia hits.

I need to see my daughter. What if something has happened to my daughter?

Having Poppy has meant that I have still remained loosely in the world, when without her I would have locked the door and climbed under a duvet.

Josephine, after a month's travelling for her honeymoon, has barely been in contact. Maybe she's in a post-wedding love bubble. Maybe she's just a bit grossed out by what's happened.

It's weird, what sex does. To a lot of people I'm different now.

You spend years building these worlds and sprawling networks that you think are carved into the earth's core and then you realise that they were floating above it, temporary, ready to be blown apart when you move house, or stop messaging, or are publicly shamed.

No messages. I wander into the kitchen and leave my phone there. I know I have had too much to drink now to speak to Ed. He's already watching my drinking. And I know what happens when people split up. It's the kind of thing that'll get flung in my face during a custody battle.

Back in the living room my lips taste it again, the harshness of that same straight vodka I've always turned to at the worst times.

I drink again.

It burns, and I need it.

Vodka doesn't mess around.

I touch my tongue to my lips and remember other times, old bouts of pain.

Of drinking vodka straight too in the days after Ollie and I lost our baby, nearly thirteen years ago.

We drove back from the hospital at 3 a.m. that night, a time we would normally have been heading to another club. I pulled the sleeves of his hoodie, which I had been wearing for a couple of months as my body had spread out beyond my own clothes, over my hands. I shook with horror at what had happened to us over the last seventy-two hours, since I had gone into labour two and a half months before my due date.

We drove past a club where we had danced with each other with smiles on our faces and beer in our hands, and it felt ghoulish. Stupid us, not knowing what was ahead. That Ollie and me weren't this Ollie and me. They were 'those people'. Those naive, drunk people who thought the catastrophes happened to someone else, someone who – don't we all think – was probably ready for them; knew somehow that they were coming. Not us. Never us. We had to think that, to believe we were protected.

I wanted to shake that Scarlett, drag her off the dance floor and scream at her to watch out.

Don't get pregnant.

Don't love.

Look what that horrible emotion is capable of.

At home, I took off every item of my clothing, wanting to distance myself from the hospital scents, the sterility, the beeps, those too-fast footsteps.

I climbed, silent and naked, into our bed, and curled up with my youthful body that had been re-formed by a baby that was no longer here. How could I escape from this when it *was* me?

And I drank, drank, drank, that same straight vodka.

I thought about single people, as I sat in bed with the bottle. About the ones without children, and they seemed wise or lucky beyond measure.

I didn't belong in our world now of parties and euphoria but I had not moved on. That meant a grotesque limbo with my stretch marks and my bleeding and no baby and two layers of deep grief that these people had never known. That meant existing at the very edges of being human, far away from most people and their centred, normal experiences.

I couldn't go out in case I saw people who I had made small talk with when I was pregnant. 'Not too long to go!' they had said last time but there was less time than we thought and it wasn't enough. Now here I was, my body absent of the baby, and my arms too. How would they small talk that?

Eventually, no vodka left at home, I went to the pub, to clubs, to anyone's party who would have me.

As I sat on a bench at 2 a.m., out of it, a teenage girl walked past carrying her strappy sandals. She glanced quickly at me, relief crossing her face: I wasn't a man; I posed no threat.

'Are you single?' I asked and she nodded.

'Stay that way,' I said. 'It's safer.'

She nodded gravely, as though the subtext was a bad break-up.

'Don't love anybody,' I carried on, believing these were the wisest words. I was twenty-three and ancient. I had discovered a truth about the universe.

The girl started to walk away. Not a man who would sexually assault her, but maybe an unstable woman. Still not ideal.

We stayed together, Ollie and I, not solid glue but more like old, tired Blu Tack that only vaguely does the job. We lost our stick sometimes but in the end we could form ourselves into a ball and keep going.

Ollie, reluctantly, began to come on nights out with me again but more as a chaperone than a boyfriend until I pressed the destruct button and pushed for the thing that would kill off lovely dancing us.

The feelings come back now compounded, extreme, but reminding me what happiness looks like when you're hurtling, fast, towards a breakdown.

I drink the vodka.

I can't access the happiness, even if I know it's there in Poppy's perfect form. It's like it's a person on the other side of a locked prison wall.

The rest of the day passes in a blur.

I think I open the door to take in a parcel.

Or did I dream that?

More vodka.

And suddenly I am waking up on my sofa, and think I am dreaming.

Because over the top of the chart songs on a chirpy reality show on TV, there is a woman's voice, in my house, saying my name over and over and over and shaking me awake. Shaking me awake, hard. So it hurts.

A woman, when I am here alone.

I open my eyes.

And there, after all of these months, is my answer.

Cheshire.

Us.

Inside.

Present.

I stare at her. And for once, she makes eye contact.

37

Scarlett

28 July

She's drunk, I can tell that immediately. Gin and slim, it'll be.

'Emma, what are you doing?' I say, sitting upright, blurry.

She says nothing. Looks around. Her eyes look darker than usual. Glazed.

'Did you knock? Did I not hear you?' I mutter, trying to buy time for my brain to catch up.

'Look at you, hey, Scarlett?' she says, slowly. 'Look at you. At home alone in such a stupor that you don't even hear somebody break into your house. I say break in, you were so drunk you left the front door unlocked. Wow. I literally turned the handle, walked in and strolled past you, snoring on the floor with a bottle of vodka next to you like a tramp.'

I wince. Don't call me that, Emma.

I stare at her. My friend, the shy one who gets talked over is gone now. Replaced.

There *was* someone outside my house last night, I think.

I had held off from calling the police because I was worried they would find nothing and that again Ed could use it as evidence of me being off the rails, delusional, drunk.

But there was someone.

It was Emma.

This isn't a one-off. This isn't about her being drunk tonight. This has a backdrop.

'You tried to get in last night,' I carry on. 'Maybe other nights. Kept going until you found a way.'

'Only last night,' she murmurs, mostly under her breath.

A happy Kylie song plays on TV.

'Me,' she says quietly. It's a one-word confession.

I am disorientated and I don't know if I can be scared in the company of somebody I know so well. If I can be scared by a woman I have seen cry and laugh and feed her baby. But I *don't* know you, I think. I have no idea who you are. And the realisation is terrifying because if I don't know who you are, I don't know what you can do.

She sits down then, on the fancy armchair I bought before we had Poppy, when we used to buy things like fancy armchairs.

'Cosy,' she says, looking up at me. She touches the chair. 'Pricey, I bet.'

You think you're so much better than us. *Us. Us.*

It wasn't Asha, in some sort of deal with Mitch, something I've thought about often after I saw them together – thought I saw them together – that day.

It wasn't Cora, suspecting that I was coveting her position as local queen bee, wanting to keep me in my place.

But Emma.

Emma looks good at the moment, even now when her voice is slurring and her head lolls.

Emma has been going to the gym, getting fit. Martha says the woman he's sleeping with is from the gym. Is this the story here? That love rival I had feared?

Emma has always been okay with silence. And right now, that's one thing about her that hasn't changed. She looks around at our house. The beams on the ceilings. The original fireplace. The empty buckets that used to be piled high with wood until we stopped bothering because fires are happiness and joy, and instead now we go to bed early in separate rooms or put another jumper on or shiver, bleak.

'Robert has left me,' she says. 'He left me a few weeks ago.'

'He's left you?' I say, trying to focus, to wake up. 'Emma, I'm sorry.'

'Oh come on, as if this is news to you,' she slurs. 'As if you don't already know.'

I shake my head, not comprehending.

'From Cora, you mean?' I say, frowning. 'She hasn't said a word. I didn't know.'

'Oh give me a fucking break, Scarlett,' she snarls. 'Not Cora. I mean you probably already know from Robert.'

I stare at her.

What does this have to do with her sleeping with Ed?

Robert is Emma's husband. The useless one; the one I've never met because he couldn't be bothered to come to antenatal classes. And he certainly doesn't sit in the coffee shops or the classes, infiltrating our new all-female world.

'How would I know Robert has left?' I ask.

She laughs in that awful bitter way; the opposite type of laugh to the one babies do at playgroup.

'Well,' she chimes, slumped in the chair. 'You know a lot about Robert.'

I wish the vodka hadn't taken its toll on my brain. I feel like I could keep up with what she is saying without that glugging around my head, engulfing my thoughts with jelly.

'I've never met Robert, Emma, remember?' I say, patiently like I'm talking to a child. 'He didn't come to NCT.'

She looks up at me, still stroking the chair like a cat.

'Don't speak to me like I'm an idiot, Scarlett. You do it all the time. Not any more.'

I'm chastised and duck my head. But I still have no clue what she's on about.

'You still haven't caught up, have you?' she snarls. 'And *I'm* the idiot. You were supposed to be the smart one.'

The laugh again.

You think you are better than us.

I stare at her, trying to compute.

'Did you send me the message about thinking I'm better than you?' I ask, removing my jigsaw puzzle pieces, replacing them in a different formation.

She ignores the question.

'Remember when I had that bad week juggling work and Seth without any help and *all* you did was talk about how much you love spending time with Poppy?' she says.

Because I feel so guilty that I miss work. That's why I had laboured the point.

'And the blog. Jesus, the way you went on about that *blog*.'

'I just . . . wanted a project,' I say, the jelly getting thicker. 'Something for me.'

Is this honestly the impression I give?

I hold my temples.

What a precarious balance it is, I think, of being happy in public but not too happy. Celebrating your wins but not being smug. Making it clear that you've had your allocated amount of shit times without spending your life moaning.

I am drained, thinking about it.

But that's not why she's done this. It hasn't helped, clearly, that she's had these thoughts about me. But it's not why. Get to the point, Emma, I think, get to your point so I can get my answers finally, about what has been going on with Ed.

I glance towards the door then remind myself, relieved, that Poppy isn't here.

I look back.

Emma's eyes flash rage.

'You talk over me. Dismiss me. Look at me like I'm this local, tedious frump,' she says, with such venom that she is

266

unrecognisable from the woman who drunk her lime and soda and ate noodles in the Peak District with me and ran behind me with her buggy.

She looks down at herself.

She *broke into my house*, I think, this shy woman with her ponytail from antenatal classes. She lurked outside until she got a window of opportunity and then, whatever the specifics about the locks, she *broke into my house*.

'You work in medicine, Emma,' I say, trying to reach her. 'You're a good person.'

'Oh Scarlett!' she shouts, flinging her head back. 'Don't patronise me, either.'

She carries on.

'We all know you only consider real work the type that's done on a beanbag in the city next to a load of people much cooler than us,' she rants, bitter. 'Or by influencers, from a shared office space in Bali. Not by us, out in the sticks.'

Us, us.

I blush. That's how I felt when we first moved. It's true. And it's awful that it was so obvious. That I was so shallow. But not now! It's changed since then, I think. It's changed so very much. You're my *friends*. You were my friends.

'You know I fucked my education because I was too busy getting off my face?' I try, to burst her bubble of my perfect career path, unblemished life.

But of course she doesn't know that. Why would I have shared that when I spend as much time as I can trying to paint the picture with the fancy soap and the good job and the designer bag and the perfect family standing next to the newborn lambs in their wellies?

'Does everybody think this?' I ask and it comes out in a croak, a whisper. 'That I think I'm better than you?'

She shrugs. 'Probably.'

I look at her, closely.

'But what about when I told you my marriage was in trouble?'

She smiles, sort of sadly. 'Yeah, that helped humanise you. But it was only because of the video. That was your only bloody problem.'

I laugh, incredulous. 'My only problem! It was a big one, Emma.'

And so far from my only problem.

She looks up, shrugs. Looks down at her hands and pauses to pick off a hangnail.

'True, true,' she concedes, eyebrows raised as she nods. 'A sex video, of all things! And then look at you now.'

Emma shakes her head in faux disbelief.

'Scarlett Salloway. Not quite the perfect woman we all thought. More like your common garden slut next door.'

Don't call me that, don't call me that.

'And still he wanted you over me,' she murmurs. 'No wonder.'

So that's it, I think. Ed has dumped her and she has fallen for him. They were sleeping together. That is where this came from.

'Are you having an affair with Ed?' I ask. 'Is that what this is about?'

She laughs.

The murmur again.

'I'm not talking about Ed,' she says. 'I'm talking about Robert.'

I can't keep up.

'You think Robert has left you for *me*?'

I am baffled. Wish again I wasn't drunk.

'Okay, you have some crossed wires here,' I tell her. 'I don't know Robert. Never met him. I'm certainly not having an *affair* with him.'

But it feels like the more I speak, the further she retreats and I am starting to feel that I will never be able to bring her back.

I look at her eyes, dark, glass, and think of her loitering outside for an opportunity to break into my house.

I'm scared, that's the truth.

I can hear her words but my mind is whirring back to my husband, to hers.

I've never met Robert, never even seen a picture of him as far as I can remember. Like I say, he doesn't come up much.

But Ed. I *know* Ed is sleeping with someone else. This has to be where this has come from, whatever Emma – drunk – is muttering about her husband. I ask again.

'Emma, are you sleeping with Ed? Is that what this is about?'

I think of them, that day in the hospital, shaking hands. Was it happening then?

I look at her. Pretty. A lot slimmer than she used to be. I hadn't noticed it happen. Clearly wasn't watching her closely.

So maybe this is a new thing, his head turned when she looked different, when he bumped into her next to the rowing machine. It would make more sense. Ed likes slim figures.

And while Emma barely knows Ed in the world that I inhabit, clearly there is an alternate universe somewhere that I am slowly being given access to and in that universe she has slept with Ed and I am the enemy.

Emma guffaws, holds her side, laughs out loud for half a minute.

'Oh fucking LOOK at me, Scarlett,' she says. 'Even a bit trimmed down, as if your husband the Instagram model would go near me. God you are stupid.'

She shakes her head. Then cocks it to one side, teacher to pupil.

'Scarlett,' she says slowly. 'I didn't sleep with your man. *You* slept with *mine.*'

Robert.

Rob?

Someone I knew when I was younger? One of those love stories in miniature?

I think.

Robert.

Rob.

Bob.

Bobby.

None of them mean anything.

But with a sinking feeling, I realise something else.

Seth has bright-red hair.

There isn't a hint of auburn in Emma's blonde.

'Emma, what's Robert's full name?'

There's a beat.

'Robert Mitcham,' she says. 'That helps, doesn't it? To connect the dots.'

Robert Mitcham.

And my stomach plummets.

Robert Mitcham.

Bobby Mitcham.

The man I found on Facebook, after Ollie told me his surname and I did some googling around DJs in Manchester. I found his first name, eventually. Bobby Mitcham.

Mitch, who I met in Manchester to ask him if he had posted a video of us having sex online, is Robert, Emma's uninvolved husband. The man who made her weep when he said that for once he would spend time with them together as a family and they would go for pizza, but then slept through it even after she shook him awake and begged, *for Seth, for Seth*, but he had only got in from a club at 5 a.m., and he smelt of Vivienne Westwood perfume.

A man who it makes sense I would have never seen around here – unless I did that one time, with Asha – because they live in the next village, not Sowerton, and my world is parks and playgroups; Mitch's is clubs and bars.

I presumed he lived in Manchester because we met there and all his reference points were there; not because he ever said it. Emma tells me freely that he is at home rarely, spends a lot of time in Manchester with friends. And now, inevitably, they are done.

Emma, or this version of Emma, watches my face as it dawns.

I stay still as she looks down at me on my sofa and I absorb this new reality and the picture I have in my mind of Emma's husband shifts to be the man I once had sex with. Robert is Mitch. The man I thought when we met up in the pub two months ago had no children and no wife but again not – in retrospect, I realise – because he told me that, just that fatherhood didn't seem to fit with the picture I saw.

And I was right, in many ways. Emma tells me often they spend no time as a family, heaving the changing bag around National Trust houses as Ed and I do. As Ed and I did.

That man I met in the pub wasn't a dad, not really. He had a child but chose to live life like he did not, making – in the process – Emma miserable and bitter. And vengeful.

She stands in front of me, this new Emma, watching me think.

'There we go.' She smirks. 'She finally gets it.'

But I don't, I think. There are so many steps I still don't understand.

'I was your friend,' I say sadly, and all that Emma does is laugh and laugh and laugh, as pop songs that we have danced together as we held on to our drinks this year play, taunting us, in the background about who we used to be, and a friendship I thought we had.

38

Scarlett

28 July

Mitch. Robert.

Emma laughs with me in coffee shops, just after she has eaten her cereal with the man I'm on the internet having sex with.

She sits there in an oversized hoodie taking a long slug of her coffee, and talks about the terrible husband who barely lifts a finger in their life and all the time it is him, a man who saw me naked.

I nod along and tut about him, this husband, this half-hearted dad, this party boy. Not knowing that he is also the man who didn't notice the slice across my stomach as I sabotaged my own life by sleeping with him in front of my boyfriend.

I think of Poppy, playing with Mitch's son. Of Emma, sleeping with him. Of a different me, sleeping with him too.

My thoughts hurtle forwards, backwards, sideways. Was there a moment that Emma changed towards me? A moment I could pin down, when she must have found out what had happened between us back in the day?

'Got it now?' asks Emma.

No Emma. Not really.

But I don't say anything out loud.

I don't say anything out loud because she is the woman now who broke into my house and is trying to ruin my life and who has a laugh that is different to her normal laugh; eyes that are different to her normal eyes.

I look at her face and there is no trace of the friend I've known. Robert is one shock but that is a second.

But then I've thought it so often lately when I've started to suspect these women, haven't I?

Did I know you? And I'm not sure I did, in the way that I wanted to believe I did.

One of the reasons I've never connected Emma to Mitch: I don't even know her surname.

I don't have her email; it's not on her social media.

I've talked about everything with this woman – the mastitis that I battled through in the early weeks after having Poppy, what's happened to my marriage, even the video.

And yet, I don't know her surname.

I look at her.

'We don't know each other really, do we?' I ask.

'Of course we don't,' she snaps. 'We were desperate for adult company. We'd have taken anyone.'

'I told you such a lot,' I say. 'I told you my worries that Ed was cheating. I told you about the video.'

Emma shrugs. 'Yeah,' she says. 'You did, babe. Bit odd really. We haven't known each other long. You want to be more careful with how much you share.'

But I had been desperate. Desperate to make friends; desperate to skip forward through the awkward parts where you exchange small talk. I wanted something to absorb me into its sphere. I wanted, as a new mum with an unsure identity, to make myself feel constructed and real. To build a whole world so I didn't feel quite so much like I had strayed into someone else's.

A feeling runs from my chest to my stomach and it is familiar.

The feeling, I think, of blaming myself, of thinking – deep down – that all of this has been brought on by me because I was bad and shameful and not good enough.

Did someone say it to me, as a teenager? That that was why I didn't have my own mum. Something is sparking a memory. Of Josephine climbing into my bed while I cried, to cuddle me afterwards, telling me I could share her mum, if I wanted. I have the feeling again, of losing my last hold on things. Of this being too much. Of not being able to breathe.

Emma walks over and shuts the living room door, leaning against it.

I stand up.

'Sit down and listen,' she tells me.

But I speak before I can stop myself. 'So it was Mitch then,' I say, deadpan and wanting to get in there first. 'Mitch leaked the video and now you hate me, because you've had to watch me having sex with your husband.'

She laughs, then, as she sits down in the chair opposite me. 'Not quite.'

Her voice slurs with the booze and something else, unknown. An edge that is unnerving.

I stay silent.

Emma looks right at me again.

'Robert has sex with *a lot* of people,' she says. 'Before he was with me, now he's with me. It makes no difference to Robert.'

'But I'm not sleeping with Mitch,' I protest.

I correct myself, out of some sort of respect to her marriage.

'I'm not sleeping with Bobby. With *Robert*. We were barely even mates then, just mixed in the same circles, went to the same clubs. What happened between us was twelve years ago. Way before you met, I would imagine?'

She nods. 'Yeah. We only got together two years ago.'

'Well then!' I say, rallying, hopeful. 'We were kids. Different people. And you and I can move on from this. It's weird, yeah, but I barely knew Mitch. He wasn't some big love of mine or anything.'

I think I see judgement in her eyes – so why have sex with him *on camera* then, why wasn't your boyfriend enough for you – or am I so used to looking for it that I see that judgement anywhere now?

'Look,' I say, picking up pace. 'I don't know why Mitch . . . Robert did this. Perhaps because he has some issue with my ex Ollie? But now I know it was him, I can move on. You can help me make sure it doesn't go up on any more sites, right? Get him to delete the video. To leave me alone.'

I think of the messages, to Ed, to me, of the threats of what could come next.

She can help, I think, surely. I sizzle with the hope of bringing this to a conclusion. I can move on.

But then I look at Emma's face. Still so different to the meek, apologetic one I've known before and I'm reminded of characters on TV dramas whose faces change shape once you find out they're the bad guy. Once you see them through the lens of evil and it's impossible to imagine the original version.

This is Emma. My friend, my enemy, the surprisingly impressive actor.

And suddenly the fear is back. Because this woman, whoever she is, waited for an opportunity to break into my house. Planning went into this. Ed wasn't here. This wasn't her first attempt.

What sort of person does that, angry or not? I picture her holding Poppy, hugging me, offering me a bite of her carrot cake. I shudder.

'I won't go to the police, if that's what you want,' I say. 'Especially when there is Seth to think of. We'll just get Robert to leave me alone and I'll move on. There's no way I could face court anyway.'

It's true.

Emma looks up slowly and deliberately and for a minute I think she is falling asleep. Has she downed something more than gin? But she smiles, lazily.

'You don't think much of Robert, do you?' she asks.

I deliberate. What's the right response, at this moment, when he has left her anyway?

'No,' I say. 'When I met up with him a few weeks ago to ask if he had done this to me, he lied to my face. Said point blank it wasn't him.'

'Do you think you're important to him?' she asks. 'More than just some girl he shagged?'

I cringe, every time I remember this is her husband we are talking about.

'Well I didn't,' I say, defensive. 'But then he did this to me. So otherwise, why?'

I focus in on the silence of the house. No baby crying. No Ed dashing from room to room picking up his jacket, his wallet, his keys. The TV has turned itself off from inactivity. No music, because slowly, slowly through this whole thing even that has gone from my life. My mood doesn't deserve music. It doesn't deserve beats or dancing or lyrics that are poetry. My mood only deserves heavy loaded silence.

The room feels small. Not in the cosy way that it does in the daytime when I read stories to Poppy in here; cuddle her in for a sleep.

Emma looks up.

'Why?' I repeat.

As soon as I have said the why out loud, my brain skips on and tries to answer its own question.

Is Mitch obsessed with me? Has he seen me around locally and remembered me? Stalked me? I shiver. Was it something that came back to him when he realised one day that his wife's friend Scarlett was the woman he'd once filmed having sex?

I'm still flitting from theory to theory, trying to work it out, when Emma speaks. And if her face has contorted into a different person's face during this conversation, now her voice is doing the same.

Unrecognisable.

Emotionless.

Bleak.

Terrifying.

Because what she says is:

'It wasn't Robert who posted the video, Scarlett. It was me.'

39

Scarlett

28 July

Emma is sitting in the hug of a grey armchair that I used to sit in to breastfeed Poppy in the eerie world of 1 a.m., 2 a.m., 3 a.m. as she tells me the story of exactly how she ruined my life.

She is relaxed about it, a little dazed, and I wonder again if she has had something more than alcohol. Drugs may well be kicking around their house; Mitch was always a fan.

But not Emma, I think temporarily, as I picture her bursting through the door of the café half an hour after everyone else, agonising over whether to have a brownie.

Not Emma.

This is a different Emma though, I remind myself.

Normal rules do not apply. Normal rules, it turns out, were bullshit.

She gets comfortable against my deep purple cushions and I feel like I am emptying out, the final traces of hope and human connection gone now.

They were all I had, those women, and if it sounds ridiculous, it is.

But this has been a ridiculous few months and I have clung to all that I have been able to cling to and slowly, slowly, it has crept up on me: Asha, Emma and Cora *were* my closest friends.

'Robert cheats on me all the time,' she says now, not a sliver of emotion in her voice. 'And I've become numb to it. The way you do to anything that happens constantly. He comes in at 4 a.m., showers, and I pretend to be asleep. I have my life; he has his.'

She slumps further back.

I listen to this new Emma, like I have listened so many times to Old Emma, and I will her to transition back.

'I thought I could change him,' she says and maybe there is something softer in there now. 'And like every smart friend has ever told me – including you actually, once or twice – of course I couldn't.'

'But what was he like when you met him?' I ask because I am genuinely curious. 'Did he settle down then?'

Emma laughs but it's angry, and I think it's angry with me.

'No,' she snaps. 'Of course not.'

I stay silent, scared I might throw our precarious balance off if I speak.

There's a gap then.

'I got pregnant quickly,' she says eventually. 'We were only casually dating. Partying a lot. I think he thought it was the ultimate rebellion. What's the craziest thing you can do when you're this party-boy DJ? His friends thought it was wild. Move to the country! Have a kid!'

'Get married,' I fill in.

Emma looks up, surprised.

'We aren't married,' she says. 'Didn't you know that?'

Of course I didn't. We've established: I know nothing. I look at her wedding finger. There's a thin band of gold around it. She glances at it too. Shrugs.

'Just fits that finger best,' she says. 'And I've always felt like we might as well be married. No difference, once Seth came along.'

I assumed, of course. I skipped the steps of actual conversation like I did with her job as we focused solely on the babies.

If I was irritated by my friends at first for not asking me questions about *the real me*, then I have done the same, I realise. Not been interested, inquisitive, curious.

Just used, for what I needed. Hours filled, advice given.

It wasn't Robert, it was me.

I look at her, this stranger.

'So what happened?' I ask as I see her eyes lose focus; her lids droop.

She is, I think, she is on something.

Emma has been pushed so far that she has got drunk at home and taken some sort of drugs.

A shrug.

'I still wanted him to stay,' she says. 'I know it sounds pathetic but I always hoped he'd grow out of it. I wanted our family together. That was my only focus. For Seth.'

I nod, empathy surging.

I reach for her hand but she pulls it away.

'A few weeks ago we had a row, a particularly bad one,' she says. 'And I told him that I knew about him sleeping with you. That this was worse than all the others, that you were my *friend*. He didn't know that. Didn't realise I knew you, of course.'

Her body crumples like a newspaper on our fire as mine stiffens.

'I wanted him to know I could act too,' she says. 'That I wasn't passive all the time. So I told him what I had done to you too. Posting the video. Sending it to everyone. I suppose I was kind of . . . proud of myself. But he was *furious*. Told me how upset you'd been by the video when he met you that day, what a disgusting thing it was to do. Said you were a nice person, and that back in the day you'd had a hard time of life. Told me some other things while he was at it. About just how low things had got for you. It was supposed to make me feel bad, I think.'

She raises an eyebrow.

I go cold. Freeze. Of course.

'You sent those messages too,' I say. 'About the other thing.'

The penthouse. The fancy gin. Emma knows it all, the grimiest corners of my past.

She grimaces.

'Say what you mean,' she mutters. 'We don't need to call it "the other thing". We can call it you having sex for money but only as long as the men had fancy pads, right? That about the size of it?'

My cheeks sting.

And even now, I'm ashamed.

'It wasn't sex,' I whisper, and I can't believe this secret, so long buried, is living and breathing in my living room. Tears of release pour down my face. 'It was escort work before I met Ollie when I was all over the place and had no job and was desperate for cash. I didn't even have a home, Emma. I had to stay on friends' sofas. Once even on a bench. I knew I was getting my inheritance from my mum when I was twenty-five and it made me lazy. I got into a lot of debt and panicked.'

She raises an eyebrow. 'It wasn't sex? Ever?'

I stay silent.

She scoffs.

The dam opens and shame floods me, drowns me, way beneath the surface.

Yes. One time there was a lot of money on offer, and I convinced myself it was a simple transaction and I did it. I slept with that man, twenty-five years older than me, maybe, and it was so much more than a transaction and the dam opened then and the shame flooded, over and over, just like now and I hated me, just like now.

'I shouldn't have to justify anything I've done in my life to you, Emma,' I say but I don't feel that way. I want to justify, like I spend so much time in my head trying to do too, to real people, to imaginary people, to myself. On a good day it works. On bad days, nothing does. I could have gone to my dad for money, instead of that man. My eyes sting. He'd have taken me in, any day, any hour. But I was too proud; still sulking about his new family. How can I have made that choice? I picture my dad knowing this and it hurts in my insides.

She ploughs forward, like I haven't even spoken.

'Robert was appalled by what I'd done to you,' she says. 'Asked why the hell I would share the video. And then said he had fallen out of love with me a long time ago but this was the final straw, he didn't want to be with a person who could do this to somebody else, especially somebody they called a friend, and he left me.'

It wasn't Robert, it was me.

This isn't a friendly chat.

I'm not here to counsel her over her marriage.

She did this to me.

Not Mitch.

Emma.

And now she has let herself into my home and she is high and drunk and angry.

My heart starts thudding. The sweat drips again.

Fuck.

Fuck.

I need to keep Emma talking, because otherwise I don't know what comes next. Will she tell Ed, tell everybody, what I did?

'And why *did* you do this to me?' I say. 'Robert made some sort of sense. But you? I don't get it, Emma.'

Emma settles back on the cushions; refocuses. Looks right at me.

'I've suspected for a long time,' she says. 'That you were back on the scene.'

I open my mouth to protest but there is no chance.

'Receipts of Robert's I found, for local places, local hotels. It's always been Manchester before, but for a while I've known Robert's been sleeping with someone on our doorstep. Knowing you two had a history, it made sense. Clicked into place.'

Her stare is intense.

'Was it still the same?' she snarls. 'After all of those years?'

I shake my head no, hard – no it didn't happen, no, no, no.

'You have no idea *how much I hate you.*' She hurtles forward. 'I was going to watch you fall apart from a distance, just do enough that he wouldn't want you any more and the affair would stop. But then he left, and I needed to stand in front of you and tell you to leave him alone. Stay away from him. And from me. I am not your friend. I hate you. You're the reason my husband's left me. You have *ruined my fucking life.*'

The tone of her voice makes me stumble backwards.

I shake my head again. How can I stay away from him? It's not happening Emma. I'm not sleeping with Mitch. No, no, no.

How quickly worlds fall apart, I think. One minute you are liked, loved. Next minute they fall like dominoes and your dad, husband, boss, friend: they all hate you, or pity you, or cringe at you, or resent you or can no longer look at you right in the eye.

But Emma does, now. And then up and down, head to toe.

'I get it,' she says. 'There I am and there you are, glamorous, confident. Alpha.'

She looks up at a wedding photo of Ed and me on the wall above my head, gestures.

'Don't believe everything you see in a photo,' I mutter. 'I would have thought that was obvious by now.'

She ignores me. It's not useful to her narrative.

'I'm not sleeping with Robert,' I tell her but she doesn't hear it.

'You had to have him, even though you already have everything,' she murmurs.

'Everything?' I shout. 'You remember that I have left my job because my body is all over the internet?'

'Yeah,' she murmurs. 'Your really good body. Having sex with my baby's dad.'

The laugh bursts out.

'Emma, you can't possibly think that's a *good* thing?' I shout, startled. 'I've had my life blown apart by this. When I watch that hideous video, I'm not sitting there thinking, "Well, at least my boobs look good." Do you have any idea how violated you feel when something like this happens to you?'

Her eyes are fire now, suddenly, and she's furious.

'No,' she says. 'I don't. I'm Miss Local. I do the weekly shop and I go in for the evening shift. I nag my partner to come home sometimes, *just this once*, before 4 a.m. I wash dishes. I try not to eat the biscuit. I feed my baby. That is literally all I do, Scarlett. This video? At least it's exciting. At least it's made you feel . . . *something*.'

And then, I see every shade of red there is at the very idea that any of this is enviable.

'It's made me *feel* something?' I shout. 'Is that why you did this? Because it worked, Emma. You made me *feel something*. You made me feel shame and horror and fear. You made me feel at rock bottom. You made me feel suicidal, at times. You made me feel desperate. You made me feel like I couldn't experience joy any more, even when I was with my daughter, because I was so horrified by what had happened to me, wondering who had seen the video, wondering who was watching it now. You made me scared that there was worse to come. Scared that everyone would think I was a prostitute, and that Poppy would think that when she was older, and that Ed would leave me and *my* family would be broken up.'

I crumble, face in hands.

'Was that the point then?' I ask, as I look up. 'That I would know how you felt, if my own marriage was in ruins?'

She raises both eyebrows.

I carry on, through my sobs. 'You made me feel like I couldn't look after my child and like I was having a breakdown and I know what that feels like too because despite what you think, my life has been hard and that has happened to me before.

'I've been at *rock bottom*, at the very darkest places. So I know, for definite, when I'm on my way there again. And I was. I am.'

I could keep going but tears are taking up breath and I run out of it and all I can do is sob and sob, as Emma stands up and moves closer, standing over me.

For half a second I wonder if she will hug me but then I remember: that was the old world.

My brain switches to fear.

If not hugs, why is she coming so close?

But she is moving away again now, staring at the wall with an Alain de Botton quote on it. Everyone got the message from that piece of evidence? *I am clever, I am arty, I am well read, I can design a beautiful home.*

'You just need to say the words to me and admit it, Scarlett,' she says, head to one side looking at the print. Slurs. She hasn't heard a word. 'Stop me going crazy. Say the words.'

I stare at her.

'Admit that you and Robert have been sleeping together all the time that we have been friends. I have to hear you admit it, Scarlett, even though he won't, for my own sanity.'

And before I can answer, she carries on.

'I've stayed close to get my own evidence, tried to make myself such a good friend that you would confess and spill, like Cora does, about the man you were seeing. I knew you wouldn't realise there was any link to me. But you're cagier. Elusive.'

She pauses.

'Even when I get you paralytic.'

I picture her, topping up my drink even when she isn't having one herself. Think of times when I've felt drunker than I should from what I think I've been ordering. Dark. I shudder.

'Okay, okay,' I say, hand up in defence. 'Okay. There's someone local who Robert is sleeping with by the sounds of what you say, with the evidence you've found. But it's not me! I slept with Mitch – Robert – once, a long time ago when I was drunk and stupid. That's it. Never again.'

She looks at me with venom. She doesn't believe me.

'It's too big a coincidence, Scarlett,' she says. 'You, moving round here. The local receipts. What happened between you all those years ago. The way he defended you. He meets up with you, then leaves me. And look at me; look at you. Once I realised you had been in his bed, I couldn't stop comparing. Beautiful, tall you. They're normally in their twenties, the women he sleeps with, but you – he'd make an exception, I'd imagine.'

She touches her nose; rolls on.

'It was this one night when I cracked. I was exhausted from getting up in the night with Seth. Robert was out again. He had left his iPad unlocked and I searched and found all kinds.

'Messages to women, pictures. Videos. I was there for hours. And eventually, I got to someone who looked familiar.'

She looks down at me.

Her eyes, these new, dark ones, drill holes in mine.

'To someone who I thought was my friend.'

She did this to me. Not a man, not an unknown. But a woman I trusted.

I think of every second of pain I've experienced through this: talking to my dad, watching my marriage unravel, seeing Poppy cry as we walked out of yet another baby group because I couldn't breathe. Felicity's face, my colleagues, the gross remarks on my Instagram, my body vibrating with fear at those messages. Jonathan the lawyer and Ed on either side of me as I clutched at my high neckline. Aunt Denise with her hand on my arm. Shame, shame, shame.

'So what?' I say. 'You decided to take some sort of revenge?'

She nods, in a daze, pacing again.

'Yes,' she says. 'Revenge.'

She looks up.

'Starting off with the video.'

My heart pounds.

'And then?' I ask.

'Funny you should ask,' she says, sitting down and leaning back again on my fancy armchair.

And I steel myself, as much as a person who is falling apart can.

40

Scarlett

28 July

'Have you caught up with Poppy lately?' asks Emma, pointedly.

I think of my phone, in the kitchen. How long have we been here? An hour, maybe, or twelve.

I go cold.

'Not since yesterday.'

Do not mention Poppy.

She laughs.

'I've got to confess, that might have a *tiny* something to do with me,' she says. 'Whoops. Ed *kind of* thinks you're an unfit mum.'

My head flicks up. She ploughs on.

'You probably know about the messages I sent to Ed a while ago,' she says, reclining on my armchair. 'I wanted him to be on the lookout too. I thought if he confronted you about your cheating, you might know you were being watched. Stop sleeping with Robert.'

Is there any point arguing with her? This is the narrative she has decided on. I shake my head, sadly. No, no.

'Did he tell you there were more messages, this week?' she asks.

A shiver runs through me.

My phone is in the other room. I can't reach my husband to correct whatever these messages say. I can't reach my husband to help me.

Although who would Ed believe anyway?

An anonymous stranger in a message or me, his wife? The answer brings tears to my eyes.

'To let him know about the affair you're having with the guy from the coffee shop,' she says, casually.

My heart starts to race. Because is there anything harder to refute than a lie that is based in truth? I think of the hangover I had that morning after the night I stayed for a lock-in with Joseph; the edginess Ed would have noticed.

I think of the evening itself. Joseph and I, heads close together and alone, knees too friendly under the table.

I think – with a shiver – of Emma, running just behind me and seeing Joseph across the street. Of her being there when I talked about him. Her seeing how often my eyes would follow him across the room. Of *her* eyes, watching me.

She would have enough to hang me, I think.

Dates, times, details, messages. She could paint this picture easily; it was like the outline had been drawn for a child in its colouring book.

'I didn't have an affair with him,' I say and she is wide-eyed now.

'Oh really?' she says. 'My error. Oh well. Too late now, Ed thinks you've been sleeping with him for months.'

I go to speak but she interrupts again.

'Not just him either. Ollie? The ex? And of course, Robert.'

Dates, times, details, meet-ups.

'Probably Ollie and Robert at the same time. We all know you, eh, Scarlett.'

She winks.

What's alarming, I think, is how she kept this hatred that is now seeping out through every single word she chooses hidden from me for so long.

Because this woman *despises* me.

'To be honest he thinks you're sleeping with anybody who will have you.' She shrugs. 'Thinks you're way, way, way off the rails, probably helped along by all the drinking I mentioned you were doing. You're not the woman he thought you were. And he tried *so hard* to wipe you clean.'

She pauses and laughs and it's too close to the bone. He did try to wipe me clean. I wanted to be wiped clean. And none of that had been healthy. Trying to eradicate a part of myself, however grimy it was. It was why I wanted to be in Sowerton; it felt cleaner, somehow. Like the less polluted air would make a less polluted me.

'Why should your life carry on like normal?' she asks. 'Why should your marriage survive when you stole my husband?'

I can see no way back; no way to undo this. It's dense and dark and it's easier to give in. I want to go to sleep. I want a mum I can remember.

'Hey there's more, babe!' Emma exclaims suddenly, waking me up, waking herself up by the looks of her eyes, wild.

And I know. Have known always that he would find out sometime. And that when he did, it would be more than respectable Ed could take. That it would finish us off.

'Of course I told him that you used to be a hooker too,' she says. 'Don't worry though, I made sure he knew it was high-end stuff. Posh apartments, right? Not drug dens and squats. So he should be fine with that?'

If I've been breaking apart for the last few months, that's the one that finishes me off with a final blow. Most of the time it was flirting and wearing tiny clothes to be stared at and pawed for money and then there was that one time but all of it, to be honest, all of it is the worst thing I've ever done. I can't forgive myself, never have been able to; I know Ed won't. I think of work colleagues knowing that too. My dad. I vibrate, and my head starts to throb. Too much, too much, too much. If it wasn't for Poppy, I could drown in shame and be happy to never see the surface again.

'It's bloody brilliant isn't it?' she says. 'And there was me thinking I'd lost my ability to be creative since I had Seth.'

'But why would you want Ed and me to split up?' I say. 'If you think I'm sleeping with Robert, wouldn't you *want* my marriage to work? To keep me away from him.'

She laughs. Mean.

'Being married hasn't kept you away from him so far,' she says. 'So that was incidental. I just wanted to ruin everything you have. The things that matter to you the most. Ed. And of course, when he leaves thinking you're unfit, Poppy too.'

I move, jump off the sofa, to get to the other room, to my phone, but she is on me. More agile since her new gym habit and I wonder if that's why she's been keeping fit, if she's been prepping for this.

She is angry too and that makes her even stronger and I am broken apart and she has me up against the wall in half a second even though she only has an inch on me, five foot seven in bare feet.

'How can you leave now?' she says. 'I haven't finished.'

And my heart pounds then with the adrenalin of trying to get out and with the horror that there is more, when I am at my limit. My Poppy, I think. Do not come for my relationship with my girl.

My insides are vibrating with fear.

It feels like I can see the trace right through me, from now, to Ed and how we are, to the video, to having Poppy, to leaving Ollie, to every night in those places with those men, to my mum, back and back and back running through me like a pipe that has sucked me dry. This is the culmination. This is the end, here.

Emma sits down too.

All Ed wants to do is protect Poppy, and he panics about anything that could harm her, and now he thinks that I, with my drinking and my strange men and my irresponsibility, could. Plus, he has met somebody else. Even if it's not Emma, it's somebody. Flick was sure, Martha too. The lines in the sand are long gone. What if they become a proper couple and I lose custody? I can't survive that, I think, and I can't breathe, I can't breathe, I can't breathe.

'A stepmum would probably be better for Poppy in the long run,' says Emma, reading my thoughts. 'Far more stable. A better example too. Plus you said it yourself, you're at rock bottom. Can you survive this? Really? Poppy will need someone, Scarlett, and you're not up to the job any more.'

The room spins and I stumble.

I said no to Ollie, just. I said no to Joseph, just. I said yes to a lot of drinks but I said no to enough, just. My mental health survived, just. Didn't it?

'What is this supposed to achieve?' I ask through deep tears. 'You want Poppy to lose her mum? Fucking hell, Emma, you have a child.'

Emma shrugs. Those eyes are dead, now. She is so far away from kindness; humanity.

'To teach you a lesson,' Emma says. 'To break up your family, like you broke up mine.'

All I can think of is Poppy.

Ed wouldn't do that to me, I think. I have to think. Then I think, again: Ed would do whatever it took to keep Poppy safe. He wouldn't keep her away from her mother, but he would keep her away from danger. If he thinks I'm both, this could go either way.

'If you're so convinced that Ed is done with me, let me phone him,' I say.

We sit in silence for a couple of minutes.

She sits back, frowns, then turns to plump the pillows that seem to be irritating her.

'That's better,' she says, looking at the cushions. And then: 'Okay, call him.'

She nestles backwards into the cushions like it's Friday night and she's looking forward to a gin and slim and a Netflix binge

– and I walk tentatively, like I might break her decision, past her to get my phone and find my husband's number in my favourites, dialling it to see if I can creep my fingernails over the cliff and cling on to the edges of my life.

41

Scarlett

28 July

I stand up as I dial, looking at Emma's face from above with that soft blonde PE teacher sensible ponytail and her long, pointed nose as she sits there in my armchair. Who the hell are you, I think, this woman who pretended to be my friend? This clichéd, kind dieter. This strange, vindictive bitch.

Each ring makes it harder to breathe. Each ring makes me feel more desperate.

Emma is deadpan when she delivers the news that we both know, by now, on what must be the seventh ring.

'He isn't going to answer,' she says, pitying. 'He can't let Poppy speak to a mum like that, knowing you're probably drunk again too. It's not good for her, Scarlett — you must see that.'

It's why she's looked so relaxed: she's known this all along.

Voicemail picks up and I know even as I am speaking that I am making things worse.

'Emma is here,' I say, tripping over the syllables like I am just learning to use my tongue. 'Emma made up those things. About me having affairs. About the . . . escorting. I only met Ollie to talk. About the video, like I told you. And Mitch. Mitch is Emma's husband. The man from the coffee shop — Joseph — is just a friend. There was . . . it was . . . I'll explain, when I see you. But I need to see you, Ed. I need to see Poppy.

Please pick up. Call me back. Come home. Emma is here and I don't know what she wants and, Ed, I'm scared.'

I'm sobbing and Emma yanks the phone from me with a firm grip before I realise what's happening.

'Ed,' she says, managing to sound calm and rational somehow to my hysteria. 'It's Emma. Don't worry. Scarlett's had a few drinks too many and she's blurry, to be honest it's been happening a lot lately, but I'm with her. I'll look after her. It might be better if you guys have space for a bit, keep Pops with you so she doesn't see her mum in this state, bless her.' And then she clicks to end the call, flicks it onto airplane mode and puts it in her pocket and I don't act fast enough to stop her.

I'm moving through treacle that's been in the fridge for hours. It's part the start of a hangover, part still being drunk, part deep, deep shock.

I look around my house, where Emma has been so many times. She's fed her baby crisps on my sofa and gulped sugary tea from my favourite mug. She's complimented my colour scheme, got nostalgic at my old CD collection and she's taken her shoes off and curled her feet under her on my carpet. She's cooed at pictures of me and Ed taken in twelve-hours-sleep-fuelled days before we had Poppy.

How, I think suddenly, have I never noticed pictures of Mitch in her house?

Then I remember: I've never been to Emma's house.

Is that odd?

Living in the next village – even if it's only a five-minute drive away – when the rest of us are walking distance from each other, with a coffee shop close by and various baby groups in the community hall, means that we default to one of ours. Now I'm wondering if that was deliberate.

I look at Emma.

'What now?' I ask.

I glance, then, at Ed's golf clubs, waiting to be put away,

propped up against a bookshelf. I had told him off about them, a danger in a room that Poppy plays in.

But Emma walks past them. To the candlestick, heavy and decorative and never in any use that actually requires a candle, much to Ed's bafflement. She examines it closely.

Will this get physical?

But if I think she might attack me, Emma already has.

Her worst was done online, in her messages to Ed, with knowledge, with a false closeness, with emails, with a misuse of intimacy.

She puts down the candlestick.

She is done.

Emma has no desire to hit me because how much worse could those blows be than the ones that she has already administered? She didn't come here tonight for violence but to ask me questions, to make me promise to end an affair that isn't real, a relationship that doesn't exist, to quiet the questions in her head.

And to tell me that she has ruined me. She has won. My life is even worse than hers; my family ripped apart even more violently. She has scored some sort of point in a game she thinks I've been involved in.

So instead, she gets up from her chair. Plumps my cushions again.

'Don't let him win,' I say, quietly, grasping at anything I can. 'Don't let him win by trying to ruin my life. There's no "women like me" or "women like you". There's just women – people – trying to get through life. That's what we're all doing, Emma.'

She stares at me.

'Delete the video, Emma,' I say gently. 'And tell my husband that I am not cheating on him, with any of those men. That I didn't do what you said I did for money. That I'm a good mum. Please Emma. Please.'

But if I think I am getting through, I am wrong.

'I want you to suffer,' she says, and her matter-of-factness is worse than anger. 'I want you to suffer what I have. To feel loss.'

The worst sentiment there is.

'I have suffered,' I say, quietly now, beaten. 'Just because people don't share their stories, doesn't mean they didn't happen. I've suffered, and I'm suffering, and what you've done has hurt me and my family, maybe irreparably. So if that was your aim, it's done. I'm not sleeping with Robert, Emma, I'm not, I'm not. Now please, can you stop.'

I taste salt on my lip, and somehow I am on the ground, in front of the fireplace like a cat, and while I am there Emma steps over me, grazing me with a bright purple trainer.

'I don't believe you,' she says.

Then she walks to the front door, opens it and leaves.

Emma, guest on
a parenting podcast

Thanks for having me on to talk about the mum blogger sex tape scandal. I know this won't make me popular. Not very #womensupportingwomen or any of Scarlett's other painfully forced hashtags. Sorry, I'm bitching already.

I meant to start by saying that I'm sorry.

No, I am.

Really.

But envy is a difficult emotion to battle, especially when you are as low as I was then.

I still don't believe that Scarlett wasn't sleeping with Robert for months, maybe longer. There was someone local. She ticked every box. Everything about it made sense.

Ever since I found that video and realised that it was my friend on there having sex with my partner, I was obsessed.

When he was on a night out, I wondered constantly if he was with her. All I could think about when I was with her was whether she was sleeping with him.

She was beautiful, my friend Scarlett, with that sporty body and the glossy bob. I knew she'd have kept him, if it had been them who'd had a child together, in a way that I couldn't.

She could have made him stay in and be a dad and get married and make a bit of tea for her when their child had colic and she was weak with hunger. And he would have loved her. In a way that he has never loved me.

I'd cry all the time, angry tears. It was overwhelming, the need to ruin her.

And so I wished terrible things upon her.

I wished terrible things upon her as we were jogging, sipping coffee, eating noodles.

I wished terrible things upon her even as she sat, jigging her tiny daughter up and down on her lap. Yep, you can blow raspberries at a child at the exact same time that you're wishing misery on their mum.

I wished terrible things upon Scarlett as she drank turmeric bloody lattes instead of coffee when I ordered my third Americano of the morning and as she flung her toned legs up on an Airbnb sofa and as she flirted with people she really shouldn't have been flirting with. God, she was greedy, Scarlett Salloway, wanted everyone to want her.

Old habits, probably.

Sorry. That was bitchy again.

Anyway, that's the story. I did it.

But I wasn't the only one.

There was someone else too.

42

Scarlett

28 July

Emma leaves my phone on the table.

She knows it's no use to me anyway.

All I can do with it now is make things worse.

I try phoning Ed again anyway. Nothing. Over and over I call, thinking that *surely* he will pick up, I'm his wife, but he ignores it. Or it's in another room, on silent, as he tries to block me from his mind. It is after 11 p.m.

But Poppy, I think. Poppy.

I pace the house, hot, panicked and feeling my brain start to twirl out of control as it does when I can't focus in on one thing.

I call, and call.

Liam and his wife too. They don't pick up their phones either, presumably asleep.

I need to get out of this house.

I need to get to Ed.

I grab the car keys and leave, saturated even in the distance between the front door and the car from rain that while I've been speaking to Emma has become torrential.

I put the key in the ignition and press a boot down on the clutch but something doesn't feel right and I realise: it's because I am drunk.

Even in my chaos, I know I can't drive while I'm drunk. Can't risk hurting somebody or hurting myself when I have – and it's the only thing I can think of that matters now when there used to be a plethora of reasons, the ones that make up a whole life and person – a child.

I sit in the drive and take my phone out of my pocket.

Who can I call, at this time of night? Who will help me?

Josephine is too far away, geographically and in her life, from this whole situation. We are so distant now; another thing the video has taken from me. I look down at my pyjamas and boots and see rock bottom.

My dad: I still can't let him see how bad things are. Still can't paint the whole picture.

Old friends are so removed now that starting from scratch on how things got here seems impossible and laboured. And so I get out of the car and run through the rain, to the only person I can think of who would let me in now, in the dead of night.

'Cora!' I shout into the silver intercom as the rain hammers down noisily. 'I know it's late. But I need help.'

And she lets me in like good friends – whatever I know about those, now – always do.

43

Scarlett

28 July

Here is that good friend, in glasses I've never seen her in before and cashmere pyjamas you want to stroke like a kitten.

'Talk about freaking me out,' she mutters as she opens the door. 'You would have to choose the night Michael is away to do a late-night surprise call. What the hell's happened?'

She looks down at my pyjamas.

'Wow,' she says. 'You do not look good, hon.'

Unlike Cora, even the 'at home in front of the TV' version. Slippers that are worth upwards of £300. Brows and lashes dark and groomed as ever. That's Cora.

'I need to get to Ed,' I hiss. 'I'll tell you everything later but first, I have to get to Ed. To Poppy. And I need you to drive me.'

She puts her hands on my shoulders.

'Calm down,' she says. 'You need to take ten minutes first to breathe. You look like you're about to collapse. You don't want to see him in this state. Tell me what the hell is going on. I'll put the kettle on.'

She looks at me.

'Actually, fuck the kettle.'

And then she goes to her drinks cabinet and takes out a bottle of brandy, the drink of the crisis, and pours me one. I don't argue.

I start speaking as soon as I have the drink in my hand.

Everything that Emma has told me in the last couple of hours is tumbling out, too fast, too messy, in the wrong order, disjointed, with the wrong emphasis. Doesn't matter. I need to expel it, as fast as I can.

Cora doesn't ask questions but I give her the answers, as she sits next to me on the sofa.

'And it was her who shared the video,' I sob, clutching my glass. 'Emma! Not even Robert. But *Emma*. How could Emma be capable of that?'

I look at her and wait for the shocked reaction, the horror.

But Cora is still staring straight ahead, no matter what I reveal, saying nothing.

I tell myself it's because she is taking in the shock. Recalibrating what she knows about Emma, her friend of twenty years. Maybe even doubting me, wondering if I've had a breakdown and invented this.

I glance at her again.

'Why are you not answering me?' I ask, uneasy. 'I'm telling the truth.'

She nods. 'Just taking it in,' she says quietly.

Right.

But still.

This isn't the Cora I know who would want the gossip, the details. To gasp and rant about Emma's disloyalty and what a bitch she is and how she plans to freeze her out of having any sort of local social life in this area, ever.

I would expect another reaction too: for her to pretend to be one step ahead of it all. '*I always knew there was something weird about her*', even if I knew that wasn't true.

I look at Cora again. Face straight ahead. Like she's watching the road while driving in bad visibility.

What's going on?

My stomach does a forward roll.

Good friends.

'What's happening, Cora?'

She stays silent.

'Cora.' I'm louder now.

'Relax,' she says. 'I'll tell you. We just need . . . a chat.'

And I stay there, because I have to trust some people, sometimes. Maybe she has important information about Emma. Maybe she *did* suspect something. Maybe this is all about to make sense.

But in the dark, with the rain angry and beating up the roof, Cora's newly built WAG mansion, out here up this isolated country road, is not idyllic, it's threatening. Same image, different perspectives. Like Emma.

Could Emma be here? I suddenly think. They are tight. Has she persuaded Cora that I'm the one in the wrong? I look around at the closed door to the kitchen. To the spiral staircase that leads upstairs. To the door that leads down to the cellar.

I glance at Cora.

'Come on then,' I say. 'Are you going to tell me that you knew about Emma?'

She nods. Shivers, in her very cold house. 'Yeah. I knew.'

I'm mad now, furious. 'When?'

She says nothing.

'What is wrong with you?' I prompt. 'God, Cora. I thought we were close.'

She starts laughing then. 'Oh come on, Scarlett, don't be a child.'

Between them, they are bastardising the last year of my life.

'When I stayed at your house? That wasn't friendship?'

She laughs again. 'No, Scarlett, that was drinking.'

She pauses. Quieter.

'And you know Emma and I have been mates for years.'

'Yeah,' I say, tears threatening now. 'So that's where your loyalty lies. Even when she's done this to me.'

Cora carries on laughing at me and suddenly, it's one too

303

many times. One too many times of being laughed at, somewhere, in some home, behind some screen, even if I didn't see the teeth bared or the sound emitted. One too many mocking tones. One too many feelings of paranoia.

'When did you figure out that it was Emma?' I demand.

Something occurs to me before she can answer.

'Does Asha know too?'

Cora laughs louder then and it's unpleasant. 'For someone who rates herself so much, Scarlett, you have a shocking sense of judgement.'

She doesn't expand.

Fuck this. I'll get a cab to Ed's brother's. I stand up to leave.

'Stay,' she says.

But I'm done, with all of it.

I ignore her and walk towards the front door.

'I think you'll want to know what I've got to say,' she says, breezy. 'Plus I've locked the gate.'

I turn to look at her and she indicates the intimidating intercom system on the wall with a remote control in her hand.

So I do as I am told and it occurs to me then that this new life of mine involves a lot of doing what I'm told.

Ed chose the house we should buy and Cora chooses the playdate locations and I traipse after them, hood up, head down.

I'm irritated, suddenly, by the realisation that in trying to be respectable, what I've become is obedient.

Cora starts speaking as I shiver harder, more deeply, and wonder why it's so cold in this house. Why on a night in, with unseasonably bad weather, Cora wouldn't have stuck the heating on.

'You think,' she says. 'That it was Emma who shared the video. And you're right. Technically.'

She pauses.

My heart beats faster.

'There were tens of them,' she says. 'These videos of women Robert had sex with. Looks like it was a thing of his.'

My shivering is impossible to hide now and I vibrate with it.

'What did you mean, "technically"?' I ask.

The flash, again.

'She came to me,' she says. 'Told me that one of the women in the videos was you. She was devastated, paranoid. Even when she showed it to me and I pointed out that it was obviously made years ago, that you must have known each other when you were younger, she was convinced you had reconnected recently and hooked back up.'

I throw my head back against the leather sofa in frustration.

'I know, I know you didn't,' says Cora. 'But she'd found all these receipts from hotels round here and was convinced there was someone he was seeing, locally. She put the two things together. Drew her own conclusion.'

She stops again.

'She thought you were laughing behind her back.'

And isn't that always what pushes us to be at our worst?

Cora continues. 'We barely knew you at the time,' she says. 'The babies were young. But I was building an impression.'

'Let me guess,' I say, defeated. 'Smug. Superior. Vain.'

'That's about it,' she replies, like it's a fact.

I feel like someone is pushing down on my chest.

'Emma *told me* about the video,' she says. 'I was just the one who pointed out how we could use it.'

We is good when you want a team to be behind you. But when you learn who has posted videos of you having sex online, *we* is worse than *I* by far. One person trying to ruin your life can be an anomaly. But when it's more than one, it becomes a conspiracy.

People have sat down together and decided to hurt you. Plotted it, planned it. Thwarted obstacles and found solutions. Laughed at their successes. Laughed at your pain. If someone does it alone, at least, there's no one for them to laugh with.

I stay silent because I know Cora will answer my questions, whether I ask them or not. And I am void of all energy. Beaten.

'Emma was angry with you,' she says. 'It built every time you told us a story about Ed and Poppy and your happy life. Meanwhile she was having a hard time with Robert. He'd be staggering in when she was up for the third time that night.'

Cora shrugs.

'And then in the midst of all that, she found these videos. She got obsessed. Convinced you were sleeping together again, that that's where Robert was when he didn't come home.

'You know how awful it is once you start comparing someone's life to yours. That's how Emma got. She thought you were thinner than her, prettier, fitter. Cooler. She was sure Robert would rather be with you. She was desperately unhappy, and every time we saw you it seemed like you were rubbing her face in it with your happiness.

'And then of course, she told Robert about the video and he started defending you – even told her what a hard time you'd had back in the day when you didn't have anywhere to live and had to stay on all your mates' sofas and even work as a hooker.'

Cora smirks.

I can't speak.

Instead, I absorb the information of what's really been happening in all those months I've been in the dark, searching for clues.

I absorb them with the chill in this mansion, feeling it seep into my skin, deeper now, into every layer. I think of the odd looks I would catch Emma giving me sometimes. How I thought she was probably shattered; I was probably paranoid.

'She called me saying he'd "taken your side" and left her,' she continues. 'And that just confirmed what she thought. That he still had feelings for you. That you were in a relationship.'

I shake my head again, no, no, no.

'It's not like Ed and I don't have issues either,' I say, quietly. 'And it's not like I've not been through bad times. I thought it was better not to moan on about what a hard life I had when I'm lucky compared to so many people.'

Cora nods. 'I said that, at first, that your life couldn't be as perfect as all those awful blog posts; that people just market themselves these days.'

I wince. Supportive Cora, telling me how much she loved my blog. How many other people add their likes then bitch about me?

'But she wouldn't have it,' Cora rolls on. 'Saw you as everything she wasn't and then, in the back of her mind, had that image there all the time of you shagging Robert on video looking hot and young.'

I snip.

'Well, I was twenty-three,' I say. 'That's why I look young. Everyone looks young when they are young.'

Already at thirty-five it feels like a generation ago.

Cora ignores me.

'She watched it over and over,' she says. 'You must have noticed a bit of a fixation on you? Yeah. You were an obsession for her. And every time she watched it, she hated you more.'

'She's pretty good at hiding it then,' I say. 'Ordering my tea. Babysitting my child. Ed thought it was a girl crush.'

Cora laughs. I feel my body start to tremble harder.

'I suppose it was, in a way.' She smirks. 'But maybe more like a stalker.'

The shaking intensifies. Who was I leaving Poppy with? *She's with one of my best friends.* She's with a total stranger. She's with my fucking stalker.

'She thought that the more time she spent with you, the more she could get a picture of your life,' says Cora. 'See if you slipped. Know if you cheated. Be close enough to you that she could work out if you had feelings for Robert and how serious it was. That was why she'd be the first to volunteer to babysit. The first to show up if you needed a coffee and a chat.'

'But there was no affair to admit!' I explode.

'I know that.' Cora laughs, loudly. 'That's why the whole thing was so hilarious for me. Her, convinced you were sleeping with Robert. You, too prim to not feel guilty for a tiny *flirt* with the guy from the coffee shop. I just sat there, watching it unfold. You've got to entertain yourself somehow on maternity leave.'

I am incredulous. 'And then?' I ask.

'And then what?'

'Well it's obvious this is leading somewhere. So why don't you get to the point?'

I am feeling brave suddenly.

But it is misplaced. Badly misplaced.

'I will get to the point when I want to get to the damn point, hon,' says Cora, ice in her voice. 'This is the problem with you, Scarlett. Even when you're behind a locked gate with no one in the world who wants to help you, you still act superior.'

I go to stand up but she pushes me back down onto the sofa, and I stay there. I am out of fight.

My whole body vibrates again.

How can I have been this dislikeable?

I suspect sometimes that I am not fully formed because I leave chunks of myself behind. One chunk in Manchester, dancing with Ollie. One chunk presenting a pitch in work, a grown-up. One chunk with my mum, maybe, wherever that may be.

I am not whole.

And I feel like reality is slipping away now, like I've lost the last millimetre of grip.

I work so hard on the image – the party girl, the successful manager, the respectable mum. Perhaps that's the problem.

I rebrand, rebrand, rebrand.

I wanted them to think I was shiny and glossy and new. And instead, this is what came across. Superior, smug, vain.

Until they forced me to expose my pain and split myself open.

I had tried to avoid that.

These women knew I had lost my mum, because people do when you have a child and she isn't babysitting or knitting gloves like the other grans because she's too dead for that.

But I have never told them about Poppy's half-sister – because that's what she would be, like Josephine is to me. I don't have the words.

And if I did find them, I know they would ruin an afternoon and send awkwardness pulsating around the room.

My body won't keep still, twitches, jitters.

Cora speaks again. 'Emma talked about it so much, Scarlett, how you'd ruined her life, how it was so much worse than seeing strangers sleeping with Robert. How humiliating it was. How maybe if he left her for you, he'd be happier.

'She was fixated. And eventually, I came up with the idea to post the video. To get her own back, and also stop you being *so bloody smug.*'

When all I really felt was fear and loneliness.

There are a lot of reasons for iciness. Is that not obvious?

I stare at Cora like she is one of Poppy's drawings, in which I try to see shapes and patterns but I find nothing that I recognise.

But then an image starts to make itself clear.

Something lurches in my insides.

'Easy to do with access to your phone a few times to get addresses while you changed Poppy,' says Cora. 'That all-staff one from your work was a *gift.*'

I breathe, or try to.

'But what did you get from it?' I say. 'That's what I don't get.'

Cora sighs, as though it's annoying that I am fixated on such an inconsequential detail.

'Look,' she says. 'Let's be blunt. I can feed this sex tape blogger stuff to the websites and they will love it. You'll be huge, in a way you never wanted to be. They're all gunning for mum bloggers, after that other one went viral.'

My heart thumps. She wouldn't do this, would she?

'Or,' she says, flippant. 'You can give me £200,000.'

She sounds like she's asking to borrow a tenner.

I think of how I have wondered so many times if this is moving towards blackmail. And at the ridiculousness of where, now, that request is coming from.

Cora is the last person I know who needs money. Except.

'I'm skint,' she says, voice cracking. 'Broke. I can't tell Michael; he'll kill me.'

I look at Cora's gleaming white walls, the expensive cushions. I think of her designer bags, of appointments and more appointments and the nanny and the fancy car and that vanity project of a job.

Then I think of how cold it is in an old house this size that needs heating on a particularly cold late summer night.

'You're taking the piss, Cora,' I spit. 'You are rich by anybody's standards.'

'*Was* rich,' she says without a beat. 'Then maternity leave happened. Not earning – yeah I used to have a real job, did you know that? – plus hours with a baby on top of you where all you can do is more internet shopping on your phone. *Lethal* combination.'

I take this in.

'It's at breaking point,' she says. 'I have so many credit card bills and I'm being threatened with legal action. Michael knows none of it and if he did . . . Well we're not in the best place anyway and he *loves* money. We won't make it, I know that.'

'You don't know that,' I say, trying to bring this down to

310

relationships, a Tuesday morning chat over a latte. 'He's your husband. You'll work it out together.'

What the hell am I doing reassuring this woman who has conspired to smash my world apart? Who is threatening to go further? It's myself I need to protect, I think, not her. But old habits. Until a few minutes ago, she was my friend.

'So the plan is to blackmail me then?' I ask. 'Is that it?'

She nods, grim, without missing a beat. Just like with Hunter, if I expected sheepish, I'm not getting it.

'That's it, yeah. Not ideal, hon. But we have something you want, the ability to not post the video elsewhere, not to tell the websites it's you and let this *really* go viral. And to keep your other secret. Not share that one with the world. And you have something we want. For Emma, it's revenge and seeing you suffer. For me it's simpler: cash. With a little cut for Em, obviously.'

Cora appraises me, sitting there on her cream sofa sodden from running here in the downpour. My hair drips globules onto the leather. She leans over, takes a very long blue fingernail and wipes one off my forehead onto the floor.

'Would put the heating on for you hon,' she says. 'But like I say, too skint.'

She stands, looking at me there, dripping, shaking.

'Emma likes seeing you broken,' she says, waving a hand around to indicate that I am demonstrating broken perfectly, right now. 'You're less of a rival to her, less likely to turn Robert's head now you're a depressed stay-at-home mum in joggers. Not so cool. Not so superior.'

Mascara, I know, is likely streaming down my face.

I stay quiet, digesting.

It's *a lot* to digest, see, when your friends turn out to hate you and then attempt to blackmail you. Discussed and disgust, all over again.

Quietly, feeling the sadness seep into my bones with the

rainwater, I look up at Cora, and then I find the energy to stand up too. Look her in the eye.

'I don't have money,' I say. 'I hate to disappoint you but even if I were willing to give it to you, which I'm not, I don't have it.'

And it's then that Cora turns. Has me up against the wall of her living room. Just underneath the giant studio photo of her face, of her bare soft shoulders.

She's not physically imposing at five foot five and an untoned size twelve but I see something in her eyes that scares me for the strength it can give: desperation.

'This isn't just me wanting a few quid, Scarlett,' she hisses, even though no one can hear her. 'Things are bad. My beautiful house will be repossessed. This is my daughter's home.'

'I get that, I do but . . .' I start.

'It's not just that, Scarlett. It's the school we've had her enrolled in since she was born. It's the cars, it's imagining what we do without the fucking nanny and the cleaner and the housekeeper who run our entire existence. It's our whole life. Everything.'

She has her hand across my neck and it's hard to get out what I want to say but I try.

'You can make more money,' I manage. 'Michael has a good job. You can get it back.'

No mention of her job because no one in their right mind thought that Cora was paying the mortgage with her Crunchie specials. But what was her former job? She's never mentioned that before. We've never mentioned a lot of things before, I think. That's been the problem.

In reality, Cora was on what seems to be an unending maternity leave with a token gesture cupcake hobby that allowed her to justify paying somebody else to raise her child. But it's me who should give her my money? Sure.

Something is happening to her, seizing her and taking over

and she pushes harder with her arm across me. I stay as still as I can like there is an angry dog or a large bee coming close. Apply the same theory to any predator, I think. Don't aggravate. Placate them. Keep them calm.

'Michael doesn't have a fucking job,' she hisses at me. 'Do you think I would be this terrified if Michael had a job?'

'What are you on about?' I start. 'In the city. With the finance company.'

She goes on about it enough; endless hints about how much cash he brings home. My details are sketchy but I know that much.

'Sacked,' she says. 'For gross misconduct. Apparently he was perving over some new starter. Truly *gross* misconduct. I was too mortified to tell you all.'

Another omission in a sea of wet wipes and rice cakes.

We stand in silence then while I take that in, or perhaps even while she does too. She looks shell-shocked at her own news.

'So you need another money maker,' I say. 'And that's me and my misery.'

She nods, grim.

'Well it's either that or sell this,' she says, indicating her fake boobs. 'But I'm knocking on a bit now. And that's more your style.'

I wince.

'Are there really rumours about me on social media? About the blogger with the sex video?'

She laughs, from her belly like I've heard so many times before but never at me. Never like this.

'Yeah that was true!' she says. 'That's what gave me the idea to fill them in. The noticeboards speculate. No one's put it together yet. But they would lap up the full story. Jesus, who knew you were such a follower, though? The second I mentioned it to you, you deleted *everything*.'

She's right. How easily I will remove parts of my life as

soon as someone tells me to, I think. Happens all the time. Ed. Cora.

'It didn't start off this big,' she says. 'I thought I'd help Emma get revenge and make a few quid to help with my credit card debt at the same time. But then Michael lost his job. I was poor growing up, Scarlett, and I can't be poor again. And don't give me that bullshit about having no money. I've seen your house. You both have good jobs.'

'No, Cora. No. I left my job. Because of the video. Did you not get that, that night in the pub?'

She waves her arm dismissively. 'But you'll get another one,' she says. 'Same sort of thing. Well paid.'

Cora has the decency — can you call it that? — to duck her head before she says the next part; to avoid my eyes.

'And I know you have an inheritance, after your mum died. Kids who lose parents always do.'

Too much, Cora. Too far.

It's like somebody has taken the wrong brick out in a game of Jenga and I am falling, toppling, away from normal boundaries.

I have weathered a lot, these years, these months, these last hours.

I have tried to be respectable.

Not any more.

Where did respectable get me?

In my house, threatened.

In Cora's house, shivering and sodden.

Online, shamed.

Cora's arm, which seemed so strong a few minutes ago, has been shoved from my neck and she is on the floor, me on top of her.

Why did I think that she controlled me?

I'm bigger than her, fitter. And I have been building up to something. Pounding the pavements wasn't enough. I need an outlet and here it is in its cashmere pyjamas, glasses on.

'Emma at least had some emotional reason for wanting to

314

take me down,' I hiss. 'But you! Money. Just money. Money that you spent on dresses and your eyebrows and *so much fucking white paint.* And now you want more, so you think the best way is to blackmail your own friend.'

I am panting now, I've become the predator I had frozen for earlier.

I pause, arm across her mouth so she couldn't answer me even if there was anything for her to say.

I am too angry to hear excuses that involve private schools and designer coffee tables.

The shaking that was from a chill earlier is with rage now, pure rage.

And I need to get it out.

'I ask again actually – was Asha in on it too? Or just two of the people I spent most of my days with?'

An image pops in of seeing Asha that day, with Mitch. Was this a whole team thing, only me on the outside? Did they come for me, target me as a group?

But Cora shakes her head, her newly dyed hair – sure, you're skint – splayed across her cream carpet like roadkill.

'Well that's one thing,' I say, sarcastic. 'Though I guess my odds of finding three utter bitches was low. Even two's quite impressive.'

I hold on to her throat then, and I think about her body, warm in bed next to me when I slept over like we were four-teen, crashed out after too many melted Mars Bars.

The friendships I've made since I've had Poppy have been similar to those teenage ones: intense, emotional. Fast.

Cora tries to wrestle away but I'm stronger and I hold her down, down, down, until it becomes like a meditation, the pressing, the holding, against a body that is moving hard and desperate against me.

How long can you stay in the moment for, Scarlett, how long, how long, how long?

Cora struggles.

But I've entered a state of mindfulness.

Far superior to the apps.

Far better than anything I get loading the motherfucking endlessly whirring time-sucking dishwasher.

I could do this forever, I think.

After living in the past so much, after spending so much time thinking of how the future looks, I have never been more in the now.

My inheritance did exist. It went on a deposit for a flat rental in Chorlton. It went on buying my way out of an old life, into a new one. It came at the right time, me turning twenty-five, as I moved out of my dad's after I went travelling and he saw that I was serious about being a grown-up. It set up my life. It went, the rest of it, into an ISA that I think now might let me get away again, from here. And she thinks I'm giving that up?

'Does the money matter now, Cora?' I ask as her eyes start to droop. 'Does it matter *this second*?'

44

Scarlett

28 July

Then suddenly, I come out of my trance.

I picture Penelope, first, upstairs snoring lightly, tiny feet, soft pyjamas.

I see Cora's face when she scoops her from the floor to go home after a playdate, loving her so much she could consume her.

I see my friend with a glass of champagne in her hand, laughing with me and laughing at herself as she is self-deprecating about her fanciness and her expensive tastes and I think that some of it was real, *surely*.

I see her with her head on her pillow, a little mascara smudged around those eyes that are now so scared.

How she had looked fifteen suddenly that morning under her duvet without her bright lipstick and her over-ironed hair and without her mouth set in its usual position, one that says *defend before you're attacked*.

I look at her face below me.

She is a person.

She's that person, and she's this person. The different versions again.

And I am a person.

I am this person who is holding my arm across her neck, and I am that person who slept with her beneath her silk sheets.

And as I look at Cora's face, which has started to lose some of the fight, my grip lessens.

When I let her go, she falls to one side, sobbing, scrabbling to get away from me. I don't look back at her as I walk to the door and she opens the gate to let me out, locking the door with scrabbling fingers and those awful nails the second she can behind me.

It still pours down and I walk home, pick up the car, drive, taking wrong turns, still too drunk really, not stopping to cry, not stopping to focus. Until I remember: Ed's brother and his family have moved and I have no idea where I'm heading to. Ed goes alone. Fuck. On the off chance, I check the sat nav history and it's in there. Ed used this car when he went to see him last week. Ten minutes later I pull up outside Liam and Jaclyn's new house.

I try to wipe some of the rainwater off me before I knock but it's pointless.

I can't clean myself even if I want to.

Now the shock has worn off I realise I am freezing and I shake uncontrollably in my sodden clothes. I think of what will happen next. I don't have Cora's money. Know I can't give in to blackmail anyway. I can report Emma and Cora to the police. Likely I will still go viral now though, as the mum blogger with the sex tape. Thoughts scramble on top of each other. I am sliced open again, like I was all those years ago. The shaking intensifies.

Ed's brother Liam answers the door to their bungalow in pyjamas and dressing gown with a golf club badly concealed behind him. The walls in the hall have been stripped bare.

'Scarlett! What the hell? Come in. Jesus.'

He opens the door but then he gives me the once-over.

I'm not sure he's yet entirely unconvinced that he doesn't need the golf club. Probably wise; you have just opened your door in the early hours to a woman who drunk-drove here after her recent attempt to strangle her friend.

How did I get here, I think? How did I wander so far from my dinner parties – albeit bought in because nobody changes that much and I always was a terrible cook – and my fancy brownies to this?

I had done such a good job.

Worked so hard.

I try to tell Liam what has happened, there in my pyjamas, with words and sentences falling out of mouth unevenly, in the wrong order. But I can't see clearly. Can't remember it all. Feel like I may faint.

The words jumble and collide and climb over each other. I try to straighten them up but don't have the capacity.

I don't sound sane – I know that.

Liam backs away, looks nervous.

'Scarlett, Scarlett, okay, calm down,' he says, edging away from me.

'Ed! Get up. Scarlett is here. I'm not sure what's going on.'

A bedroom door opens and Ed bustles down the hall in his pants and a T-shirt.

Liam places a gentle hand on his brother's shoulder. Leaves. Comes back a few seconds later with a towel which he passes to Ed rather than me, then heads down the hall, closing his and his wife's bedroom door audibly and leaving us to it.

Ed and I look at each other. And I think I have run out of emotions to feel. Is that possible? To exhaust them all and be hollowed out?

I am done feeling it all and dealing with it and analysing it and trying to save it. I am done tending and lamenting and blaming.

'Why didn't you answer my calls earlier?' I say quietly. Ed doesn't miss a beat.

'I turned my phone off, Scarlett,' he says, as he silently pats me and my pyjamas dry in the hall like I'm a wet dog. 'I needed an early night and Poppy was in bed with me. I didn't look at it. What the hell has happened?'

I stand still, obedient.

Ed looks scared. He glances nervously towards the bedroom door, where Poppy sleeps. I try to move towards it and he blocks me, with an arm.

'She does not need to see you like this, Scarlett,' he hisses. 'And it's the middle of the night.'

I stare at him. Think about what he could have saved me from this evening, if he had just answered the phone to his wife.

'So you didn't listen to the voicemail?' I say.

He shakes his head.

'It was Emma,' I say to Ed.

What follows is another diatribe of nonsense and what sounds like hyperbole as I speak of blackmail and coercion and a show-down in a WAG mansion.

'I did flirt with the guy from the coffee shop but that was it, Ed,' I say. 'Nothing happened, I swear. But Emma thought I was sleeping with her husband Robert – Robert is Mitch, the guy from the . . .'

'Video,' fills in my husband, grimacing.

I look at him then, closely. His hair has moved even further towards grey lately, sticking up now as it does when it doesn't contain product. It feels like months since I've seen him like this, sleepy and exposed.

I notice the lines around his eyes and from nothing, I feel everything at once.

'You act like it is a terrible thing I did, Ed,' I say. 'Sleeping with other people such a long time ago. Shall we talk next about who you're sleeping with now?'

Perhaps it wasn't Emma. But what Flick and Martha said still exists.

'What are you on about?' he says but he's always been a terrible liar and now is no different. His cheeks colour; his voice shakes.

'Can I ask you something, Ed?' I say, calmer now, somehow.

'Would you have supported me more if you weren't seeing someone else? Or was the video enough to kill us dead anyway?'

Ed sighs. 'Sleeping with someone else?' he says but the cheeks are redder, the vibrations more audible. 'Who am I supposed to be sleeping with?'

'I don't know, Ed,' I say. 'You would know that, not me. Someone from the gym?'

He refutes and blusters. Then he pauses. 'And also, I did support you!' he says. 'I got you a lawyer's appointment, went there with you.'

You, you, you. Still no we.

'I was having a crisis, Ed. You're my husband. That's the 101 level,' I say. 'I needed emotional support, comfort, love, a hug to tell me everything was going to be okay.'

He ducks his head because he knows he can't claim to have given those things.

'You didn't comfort me, Ed. You never comforted me.'

'Well aren't I the worst husband?' he mutters. 'You've not exactly been perfect, Scarlett.'

That inflames me again. 'Somebody has just tried to blackmail me, do you understand?' I yell, and he hisses at me to quieten down. All the bedrooms are on the same floor as us. If I shout like this I'll wake Poppy. I'll wake Liam again. I'll wake Liam's wife and their three kids.

'I don't give a fuck, Ed!' I scream. 'I don't give a fuck if I wake up everybody!'

Ed raises an eyebrow and puts out a placating hand.

Patronising bastard, I think, patronising *bastard*.

'Let me get this straight,' he says. 'Emma tried to blackmail you.'

'No,' I simmer, impatient for him to understand. 'Cora did. Emma posted the video.'

He furrows his brow, this man who is supposed to support me, who has let me deal with all of this by myself, and made me feel grubby, all the while sleeping with somebody else.

'And these are the women we met at NCT, right?' he says, sceptical.

I nod. 'Just because they know nursery rhymes, Ed, doesn't mean they can't be cruel too,' I snap. 'They are human beings. They don't exist in a box.'

'But why would Cora want money?' he says. 'Isn't she the one who's loaded? With that big house off Woodland Lane?'

I nod. 'But their financial situation isn't what I thought,' I say.

What is?

I look at him.

He pats me more with the towel and it's so pointless that it's making me furious. I shake him off.

'Again, you're not supporting me!' I shout. 'My life was at risk tonight. Emma broke into our house. And you weren't there to help me because you'd given up on us, when I stayed and tried and clung on.'

He ignores the last part – typical Ed, zoning out on the emotional element. He interrupts me.

'Emma? But it was Cora who asked for money?'

He is more like a police interrogator, trying to pick holes in my story, than a man who stood up in front of one hundred people and said he'd love me for our lives.

I stare at him, incredulous.

And suddenly, I fly. 'You, you, you!' I scream. 'All I've been through tonight, all I have been through, and you start accusing me of lying when it's you who's having sex with someone else.'

'I'm not accusing you of lying,' he says as I hit him and he puts his arms up. 'Stop that, Scarlett, stop that. How can you be the one going for me when I know what I know about you now? That it's not just threesomes. According to these anony-mous messages I've been getting, you cheat on me. And you used to be a *prostitute*, for god's sake.'

The fog drifts in again that was there earlier in the night with Cora. And I roar in fury.

Arms that could almost strangle a friend are more than enough to beat at a man, hard, ferocious.

I am powered by his not backing me, by his doubting me, suspecting me. By him leaving me so alone that I felt I needed to confide in and put everything in the hands of women I barely knew. By him being so distant from me that I honestly believed I was closer to them than my husband.

That raised eyebrow and those barely perceptible sighs and that fucking *arm*, telling me to calm down when my world had fallen apart and he *wasn't listening*.

I could just about weather public shame but private shame emanating from my own husband – maybe that was the form that would tip me over the edge.

And as I beat at him his voice rises up in the chaos and he says to me, clear, 'You know, it might be time to stop being so obsessed with who did this or trying to accuse me of things and accepting that *you* slept with those men and made a video of it. It's all *somebody else's fault* or it's because of the booze or it's because you lost the baby. But really, Scarlett, is that just a way of persuading yourself that it's not your fault, how you used to live? Take some bloody responsibility.'

All of our good moments and our close moments didn't matter in the end, I think, versus this. I learnt too late that my husband thought it was bad that somebody shared a video of me having a threesome but if he truly admitted it, he thought it was worse that I had done it in the first place.

I let him finish, because I want to hear it all.

'And all of this business about me sleeping with somebody else? That's a complete falsehood.'

I stare at him and make a split-second decision.

'Let's see, shall we?' I say, and I walk out and open the car door and start it in the dark, forgetting to turn the lights on. I

323

shout behind me. 'Because on the way here I realised I've never been to Liam's new house so I put the address in the sat nav, and in the recent history was a random address in Chorlton. We don't have much reason to go to houses in Chorlton at the moment, do we, Ed?'

Ed reddens.

'The only good thing about the fact we used to live there is that I know it pretty well. That's the street just on the left after the wine bar, right? God, we used to love their Chablis, didn't we? Little sharing platter on the side on a Friday night after work.'

I pause.

'Or maybe for you, there's no "used to" about it.'

I pull out hard, screeching into reverse to turn out of Liam's drive and head to Chorlton where Ed and I used to nip out for brunch and watch films under a blanket on our sofa and kiss and dream about a future that was incomprehensibly old, with a garden and a baby and a wedding, thinking it would be rose-tinted when really it is edged in grey.

I pull out to drive back into our past and see what is lurking there, and how long it's been lurking for. A few months? Our whole marriage? Did it start before Poppy was born, or was it in that newborn phase, when I thought we were such a unit?

I pull out to find out if this is true and who it's been happening with. I will look at this woman right in her sleepy, middle-of-the-night eyes and ask if it was before my sex tape was sent to everybody, or after, when she started sleeping with my husband. I will wake her, whatever time it is, whoever she is, and finally, I will know everything. Finally there will be no more limbo.

But I pull out too fast, too irresponsibly, miles away from the mum driving of the daytime with its mirror checks and its car seats and its slowness.

And its sobriety.

Because yes, I also pull out of Liam's drive ignoring the fact that I am too drunk to drive, still, the rationale of earlier having left me now and on the drive over here as the events of tonight spiralled.

I hear a shout. Ed's lovely accent-free voice, the one that I used to tease him about when we met, gently, inexplicably, because I barely knew anybody else who didn't sound like they were from the heart of Manchester.

My husband's lovely voice shouting stop to me, shouting no, shouting Scarlett, shouting please, shouting listen. And then the thud.

And it's only when I feel that thud I've never heard the car make before that I know that I have hit him, Ed, and that as I step out of the car in what feels like slow motion, there is no sound coming from him.

This man who kissed my head at the hospital. This man who put the hot water bottle on my feet in our new bed. This man who poured me a glass of wine. The man who told me, as Poppy came into the world, that she was a girl, and knew what that meant to me and held me as we wept together.

And as I round the back of the car, I see Ed, not moving and I crouch down to check him, to revive him, to tend to him.

'Be okay, Ed, be okay,' I murmur in his ear, and then I stand up and look up for Liam, for Jaclyn.

'Call an ambulance!' I yell, though I am scared simultaneously because my drinking will have repercussions. Huge ones, potentially – depending what happens next. But what else can I do?

I look up.

But it's not Liam or Jaclyn at the door.

Instead it is my daughter. Gummy smile, sleepy eyes, in her baby pink pyjamas with elephants on them. She holds her toy dog close to her soft tummy. Her chubby feet are bare.

She is excited to see me, my love, after we have been apart. But her smile fades and she is simultaneously worried, because her dad is on the ground and I am stood above him, screaming.

45

Scarlett

Three years later

'This is really not the ideal place to raise a child,' he says, as Poppy heaves her scooter in through the door of our tiny flat, leaving the latest batch of scuff marks on the wall.

I mutter about it too on a weekly basis but I'm smiling.

We are home.

This home is in central Manchester, the place I thought I had to flee from for the next phase of life, because I would be too old to be there in my thirties and there was a sleepy pub that did a good roast dinner in the countryside calling my name. They were the rules; that was the trajectory.

But now a moderately rough bit of town is where late thirties me puts the chain on at night, double bolts the door and calls home.

Turns out, there are all kinds of ways of doing things.

Poppy needs space, and she gets it. We just have to work a bit harder to get it than opening the back door and pushing her out of it into a big, luscious Sowerton garden with its very own swing.

Ideal places to raise a child can be far from ideal if they create miserable parents who feel like a section of their insides have been hollowed out because they don't belong there, because for them it is wrong, wrong, wrong.

People are different. I need the city. I need songs. I need to dance. I need noise. I need edge and culture.

Nobody wrote a rulebook for a life and there's a reason. Something was right, and I tried it, and something else was right, and I am trying that. Now though, I try not to bury all the old versions of life, all the old versions of me. I try to let them live too.

I am back at work; a new job at a painfully cool agency that I got partly thanks to an incredible reference from a guilt-ridden Felicity who I catch up with regularly for a drink and a conversation in which we try to avoid the topic of the time we watched me have sex.

Martha comes too. I apologised for being so distant when I moved; she said no, it was her. She had been dealing with a new situation, trying to be a step-parent to her boyfriend's daughter and she was drowning. She had to retreat. I had been too focused on me to think about everyone else's narratives. Everyone else's battles.

I stop at two wines these days. I should probably quit altogether; there's no doubt I see alcohol as a crutch and I definitely abused it for a while. But I'm a work in progress. Leave that with me.

Now I don't mind being a work in progress though; I don't mind looking grimy. I don't mind having a past. I don't mind that I am, like most, a little bit fucked up.

Sometimes I am almost glad the video was uploaded that day, and that Emma and Cora did that to me: it pressed restart on my life, and restart was what I needed. Everybody needs restarts sometimes. Life's never one long go.

I am even *almost* able to laugh about the thing that ruined my life. Mostly because I've realised: your life being ruined isn't always a bad thing. There might be a better one available.

It takes me a long time now though to make new friends not least because those websites did write posts on me, the mum blogger with the sex tape. Anyone in my life who didn't know – though there weren't many anyway – was filled in after that. Cora denies that she leaked it, in the only contact we've had since, but I'll never know.

Whatever happened afterwards though, on the internet what Ollie, Mitch and I did is there forever. I am the mum blogger with the sex tape. In my lowest moments, I worry that everyone who meets me sees me as solely that.

Joe often tells me I need to let people in more. That not everybody's like Emma and Cora, whose names I struggle to say still, like they are Voldemort, when what happened then comes up.

That's right. Joe – Joseph – and I are together. Not married – I'm not sure I am up for doing that again – but we live together. Poppy likes Joe, although, nearly five now, she can't say that he's my boyfriend without giggling.

It's odd, doing new love with the responsibilities of now. There's a romanticism that's curtailed when you can't lie in on Sunday mornings and have sex all day and eat like teenagers and worry about nothing. When you're not getting to know each other at a time when the most grown-up thing you had ever bought was a £20 lamp and it still felt incredible that you were allowed to go to Greece together and share a bed and being an adult was very much like being in a play at school. Like it was with Ollie.

For most people, flirtations with the barman end there, in a bubble of what ifs flavoured with tequila slammers and scented with heavy aftershave. You may have the occasional thought of maybe, maybe, but that's it, because you would never smash your real life up for something so pretty and frilly and young. You would never get the chance.

Now though, the barman and I put the bins out. The barman checks if I've called the landlord about the dishwasher. I remind him to take Poppy's school uniform out of the washing machine and he reminds me to drop that bag into the charity shop when I'm passing. He works hard, getting up at 5 a.m. to manage a coffee shop in the Northern Quarter. Sometimes he works from home at the other end of the day, coding too, for friends; people he meets at the shop. We're not rich, far from it.

Every now and then, we go dancing because it wasn't just youth, music is something that formed me and continues to form me and we live in a place where we can embrace that. When I turned thirty-eight last week, we hired out a room in a club and danced until the early hours. Ed is no longer here to turn the volume down to the level of background noise that is only acceptable during the hot stone massage you booked on Groupon. Conversely, Joe loves dance music too and he comes into the room, turns the music up to booming, spins me round and we rave in the kitchen as he whispers into my hair that he loves me and I'm back there, twenty-three and euphoric but with these grey roots now and a messy, messy mind.

I can't believe that I did that to Cora, that I was capable, and sometimes at 3 a.m. it makes me wake up screaming, as Joe holds my head and whispers that it's okay. He knows what happened. The clearest thing you have is your sense of self and when you are so low that it has disappeared and you don't recognise your own actions and the path you chose to take, it is truly, truly terrifying. I know now I had a breakdown after the video was posted and what I did to Cora was the culmination of it. I've had a lot of therapy; the therapy I should have had fifteen years ago when my baby came too early. Or maybe even before then, before I reached adulthood, after I lost my mum.

Jonathan White and I reported Emma to the police for posting the video. Despite new guidelines meaning that she could have gone to prison, she had no previous convictions and was given a caution and a fine. Part of me was relieved, for Seth.

I never reported Cora; too scared that she would report me too for what I tried to do to her and terrified that would mean I would be taken away from Poppy. She still 'makes' cupcakes.

Neither of them has ever exposed me for what happened in the penthouse, or when I used to go out with those men. On bad days, I get scared it will come out, one day. On others I think neither of them would poke me a second time, for fear I would report them or strangle them, neither being a strong option.

Emma spoke to a parenting podcast about the whole thing though I suspect Cora was behind that. Maybe I'm doing Emma a disservice thinking that though, underestimating her again. There's nothing I can do about it legally. She still doesn't believe I wasn't sleeping with Robert.

But here is a lovely thing. When Asha had her second child Rupert last year and planned to have a naming ceremony for him, she asked me to be a kind of equivalent of a godparent, despite me being – our favourite in-joke – a sexually deviant heathen. Because we're friends now; the proper kind. That was there to be discovered, like it is anywhere. I was just rushing to the finish wanting a twenty-year-old friendship style closeness with everyone I met, immediately, without seeing how things developed naturally, which was never going to work. Instead we built it slowly, Asha and I. Long lunches going over this hideous thing that had happened within this circle that we had formed. Frank conversations. Hugs. Longer dinners talking about our past loves, past hurts. Confessions. More hugs.

Honest talks about Asha's anxiety, her need to control situations, how she feels like she missed out on a lot of the fun of having a baby because she was tidying the kitchen, refusing to give a bottle of formula, worrying there was something bleak around the corner coming for Ananya. How it was too late really by the time she listened to someone speak about their postnatal depression on the radio and stood next to her fridge holding a butternut squash and crying with empathy and with regret that this epiphany hadn't happened to her earlier. That she worked for a mental health charity, and didn't spot when she had mental health problems, which for her is difficult to fathom.

I think of how I rolled my eyes at Asha and I cringe. She couldn't control her mind, she tells me, so she worked outwards. There's always a story. I'm angry with myself for just looking – or rolling my eyes – at the surface.

In the same way, Asha tells me that she feels she played her part in what happened to me as well. Yes, Cora would make comments that I was smug and she wouldn't be able to convincingly disagree with her. Because she thought I was a little aloof too. That I mocked Emma, and it was unkind. That sometimes she presumed I was laughing at her too. I cringe at that because it's true. Asha is an intelligent woman who works in a job that's way more important than mine and reads historical fiction and has a Google-worthy knowledge of contemporary artists and I reduced her to ironing and *shoes off, girls* because I was so paranoid about this new life of mine, so defensive and scared of changing.

Yes, she says too, she thought that while she was drowning in postnatal depression, I was sailing through. *Why didn't I tell her about the baby that I lost?*

Did I need to saw myself open, I ask her, for people to see why I was sealed shut? She doesn't know the answer. I don't know the answer. None of us know the answer. There isn't one.

I saw myself open now though and glance inside regularly when I am alone or at therapy and I see that I *was* smug, yes, and bitchy, then ten minutes later I was sorry and kind and quite a decent person. I see that I was aloof, because I was working so hard on that respectable persona. I see that – mostly because of the blog – I was so fixated on what everybody thought my life looked like that I stopped caring about what *I* thought it looked like. What it felt like.

It's not straightforward. Characteristics have always tripped over each other. You can be lonely when you're surrounded by friends, a bitch when you're paranoid. Envious when you're happy. You can even be having sex with two men, looking like you're enjoying it when you're heartbroken and grieving for a baby that wasn't to be and a relationship that you knew couldn't weather what was happening. When I had sex with both Ollie and Mitch that night, all of that was true. When the video pinged into people's inboxes all those years later, none of it was visible.

To the people who judged me on the basis of that, I can't say much. I judged too.

Asha and I go for walks, drink coffee on hard days, and the turmeric lattes which I know from Emma's podcast appearance irritated her so much, on slightly easier ones. It hurt that she did that. And who had given her the idea of monetising her own life? Me. Her old pal Scarlett and her ill-fated blog.

I never went back to blogging and I don't miss it. I don't miss hiding in toilets to watch the likes roll in. My new life isn't available to be rated.

When Asha took a maternity leave opportunity for her and her family to go to see her sister for six months in Australia, Joe and I booked flights: we are headed out with Poppy in a couple of months, Poppy old enough to stick headphones on and put her face in an iPad now. We can't afford it but we're doing it anyway. Joe has heard about a grungy old coffee and vinyl shop that he wants to visit and scope out. He's thinking tentatively about looking for investment to open something similar here. Music's something we love together. A strong coffee when we're shattered isn't far behind.

You're wondering if Ed died, aren't you?

I wondered too, as I saw him there on the ground, and I shook in terror for Poppy.

He lay there, still.

She watched, and cried.

I regret doing that to her, every day.

But then he is a man who did something as old as time, and made a woman feel ashamed for having a body, ashamed for having sex, I thought, as I stood there in the stillness.

A man who thought I brought it on myself.

Stillness.

A man who thought I should be punished.

Still, still.

He is a man who pushed me and pushed me and pushed me.

Was he a man who deserved it?

I'm not sure.

But you know what, I didn't deserve any of it either.

And then the stillness was broken as Ed's brother Liam and his wife Jaclyn appeared and their sleepy kids a second later, and they raced into action and got Ed up off the ground and though he couldn't walk and needed an operation later down the line on the ankle I had managed to run over, he was okay. Okay enough to reassure Poppy.

It doesn't matter now how much Ed tells his family we must move on. It doesn't matter that Ed and I are civil, having talked at length about how toxic our relationship had become and how it is right that we are not together. How Ed had even admitted that he had been seeing a woman from the gym – yes, she lived in West Chorlton, yes that was her in the sat nav – for months when we were still together, though they have long since fizzled out now. How I told him that I know I wouldn't have looked at Joe if we had still been in love but we weren't; hadn't been for a long time by then. How sometimes people grow apart not together, and that's just how it is.

How the hugs that we shared after I had run him over had more emotion than they'd had for a long time in our marriage, filled as they were with relief and closure and knowing that no matter what, we will always be Poppy's parents.

'I only slept with someone for money once,' I told him. 'Please believe that.'

And he did, eventually. Though I suspect on some level he thinks there's little difference between that and the rest of what I did: the escort work. I was paid money to flirt, to sit next to men while I wore short skirts, to laugh at their jokes. Ed is black and white. But the thought has tortured me over the years too. The reasons why go out of the window again and all there is in those moments is shame, shame, shame.

Ed tells his family that I am Poppy's mum. That he doesn't want to report me to police because I had been drinking too and that would impact her; as long as I agree to a better shared custody agreement than the courts would give him so that Poppy spends half of her time with Ed, in the countryside, in all of that much-lauded outdoor space. In truth I wonder if he didn't report me too because he wouldn't want to be a full-time parent. God, imagine, Ed. How awfully modern you would have to be for that. When Poppy is with Ed I miss her so much it hurts my insides but what choice did I have? It was that or an ABH charge. He is her dad. I go dancing when it hurts too much; I stay out late so I forget.

Epilogue

Cora

After

Hunter, then, was never the real other man.

It *was* the name of my yoga teacher, that bit was true, but Hunter and I never got closer than a hand on my back for an adjustment to my plank.

I just thought that was a nice detail.

No. The man I was really having an affair with was called Robert.

Mitch, some people call him.

Robert slept with Scarlett, had a baby with Emma, and then – after we met one night in a fancy bar in a village nearby four months after I had Penelope – he began an affair with me. I realised he was Emma's partner about a month in; saw them walking around a supermarket together. It jolted me, sure, but I wasn't willing to give it up. When I told him I knew his wife, he felt the same.

Asha knew about it. Saw us once when she was at a wedding at a hotel we were at together and tried to persuade me to stop it. She even had a word with Robert once when she saw him in the street. She ran when she thought she saw Scarlett watching them; she had no desire to spread the gossip further. Sweet, sweet Asha. I'm rolling my eyes now, can you tell?

But here is the thing about Robert. He is an uninvolved dad, a cheating husband but when your life is dreary and you're worried you've hit middle age and you're in a monotonous relationship, he is an antidote better than the lines of coke he suggested we take together a few weeks ago.

Robert and I book hotel rooms and pretend we don't have children and order room service and have sex. We go to clubs and bars and casinos.

All paid for by Robert because my money worries, unfortunately, are real.

When Emma told me about the video she had found, blackmailing Scarlett seemed like the obvious answer. I pushed Emma into it really, got into her head about Scarlett and played on a lot of the insecurities that are right there for everybody to see with Emma. *Yes, Emma, Scarlett does think she's better than you. Yes, they probably are still sleeping together.*

Don't be a doormat, Emma. Don't let her get away with it. She's laughing at you, Emma, while she pretends to be your friend.

It helped deflect attention from me too. Because yes Emma, Robert was sleeping with somebody local. You got it right. You just had the wrong neighbour.

Nobody likes to be laughed at and believing that someone's doing it is a trigger for most people, dating back to the first person who bullied you, whether they were in the school playground or sitting next to you in the office. Everyone remembers the feeling. And everyone feels a surge of rage at the idea of anyone making them relive it.

So I waited for Emma to deliver Scarlett to me. She would come of course, needing me after receiving such a blow as Emma delivered. You need your friends at times like that.

But of course my blackmail attempt didn't work, with Scarlett rejecting it and telling me she didn't care if the world saw her have a threesome, if she was famed for being the blogger with the sex tape. She'd rather deal with that than capitulate to me. That anyway, there was no money.

So now, I need a new plan.

'If Emma is away next weekend with Seth, I could come to yours?' I say to Robert, tracing a long fingernail down his back.

He and Emma got back together, recently. He says he can't afford to live in his own place. And, he points out, he doesn't see me leaving Michael. We both know what this is. Though we'll see how long he stays around when he gets wind of Emma's podcast appearance.

Robert and I are lying naked under icy white sheets in one of Manchester's best boutique hotels. No kids allowed; it's one of my favourite jokes to glare at them if I see them while I'm out with Robert, as though I hate them; as though I haven't made one all of my own pretty recently, as though I don't spend most of my time wiping dripping noses just like these parents are doing, the ones I pretend I find disgusting.

Robert looks apprehensive. But then he shrugs.

'Sure. At least we save some money on hotels.'

He looks around pointedly. I don't do four star. Five only. I reach to the side of the bed for my champagne glass.

In truth too, Robert doesn't care if I leave an earring or a lipstick at his house: he's so flagrant about his affairs, and Emma still ignores anything she finds. They are back together in name only really.

So I pack my expensive lingerie and I go on holiday to Emma's house. And when Robert is in the shower on Sunday morning, I go on the laptop where Emma told me she found the video of him and Scarlett, and – she was clear on this part – probably everyone else he's ever slept with.

Which included his partner. I know that as Emma told me, sickened that she was filed away with 'everybody else'. Sure, Emma; that's the problem. Not your husband having sex with other people and filming it, but his filing system.

I hear Robert singing in the shower – something from the old days, Noughties dance music that would send you crazy if you were on edge anyway. Bloody hell, Robert, let it go. I spray a little of Emma's perfume on my wrist, smell and wince: not good. The kind of thing we used to spritz in Boots on Saturdays together when we were thirteen. Emma, hon, time to move on.

And then I shut everything down. Because I've emailed the file I need to myself now.

Dearest Emma, who sat next to me in double history and then twenty years later at NCT classes.

Emma might not be as rich as our friend Scarlett but at least she should give me something to pay off a couple of credit cards, buy me some time, keep me in coffee.

Give me the money, and I promise not to post the video of you and your partner Robert with your naked body that you're so self-conscious of anyway, exposed to the world. And you've just seen how that can topple over a life, Emma. *Nobody* wants to be the new Scarlett Salloway.

Acknowledgements

These acknowledgements come to you from the lockdown of 2020, so don't be surprised if I get extra sentimental; I've not hugged anyone outside of my immediate family for over a month. Book acknowledgements feel like a chance to give a few virtual hugs and a virtual cheers with a definitely not virtual glass of wine, at least.

First, a note to my own 'mum friends'. All of you are lovely, none of you have tried to ruin my life, all of this is a work of fiction. A special shout-out to my own NCT crew too, especially my good friends George and Anna who are always there with a strong cup of tea, wise words and reassurance that no, it'll be fine that he's eaten the Play-Doh. And to Beccy, my partner in crime through the newborn years, 'mum friends' don't come much finer than you, my love.

There are quite a few people to thank for help with research on this book. Yair Cohen at Cohen Davis Solicitors for legal knowledge, Matt Pyke from Fly High Media and Melanie Smith at Run 2 Media for the digital marketing background. My dear friend Charlotte Kewley, AKA The Little Stylist who patiently conducted a blogger/ Instagram 101 lesson to someone who can barely remember to add a hashtag. To all the people that got back to me on Twitter about noughties dance music, you improved my book and my Spotify playlists. Both are appreciated.

Mike, thanks for Manchester knowledge and tip-offs. If I

trust anyone to know where the cool spots are, it's you, so keep eating brunch and drinking wine, just for me, in case I need help again, will you? And to Mike and the rest of my school friends, Vic, Zo, Helen and Suse; the support you gave me when my first book came out was such a special thing and I'm lucky to have had you all in my life since we went to school together about, erm, eight years ago. Yes, that's the right number. Definitely eight(een. And the rest). The same is true for all of my friends, especially the power crew of women's magazine alumni, who've spent the last year championing my books and whooping in my corner. Thank you.

When I wrote my epic acknowledgements for *Through The Wall* – that's allowed for your first book, isn't it? Don't worry, I'll try and keep it shorter for this one – one person I didn't mention was THAT teacher, you know the one, the one that makes a difference. So just on the off chance you ever see this, the Miss Brophy who taught English at Rainford High School around, erm, 2012 (ok fine, the late nineties) and dragged me away from Point Romance and over to the Brontës, you made a *big* impact on me and the breadth of my reading and that's something I have reason to be grateful for from both a personal and a professional perspective. I'm sure I'm not the only one. What a teacher.

To Lucy and Daisy, the support crew of the Diana's Dames WhatsApp group for a policy that we must always start a conversation mildly hysterical, paranoid and irrational and end it as vaguely reasonable human beings. You know, for writers.

On the publishing side of things, thanks to my editor Phoebe Morgan for her patience, expertise and brilliance. As I've mentioned, this book was edited during Covid-19 lockdown when we were all in shock and finding our feet with a whole new way of working, but Phoebe ploughed on regardless and utterly professional to make this a better book, as she always does.

To the Avon massive; from every awesome member of the team to the authors that have welcomed me into their crew in such a kind way. I burst with pride at being part of what is without a doubt the tightest knit, most hardworking gang in publishing. Special note to Sabah Khan, obviously, because she is obscenely talented and none of us could function without her.

The same is true for my agent, Diana Beaumont. Diana, I may have been waving at you this time round over Zoom instead of across a table with extra mashed potato but your support has been felt keenly, as always. I hope we work together on many books to come. Hopefully then out of lockdown, with an extra big hug and an extra large wine. Thanks too to the rest of the Marjacq team, notably Sandra Sawicka and Leah Middleton.

To Luke, I need to take this opportunity to say that I'm sorry I gave the *Through The Wall* baddie your name. You are very definitely not a baddie. Now please let us still come and swim in your pool in Miami.

To everyone that supported my first book, from bloggers to reviewers to local book shops and radio stations; every kind word spurred me on to start again with a blank page for round two and write *The Baby Group*, even when a *tiny bit* tired with a newborn. So a huge thank you.

To my family, especially Mum, Dad and Gem for unending support, enthusiasm and (Gem) Facebook posts. To Grandad, I wish you'd been around for this. You'd have loved it.

And of course, thanks to Simon for entering into this parenting/work tag team system of ours, which means that every week I get to write calmly at a laptop one minute and hurl myself around a baby group pretending to be a lion the next. These years are unique and non-stop and special and I would not change one tiny thing about them. Which brings me to my two incredible boys, whose smiling, generally food-covered faces put everything in the world – including book edits – into perspective. Thanks to the three of you for being my team.

Lexie's got the perfect life.
And someone else wants it. . .

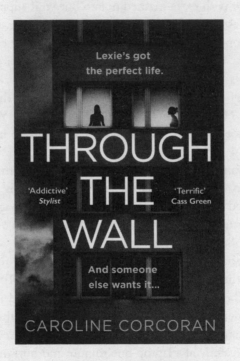

Lexie's got
the perfect life.

THROUGH
THE
WALL

'Addictive'
Stylist

'Terrific'
Cass Green

And someone
else wants it...

CAROLINE CORCORAN

A heart-racing psychological thriller
perfect for fans of Louise Candlish
and Adele Parks.